Bone, Fog, Ash & Star

A **free** eBook edition is available
with the purchase of this print book.

- -

CLEARLY PRINT YOUR NAME ABOVE IN UPPER CASE

Instructions to claim your free eBook edition:
1. Download the BitLit app for Android or iOS
2. Write your name in **UPPER CASE** on the line
3. Use the BitLit app to submit a photo
4. Download your eBook to any device

www.coteaubooks.com

THE LAST DAYS ⊕F TIAN DI

BONE, FOG, ASH & STAR

BOOK THREE

CATHERINE EGAN

Edited by Laura Peetoom
Designed by Jamie Olson
Typesetting by Susan Buck
Maps by Jonathan Service
Printed and bound in Canada at Houghton Boston

Library and Archives Canada Cataloguing in Publication

Egan, Catherine, 1976-, author
      Bone, fog, ash & star / Catherine Egan.
(Last days of Tian Di ; book 3)
Issued in print and electronic formats.
ISBN 978-1-55050-593-1 (pbk.).--ISBN 978-1-55050-594-8 (pdf).--
ISBN 978-1-55050-779-9 (epub).--ISBN 978-1-55050-784-3 (mobi)
      I. Title. II. Title: Bone, fog, ash and star. III. Series: Egan,
Catherine, 1976- . Last days of Tian Di ; bk. 3.
PS8609.G34B65 2014   jC813'.6   C2014-903752-X
                                                 C2014-903753-8
Library of Congress Control Number   2014938365

2517 Victoria Avenue
Regina, Saskatchewan
Canada   S4P 0T2
www.coteaubooks.com

10 9 8 7 6 5 4 3 2 1

Available in Canada from:
Publishers Group Canada
2440 Viking Way
Richmond, British Columbia
Canada   V6V 1N2

Available in the US from:
Orca Book Publishers
www.orcabook.com
1-800-210-5277

Coteau Books gratefully acknowledges the financial support of its publishing program by: the Saskatchewan Arts Board, The Canada Council for the Arts, the Government of Canada through the Canada Book Fund, the City of Regina, and the Government of Saskatchewan through Creative Saskatchewan.

FOR
JAMES AND KIERAN,
WITH ALL MY LOVE

Map of Di Shang

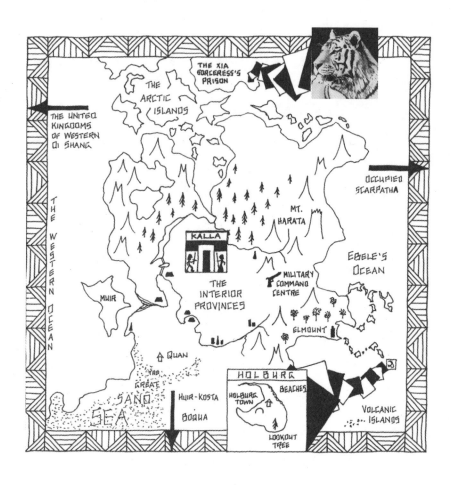

Map of Tian Xia

BONE

CHAPTER

1

She clung to his broad, furred shoulders with her knees, her hands deep in the feathers of his neck. She clung to him while overhead the blue sky spun and beneath them the rolling, golden dunes flashed by. She thought the joy of it would burst her chest open. The world was only sand and sky and speed, his shoulders between her knees, his feathers in her hands.

And then she let go.

She fell, plunging from the sky toward the ground. The wind roared in her ears. She stretched out her limbs, she closed her eyes, she thought of the dark wings, she thought of flight. The ground rushed closer. She opened her eyes and her heart nearly stalled. Just before she hit the ground his bony talons closed around her and she was borne up again, back into the blinding blue of the sky.

This was the third time and she'd had enough. She climbed up his legs and pulled herself expertly onto his back. She wrapped her arms around his feathered neck and shouted, "Let's go back."

He swooped round in a great semi-circle. Over a mountain of sand stood fifty or more peaked, brightly coloured tents: the Sorma camp. They landed by a trio of disgruntled camels.

The gryphon became a boy, tall and lean, with lively dark eyes and a laugh tugging at the corners of his mouth. As always, when she looked at him these days, she felt an odd pain she couldn't give a name to, a longing that made it hard to speak for a moment.

"Nay our most successful flight, Cap'n," he said.

She drew a breath. The air was bone dry.

1

"If you keep calling me that I'll turn you into a toad. Permanently."

She pulled her dark, corkscrewing hair back from her face and looked away from him at the ugly camels.

"Still no sign of them," he said, scanning the sky. "You're sure they're coming?"

"I'm sure."

"I could have gone to get her. I dinnay see why Foss has to go out of his way."

"I dinnay know either, Charlie. It was her idea."

The corners of his mouth turned down suddenly, changing his face. His eyebrows came together and he gave a sullen shrug.

"Lah, they'd better be here. It's your birthday."

She nodded and gave a half-hearted laugh. She wanted to stroke the frown away, ask him what was the matter, but he wouldn't tell her – she knew that much.

"I'm parched, aye. Let's see if they'll ration me extra water on my birthday!"

Charlie had been dropping Eliza from the sky for weeks now. They wanted to see if she would turn into a raven. Every time they failed she felt rather embarrassed by the whole endeavour. After all, how absurd it was to think she might suddenly become a bird! And yet she dreamed of flying every night, and when she woke there were long dark feathers in her bed.

She had wanted to spend her sixteenth birthday in Holburg. With her best friend Nell at school in the capital and her parents in the desert with the Sorma, she hardly ever went back to the island. It was the closest thing to home she'd ever had and she missed it terribly. She came close to asking her father if they could all go back for her birthday but she knew it was impractical and, in the end, she held her tongue. Her mother was far too weak to make the journey. It would be selfish and unfair to ask her to do so. And so Eliza's birthday party was held in the middle of the Great Sand Sea. The Sorma were midway on their journey from one oasis to another and there was not a speck of green to be seen for hundreds of miles around. There was nothing to see at all but the undulating sand dunes, changing colour with the light. Eliza felt uneasy and restless out here without trees or water or anything alive but her father's resolute tribe. Still, it didn't matter really. The main thing was that everybody she cared for would be here, all together in one place for once.

Eliza's birthday was in the spring. It was more than a year since she had made the decision to leave the Mancer Citadel forever, and it had not been an easy year. In her chest, next to her heart, she bore the Urkleis, which the Sorceress Nia had Made. In taking possession of it, Eliza had been able to defeat Nia, who remained frozen in the Hall of the Ancients in Tian Xia. But Eliza felt in her chest, every minute, the limitless depth of Nia's rage. It was a strain that showed in her face, thinner now, with hollows under her eyes.

She had continued her study of Magic with Foss, the Mancer Spellmaster and Emmisarius of Water – and the only Mancer she trusted. He came to her in the desert with books and gossip from the Citadel. He was the Mancers' only link left to the Shang Sorceress. Eliza knew they hoped he would bring her back eventually. She knew even that the idea of bringing her back by force had been discussed and each time rejected. They needed her to be willing, but she would not budge. She wanted no part in the business of the Mancers, with their carefully guarded secrets, their desire to control her and make use of her power. Above all she swore she would not return so long as Kyreth, once the Supreme Mancer, was given asylum in spite of his crimes.

"Perhaps they've been held up."

Eliza was lying in the shade outside her tent when her father, Rom Tok, came and sat down next to her. He ran a hand over her unruly hair and smiled down at her. The sun was getting lower. In an hour or two it would be nightfall.

"Maybe," Eliza said lazily.

"Why don't we begin the party without them?" he suggested.

"No," said Eliza. There was a flutter of dark wings somewhere within her and she sat up, breaking into a grin. "They're coming," she said.

A moment later they all saw the bright speck of gold on the horizon. As it drew nearer, it became recognizably one of the Mancer dragons.

The camels edged away, uneasy, as the huge, shimmering dragon landed close to the camp. Foss came towards Eliza with open arms, his fair hair and white robe billowing in the afternoon breeze, his eyes as dazzling as the sun itself. Before he reached Eliza, Nell had raced past him and hurled herself onto her best friend.

"Happy birthday!" she cried.

Eliza laughed and hugged her, then pulled herself out of the embrace to greet Foss. Now all was well. Everybody was here. It didn't matter that they were in the middle of the desert instead of on Holburg. This was as much as she could hope for.

They ate figs and olives as the sun went down and the moon rose. The surrounding dunes went from deep gold to fiery red to ghostly white. The Sorma played music and they all danced around a fire on the cooling sand. Eliza's mother Rea sat on a blanket and clapped her hands while the others danced, her red hair bright by the firelight. Rom danced circles around her and she laughed up at him.

When they were tired of dancing they set off fire-flares into the desert sky.

Nell and Eliza lay side by side on the sand and watched the fire-flares explode into dazzling showers of colour.

"I'm glad you're here," said Eliza. "I know it's nay easy for you to take time off right now."

"Lah, I couldnay miss your birthday!" said Nell. "Anyway, I

brought my notes with me." She pulled a cream folder, thick as a book, out of a stylish satchel to show Eliza. "This is it. Everything I'll need for the Austermon Entrance Exam."

Austermon was the top university in the Republic. Nell had her sights set on studying cetology there with the renowned marine biologist Graeme Biggs. With top grades and countless academic awards from prestigious Ariston Hebe Secondary School, Nell was certain to be accepted, but she needed to a win a full scholarship if she was going to afford it. That meant acing the notoriously difficult entrance exam, as well as the interview.

"I've got my own shorthand, aye, and I've been reviewing nonstop," said Nell. "I dinnay recommend trying to study on the back of a dragon, though. I lost a few pages, and I had to get Foss to make the dragon land so we could look for them. They'd fallen in the top of a tree and it was very awkward getting them all. He got a bit annoyed with me, I think. It's hard to tell when he's annoyed, though, dinnay you find?"

Eliza laughed, and then said carefully, "Charlie was disappointed that you didnay ask him to come get you."

"It just seemed easier this way," said Nell. "Besides, I like dragons. Much smoother ride, aye."

Eliza rolled over on her side to look at her friend. Nell's face was lit up by the fire-flare exploding overhead, her violet eyes reflecting the shower of brilliant sparks. Her light brown hair formed a pool of silken waves around her head. She was a beautiful girl and perhaps too much aware of it.

"Is everything all right between you and Charlie?" Eliza asked. "He thinks you've been avoiding him. And it's true we've hardly spent any time together this past year. The *three* of us, I mean."

"Everything's fine," said Nell airily. "I've just been busy. And lah, you're the one who's really my friend. Charlie's your friend and of course I'm fond of him too, but I cannay make time to see him when I've got so much studying to do."

"All right," said Eliza. "But I think his feelings are a little hurt."

Nell rolled her eyes. "He's a mite oversensitive. He hardly showed his face in Kalla for months after we got back from Tian

Xia. And now he thinks *I'm* avoiding *him?*"

Eliza sighed and dropped it. She didn't want to argue tonight and it would inevitably be sticky getting in the middle of whatever had come between her friends. It was true that Nell was under a lot of pressure lately. She decided to wait until after the Austermon exam to broach the subject again.

"I think that's it for the fire-flares!" shouted Rom.

Nell bounced upright. "Let's give Eliza her presents!"

The others laughed.

"Now is as good a time as any," Rom conceded.

"I agree!" said Eliza.

"Mine first!"

The sat around the dying fire. Foss looked like a golden giant, beaming and luminous among the dark-skinned Sorma – Eliza's grandmother Lai and her toothless grandfather Kon, her many aunts and uncles and cousins. Rom sat with his arm wrapped around Rea and she rested her head on his shoulder peacefully. From her satchel Nell pulled out a perfectly wrapped box with a purple ribbon around it and handed it to Eliza. Inside was a leather shoulder strap with a long beaded scabbard attached.

"I made it!" said Nell proudly. "It's for your dagger, aye. So you can look a little more stylish while you tote that thing around! Look, you wear the strap across your chest like this. You can move the scabbard so the blade is against your back or at your hip. See?"

Eliza hugged her friend, touched that even while she was cramming for exams Nell had found the time to make her something special.

Most of her presents were handmade. Her grandmother had woven her a sturdy backpack of camel hair and her aunt Ry had made her a jaunty little cap. Her father had carved her a chess set with hinges at its center, so it could fold up into a little box. Foss, predictably, had brought her a book: *Legends of the Ancients*. It was an unexpected gift, since Foss had originally objected to her wanting to read it at all, insisting it was mostly rubbish. Written centuries ago by an eccentric Mancer and now mostly discredited, it contained some of the more far-fetched theories regarding the Ancients, which Eliza had begun to take an interest in.

"So you've changed your mind?" Eliza asked him laughingly. "You think this book might have something useful in it after all?"

"Not a bit," replied Foss. "No, I think it is arrant nonsense, but it is your birthday and you may read it for pleasure, remembering always that there is no evidence at all to support these wild speculations!"

"I've brought some presents back from your friends in Tian Xia," said Charlie, handing her two small parcels.

The first was from Swarn, the Warrior Witch, who trained Eliza in potions and weaponry. It was a slender white cylinder with the centre bored out and a mouthpiece at one end. Eliza examined it, puzzled. It looked almost like a flute, but a bundle of black darts was attached to the side of it by a tight loop of wire.

"That must be dragon bone, aye," said Nell, leaning forward eagerly to get a better look at it.

"But what *is* it?" wondered Eliza.

She handed it to Foss and he turned it over in his big gold hands. He took one of the darts and sniffed it, then placed it in the hole at the end.

"Try blowing in the mouthpiece," he suggested. "Point it away from us, please."

"And away from the s!" piped up her grandfather, Kon, in the Sorma dialect.

Eliza put the cylinder to her lips and blew. The dart hissed away into the night.

"You will have to ask Swarn," said Foss, "but I think the darts contain *verlami*, a substance that paralyzes."

Eliza laughed dryly. "Swarn has a funny idea of what a sixteen-year-old needs," she commented.

"Let's see what Uri Mon Lil has got you," said Charlie.

The wizard's parcel was wrapped in a delightfully soft, silvery substance that fell away under her touch. At the centre of it lay a little amber dropper with what looked like smoke inside. Attached was a card written in the wizard's spidery hand: *My dear*

Eliza, here is a pleasant dream to celebrate your first sleep as a young woman of sixteen! Do come and visit us in Lil soon. Your affectionate friend, Uri Mon Lil.

Eliza smiled. "How just like Uri!" she said.

"When the Sorma turn sixteen, we send them out into the desert for twenty days and they have to find their way back to us," said Lai, speaking rough Kallanese out of politeness towards the visitors. "But in your case…you have already proved such a test unnecessary."

"That sounds like a rotten birthday," said Nell. She had slipped a couple of pages out of her folder and was scanning them by the fading firelight.

"I've got something for you too," said Charlie softly in Eliza's ear. "But I'll give it to you later, aye."

And her heart began to race like when she'd been falling through the sky, braced for impact.

The Sorma were raking sand over the glowing embers and tents had been set up for Foss and for Nell. It was close to midnight, the moon a bright sliver in the sky. Charlie drew Eliza aside and they walked a little way from the camp.

"Lah, this is your present," he said, handing her a piece of paper. "Or, this is nay it *exactly* but it tells you what it is."

Willing her hands to stop trembling, Eliza unfolded it. It was a map of the Western Ocean. Marked out in the centre was a little dot, which Charlie had labelled, *Eliza*.

"I'm almost sure it's nary been discovered," he said in a rush. "It's an island just about ten miles around. You cannay find it on any other map. White beaches and a jungle full of birds and lizards and snakes. There's a lake on the island too, a small one, and *seventeen waterfalls*. A tiny island but seventeen waterfalls, aye. I've named it after you. Whenever you have time, I'll take you there."

"Charlie," she said. Her voice sounded hoarse and strange.

She cleared her throat and looked up at him. He was watching her nervously. "That's a wonderful present, aye," she said. He broke into a smile.

"I thought you'd like it," he said, relieved.

"I do. Thank you."

She folded it up again and pressed it between her fingers. Besides Nell, Charlie had been her closest friend for nearly four years now. Whatever it was she felt for him she thought she had always felt, but as she got older it became more urgent somehow. Lately she found it hard to look at him without her heart quickening, and when flying with him the joy was less in the flight than in the excuse to put her arms around him. His uncomplicated friendship was not enough for her anymore. She had said nothing to him of this, at first because she wasn't sure what she wanted, and then because she was afraid of what he would say if she told him. After all, he had never given her reason to believe that he felt anything but friendship for her.

Alone under the desert sky, she knew she had to tell him, here, now; that there would be no better time for it. But fear froze her tongue.

Have courage, she told herself sternly. You are a Sorceress, and you have done far more difficult and dangerous things than confess your feelings to a boy.

But he wasn't just a boy, of course. Not literally, for he was a Shade, a shapeshifter, but also because he was *Charlie*, her beautiful Charlie. What could she say to him that would not sound ridiculous? She took a deep breath. It was her birthday. They were apart from the others, hidden by the dark. Suppose she said nothing. Suppose she just took his hands, stepped a little closer, and kissed him.

"Are you sure you like it?" Charlie asked, becoming uncertain. "You look a bit funny, aye."

"No, I'm…it's something else. Charlie…"

His expression changed and he took her hands in his. "Eliza! You've got me worried now. What's going on?"

There. He was holding her hands. All she had to do was step

closer. Why couldn't she? Well, she couldn't. So she would have to speak.

"I'm sorry," she said feebly. "This is strangely difficult."

She was cut off by the jolt of her heart and the screaming of ravens, wings beating all around them. The ravens were her Guide and they were telling her something but in her shock and confusion she couldn't make it out. A sudden fog slithered around their ankles and up, engulfing them. She let go of his hands, reaching for her dagger.

"Stay still," she said.

A faint whistle and something skimmed her ear. Out of the mist, leaping, somersaulting, flying, came a horde of beings as graceful as acrobats, their clothes and skin and flying hair ash-white. They had no eyes or mouths, just strange blank faces ringed with streaming hair like white flame. Some held curved, glinting swords, others large powerful bows from which arrows rained. Eliza raised a barrier around herself.

"Foss!" she shouted. She had lost Charlie in the fog, didn't know where to put her barrier around him. "Foss!" she cried again. Then she saw Charlie face down in the sand.

As quickly as it had fallen, the fog lifted. The beings were gone, leaping and spinning over the edge of the dune. She ran to Charlie's side and turned him over.

He was riddled with arrows. He had not even had time to change into something else.

Foss and her father were at her side in seconds, Nell following close after hollering: "What? What? What?"

"Where are the healers?" Eliza pushed her father back towards the camp. "Get the healers!"

"Oh, the Ancients." Nell sank to her knees at Charlie's side. A mottled, smoky substance poured from his mouth and nose and eyes.

"A spell, Foss, a spell." Eliza's words spilled out of her like tears. The Mancer's hand was heavy on her shoulder.

"It is too late for spells and healers, Eliza Tok," he murmured.

"No." She shook her head.

"Oh, the Ancients," said Nell again. She held Charlie's limp hand in hers and looked up at Eliza, her face ashen. "He's dead, Eliza. He's dead."

She shook off Foss's hand.

She thought: No.

Ravens filled the sky, covered the ground, their wings stirring up a great wind.

She opened her mouth and screamed and when she screamed the ravens screamed with her. They screamed words she had never learned, didn't know she knew, and with those words she tore a hole in the world and stepped through it.

CHAPTER

2

The Supreme Mancer Aysu was looking into the Vindensphere. In it she saw the boy lying dead in the desert, the others surrounding him; she saw Eliza frantic, shouting orders. Then the Vindensphere filled with ravens and went black. She looked up, staring into the darkness of the room.

"Oh, horrible," she murmured. "What has happened to me? How have I become a murderer?"

A voice behind her rumbled, "He was a spy among us here once and a threat to the continued line of the Sorceress. You have done what was necessary."

"Necessary?" She laughed a brittle, unhappy laugh. "This is madness, I am mad! What if she learns that the Mancers are behind the murder?"

Her eyes flared brighter and she tried to stand. Kyreth's hands on her shoulders pushed her back down into the chair. She felt all the strength drain from her body. What did it matter? What could she do? She remained seated, slumped forward slightly.

"That is what will bring her back to us," he said.

Cold beneath her feet. Not cold stone or cold grass or cold anything she could name. Only cold. The darkness engulfing her was not an absence of light but a thing in itself – a thing with purpose and a kind of hunger. There was no air – that was the thing she noticed first. She rasped a spell, conjuring enough to breathe. Her heart beat against a kind of pressure, as if a strong hand were wrapped around it. A whisper of wings led the way and she followed. She sensed a great number of other beings walking near her but she couldn't see or hear them. She murmured another spell and conjured a light but the light was swallowed instantly by the hungry dark.

She walked with the soundless, invisible others and gradually her eyes adjusted. She saw shadows all around her, walking. Some of the shadows were shaped like people, some like animals or other beings. They kept pace with one another, neither hurrying nor loitering. They kept their eyes straight ahead, fixed on the encompassing dark. Eliza could hear running water.

At length they came to a river. Without faltering, the shadows walked straight into the river and were swept away by its powerful current. The river was full of bodies, only their heads sometimes visible above the black rushing water. Eliza stopped at the bank of the river and felt the strange pull it exerted. She too wanted to step into it and be carried off. She dared not look at it too long, for when she did it seemed to call to her. It was as if the water was telling her, *For too long your feet have borne the burden of carrying you and you have never known where you should go. Let me take you now.* She walked along the river in the direction that it flowed. She walked alive in the place of death until the river poured between two colossal dark paws and disappeared.

Eliza looked up. Crouched over the river was a giant panther with a starved face and eyes each as vast and cavernous as the caldera of a volcano, shining with black flame. It was looking right at her.

Go back, said the panther.

Its voice was inside her bones, behind her eyes; an empty voice, echoing and insubstantial.

The black current swept countless beings between the paws of the panther and they vanished.

I know who you are, said Eliza. The words made no sound. Her voice had no power here.

The panther said again, *Go back.*

Dragons, humans, centaurs, eagles, witches, giants, foxes, trolls – she saw them carried by the river to oblivion between those paws. With a jolt of horror, she saw a gryphon. Not just a gryphon – *Charlie*. Even as a fast-moving shadow in the dark water she recognized him, she knew him. Before she could move he swept past her like the others, disappeared.

The shock of it froze her for a moment and then her mind began to race. The panther spoke to her again: *You cannot follow him. This is the edge of things. You have to go back.*

She knew it was true but in the moment she saw Charlie, her beloved Charlie in his gryphon form flashing by and disappearing, she wanted nothing but to disappear also, to be swallowed by whatever lay beyond those paws. Her grief opened her wide, drew her apart from herself. It weighed her down and pulled her towards the black water. The river called her more surely now, claimed her. She felt it lapping at her feet. She looked bleakly into the water at the beings it carried through the dark. Though at first she could not say why, certain creatures caught her eye in particular: a grey cat, a wolf, a donkey, a half-hunter, but it meant nothing to her until she saw a small, dark-haired woman she recognized: Missus Ash. Missus Ash, who had taken care of her when she first came to the Mancer Citadel as a terrified twelve-year-old, and who had turned out to be only one guise of the Shade. Then she understood that every form Charlie had ever taken was distinct in this river. She could not save them all, but she could save the one she loved best. She scanned the water for his face. What if he was lost already?

She caught sight of him at last, her own dear Charlie in the shape of a beautiful seventeen-year-old human boy. His face was calm and pale as the water bore him towards the panther. He did not struggle or try to swim.

"Charlie!" It took all her will to make a sound but he did not seem to hear her. There was no time to consider. Eliza threw herself into the river. It wrapped itself around her hungrily.

The cold was unlike anything she could have imagined. What breath she had left, it stole from her. It froze her heart and lungs and drew her racing towards the void. But Eliza was a strong swimmer. She drove herself through the black water towards Charlie. She wrapped one arm around him tight and struck out, legs kicking, one arm wind-milling, struggling for the shore.

The water carried them fast, poured over her head and into her mouth. The taste was death, the simple blackening end to all. She gagged and coughed it up again, pulled herself through the water, pulled Charlie. The great paws loomed. The water filled her veins with its icy darkness. Her heart choked on it. She could not reach the bank and so she grabbed the paw with her free arm. She clung to one silken claw, there at the drop where the river disappeared. She held Charlie to her and she begged.

Let me take this one. I'll go back, but let me take this one with me. No. This one is mine.

A rush of wings inside her skull, and then outside, all around – her ravens swarming around the panther's thin, ravenous face, cawing.

He is mine! Eliza screamed with something other than her voice. She shook the dark, wrung the airless void. *He is mine! Give him to me!*

The panther opened his awful mouth and snapped at the swarming ravens. His teeth flashed white, his tongue was red as flame. The ravens retreated and then dove at him again, cawing, shrieking.

Give him to me! Give him to me! Give him to me!

She dragged Charlie over the giant paw to the bank, the cold nothing that lay on each side of the rushing water. Her ravens filled the emptiness with black beating wings and screaming voices.

Give him to me! Give him to me!

The panther roared. The river roiled.

Give him to me. She sobbed, holding him in her arms, rocking him. His cheek was ice-cold against hers. *He is mine.* She wept and the ravens beat their wings in a frenzy. *He is mine. Give him to me.*

Go back! The panther roared again.

She held him to her. The river swelled and poured over its banks, rushing around them. The ravens formed a towering black column, spiraling around her, the wind from their wings pushing the water back so it swept around her but did not touch her. In the centre of this storm of ravens, in this gap in the roaring river of death, she held him. Her lungs ached, her heart strangled. Water and ravens spun about her. She opened her mouth and felt Magic pouring out of it. The crouching panther lurched to its feet, a great tail lashing somewhere in the dark. Fiery-tongued and roaring he pounced. The Magic pouring from Eliza's mouth split the dark. Holding the boy close, she burst through the sky, plummeting. Charlie would catch her as he always did. Or she would become a raven at last, this time, and save them both.

He is mine, she whispered, and they hit the ground. The violent jolt brought sweet air rushing back into her lungs. Her heart began to beat again, slow and frozen from the awful water. She hung onto him, Charlie full of arrows, Charlie bleeding terribly, but alive.

Nell was staring at her, wild-eyed, mouth open with a question she couldn't put into words. Foss took her by the shoulders, hard.

"What have you done, Eliza Tok?"

"Healers," she gasped. They were there already, surrounding Charlie. She heard their low murmur, smelled the herbs beginning to burn. He was alive. Barely, but it was enough. If he was alive, the Sorma could help him.

"Eliza!"

She looked up into Foss's flaming eyes.

"I brought him back," she said, trying to sit up. His face began to spin and fade and she fainted.

When Eliza woke up she was alone in her tent with Foss. She leaped to her feet, dagger in hand. Immediately her knees gave way and she crashed back down onto her mat.

"What happened?" she cried, then couldn't really think what she meant.

"Is Charlie all right?" she asked next.

"The Sorma healers are with him now," said Foss quietly. "He will live."

She nodded her head and felt how weak she was. She leaned back onto the cushions, let the dagger slip out of her hand.

"You went where you should not have gone, Eliza Tok," he murmured as sleep swept over her again.

When she woke up a second time her head was pounding. Her mother was seated in the corner of the tent chewing on a fingernail. Her father was cross-legged at her side, holding her hand. The entrance was tied open to let in the cool night air and Foss paced back and forth before it.

Rom smiled at her when she opened her eyes. He said to the others, "She's awake."

"Thank the Ancients," said Rea.

Rom ran a hand over her forehead. His hand was very cool. "How do you feel?" he asked.

Her tongue felt swollen in her mouth when she answered him: "Fine. Lah, no, terrible actually."

"You have a fever," said Rea. "But you'll be all right. Your friend Charlie seems to be stable as well."

Eliza glanced at Foss, still pacing, his head down.

"*Am* I going to be all right?" she asked.

His eyes were the colour of sunset when he looked at her.

"You look well enough, Eliza Tok," he said. "But I do not yet know the consequences of what you did. Only that it is unwise to make an enemy of the Guardian between life and death."

"Drink some water," said Rom, handing her a cup.

Nell peered into the tent.

"Can I come in yet?" she asked.

"Hello, Nell," called Eliza.

"Oh, thank the Ancients!" Nell gasped, bounding past Foss and hurling herself onto Eliza to hug her. "I just looked in on Charlie. He's still out cold but the Sorma dinnay seem too worried. They say they've seen worse, aye." She laughed a bit at that. "What happened, Eliza? He's shot full of arrows!"

"I was going to ask *you* about that," said Eliza to Foss. "We were just…we were talking, aye, and then there was a fog and I *knew* something was going to happen but I didnay know what. And then –"

"The Thanatosi."

"The what?"

Foss bowed his head. He seemed strangely reluctant to speak.

"The Thanatosi are a…well, I don't know exactly what they are. A sort of mystical tribe perhaps."

"Tian Xia worlders," said Eliza.

"Of course. They are assassins, essentially. They can be called upon only by Great Magic and once they have been called no power known can stop them from pursuing their goal. From what little I know, they are notoriously difficult to kill – perhaps impossible. I have never heard of them failing, giving up or being defeated."

"Will they be back?" Eliza struggled to sit up again. Her limbs felt hot and weak.

Rea, Rom and Nell were all gaping at Foss in horror.

"They will," said Foss. "As soon as they sense their prey is still alive. I have put a barrier around the camp. We are safe for the time being."

Nia, thought Eliza immediately. But no. The Urkleis, which bound Nia, was still in her chest. She could feel it: Nia's power turned in on itself in a furious deadlock, pulsing like a second poisoned heart in her chest. Nothing had changed. Nia could not have called the Thanatosi.

"Who wants me dead?" she asked, a bit tremulously.

"Eliza," said Foss gently, "*you* were not the target. They achieved their goal, if only temporarily."

It took a moment for this to sink in.

"Charlie?" she blurted.

"It makes sense," said Nell. "He's been around forever, aye, and he is sort of a difficult personality. I imagine he's got loads of enemies."

"But enemies powerful enough to…" Eliza paused.

"What are we going to do if we cannay repel them?" asked Nell. "I spec the Mancers can get rid of them, nay? I mean, I know you dinnay want anything to do with them anymore, but for something very important like this…lah, we need the Mancers, nay?" This last she directed at Foss.

"Foss?" asked Eliza. She was beginning to feel faint again.

He met her gaze with a sorrowful face.

"I fear that you cannot rely on the help of the Mancers in this matter," he said.

"That's ridiculous!" cried Nell. "We'll persuade them! We'll –"

"Hush," Rea said to her sharply, which startled Nell to silence.

"Foss." Eliza struggled to keep her voice steady. "Tell me what you know."

"I do not *know* anything," he replied. "But Great Magic was worked in the Citadel recently. I had no part in it but I felt it of course, we all did…the kind of Magic that might be used to summon a great being. Or call the Thanatosi."

Eliza shook her head. No words would come.

"I do not *know*," Foss repeated. "But it seems possible, even likely, that the Mancers called the Thanatosi to kill your friend."

CHAPTER
3

Charlie woke with a start and shouted, "Help me! I'm drowning!"

Somebody grabbed his hand and the world swam into view. He was lying in a tent lit with candles and the somebody holding his hand was Eliza. The candlelight threw shadows across her face, with its pointed chin, beaky nose and serious black eyes. She had such an odd look on her face, like she'd just put something very hot in her mouth and couldn't decide whether to swallow it or spit it out.

"Bad dream," he muttered. "What're you doing in here?"

"Do you remember what happened?" she asked, her voice high and strained.

Charlie thought about this a bit, then said, "Something definitely happened. I cannay move. Why cannay I move?" He kicked his legs in a sudden panic. "Oh. I can move. Then what's wrong with me? Something's different, aye."

"There were...assassins," began Eliza.

"Forsake the Ancients!" Charlie sat up in the bed and stared at her. His face had gone quite white.

"Charlie?" she said anxiously.

"Eliza...*I cannay change.* I cannay change. *Why cannay I change?*"

"I couldnay...I could only save part of you. This part. The human part. I'm so sorry, Charlie."

"Start again. Oh, by the Ancients. Start all over again, Eliza. Why cannay I change?"

She told him what had happened and he held a hand to his

chest as if aware of his beating heart for the first time.

"I'm just a person," he said dully when she had finished. "Lah, I'm just a *person*. What good is that going to do me?"

"Some of us manage to live with it," said Eliza. "The real question is why the Mancers would send assassins after you."

"You're nay just a person, you're a Sorceress," said Charlie. "It's nay the same thing. You can do Magic."

Eliza took a deep breath.

"How are you *feeling*, Charlie?"

"Like I've been shot with arrows and killed and drowned and then dragged back. I cannay change, I cannay protect myself and there are assassins after me. Otherwise, fine. It hurts to sit up, though."

"Then dinnay sit up."

"No. I want to sit up." He looked at her for a moment. "So you brought me back from...lah, being dead."

"Yes."

He paused to ponder this, and then said, "Thank you."

She gave a nod and he laughed feebly.

"Ouch. It hurts to laugh too. I dinnay recommend being shot with arrows, Eliza. Keep that in mind. And *thank you* doesnay begin to sum it up of course. I dinnay know what to say to you."

His hand was still in hers. She looked at it.

"I couldnay let you go. Charlie, do you remember just before the assassins came? I was about to tell you..." Her sentence trailed off as Foss swept into the tent.

"Ah!" he said. "You are awake. And alive! Well done. A far better state than the alternative, or so we tend to think, though we've no empirical evidence to back it up. The Thanatosi are back."

"Already?" cried Eliza. She ran to the entrance of the tent. It was just after dawn. Outside the camp, the desert was obscured by fog. The wheeling white bodies of the assassins spun along the edges of Foss's barrier.

"Thank the Ancients we have a Mancer here," said Nell, who had been waiting outside. She was pale, and there were shadows under her eyes. "Is he awake?"

"Yes."

Eliza could not tear her eyes away from the swift-limbed Thanatosi. They moved in a white blur, feet flashing, bright blades swinging. But they could not enter.

"We need to discuss our next move immediately," said Foss. "Come, Eliza Tok. And you too…Eliza's friend."

"You still dinnay know my name, do you?" said Nell in disbelief. Foss pretended not to hear her, and the two girls followed him back into Charlie's tent.

"Everything OK?" Charlie asked weakly.

"For the moment," said Foss. "I assume you have realized that you are no longer a Shade."

Charlie nodded. Nell gasped and began to ask a question but Foss carried on, cutting her off: "You will live out your life as a mortal human now. No doubt you will adjust. However, if we do not hide you from the Thanatosi it will be a very short life indeed."

"Hide me where?"

"Ah! Excellent question, quite to the point." Foss paused. "I do not know."

"Foss," said Eliza, "do you have *any* idea why the Mancers would be trying to kill Charlie?"

He shook his head briefly, a gesture that might have meant *no* or *not now*. She let it drop, a cold creeping feeling around her heart. She thought perhaps she knew the reason.

"The *Mancers!*" exclaimed Charlie, recovering from his shock just enough to get angry. "Typical crazy controlling Mancer behaviour! No offense, Foss. Kyreth *said* they were going to let me off the hook for spying, aye, but I should have known better than to believe it. Still, sort of late for them to change their minds, nay? I mean, that was *years* ago."

"We can come to that later," said Eliza. "A hiding place is the most important thing now."

"The Thanatosi are relentless," said Foss. "They will never stop seeking their prey."

Charlie slumped back against the pillows.

"I know where we can go, aye," said Nell suddenly.

"We?" said Charlie. She ignored him and held out her hand to Foss, as if offering it to him to kiss. He looked at it in surprise. On her finger, she wore the ring Jalo the Faery had given her when they parted ways in Tian Xia.

"The Realm of the Faeries!" she said. "Jalo can give us sanctuary. These Thanatosi or whatever you call them, lah, they wouldnay be able to follow us there, would they?"

"True," said Foss. "If the Faeries were willing to give you sanctuary, you would be safe. The Thanatosi cannot enter that Realm uninvited."

"What's this *we* and *us* business?" asked Charlie. "You dinnay need to hide."

Nell turned on him, her violet eyes flashing angrily. "Do you really think the Faeries would take *you* in by yourself? If I go with you, Jalo will help. But I dinnay remember him being terribly fond of *you*, lah. Seeing as the first thing you did when you met him was try to kill him."

"If you can call finding him with a sword at your throat *meeting* him," huffed Charlie.

"Stop it!" said Eliza. "Nell is right. Jalo would help her but I'm nay sure he'd help you alone, Charlie. Can you do it, Nell? I know you've got this exam coming up."

"I'll bring my notes. I can study in the Realm of the Faeries as well as anywhere," said Nell lightly, as if they were proposing a drive to the seaside. "As long as I'm back in time for the test. I've got a month, aye."

"Then I've got a month to stop the Thanatosi once you two are safe. We should leave right away."

"We?" said Charlie again. "So you're coming too? We're all going to the Realm of the Faeries together?"

"Someone has to get you safely to Tian Xia," said Eliza. "Once you're in touch with Jalo, I'll be comfortable leaving you alone. But until then I'm nay letting you out of my sight. Will you come, Foss? We'll need barriers."

"Of course," he said. "We will leave at once."

They packed up their few belongings quickly. Of her birthday gifts, Eliza brought with her the peculiar weapon Swarn had sent, the scabbard Nell had made her, into which she fitted her dagger, and the backpack her grandmother had woven, which she filled with supplies. The rest she left with her father. Charlie limped out of his tent, Sorma herbs packed against his tightly bandaged wounds. He looked at the Thanatosi, still leaping and spinning and swarming along the barrier in eery silence.

"Makes me dizzy watching them, aye," he said flatly. "Do they nary stop moving?"

"Look at that! They can turn right upside down. Like gravity doesnay apply to them!" exclaimed Nell. "It would be fascinating to be able to study one of them in a lab. See how they work, aye. Like those jumps they make. How do they *do* that?"

Charlie gave her a faintly disgusted look. "You're creepy when you get all scientific," he said.

"Come," said Foss. "They cannot stray far from the ground. We shall be out of their reach in no time." He gestured towards the waiting dragon.

Charlie grimaced. "I'm nay sure how I feel about sitting on some flying beast's back. I'm usually the back, aye."

"Nay anymore," said Nell, a bit cruelly.

Rom came out to see them off, supporting Rea with one arm.

"So you're off again," said Rea, squinting in the sun. "You'll be careful?"

"I always am," said Eliza. She kissed her mother on her cool cheek, struggling to ignore the hum of the Urkleis as she did so. Then she threw her arms around her father and hugged him goodbye.

"Take care, my girl," he whispered.

"I'll be back soon," she said. "We'll play chess with my new set." He kissed her and smiled. "You're all right, then?"

She nodded. "It was a good birthday, up until the assassins."

Foss helped Nell and Charlie onto the dragon's neck and

seated himself just before its wings. Eliza climbed up the gold-scaled back. The dragon swiveled its neck and watched her with one brilliant eye. Dragons knew a being of power when they encountered one and this dragon had flown with Eliza before. She seated herself on the middle of its back, behind Foss, gripping the golden spike in front of her. Foss called out a command and the dragon leaped into the air, its huge wings accordioning out. Below them the barrier crumbled, but the Thanatosi were no longer interested in the Sorma camp. In a swirl of white limbs and flashing swords, they came leaping across the desert after the dragon. The dragon beat its massive wings, climbing higher and higher into the sky and leaving the Thanatosi behind.

They crossed the great stretch of desert to the eastern coast, stopping only briefly for silent meals. They ate quickly, stretched their legs and then resumed their positions on the back of the dragon.

When Eliza spied blue sea on the horizon she felt tears spring to her eyes. How she missed the sea! The dragon began a joyful downward swoop towards the white-capped waves, but rose again at a stern command from Foss. It was another hour before they reached a chain of volcanic islands. The archipelago, and Holburg, lay to the north. Their destination was a long-dormant volcano, whose crater had collapsed into a deep cavern, large enough even for the dragon to enter. They descended with slow wing pulses to a pool of black water, the ring of dusky sky receding above them.

"Fascinating," said Foss, climbing off the dragon and splashing in the water up to his knees. "I do not think the Mancers know this entry to the Crossing."

"Charlie knows all the entries, aye," said Eliza.

"We cannay know if he knows *all* of them," pointed out Nell, ever logical. "I mean, he wouldnay know about the ones he doesnay know, would he?"

Charlie snorted.

"I must confess I'm rather excited," said Foss. "I've been an Emmisarius for a short time only and there has been no cause for me to make the journey to Tian Xia. This is the first time that I will see that other world. May I command the Boatman, Eliza?"

"Be my guest."

Foss began to intone the words: *My power spans the worlds and that between the worlds, my power spans the skies and seas of Tian Di, my power is undivided.* He seemed to find it effortless. Though he was her teacher and a source of seemingly endless knowledge, it was rare that Eliza was able to witness displays of his power. The tremendous barrier that morning, covering all the Sorma camp, and now this commanding of the Boatman, reminded her what a powerful being he truly was.

A boat took shape on the water as he spoke, its sail full, its boards ash white. The ghoulish boatman, knotted muscle and bone and blood vessels visible through his translucent flesh, stood at the helm to greet them.

"So this is the Boatman!" said Foss.

"Emmisarius of Water," the Boatman greeted him in an awful scraping voice, like a blade on stone.

"Greetings," said Foss, bowing. The Boatman stepped aside and all four of them were permitted to board the wide, flat sloop, unchallenged. The boat slipped away through the water and the darkness of the cavern, emerging quickly onto a misty grey sea. Nell settled down near the front of the boat and took her folder out of her satchel.

"Can you give me a light, Eliza?" she asked. "Or praps Foss could just look over my shoulder and keep his eyes nice and bright."

"Dinnay you want to get some sleep?" asked Charlie.

"I'm fine," she said, barely looking at him. Eliza conjured a light for her friend to study by, then lay herself down on the pale planks. She felt a chill around her, within her: a memory of the dark water of the river of death, as if it were flowing through her and mingling with her blood. When she closed her eyes, she saw hundreds of ravens trying to take flight and yet somehow fastened to the ground, while somewhere there was a sound like a great tail lashing the air.

It was a long time before she slept and it felt like a very short time before she was woken again by the spine-chilling baying of the hounds of the Crossing. They were deep in the white mist of the Crossing now but she could still make out the forms of the others. Charlie was on his back – she had to look closely to make sure his chest was rising and falling. Nell was slumped over her folder, fast asleep. Foss sat against the gunwale, his eyes bright discs of flame in the mist. She glanced at Charlie again, to make sure he was sleeping.

"Foss?" she whispered, crawling closer.

"Yes." His deep voice soothed her, gave her the courage to ask the question that was tormenting her.

"Do you really think the Mancers are responsible for calling the Thanatosi?"

"I do. Not all of them, naturally. I cannot know for certain who took part."

"Kyreth."

"I assume so. But not alone. He could not have done it alone."

"Because they're afraid…they're afraid I'll do what my mother did."

This was terribly vague, but Foss understood.

"I believe so," he said. Eliza's heart sank.

For thousands of years the Shang Sorceress had lived with the Mancers, learning to use her power under their tutelage. When she came of age she married a Mancer and bore a single daughter, heir to her power. Once the continuation of the line was established, she went into the worlds and performed her duty, guarding the Crossing from any being who did not belong in Di Shang. This had been the unfaltering way of things until Eliza's mother, at the time an unusually powerful and rebellious young Sorceress, fell in love with a young Sorma man, Rom Tok. She married him in secret and bore him a daughter, thus diluting the line of the Sorceress as far as the Mancers were concerned. Though none of them had ever spoken to her of the matter of an heir, Eliza had known she would be expected to marry a Mancer one day. It was one of the reasons she would not go back to them. She would not be told whom to marry. But somehow they knew, *Kyreth* knew, that she had feelings for Charlie. They were eliminating the competition, hoping to prevent her eloping with a non-Mancer as her mother had done. Now that Foss had confirmed her fear, she did not want to discuss it further. The fact that Kyreth would enlist some of the Mancers in a plot to murder Charlie, her dear Charlie, for fear that she might one day choose him over them, made her nearly sick with rage. If she was to stop the Thanatosi, she would have to begin with the Mancers.

The whiteness closed about them, until they could not see one another at all, and then blew away all at once. They were sailing on the green lake of the Crossing, the fiery sky of Tian Xia blazing above them. Around the lake curved the great black cliffs, carved with images of unrecognizable beings and unreadable symbols.

Nell woke up and put her papers back into her folder in a hurry. She looked a bit green.

"This is your third time, aye," said Charlie gently. "Shouldnay be so bad."

Eliza handed her a little sack of herbs from the Sorma. Nell held them close to her face and inhaled deeply.

"Not an easy journey for a human," noted Foss.

"Or anyone going where they dinnay belong," said Charlie. "I got hellishly sick crossing over to Di Shang the first time, but it seems like after a few times you build an immunity. Like you have enough of that world in you to make you belong a little more. Then there're people like Eliza, aye, who dinnay get sick at all, either way. Belonging to both worlds, I spec."

"There are no people like Eliza," Nell said, glancing up from her sack of herbs for a moment. "Oh, the Ancients, I feel awful."

"And the Mancers?" asked Foss.

"Lah, you're really Tian Xia worlders, nay?" said Charlie. "But you live in Di Shang. So you should be all right either way, I spec."

Foss looked thoughtful. As they drew closer to the towering black cliff that frightened Eliza every time, Foss became very interested in the symbols carved there. "If only I had the Book of Symbols with me!" he cried. "I do not think all of these have been deciphered, you know... though it ought to be possible, with the book." His face fell, light fading from his eyes slightly. "It is one of the Books Nia drained. It has been a tremendous job, Eliza, trying to repair the Old Library, and we have only made the smallest beginning in a year's time. We have repaired the Book of the Ancients and many other Great Texts. But the Book of Symbols is still empty. Such a shame."

Nell curled into a ball and whimpered, clutching the bag of herbs to her face.

"Almost there," said Eliza, squeezing her shoulder. "Just hang on a little longer."

"Are the Thanatosi crossing also?" Foss asked the Boatman.

The Boatman grinned hideously and did not reply.

"You cannot tell me?" asked Foss. "Fascinating. I have much to learn about the way of things. Not everything can be learned from books! Well, we must assume they are. I will prepare a barrier."

"Crossing at the same time?" Nell asked, giving him a white-faced, miserable stare. "How?"

"The Boatman, as I understand it, is not constrained by time and space in the same manner that beings more rooted in the worlds are," said Foss. "But it is quite beyond our minds to comprehend it."

Nell groaned and shut her eyes again. Eliza held her hand. Foss knelt aft and murmured to himself, preparing a barrier. The black cliff loomed up before them and then opened into steps.

"Come quickly," said Foss, rising. They followed him off the boat and up the steps while the boat faded away to nothing behind them. Eliza and Charlie supported Nell between them.

At the top of the steps they faced the temples of the Faithful, great red-earth domes still being repaired since Nia had destroyed them. The Ravening Forest scooped around the eastern horizon, a green half-ring. The very land and air here seemed to thrum with Magic.

"I wonder if they've chosen a new Oracle yet," said Charlie, looking at the temples.

"Should we take shelter?" Eliza asked. "We could go to the Faithful but I hate to put them at risk after everything they've been through."

"We will stay in the open," said Foss. "We want to see our enemy approaching. First, do what you must to contact the Faery."

Nell turned the crystal in her ring and said, "Jalo, please come and help me. It's Nell, aye. Thank you." She looked around at them all, suddenly doubtful. "What if it doesnay work?"

"It will take him time to reach us," said Foss. "But the gemstones of the Faeries are known to possess a great variety of powers and I am sure the ring does what you have said."

He paced out the outer limits of the barrier he had prepared and uttered the final words of the spell. It formed a dome over the little group and their dragon, visible only by the slightest shimmer in the air. Nell sat down on the dry red earth and pulled her folder out of her satchel again. Moments later she was entirely lost in a physics problem. Foss looked over her shoulder curiously.

"Ah, but you see, this neglects the Magic element," he said, pointing at the problem with his long, golden index finger. "If you look at this problem from the perspective of Deep Physics it becomes much clearer. Matter is not only matter, it is *imbued*, one might say…"

"I dinnay need to know about *Deep* physics," said Nell impatiently. "That's nay going to be on the test."

"*Not on the test?*" cried Foss. "At Austermon? The most prestigious university in Di Shang? I myself have written a letter to the President of the University, commending him. It is outrageous that they should not require any knowledge at all of the Deep Sciences. I shall have to write to him again."

Eliza's heart gave a thud and a raven appeared on Nell's head with a squawk.

"Foss!" she said, drawing her dagger. The cliff behind them opened into steps. Fog poured up it, covering the barrier but not penetrating it. Arrows fell off the barrier and swords struck it uselessly. In the fog they saw the featureless, oblong faces of the Thanatosi, with only the slightest depressions where eyes ought to be and the slightest protrusion where a nose ought to be. Their hair floated about their heads as if they were underwater. The four companions drew close to one another inside the barrier.

"Are you sure they cannay get in?" Nell asked, clutching her notes to her as if she was protecting a beloved child. "Eliza, why is this raven on my head? Its claws are scratching me."

Eliza jerked her head at the raven and it flew to her shoulder, disappearing as soon as it alighted.

"The barrier will hold," said Foss. He couldn't resist adding, "If you had some knowledge of Deep Mathematics you might have more faith in the barriers of the Mancers and how they come to be. It is like asking if the sky will fall. It is not easy to make the sky fall, is it?"

"I've nary tried," said Nell primly. She glanced at Charlie. "Are you all right?"

Charlie looked pale. "It's just strange, aye, to think that if they *did* get through the barrier I couldnay change. I couldnay do a thing. They would just rip me apart."

"Fear not!" said Foss, becoming a little annoyed with all this talk of the barrier not holding. "They will not give up but nor will they break the barrier. You would be safe for a lifetime within it. Of course, that is not ideal."

"Can you make a *moving* barrier?" asked Nell eagerly. "Then he *could* just stay in it forever."

Foss sighed. "Those who understand nothing of Magic think *anything* is possible," he said to Eliza, who smiled at him. To Nell he said, "Some permanent barriers move, but only on a set course. Charlie would not be able to set the course himself and so would not be able to move about freely. It is, as I say, not an ideal solution."

Eliza thought privately that if the Mancers were behind this, then barriers would not keep Charlie safe for long, in any case. Any barrier that Foss could raise, the Mancers could tear down.

"I'm just trying to help," said Nell. One of the Thanatosi went spinning by her and she moved closer to the center of the barrier, uneasy. "I dinnay think I'm going to be able to study while they're cartwheeling all over and waving those big swords."

"Cannay we fight them?" asked Charlie. "I mean, nay *we*, but *you*, praps?"

Foss shook his head. "I am not an expert on the Thanatosi but I have read that killing them is not a simple matter. I think it is better not to try, at least until we know more."

"Why dinnay we try to eat?" suggested Eliza. "We're going to be here a while."

They made sandwiches and tried uselessly to ignore the swift-limbed assassins. The light drained from the sky, darkening behind the fog of the Thanatosi.

"I had hoped to see the hanging gardens of the Sparkling Deluder," said Foss. "They appear in the south, no?"

"Yes," said Eliza. "They're beautiful, aye. Hard to describe."

He smiled. "You have seen much of the worlds, Eliza."

"I spose I have. Is there going to be trouble for you, Foss, when you go back to the Citadel?"

His eyes dimmed and flickered. "We shall see. I have done nothing against Mancer protocol. My continuing contact with you is encouraged by the Mancers in general as well as by Aysu. That I should act to assist your friend is entirely natural. It will depend on how powerful a faction Kyreth controls. And where Aysu stands."

Eliza's heart sank. She hated to think of putting Foss at risk for her sake.

"Do not fear for me, Eliza," said Foss. "Things are...complicated in the Citadel, but I trust Aysu. It is good that she is our leader now. And whatever the consequences, I am glad to have seen even a glimpse of this world, to feel its ground beneath my feet." He pressed his hand flat against the earth. "So different from Di Shang. It is strange. Perhaps its because Di Shang is ruled predominantly by the laws of nature and the Magic of Mancers has its roots in nature, but I am weaker here somehow. I have less to draw on, or perhaps there are more forces working against me. I do not know."

"But the barrier *will* hold?" Nell piped up.

"I can still call forth an impenetrable barrier," Foss replied irritably. "I am a Mancer, after all, even here."

"Good." Nell pulled her jacket around her for warmth. "I'm cold."

"Me too," said Charlie. "This is awful, lah. I cannay even turn into anything furry."

"Will you stop with that?" grumbled Nell.

None of them slept well inside the barrier while the Thanatosi pressed their strange faces to it, flashed upwards or to the side with swift kicks, running up and over the barrier on their hands, for the thousandth time bringing a blade down. They ate most of the provisions the following day and conversation was minimal. They were all beginning to be afraid that Jalo would not come.

Late in the afternoon the fog of the Thanatosi was suddenly scooped up and the assassins were flung aside in a golden net. Jalo was hurtling towards them on a myrkestra. He veered away from the barrier at the last minute, then alighted and stepped inside it at a gesture from Foss. With golden hair, ever-changing eyes, and the ageless beauty of all the Faeries, he looked entirely out of place in this bleak, rocky landscape. He made a courtly bow and kissed Nell's hand, his feathered cloak swirling elegantly with every movement.

"A pleasure!" he cried. "How I have hoped that I might be of assistance to you some day! You and your friends, of course."

"Hello, Jalo," said Nell, beaming up at him. He was even lovelier than she had remembered.

Jalo gave Eliza a deep bow, Charlie a brief nod, and then looked at Foss with thinly disguised disdain.

"We are glad you have come," said Foss, sounding not quite as sincere as he had hoped to.

"Hm," said Jalo. He looked at Nell. "You have brought a Mancer with you," he stated flatly.

"Ye-es," said Nell, looking to Eliza for help.

"As you can see, we needed a barrier," said Eliza awkwardly.

"No need now!" said Jalo triumphantly. The tumbling mass of the Thanatosi in the net roiled and spun several yards from the barrier. A sword cut through one of the strands and one by one, mist around their ankles, they came spilling out and back over the barrier.

"Indeed," said Foss a bit smugly. The Faery shot him a hateful look.

"I'm *so glad* you're here, Jalo," said Nell hurriedly. "I was worried you…lah, that you might nay be able to come."

"You wound me with your doubt!" he cried, clapping a hand to his heart.

Charlie rolled his eyes at Eliza, who stifled a grin.

"I didnay *really* doubt you," Nell assured him. "I just didnay know if the ring would work. But it did, aye, and you're here, and we need your help! The Thanatosi are after Charlie…and me. They're after both of us, lah, and we dinnay know why, but we need somebody really powerful to help us."

Eliza thought she was laying it on a bit thick but the Faery seemed enchanted.

"Whatever I can do. However…well, there is a slight problem. The Thanatosi are devoid of feelings or senses beyond their sense of their prey and the instinct to kill. Thus Illusion and Curses, which work primarily on the emotions or the senses, are not terribly effective. And from what I hear, it is useless to kill them, for there are always more. Well, I suppose we could *try*."

"Unwise," said Foss briefly. Eliza gave him a warning look.

"Praps we could *work* on *that*," said Nell, "and in the meantime praps we could have…oh, sanctuary or something? In the Realm of the Faeries. Where we would be safe, aye."

Jalo looked pained, but assented immediately. "You have but to ask, Nell, and I will do whatever I can for you. However, the Mancer will not be permitted to enter our Realm. And the

Sorceress…well, as I'm sure you can understand, Sorceresses are not terribly popular either."

"We are not coming," said Foss stiffly.

"Oh!" said Jalo, beaming. "Well, good. That's no trouble at all then. Just the two of you?"

Nell nodded, giving him a coquettish look Eliza had never seen.

"Then we part ways here," said Foss.

Eliza gave Nell a tight hug and then Charlie. "Be safe, you two. I'll come for you as soon as I possibly can." She gave Nell a stern look and whispered, "And *behave* yourself, lah!"

Nell pretended not to know what Eliza was talking about. She took off the ring and gave it to Eliza. "Call Jalo with this," she said. "Now that we know it works!"

"Thank you, Eliza," said Charlie solemnly. "For my life, I mean."

She could not reply, clutched suddenly by the awful fear that she might never see him again.

"Shall we?" Jalo gestured at the Thanatosi and a golden net sprang from his hand. It struck the underside of the barrier and then vanished. He gave Foss an annoyed look. "How can I get them out of the way when you've got your clunky barrier up?" he demanded.

Foss's eyes grew so bright that they all had to look away, even the Faery.

"Very well," said Foss. "I will collapse the barrier, but you must be ready the instant I do. The reflexes of the Thanatosi are at least as quick as yours."

"Nonsense," scoffed Jalo.

Foss uttered a phrase. The Thanatosi were plunging onto them and at the same instant Jalo had them in his net, sending them rolling off with a deft flick of the wrist.

"Quickly now!" he cried. "Nell, on my myrkestra. You will follow," he said to Charlie.

"Wait!" cried Charlie. "I…I cannay follow. I need to ride the myrkestra too."

Jalo gave him a look of surprise.

"I'm nay a Shade anymore," said Charlie. "I cannay change."

"Oh?" said Jalo. "Very well, both of you. Poor myrkestra will find it a tiring journey, I think."

"*Hurry*," begged Eliza, looking anxiously at the Thanatosi. "Cannay you just trap *them* in a barrier?" she asked Foss.

"Ah!" he said, as if he hadn't thought of it, but Charlie and Nell and Jalo were already on the back of the great white-grey bird, which took to the sky. The Thanatosi spilled from the net and followed on the ground. They moved like a film skipping too quickly for the eye to see, jumping great distances in a flash.

"Well, they are away now," he said. "There is little point in trying to hold the Thanatosi within barriers, Eliza. As Jalo says, there are always more of them, the Ancients only know how! Your friend will be safe in the Realm of the Faeries. Now...what will you do?"

"I'm coming back to the Citadel with you," she said.

Foss looked at her, astonished. "Why in the worlds?" he asked at last.

"I was glad to part ways with the Mancers, Foss, but they've chosen a war with me instead," Eliza said darkly. "And that's what they're going to get."

CHAPTER

4

$\mathcal{F}$oss and Eliza stepped out of the dark wood in the northeast corner of the Citadel grounds. Eliza felt immediately how the Citadel welcomed her, was glad to have her back. She had never really been comfortable or happy here, and yet seeing the Inner Sanctum at the center of the grounds, the giant trees around the lake where she and Charlie used to play, the flower gardens and the bright swooping birds all enclosed by the white walls with towers at each corner, she felt strangely as if she was coming home. After all, she had spent the best part of three years here – longer than she had lived anywhere besides Holburg.

Aysu was waiting for them, hands clasped before her, eyes like dying stars. She no longer wore the robe of a manipulator of water, marked with a black crab like Foss's robe. Now she wore all white, for she was the Supreme Mancer. Her posture, though erect, suggested a great weariness.

"You have returned to us," said Aysu to Eliza. "The Mancers welcome you."

"Thank you," said Eliza. She hoped desperately that Aysu wasn't involved in the attempt on Charlie's life, but there was something about the Supreme Mancer now that made her uneasy. The peculiar brightness of her eyes, the tenor of her voice, the extreme tension of her stance, all gave Eliza the sense that something was not quite right.

Foss bowed deeply, saying, "Your Eminence."

Aysu gave him a brief nod of acknowledgement and Eliza noted the approval in it. Well, he would be given credit for bringing her back and that was good. She wanted to keep him out of trouble.

"Is Kyreth here?" Eliza asked bluntly.

"He is," said Aysu. "He labours still under Nia's Curse, though we have given him as much peace from it as we can. He is one of us, Eliza, and that cannot change. But you do not have to see him unless you wish it."

"Keep him away from me."

Aysu nodded assent.

"I think the Sorceress would like to rest after her journey," suggested Foss.

They crossed the grounds together. Aysu walked with them in silence to the south wing. What was there to say?

"I'll have my lessons with Foss as before," said Eliza at last. "Do you want me to study with you also?"

Aysu looked surprised by this. "Is that what you wish?" she asked.

"No," said Eliza. "Kyreth used to read the Old Texts to me and...talk. They were nay very good lessons. I'd prefer just to study with Foss."

"Then that is what you shall do," said Aysu, relieved. "I have no wish to interfere with the Spellmaster's lessons."

It was familiar but it didn't feel good to be back, Eliza decided. They entered the south wing and she felt herself dwarfed by the giant hallways. How had she ever gotten used to the scale of this place? They parted ways with Aysu, who returned to Kyreth's study. Her study, now. Foss and Eliza made their way up to the guest rooms, where Eliza's bedroom had been.

Foss said goodbye to her in the doorway and she sat on the bed in her old room. This was the bed she had woken up in four years ago, when the Mancers had first brought her, unwilling, to the Citadel. Before she had even known what she was. It did not seem such a long time – four years – and yet she was barely the same girl anymore.

The room had been left untouched. The clothes she had left behind were still folded in their drawers, the books she had been studying before that fateful winter festival were still piled on the table and on the floor. Her old notebooks, full of her practice passages in the Language of First Days, were under the desk. She flipped through them absently, noting how her characters had improved, and thought about what to do. She looked out the window and saw a flock of ravens in the grounds. She smiled, comforted. She was not really alone.

Aysu stood in her study facing the blank Scrolls on the rear wall. They had been silent since Nia's invasion of the Citadel. Without the Scrolls she had no access to the kind of wisdom and prophecy Kyreth had made frequent use of and she knew that as a result many of the Mancers considered her leadership to be sorely lacking. Until now, she had not even been able to compel the Sorceress to return. Though it was due to Kyreth that Eliza had left in the first place, that seemed to have been forgotten. As the majority of the Mancers now saw it, when Kyreth was Supreme Mancer the Scrolls spoke and the Sorceress lived in the Citadel and all was as it should be. At least Eliza was back now. That was good.

"Indeed, the Sorceress and the Mancers have been linked since the beginning," said Kyreth. Aysu tensed. He had been Listening to her thoughts again. "But why do you think she has come? And how long do you think she will stay?"

Aysu turned. He sat on the other side of the desk. The desk that had been his, once. He had destroyed it and, though it had been repaired, the cracks still showed. She would have liked to resist, for she longed to rest, truly rest, but she found herself looking reluctantly into his eyes. They were so hot and bright. They held her fast.

"Why she has come…" she repeated dully.

"The important fact is that she is *here*, and *now*," said Kyreth. "We cannot allow the opportunity to pass. We must act quickly. Do you understand me, Aysu?"

And how could she fail to understand? His will was sharp and steely as a blade. Tormented shadows clung to it. When faced with a will so terrible, so unfaltering and sure, what could she do but submit?

The following day, Eliza did not go immediately to the Library for her lesson with Foss. She went out into the grounds and climbed the great oak tree. The tree fort she and Charlie had built still hung from its uppermost branches. From there she had a good view of the Inner Sanctum. When the gong rang, the Mancers filed out from every wing. There were more than two hundred of them, but she knew she would recognize Kyreth, even from afar, when she saw him. She did not see him among the manipulators of fire, water, metal and wood streaming out of each wing towards the white dome. Of course, the chambers of the manipulators of earth were within the Inner Sanctum and so she could not see them crossing the grounds. She realized she did not know to which group Kyreth belonged. She had only ever known him as the Supreme Mancer. When all the Mancers had disappeared into the Inner Sanctum and their chanting had begun, she climbed down from the tree and ran across the grounds to the Library. Foss was waiting for her there, his eyes bright with anxiety.

"I feared something had happened to you," he said.

"Sorry," said Eliza. The smell of the Old Books comforted her. This place had always felt like a sort of sanctuary, but it had changed too. The marble bookcases, rising up like sheer cliffs towards the ceiling far above, stood mostly empty. Books were piled around the bottom of the bookcases, Mancer-height, filling the aisles. She felt their emptiness.

"Those that are upright on the shelves have had their text returned to them," said Foss, pointing at the stacks around them. "The books that lie in piles are still empty. Most of them, as you can see. Perhaps we can spend our afternoons with those."

"I'd love to help you with it, Foss," said Eliza. "But I might be doing other things, lah. Things you dinnay need to know about."

"Indeed, it is best I do not know," he said hastily. "Very well. Under the circumstances, the theory and practice of barriers seems a good beginning point for today's lesson."

Eliza laughed. Even though she knew he couldn't protect her if the Mancers meant her ill, it made her feel safe to have Foss on her side.

"Foss, is Kyreth a manipulator of earth?"

Foss looked startled by the question. "No," he said. "He is a manipulator of fire."

"Then he doesnay work Great Magic with the other Mancers these days?"

"He does not."

"Why?"

"I do not know," said Foss. "I rarely see him. I feel his presence, sometimes, and the Curse upon him. I know he is here and working Magic of some kind. If he were a manipulator of water I would feel more."

"Do you think the manipulators of fire feel a particular loyalty to him?"

Foss looked at her pleadingly, his eyes dimming to a pale yellow. "I do not know, Eliza."

"I'm sorry," she apologized. "One more question, and you dinnay have to answer it if it's…difficult. Every day the Mancers do the Magic separating the worlds, nay? And from what I understand, which is nay much, lah, they call on the power of nature and transform it into Magic and the Supreme Mancer directs the Magic. Would it be possible for the Supreme Mancer to *misdirect* the Magic of the Mancers? Do something else with it?"

"Of course not," said Foss. "No, no, Eliza, it is not so opaque as that. The spell separating the worlds was essentially completed by Karbek in the Middle Days. What we do is simply pour our Magic into that same spell to keep it working. We sow our Magic into Di Shang, deep into the world, so that it may pull apart from Tian Xia."

"That doesnay make any sense," said Eliza.

Foss looked startled. "It is Mancer Magic, Eliza Tok, and at a level you have not yet attained. Are you going to interrogate me further or shall we begin the lesson?"

She saw she had offended him and was immediately sorry. "All right," she said. "Let's talk barriers, aye."

Later that afternoon Foss made his way down a long hallway and knocked on the wall. A door appeared and opened. Inside the study Aysu sat hunched over the big marble desk. Her eyes were dim now, like echoes of light.

"Foss," she greeted him. "Please sit. How is the Sorceress?"

"She is well, I think."

"We are all pleased you were able to prevail upon her to return at last," said Aysu.

Foss bowed and sat down.

"Do you think she will stay?" asked Aysu.

"I hope so," said Foss.

"As do we all. Foss, I know you are fond of her but I ask you to consider the situation objectively for a moment. She is unreliable. She cannot be depended upon."

Foss struggled to keep his expression neutral. "Perhaps you are unfair to her," he said.

Aysu smiled but the smile was strained. "The Mancers have never been weaker than we are now. This is a dangerous time. These troubles with Kyreth have been demoralizing. We do not control our Sorceress. The Scrolls are silent since Nia broke into the Citadel. It is important that we work together towards a more stable future."

"Of course," said Foss cautiously.

"Good. As for the Sorceress: Eliza's power is diluted, as you yourself can see, by her human father. She is not nearly as strong as past Sorceresses her age. Compare her to her mother."

"Rea was unique," interrupted Foss. "It is an unfair comparison."

"Maybe so. That is not the point. I recognize that Eliza came to us at too great an age for her loyalty to lie entirely with us. Many exceptions have been made for her. But it is essential that her daughter be Mancer-born. On this we cannot compromise. And sooner is better."

Foss had not been expecting this. In retrospect he realized he should have. But he could not hide the shock that appeared instantly on his face.

"She is not a child any longer," said Aysu impatiently. "She is sixteen years old. That is old enough to marry and bear a child. So it was with the Sorceresses of ages past. We do not wish to force her into an unhappy marriage, naturally. And so I ask you to father the next Sorceress. Eliza cares for you, she trusts you. She will accept it."

Foss staggered to his feet, nearly knocking over his chair.

"No," he said. His tongue was like a stone and the word fell heavy from his mouth. "She is like a daughter to me. I cannot. And she is too young. She is still too young. I beg you…"

"Very well. Sit down, Foss." Aysu gestured at the chair again and he sat. "We will not compel you. I only thought that you were the choice she herself would be happiest with. Obrad, of course, is eager for the honour."

"She will not accept him," said Foss.

"She has no choice," said Aysu.

Foss stared into her suddenly too-bright eyes. They blazed with pain. He rose again, but slowly this time, reining in his outrage.

"Your Eminence," he said very softly, "I think you are unwell."

Aysu's eyes flared up and died down again. "Your concern is unnecessary," she said icily.

"Aysu." He spoke almost in a whisper, leaning towards her over the desk. "Are you there, Aysu?"

She rose to her feet abruptly, backing away. "Enough, Foss. What is this?"

"Only the concern of a friend," he said gently, his face full of compassion now. "You have been speaking with Kyreth."

"As is only natural," she retorted.

"You have been speaking with him too much. You are still strong, Aysu, and you may rely on the manipulators of water. If you need us, if you need our help, you need only to say so."

Something in her seemed to crumble at his words. Her shoulders fell and she cast her eyes down at the desk.

"I am tired, Foss," she said. "It is not easy."

"Keeping him in check, you mean." This was dangerous, Foss knew, but he felt a slow willingness in his old friend to speak about the matter. "Perhaps it was a mistake allowing Kyreth to stay among us. He will not be relegated to the sidelines. His influence is too strong for you to resist alone. You need help. I think we should discuss again whether it is safe to have him here among us."

"We cannot cast him out," said Aysu. She glanced about the room nervously, as if Kyreth might be watching them. "The Mancers would not accept it. You know as well as I do that he has the support of many of them. And it is only natural – there is no denying that things were better under his reign. Besides, he is... he is doing something important."

Foss felt a chill. "I know the Mancers lend him power," he said. "You have approved it. But to what end? It cannot be good."

"Do not challenge me, Foss!" Aysu blazed, her spine straightening again. "It is my decision that Kyreth's work be supported by the Magic of the Mancers and that the nature of it remain confidential for now. Believe me when I say it is something we will all be grateful for eventually."

At this, Foss's anger got the better of him. "If you mean summoning the Thanatosi, let me say now that I shall never be grateful for the calling forth of that murderous tribe!"

"Foss!" cried Aysu, turning very white. "What are you talking about? The *Thanatosi?* What do you mean?"

"Kyreth's work..." Foss's words died in his mouth. "You said..."

"I said nothing of the Thanatosi," she said coldly. He felt her drawing away from him again and he feared he had handled the meeting very poorly indeed.

"I wish to rest. Leave me." She waved her hand at him and

sank back in her chair, touching her other hand to her forehead. He had to conjure his own door on the way out.

Eliza waited until dark fell. She wanted to explore a bit while the Mancers were sleeping and less likely to notice her movements. All afternoon she had stayed out of the way, lurking about the Library. Whenever she encountered a Mancer she saw the relief in their faces as they bowed to her and welcomed her back. It made her uncomfortable. She felt like a hypocrite smiling and thanking them, simultaneously guilty about her deceit and furious at the possibility that this Mancer or that may have been involved in summoning the Thanatosi.

She walked swiftly down the hallway to the southeast tower. According to the Chronicles of the Sorceress, her grandmother Selva had been killed in an attempt to steal one of the four Gehemmis, gifts of the Ancients, from the Realm of the Faeries. But Eliza was sure she was alive. She had seen her. Her grandmother had saved her from harrowghasters. Her only regret in leaving the Citadel behind had been the thought that she would never know what had truly happened to her grandmother. Now she was going to put that right.

Many Mancers, Foss included, doubted the very existence of the Gehemmis. The Chronicles had it that a Sorceress named Lahja had successfully retrieved one Gehemmis from the Horogarth of Tian Xia four thousand years ago. If her grandmother was indeed alive and in the Citadel, if the Gehemmis existed, and if one of the Gehemmis was in the possession of the Mancers, these were secrets Kyreth had guarded very carefully, not only from Eliza but from the other Mancers. Eliza needed to know his secrets. She would begin with the only secret she had caught a glimpse of: Selva, her grandmother, Kyreth's wife, and the former Shang Sorceress.

She reached the tower and paused. There was no way to enter without alerting the Mancers. She pressed her forehead to the wall, closed her eyes, and opened her mind to Deep Listening. *Are you there?* She reached with her mind. *Grandmother? Are you there?*

To her amazement, the wall fell away instantly. She stumbled and found herself in the flower gardens of the Citadel in broad daylight. Her grandmother Selva was approaching her, smiling. Her cropped hair shone white in the sun and her black robes flowed about her. She carried a white staff the length of her forearm and a long serpent lay across her shoulders, tongue flickering. Bees buzzed around her face and limbs.

"What happened?" asked Eliza, stunned at how easy it had been. "Where are we?"

"Isn't it interesting?" exclaimed Selva. More bees abandoned the flowers and swarmed about her face as if she was made of nectar, but she didn't seem bothered. "I didn't think anybody else could come here with me. Sometimes I wish he would come; I walk and wait for him, but he cannot. I suppose it's because he is not a Sorceress. I miss walking in the garden with him. When I was a young girl about your age, we walked together for hours and he told me so many things, so many things! This is my sweet relief and I can find my words more easily but always I have to go back and then there are rats and I don't know what I am saying. He comes and I am not myself. He is not himself either. But you, you are so whole, and you have found your Guide, dear girl! I am so glad for you."

Eliza realized that a large raven was perched on her own shoulder.

"Are you in the tower?" she asked.

Selva glanced back at the large white tower that shone in the sunlight. Bees formed a noisy halo about her head. The serpent slithered down her body and lay coiled about her feet.

"Do you know," said Selva then, not answering the question, "he says that I am under a Curse!"

"Yes," said Eliza. "Is it nay true?"

"A Faery Cursed me," said Selva dreamily. "Jumbled my mind! But there are no accidents. Don't be fooled. Now every stone and every tree has secrets to tell me. I know about you. I know all about you. I watch you and I am so proud, so proud. Look at that brave girl, I think to myself."

"I want to help you," said Eliza.

Her grandmother laughed and gave a little caper. "It is lovely in this garden!" she said, plucking a flower. The flower wilted at once and turned ashy grey. The garden shimmered and darkened for a moment.

"Careful, careful," whispered Selva. She came creeping closer to Eliza on her bare feet. "It is I who will help *you*. Oh, we cannot stay long, we cannot stay. They say a gift may be a curse, but a Curse may be a gift as well, and who is to say? Am I under a Curse, or is the Curse under me, holding me up where I can see things? I know secrets. I know who is in *that* tower."

She pointed at the northeast tower.

"Who?" asked Eliza.

Her grandmother winked. "I will ask the stones to show you. They are my friends and I can go where I like. I am a part of this place. They think it is their place. Well, so it is, so it is. Simathien built the Citadel but did not Zara help him? This place is loyal to us as well. Ah, the stones will tell *me* things and I can speak to marble and gold and I can crawl inside the walls and look out. It's a shame, that other one, the *bad apple*, she used me you know, trampled right over me, got inside. Got to him. I couldn't help him but I helped *you*, didn't I? Never mind, all done, all finished. I can come to the garden whenever I want, stop it, stop it!" The bees were swarming about her face now. "I can't see you!" she cried to Eliza. The flowers all around them were wilting, dipping, turning black. The grass melted to tar and the sky went fast from day to night. The bees formed a dark cloud all around Selva but with her staff she pointed to the northeast tower. The sky crumbled into dust and Eliza found herself still in the dark hallway with her forehead pressed to the wall of the tower. It took her a moment to gather her thoughts.

"Thank you," she whispered, running a hand along the wall.

To reach the northeast tower she had to go through the portrait galleries. It was an eerie feeling, all those Mancer eyes watching her from the paintings as she ran by. By the time she had passed through all the galleries she was out of breath. She slowed as she came to the narrow hallway that wound around the outside of the tower and joined with the north wing and the Library. She touched her fingers tentatively to the wall of the tower. It parted before her. She cringed, expecting a siren to go off, but there was no sound. The Citadel itself was working this Magic on her behalf, or on her grandmother's.

It was dark and cold inside the tower. She was standing on a broad stone ledge that ran full circle round the inside wall. There was a gap of a few feet between this ledge and a spiral staircase that wound up the center of the tower. There seemed to be a ledge like this one at the level of each floor of the Citadel. She jumped from the ledge to the staircase, wondering whether to go up or down. There was a rush of wings up ahead of her and so she went up.

She had been climbing for quite some time when she rounded the final curve and almost hit her head on the solid stone ceiling. The staircase simply stopped, going nowhere after all. She sat down on the steps to catch her breath. She felt something crawling inside her sleeve suddenly and shook it. A bee flew out and straight up, disappearing through the ceiling. Eliza nearly laughed. When she touched the ceiling, two stones parted quietly. She climbed through the narrow space and into a broad, circular room lit with lamps. Lying huddled on a divan, teeth chattering, clutching a book to his chest, was Malferio, once King of the Faeries.

She had barely a moment to take in the stacks of books, the jars of powders and liquids and the boxes of talismans that cluttered the room. Malferio looked up at her and screamed, a scream of pure terror. He threw the book he had been clutching at her. The Urkleis gave an awful wrench in her chest. Eliza turned tail and ran back down the spiral staircase. Malferio's screams chased her, echoing in the dark passage. She rounded a curve and ran straight into a body, which knocked her back onto the stairs.

She landed badly. Pain shot up her back from her tailbone. Kyreth's face loomed over her.

CHAPTER

5

"Eliza," said Kyreth in his beautiful, sonorous voice. "What a pleasure to see you. Welcome back."

The brilliance of his eyes lit up the stairway. She noticed immediately that they were between two floors and so the nearest ledge was quite a long drop down. There was no way past him.

She scrambled to her feet painfully. Ravens gathered behind her, lining the stairs.

"You have no reason to fear me," he said, with a nod at the ravens. "I have only ever wanted your safety. Even now, I would protect you against any who wished you harm."

"What's your idea of harm?" asked Eliza, her voice trembling with rage and fear. "Does killing somebody I love count as harming me? Because frankly I'd prefer a more direct approach."

Kyreth smiled thinly. Malferio's screams from above were dwindling into sobs.

"What are you doing to him?" asked Eliza.

"Isn't it obvious?" asked Kyreth. He reached towards her with his hand, as if to touch his fingers to her chest, above her heart. Eliza backed away up the stairs, slipping a little. The ravens drew closer around her, cawing.

"You still bear the Urkleis," he said. "It is a burden."

"Yes." She took another step back and added, "If you try to touch me again, I'll kill you."

Kyreth acted as if he had not heard this. "I am going to lift your burden, Eliza. You pretend to be used to it but you will never be used to it. You feel within your very flesh and bone the hatred and the hunger for freedom of she who sought to annihilate you.

49

In that room above lies the key to Nia's Immortality. Under her Curse he wishes only to die, and so he shall. When that happens, the Xia Sorceress will die too, and you will be free of the Urkleis."

"You're going to kill Nia?" asked Eliza. In spite of everything she felt a bewildering wave of sorrow. "Your own daughter."

"She is no daughter to me," said Kyreth, his terrible eyes boring into her. "Rea is my daughter."

Eliza said nothing.

"What we love is the same," he said to her in a low voice. "What we hate is the same. What we wish for is the same, Eliza. This is where you belong. It is good that you have returned."

"You lied to me," said Eliza bitterly. "You lied to me about everything."

"Don't be childish, Eliza. When did I lie?"

She turned her eyes from his, for there was something in them that sought to hold her or consume her. "You told me my grandmother was dead," she said.

"There are many kinds of death, Eliza Tok," murmured Kyreth.

"There are nay many kinds!" she shouted, looking straight into his face for an awful burning moment. "I've seen the Guardian between life and death. I've been to the river. There is one kind of death, Kyreth. One."

"Sixteen years old, in love, and you think you are wise," he said dryly. "What have you seen that I have not seen? Nothing. What do you know that I do not know? Nothing. You have lied to *me*, Eliza, countless times, endangering yourself and the Mancers. A selfish adolescent, unfit to be called the Shang Sorceress, oblivious to your duty, obsessed only with your own inner circle, your own inner world." He said this entirely without emotion but he stepped a little closer as he did so. The ravens screamed, more and more of them appearing on the stairs. Eliza wished they would fly at him, attack him, but they did not dare go near him.

"Let me by," she said in a tight little voice.

Kyreth did not move. His eyes burned still brighter.

"Let me by," she repeated, more forcefully this time.

"How did you get in here, Eliza?" Kyreth asked her softly.

There was something terrible in his eyes, something dangerous. She did not think. She leaped off the stairs to the ledge below. A second bad landing, this time twisting her ankle. She pressed her shoulder to the wall but it did not make way for her. She pounded against it with her fists and her ravens swarmed in a panic about the tower.

Above her, Kyreth gave a joyless chuckle.

"Go back to bed, Eliza," he said and made a gesture with his finger. A door opened in the wall. Eliza limped out into the hall. Her ravens streamed after her and the door shut behind them, disappeared. She did not look back but went as quickly as she could on her hurt ankle, back through the galleries under the endless eyes of the Mancer portraits, to the south wing and her room, where she crawled into bed. Her ravens formed a black, feathered wall all around her, but they could not comfort her once sleep came.

In her dreams, the black panther from the river of death gnashed his teeth at her and growled, *You cannot steal from death. You will bring me your beloved,* and the Oracle of the Ancients, the one Nia had killed, hissed the prophecies that had haunted Eliza for years now: *Yours is the lonely road. You will lose all those you love. You will cut out your own heart.*

Eliza's ankle was swollen and sore when she woke in the morning. A stab of pain shot through it as soon as she tried to stand. She forewent her usual scavenge in the kitchen for breakfast and instead limped straight to the Library. Foss was seated at the broad mahogany table where they used to have their lessons, open books spread out all around him. He was drawing a chart on a long scroll whose other end spilled off the table and lay on the floor in great curls.

"Kyreth has Malferio in the northeast tower," she told him,

limping to her chair and sitting down. Sitting hurt almost as much as walking – she had given her tailbone quite a crack when she fell the first time.

Foss looked up sharply. "Are you hurt, Eliza?"

She shook her head. "Nay badly. I think I sprained my ankle. I ran into Kyreth last night. He's gone insane, Foss."

"He is still deep in Nia's Curse," said Foss. "He is driven as much by fear as the lust for power. Together, a dangerous combination." He cleared his throat. "I have been rethinking the matter, Eliza, and I have concluded that you should not stay here. It is not safe. I will speak frankly with Aysu and find out what can be done for your friend the Shade…Charlie. But you should not be here."

"I cannay leave yet," said Eliza.

Foss passed a big golden hand over his forehead. He looked very agitated. "Malferio is here," he muttered. "I did not know."

"Kyreth is up to something. He has Malferio because he wants to kill Nia. If Malferio dies, so will Nia; his Curse will be lifted and he'll get credit for defeating her. Obviously he wants Charlie out of the way too. But he's just clearing the way for something else. Lah, I know he wants me to marry a Mancer and have a little Sorceress daughter that he can control better than he can control me, but there's something else going on. Something bigger. I'm sure of it."

"That may very well be so," said Foss. "And it is all the more reason for you to be away somewhere safe. Winning Aysu over and ridding her of Kyreth's influence is the key and I am well on my way, Eliza. I think it would be best if you joined your friends in the Realm of the Faeries or went to Swarn for protection."

Eliza shook her head distractedly. "I'm on his trail, aye," she said. "I'm going to find out what he's up to and once I have something over him that I can use…lah, then I'll use it somehow, I spose." She peered across the table at the chart he was working on. "What are you doing?"

He beamed, eyes brightening. "I am charting the separation of the worlds. Do you know, it has never been done before!

There are some scattered records, of course, but nothing that can give us a clear idea of how long it will take. The peculiar thing is that the separation seems to be gradually slowing down. Rather like pulling apart something made of flexible rubber. It is not so difficult to stretch the two halves a certain distance, but as they get farther apart the pressure increases and it becomes more difficult. Either they will snap apart all at once or the force holding them together will be greater than the force pulling them apart and the process will grind to a halt. I believe that is what is happening, Eliza."

"I thought you were going to research the Thanatosi," Eliza broke in, but Foss was so animated that he barely heard her.

"Even more peculiar, Eliza Tok, is that there is no record at all in the Old Library of Karbek's spell – what was done, *how* it was done. The *original spell*, I mean! Nothing! How can this be? I suspect that there *is* a record of the spell somewhere but it is hidden. Or missing. Even stolen. I do not know, but it is shocking that we have not kept the text under close watch, guarded it as an object of great value. We Mancers pride ourselves on our *curiosity*, Eliza, for above all other beings we seek answers, knowledge. We keep meticulous records, as our Library attests! And yet all our questioning is turned outward, never inward. We are perhaps too docile, too incurious, when it comes to ourselves."

Eliza put her head down on the table and faked a snore.

"Yes, Eliza?" Foss asked dryly, stopping his monologue. She raised her head and grinned at him.

"Sorry. Do you know what's in the other towers, Foss?"

"I do not. Please pay attention. Do you see what I am saying? You made me think of it yesterday when you told me the Magic we worked made no sense. I realized that I myself only partially understood the great work we have all undertaken. I, the Spellmaster! There must have been a text in the Library at some point outlining Karbek's spell, but Eliza, it is *gone*."

"It's nay one of the books Nia drained?"

"No. I do not mean it is empty. I mean there *is no record* of such a book! I have checked all the indexes more than once. I know, at least, what the empty books *were*. A description of Karbek's spell was not among them."

"You think Kyreth might have the book you want," said Eliza, the connection dawning on her. "In which case he was up to all kinds of mischief as a young Mancer – trying to take over the line of the Xia Sorceress, sending his wife off to the Realm of the Faeries for the Gehemmis, stealing and hiding important books. What does he want?"

"Look at this, Eliza Tok. Come, sit over here."

Eliza groaned as she moved to sit next to him. Her ankle and tailbone were throbbing and she was exhausted from the night's adventures and the tension of being back in the Citadel. However, all these worries fell away as she examined Foss's chart.

"You're right," she said, interested. "The separation of the worlds *is* slowing down."

"The Mancers are weakening," murmured Foss. "Perhaps. Perhaps."

"Perhaps what?" asked Eliza.

Foss shook his head. "I do not know. Something different is needed. But to know what, I must see the Original Spell. I will speak to Aysu."

Eliza tried to be diplomatic. "I can see how this might be important, aye, but it could be a wild goose chase, too. And we dinnay have time for a wild goose chase. Have you done any reading at all about the Thanatosi?"

"Indeed I have, Eliza. My research on calling off the Thanatosi has turned up nothing, I regret to say. But do *not* be discouraged! It is too soon to give up hope, Eliza Tok! It is much too soon!"

"Thank you for helping me, Foss. I hope you're nay putting yourself in danger."

"It is my nature, I suppose," he replied cheerfully. "All the books on the Thanatosi are there on the floor. Look through them if you like. I will take this to Aysu."

He gathered up the loops of paper in his arms. Eliza fondly watched him go before settling down to read.

Aysu was staring at her hands on the desk as if they did not belong to her. A knock came and she started. She could not remember what she had been thinking, what she had been doing, how long she had been sitting here. She looked at the wall, full of trepidation. She was troubled by her trance this morning. The black crab that should have led her to a vision had been washing listlessly against the shore, as if lifeless on the waves. The knock came again. What could she do? She drew a symbol in the air with one shaking finger and the door appeared and opened. It was Foss. She felt a mixture of anger and relief.

"Spellmaster," she greeted him, as civilly as she could.

He bowed. He was holding something in his hand. A long scroll. Perhaps this one would speak to her.

"Pardon my intrusion," he said very formally. "If your Eminence would look at this?"

She nodded. With a flourish he unrolled the scroll across her desk. As she looked at it she felt a shadow around her heart, a frightening constriction in her throat. It made no sense to her at all, these marks and scratches on paper. She could not focus her eyes, she could not read it. It meant nothing.

"What is this?" she asked angrily.

"I have been charting the progress of the separation of the worlds," explained Foss, very animated. "Do you know it has never been done? I thought…"

"Kyreth is right about you!" cried Aysu, pushing the scroll off her desk so it tumbled looping to the floor. Foss took a step back, amazed. Aysu strode around the desk, walking over the scroll so she was eye to eye with him.

"You *seek* trouble," she hissed. "We Mancers have always worked together, worked as a group, and yet you are always off on some investigation of your own. We brought writing to the One World! We collected all the knowledge of the past and recorded it for posterity! We have been the protectors of humankind for thousands of years! The keepers of the Sorceress! Why do you seek always to undermine, to sow discontent? Why did you come to me with tales of Kyreth's misdeeds, why did you let the Sorceress leave at all? All might have been well had you not chosen to interfere. Oh, Foss!" She was breathing heavily.

Foss put his large hands on either side of her face. He began to murmur and she felt the ocean rocking beneath them, she felt the rains pouring down from above. She felt a deep thirst, felt how she was scorched to the skin, dried out, full of hot flame. She let herself soak in his words; she drank her fill of them. She let the deep, dark oceans hold her for a time.

The next thing she knew, she was seated in her chair. Foss knelt at her side and his hand was on hers.

"Aysu?" he said.

"Yes, Foss," she replied. She took a deep breath.

He smiled at her. "It is you," he said.

She nodded. "I am sorry."

"No need to apologize. You have always been a friend to me, Aysu. Now I wish to be yours."

"Thank you." She was so tired. Just making the words was difficult. It was as if she had put down a great weight. Before she could rise and carry on her journey she needed to rest.

"You must call together the manipulators of water," he said. "You must ask them for their strength. You must rely on *us*, Aysu, and not see Kyreth for a time. I do not presume to give the Supreme Mancer orders but this is for your own good. He hungers for power and he has asserted his will over yours. You have been dragging it around like a great chain around your own power. You can be a great leader. I have faith in you as a leader. But *you* must lead us, Aysu. Not Kyreth."

"He is stronger than I am," said Aysu. "Even Cursed and mad, he is so much stronger than I am."

"Perhaps. But he is not stronger than all of us, Aysu. It is time to take a stand."

She nodded weakly and squeezed his hand.

"Thank you," she said. "I will gather the manipulators of water tomorrow. Today I must rest."

Foss gathered up his fallen, trampled scroll and spread it out on the desk again.

"Look," he pleaded. "Look."

Aysu examined the scroll and this time she saw what he meant. She went over every inch of it. When she was done she said, "Continue with your work, Foss, and keep me informed. What you are doing is important."

Foss bowed gratefully. "Thank you, your Eminence."

She smiled at him, her real smile as he remembered it from before she became Supreme Mancer.

"Be careful, Foss," she said.

"And you, your Eminence."

∞

The day was growing late. Soon she would retire to her chambers. Foss was right, she had been drawn entirely away from herself, but it was not too late to set things right. She walked slowly to the Library. What Foss had showed her on the scroll was unsettling. She trusted him but she wanted to double-check. It was possible that the Spellmaster was mistaken. He was powerful but not infallible. It seemed so improbable that the Old Library would contain no text of Karbek's spell at all. She must be certain he had not simply overlooked it. It would not do to take action or speak to the other Mancers until she was sure he was right.

As she made her way among the bookshelves in the Old Library she thought she saw a flicker of movement, something small and dark by the windows at the back. She froze, then shook away her fear. She was the Supreme Mancer in her own Citadel. What did she have to fear? She walked swiftly to where she had seen movement. There she found Eliza by one of the long windows, bent over a book.

"Pardon me!" she exclaimed, startled. Eliza looked up and closed the book hastily. It was one of the Histories, Aysu noted. The Thanatosi. She felt a strong desire to snatch the book from the young Sorceress and interrogate her.

"Are you all right?" asked Eliza, for Aysu had begun to sway slightly, her eyes growing brighter and brighter.

"Yes! Yes!" All at once she was Aysu again. "I am here for a book."

"Lah, you're in the right place, then," said Eliza, rising and sidling around the Supreme Mancer.

She is afraid of me, thought Aysu sadly.

"Goodnight!" she called after Eliza, who disappeared among the bookshelves. She bent down and picked up something that Eliza had dropped. It was a soggy towel wrapped around a block of melting ice. What could she be doing with such a thing? Was it part of a spell? Fear washed over her again.

I am going mad, thought Aysu. The Citadel is against me. The Sorceress does not trust me. I am not fit to be Supreme Mancer.

"I must agree with you."

His voice in her ear. His hand on her shoulder. She thought of the dark ocean, the rain, but it was too late. She could not fight him now.

"This is not what I wished but time has run out," said Kyreth. "I am sorry, Aysu."

"Never mind," she said faintly. "It doesn't matter."

"No," he agreed. "I suppose it doesn't."

His blade slid into her, through her heart. The oceans and rivers poured out of her. She crumpled to the Library floor, her eyes fading, and watched his feet walking away, the blade at his side. Darkness closed around it all. She caught a flash of the black crab washing against the shore. Then it was gone.

CHAPTER

6

Eliza fled the Library and went to look for Foss. She knew she was not permitted to enter the Mancers' chambers but she was frightened. She wanted to tell him how Aysu had looked, that awful glare in her eyes, the way she had been swaying back and forth. The Supreme Mancer was slipping.

She made her way to the warren of torch-lit stone rooms under the Library, where the manipulators of water slept. She had bandaged her ankle and kept ice on it for much of the day but it was still sore and she couldn't put her full weight on it. There was a crab on the wall marking Foss's chambers. She knocked and waited. No reply came. She touched her fingers to the black crab and hesitated, then drew the symbol Foss had taught her with her index finger. It was his own private symbol for his door. The door appeared and swung open soundlessly. The Citadel did not protest.

Foss's chambers were made up of three connected rooms with domed ceilings and high arched doorways between them. In one room cushions were arranged on the floor on either side of a low table. The next room contained only a long, tidy bed and a desk, and the third room was lined with empty bookcases. The lack of books was so uncharacteristic of Foss that she felt a chill run through her.

"Foss?" she called hesitantly, as if he might be hiding somewhere. But there was nowhere to hide; his chambers were empty. Disappointed and increasingly afraid, she crossed the darkening grounds back towards the south wing. As she approached she noticed a number of Mancers entering the south wing, rather more of them than usual at this hour. She hurried after them and headed up the marble staircase. Hearing footsteps behind her she froze, then spun around. It was Ka, Emmisarius of fire. He gave her a polite bow without breaking his stride.

"Hello." Her voice came out high and nervous. He swept past her and turned down the hallway.

"Where is everybody going?" she asked.

Ka glanced back over his shoulder and there was something sorrowful in the look he gave her.

"Some matters of no great importance to be discussed before nightfall," he said. "Goodnight, Eliza. Welcome back."

"Thanks," she said. "Goodnight."

She hesitated on the stairs as he disappeared from sight, wondering whether or not to go back and look for Foss to tell him about this new development. But if he was not in his chambers and not in the Library, perhaps he too was attending this unusual evening meeting. In any case, it could wait until morning, she decided, and made her way back to her bedroom.

Tired though she was, she did not sleep well. Ravens hopped about the room in agitation, occasionally cawing and waking her. For a while she tried to ignore them but at last she rose and went to the window. The grounds were quiet. Still, there could be no doubt *something* was going on; she ought to be ready. She got dressed and fastened the shoulder strap and scabbard Nell had made across her chest. Her dagger was not in the scabbard and she had a moment of panic before remembering that it was under her pillow. She had taken only a step towards the bed when her bedroom door flew open. There came a blinding flash and a great force threw her back against the far wall, knocking the breath out of her. She stumbled to her feet, gasping. Five Mancers had entered her room. She knew from the emblems on their robes, the black crab, the red bird, the yellow human, the white bear, and the blue serpent, that they were manipulators from each of the five houses: water, fire, earth, metal and wood. Any Magic combining all five of these forces was terribly strong. The room was full of ravens all at once, diving at the chanting Mancers. Five voices spoke a word together in the Language of First Days: *Bind.* It was the final word of a spell prepared in advance. The ravens were gone, not a cry, not a feather. A ring of fire appeared around Eliza's waist. From this ring a shimmer of light emanated, surrounding her like a shell. She touched her hands to it and withdrew them with a sharp cry. It was white hot.

"What's going on?" she asked in a high voice, despising herself for the fear she knew they could hear and sense. "What are you doing?"

"Excuse these extreme measures," began the manipulator of metal a bit sheepishly. The manipulator of wood said gruffly, "Hush," and the other fell silent. They turned and left.

"Help me!" shouted Eliza, without really meaning to. After all, who would help her here? Her voice bounced thinly inside the barrier, contained. She knew without trying that she could not do any Magic that would penetrate it. This was no ordinary barrier. She did not cry for help again. Now that the shock of it had passed she was more angry than afraid. There was nothing to do but wait and stay calm, if that were possible. Whatever they intended, she did not think they could be planning to hurt her.

Hours passed. The sun rose. No one came.

Finnis, manipulator of water, hurried across the grounds. He had been summoned to the Supreme Mancer's study. Last night before sundown he had felt something terrible, something that had turned his blood cold, cloaked in a heavy secrecy. He did not know what it was but he had been unable to sleep and had considered going to see the Emmisarius of water. In the end he had been too shy to disturb Foss at night, so he remained sleepless and unsure until morning. In his morning trance, the black crab raced along the sand, the tide close behind, and as it ran the crab swelled to twice its normal size. The vision had been full of fear but told him nothing useful. Should he mention it to the Supreme Mancer? But perhaps it was nothing. Finnis was still a novice, only recently granted full Mancer status and allowed to partake in the daily goings on of the Citadel. He did not wish to be seen as immature or easily shaken. He feared that perhaps his poor sleep had disturbed the others and he was to be reprimanded. He knocked on the wall. A door opened and he entered.

Four of the Emmisariae stood before the Supreme Mancer's desk: Ka, Anargul, Obrad, and Trahaearn. When he entered, they stepped aside for him. It was not Aysu seated behind the desk as he had expected. It was Kyreth. Finnis froze, paralyzed by his confusion.

"Welcome, Finnis," said Kyreth in his deep voice. "I apologize for the disruption last night. I imagine you slept poorly."

"Yes," said Finnis weakly.

"My fault," said Kyreth with a swift, crumbling smile. "Matters got out of hand. Foss destroyed the Vindensphere. He is in the dungeons awaiting charges. Aysu is missing and we suspect he had something to do with it. It would appear we are in need of a new Emmisarius immediately. I wish to offer the position to you."

Finnis did not know what to say. It was absurd, a joke, surely. But no, they looked too somber for that. What could he say?

"I…I would be happy to accept. Such an honour." He looked around at the others, who were regarding him calmly. "But surely Foss would never wish any harm to Aysu?"

He could not help saying it. The idea was ludicrous, after all. A slight tremor ran through the room and the others averted their eyes. Kyreth rose to his feet and came slowly round to the front of his desk, where the Emmisariae stood. Finnis wished he could unsay the words. But the Supreme Mancer spoke as if he had not heard them: "I am glad that you have joined us. You are young, but most promising, Finnis. I have had my eye on you. I think you will do well."

His eyes fell on Anargul then. She dropped her head. Finnis saw she was mortally afraid.

"I do not wish to hold grudges," Kyreth said. "You spoke against me once, Anargul. Where stand you now?"

"Your Eminence, I was wrong," she said. "This past year has seen nothing but dissonance and difficulty among the Mancers. I welcome your return to power and I hope you will accept me, unworthy though I am, as your Emmisarius."

"I am glad to have you with us, Anargul," said Kyreth. "It is the season of your ascendancy. You must lead the Emmisariae. This new member in particular will need your guidance."

She fell on her knees and bowed. He touched his fingers to her forehead. They each did the same in turn, including Finnis. Then Kyreth returned to his desk and sat down. Finnis noticed that the desk was riddled with cracks, like the ground split by an earthquake.

"There is much to be done," said Kyreth. "Today the Shang Sorceress and Obrad will be married. For this, all the Emmisariae must be present and I myself will conduct the ceremony. Gather the necessary items and take them to the Marriage Hall in the Inner Sanctum. That is all."

Kyreth nodded to them and they filed out. Only Obrad stayed behind.

"Thank you for this honour, your Eminence," he said.

"She will not welcome you, Obrad," said Kyreth.

Obrad bowed his head. "It grieves me. But I hope she will come to accept it."

"Indeed, no doubt she will. But in the meantime she must be subdued. Do you understand me?"

Obrad looked up at the Supreme Mancer questioningly. Kyreth handed him a vial of dark liquid.

"This will serve the purpose," he said. "She is held in a barrier in her room. Feed her the potion and bring her to the Inner Sanctum as soon as it has taken effect."

"What will it do?" asked Obrad uncertainly, taking the vial from him.

"It will make her willing," said Kyreth. "Go. Fetch your bride."

⤫

She looked tired and frightened, he thought.

"Obrad?" She peered at him through the glare of the barrier. He saw understanding dawn on her face, and then fury.

"Stay back," she said. "Another step and you will see what a Sorceress can do."

Obrad held up the glass vial Kyreth had given him.

"I think you will change your mind," he said, "after you have a drink of this."

He stepped closer, then hesitated. Kyreth had given no advice on how to administer the potion. Suppose she simply spat it back in his face? Would it work if she swallowed a mere drop or did she need to drink all of it? He circled her, pondering this. Her black eyes burned with hatred. The whole thing was unpleasant, horrible, he thought.

"This is what is necessary," he told her. He meant to sound placating, but it came out angry. "If you were not so stubborn, so selfish, these measures would be dispensed with. You do not understand the history, the traditions –"

Something sharp struck him on the ankle. He looked down and saw a long black snake, twice as thick as his arm, spread across the floor of the room. Its head was poised for another blow. Stunned, his mind confused, he began to raise a barrier. It struck again, too quickly. The pain was blinding for an instant and then his leg went numb. He felt the poison in his blood.

"What snake?" he heard himself say, as if from a great distance. He fell heavily, dropping the vial, whose contents spilled on the floor.

Selva entered the room, her eyes meeting Eliza's through the barrier.

"Thank you!" Eliza took a deep shuddering breath. "Is he dead?"

"Paralyzed," said Selva softly. "I have had too much of killing in my day."

"I need to find Foss. Can you break this barrier?"

"Listen to me," said Selva, her pale eyes intense. "Listen to *me*. You need to find the Gehemmis. I know. I know where it is hidden. There is a secret treasury in the northwest tower and that is where you must go. You must go there and you must get the Gehemmis. I wanted to bring it to you but there is no time. You must take the Gehemmis and go to Tian Xia, and you must collect the other Gehemmis. It is terribly important, my dear, that you do this."

"But why? What are the Gehemmis?"

Eliza was still trembling and Selva's strange way of speaking was making her head spin. She wanted to get out of this barrier and get her dagger. That was all she could think about. She was horribly afraid of seeing Kyreth appear at any minute at the door, or some other Mancer.

"Why, they will tell you what they are!" said Selva, and suddenly she laughed and her eyes sparkled. "My poor child. This barrier is made to hold a Sorceress. You cannot break it and neither can I."

"Then how will I go get the Gehemmis?" She could hear the panicked pitch of her voice but she could not control it.

Selva ran her hands over the outside of the barrier and her palms blistered from the heat. She seemed hardly to notice.

"To hold one Sorceress," she said and laughed again. "Do you remember how we met in the garden? How unusual!"

"I remember, aye," said Eliza.

"And Nia, she reached inside you, didn't she? Right inside you."

"Yes." Eliza shuddered.

"Come. There is something between us that is greater than this small Magic! Remember how you came into the garden with me."

Eliza closed her eyes. She tried to lean against the barrier. It was too hot. But then she felt Selva opening, her grandmother opening into something wide and cool like a wind. There was no barrier between them. How could there be? Eliza stepped into her. When she opened her eyes, she was facing her grandmother from the other direction and Selva was inside the barrier. Her ravens were flapping freely about the room. Selva's snake had disappeared.

"Go," said Selva. "Quickly, child. I cannot help you any more but the stars whisper to my bones that only you can do this."

Eliza grabbed her dagger from the bed, her few belongings in the camelhair backpack, and ran.

The ravens shot off in every direction, high against the ceiling, coasting on quiet wings. She could see what they saw, not with her eyes but somewhere in her mind. They were her sentinels, telling her when the coast was clear. Gritting her teeth against the jarring pain in her ankle, the throb in her tailbone, she raced up the stairs at a lopsided gallop. It was safer to stick to the upper floors, where it was generally quieter. More Mancers would be coming for her soon. She ran around the southwest tower and entered the west wing, the Treasuries. She paused and listened. Her ravens were her eyes, but they could not be everywhere and she was anxious lest they be seen. No sound, and so she hurried along the uppermost hallway. She could feel the barriers on the walls here, the power of the unseen doors keeping out those who would steal the treasures of the Mancers. The Citadel was on the side of the Mancers and yet, in some ways, it was on her side and her grandmother's side too. She couldn't be sure if it would betray her or protect her. She didn't want to take any chances. She lurched and hobbled the length of the Treasuries, came to the next tower and went around it into the Library, where she was always authorized to make a door and enter. Foss had fought with Kyreth for that right for her; it had been reluctantly granted a few years ago and never revoked. The wall opened for her and she ran to the back of the Old Library and Foss's supply shelf. Here he kept all the items for potions. She hastily grabbed what she needed. She had nothing to hold the potion and so she emptied a jar of powdered nettle root right onto the floor and mixed together the things she needed in the jar. She whispered incantations as she worked, kneeling behind the stacks, her ravens keeping watch. The task of performing this simple Magic calmed her somewhat.

Through one of the ravens high on a bookshelf she saw Ka enter the Old Library and she froze. He was coming her way. There was no time to finish the potion. Hanging onto the jar of ingredients she had mixed already, she grabbed a dropper from the shelf containing the spinal juice of a Tian Xia invisible eel and crawled quickly along the wall. Ka stopped several feet away, just two bookshelves over from where she was. He was looking for something and found it. She was concentrating so hard on watching him through the raven that she barely noticed what was in front of her until she put her hand on a book. It was the book she had let fall yesterday evening, the History of the Thanatosi. Next to the book, a large golden hand lay across the floor, the arm hidden around the next bookcase. Eliza gasped, then clapped a hand over her mouth.

Ka had good ears. He froze, the book he had come for in his hand. Through the raven she saw the title: *The Book of Union*. For a moment, neither of them moved. Then he looked up and locked eyes with the raven watching him from a bookshelf high above. She was out of time. Eliza held the dropper over the jar and let fall four, five, six drops, muttering the incantation as fast as she could. Ka stared at the raven and listened. He heard Eliza's voice and began to walk towards it. She threw her head back and drank half of the potion. It worked immediately. She watched her hands around the jar as they became translucent and disappeared. The jar disappeared too, a moment later. Awkwardly, since she couldn't see it, she put the lid back on. Everything she was touching at the time she drank the potion had become invisible. She could see right through the floor to the level below. Ka was almost upon her now. She crawled quickly away from the invisible patch of floor, around the bookshelf, to where Aysu's body lay.

The blood pooled around the body was like liquid light. Her eyes were dead caverns. Horrified, Eliza huddled next to the corpse of the Mancer. Ka had seen the invisible patch of floor and the Mancer hand. He rounded the corner and stood over Eliza and the terrible sight of Aysu's body. Eliza looked up at him, his face constricted with grief, the light of his eyes fading to a pale glow.

"Oh, my friend," he said, very softly.

He looked around and Eliza could feel him listening. She did not breathe.

"Eliza!" he called suddenly and she jumped. His eyes fixed on her, though she knew he could not see her. He began to murmur under his breath. She caught the words: it was a spell of Deep Listening. He was searching for her mind. Still holding the jar tight, she leaped to her feet and fled the Library. She heard him behind her. Ravens came soaring down from the ceiling, multiplying, swarming about him with their screeching and cawing. She left him calling up a barrier to fight them off. She ran to the northwest tower, the pain in her ankle screaming its violent protest. There was no time even to think of the best order in which to do things. She pressed her invisible hands to the wall of the tower, writing symbols on the stone with her fingers, speaking every spell she knew to conjure a door, but the wall resisted her. She put the jar with the remaining potion in her backpack, drew her dagger, and took a deep breath. The blade went through the wall as if it were butter.

Kyreth was waiting in the Marriage Hall of the Inner Sanctum with Finnis, Anargul, and Trahaearn. They had gathered together the necessary objects: the ritual cups, the double-flute, the bells of Sinath-Mag. Soon Ka would come with the book and Obrad with the bride. The Marriage Hall was a smaller room off the Main Hall, with a domed ceiling and a line from the Book of the Ancients regarding the virtuous nature of marriage running around the top of the wall. Kyreth, who would officiate the ceremony, was seated on a long, tasseled bench. Two pillows had been placed on the floor before him, where the couple would kneel.

But something was holding them up.

"It should not have taken Obrad this long," Kyreth said, rising.

"Shall I go and check?" asked Finnis, eager to please.

Kyreth replied, "I will go myself. Remain here." He swept out of the room. Crossing the grounds, he sensed something was wrong. He thought he saw a raven watching him from one of the trees but when he looked up it was gone. He paused and searched his mind. Nia's Curse sometimes brought his fears to life, made him see terrible shadows that were not there in reality. He could not be certain about the raven. He made his way more quickly to the south wing.

He had spent months preparing a barrier to bind a Sorceress. She could not possibly have escaped from it, even if Obrad had failed to administer the potion correctly. Though she was getting stronger, surprisingly stronger, he was confident the barrier would hold. He told himself these things as he made his way up to her room and pushed the watching raven out of his mind. But when he entered the room his fears were confirmed in the most terrible way.

"My dear," said Selva. She stood ringed with fire. Through the gleam of the barrier her skin and hair had a golden hue. She looked almost like her younger self. Obrad lay on the floor, stiff as a board.

"Selva." He stepped closer to her. Rage slithered up from his belly like a black snake. "What have you done?"

"It was whispered to me by the creatures of the ocean floor and the celestial orbs. She must finish it. But you are angry, I see you are angry."

"Yes." He took another step towards her. "I am angry."

She shook her head at him, her eyes widening. "I know what you are thinking. Terrible! Terrible! You must not do it. We were in love once. Do you remember? In the garden?"

"I remember everything," he said. "Where is Eliza?"

A terrible siren rent the air.

CHAPTER
7

The tower wall was thick. In spite of the tremendous properties of her dagger, cutting through it took longer than Eliza had hoped and now the siren had alerted the Mancers. It was as if the Citadel was screaming with rage and pain. Eliza kept on slicing and slashing. She felt rather than heard the Mancers coming and squeezed through the wound she had gouged in the wall. She found herself on a ledge like the one in the northeast tower, facing a narrow staircase spiraling around a central pillar. She leaped from the ledge to the stairs. Though she tried to land on one foot, she couldn't altogether protect her hurt ankle and the impact made her cry out. She climbed as quickly as she could. There was no sound of pursuit. A raven peered through the dagger-torn wall she had left behind her at the Mancers milling outside it. They were too large to fit through and clearly none of them were authorized to make a door in any of the towers. She had a little time yet, then.

When she got to the top of the stairs she had to cut through the ceiling into the room above. Selva, in her barrier, could not speak to the Citadel on Eliza's behalf anymore. It was exhausting work. Eliza's arms ached and she felt as though her head would split open from the Citadel's screams. When she had created a large enough gap she hauled herself up into the room. Immediately two halves of a spherical barrier swept down and closed around her, lifting her up and spinning about the room at high speed. Terrified of being dashed against one of the walls, she cut through the bottom of the barrier and tumbled out onto the stone floor. A barrier on the ground beneath her lifted her up at a terrifying speed as if to crush her against the ceiling. She rolled off it barely in time, landing hard again on the ground below. Another barrier fell upon her and trapped her there like a bug beneath a glass. She lay still this time, lame and bruised and feeling, for a moment, entirely helpless. The room was booby-trapped with deadly barriers. Worse than that, it was empty. She saw nothing at all that could be the Gehemmis, whatever it looked like. Had she come to the wrong tower? Had Selva said the southwest tower? But then why go to such trouble with barriers in an empty room? No, the Gehemmis must be hidden here somehow, hidden by Magic. Invisible, just like her. So now the invisible Sorceress had to find the invisible treasure in a room full of invisible barriers. It wasn't safe to move until she figured out where the Gehemmis was. She could not think or see clearly while being spun about or nearly flattened. She cut a hole in the barrier she was under and ravens flew out of it, into the room. The barriers fell upon them, sweeping down from the ceiling and up from the floor, snatching up her poor ravens, trapping them and hurling them about. Safe under her own barrier trap, Eliza watched closely. Within the storm of ravens in barriers, there was a space of inactivity near the wall on the other side of the room. It must be the Gehemmis.

She took a few deep breaths and let them out slowly. She shut out the pain in her ankle; she shut out her fear. She memorized the movement of the barriers and then she was ready. She sliced the barrier she was under wide open and made a dash across the room to the empty spot, dodging the barriers that were still chasing and trapping her ravens. She groped about madly and her hand struck a barrier over the wall. There. She cut through it and reached inside, feeling along an invisible shelf. Her hand closed over something oblong and smooth and all the ravens cried out at once. She would have to hope she had it. She dodged and ducked and rolled her way back to the space she had cut in the floor and slipped through it back onto the stairs. She heard footsteps coming up and immediately jumped down to the nearest ledge. Trying to land on one foot again, she fell and let out a sharp gasp.

Fortunately the Mancers were not close enough to hear. She crouched against the wall as they came into her sights and hurried by her, newly authorized to enter, up the stairs towards the top of the tower.

She waited until she could no longer hear their footfalls echoing and then jumped back onto the stairs. She limped past the wall she had cut through to get in, all the way to the very bottom, by which time she was winded and terribly dizzy. She held her dagger firmly in one hand and in the other hand the Gehemmis, if such it was. Once she was at the bottom she set about cutting through the wall again, through to the north wing and the chambers of the manipulators of water. Once again the Citadel screamed in deafening, sickening protest, but nobody had made it to the wall by the time she squeezed out. Beneath the chambers were the dungeons. She opened her mind to Foss and made her way cautiously, quietly now. The chambers were deserted. There was no barrier barring her way down the narrow staircase to the dungeons. She followed a glimmer of light through the warren of cells to where two Mancers stood guard, not speaking to each other. The light came from their eyes, bright and alert. Eliza sent one of her ravens winging down the hallway past them, and then another.

The Mancers started but did not move. The ravens set up a terrible cawing around the corner. Still the two standing guard did not budge, though they exchanged agitated glances.

"She is here," one of them muttered. Eliza gave up on making them move and inched closer. She crouched against the wall directly across from them. Behind them she could see a small cell and Foss's shape sitting down. She caught the glow of his eyes, brilliant and knowing. She opened her mind to him again and this time she felt him respond.

I'm going to get you out. We need to go straight to the dark wood, get to Tian Xia.

His reply came to her like a scorching blaze that made her wince but she was able to take it into herself. *It will be impossible to get to the Crossing through the wood. They will be expecting it.*

He was right, of course. That way was no good. They would have to steal a dragon.

The dragons too will be under guard. We must go on foot.

Very quietly, very slowly, Eliza took from her backpack the weapon Swarn had sent her for her birthday. The two ravens in the hall swooped up and down, cawing, to mask any sound she might make. The Mancers were still as stone, waiting, listening. She found the mouthpiece, fitted it to her lips, and then placed one of the little darts into the other end. She aimed it at one of the Mancers and blew softly. It caught him in the neck.

He fell like a stone. The other one stared down at his fallen companion in a momentary panic and Eliza blew a dart into him as well. He too fell instantly. She rose and stepped over the fallen Mancers, cutting through the barrier with her dagger. She reached for Foss's hand.

"You have more of the potion?" he asked her.

"Of course." She fumbled with her invisible backpack again and placed the jar in his hands. Within seconds, he too was fading out of sight.

"We had better stay very close to one another," said Foss. "Come. There is a way out through the dungeons."

"I know it," said Eliza, limping after him.

"Ah yes," said Foss. "I forgot how much mischief you've gotten up to in your time here. Useful, in the end. Your footfalls are uneven. Are you hurt?"

"My ankle, still."

"You said it was not bad yesterday."

"Lah, that was before I had to do a whole lot of running and jumping."

"Come, I will carry you."

Foss crouched down as he spoke. Eliza gratefully felt for his shoulders and put her arms around them, climbing onto his back, the way she'd climbed onto her father's back when she was a little girl. Her weight was nothing at all to Foss and he continued swiftly through the dungeons to the caverns that the dragons used. They followed the vast tunnels to an iron door, the only exit from the Citadel into Di Shang, and deeply enchanted.

"The thing is," said Eliza, "I've been out this door before, aye. And I'm nay sure…"

"Quickly, Eliza," said Foss. Mancer voices echoed somewhere in the caverns, not far. She sent back a cloud of ravens to obstruct them and set to work on the door. She could feel the deep fury of the Citadel as she cut through the enchanted iron. She would not be welcomed back a second time. This was the end of any pretense of goodwill she could claim between herself and the Mancers.

Once she had cut out a space wide enough to fit through, she and Foss looked out. The door opened onto a cliff.

"Oh!" said Foss, dismayed.

"We've got to climb," said Eliza.

Eliza had spent much of her childhood scrambling up and down trees and rock faces and the like and was, by any standard, a proficient climber. Even she was daunted, however, by this long ragged drop to the canyon floor below. Thinking about it would only make it worse, she knew that much, and so she lowered herself out of the doorway and scrabbled about with her unhurt foot for a foothold. Fortunately the cliff was covered with bumps and crags and roots. The soles of her boots were worn smooth and so she kicked them off, letting them fall. Her bare feet would give her a better grip.

It was several seconds before she heard the soft thud of her boots landing far below and this shook her confidence somewhat. She clung to a little ledge of rock with one foot, letting the hurt foot rest against the rock face. Still hanging on to the bottom of the doorframe with one hand, she reached down and found a root with her other hand. She held it fast and let go of the door frame. She pulled her center of gravity in, towards the rock, then drew her dagger and drove it into the cliff.

"Give me your foot," she hissed to Foss. She reached up and

felt his large foot against her hand. To her surprise, it was bare and soft. The Mancer robes brushed the ground and it had never even occurred to her to wonder if they used footwear of any kind. She guided his foot to the dagger. "Come on, down next to me," she whispered.

"I do not think I can climb down a cliff, Eliza Tok," he murmured back.

"You can. Dinnay think about it. Follow me," she ordered him fiercely.

"I cannot see you."

"Follow my voice."

It was an arduous and painfully slow descent. Eliza used her dagger as a handhold for herself and a foothold for Foss to steady himself on with every further movement downwards. After they had been climbing for some time, she at last allowed herself to look down, but the canyon bottom seemed barely closer at all. Worse, their escape route had been discovered. The iron doors flew open and a dragon soared out of the Citadel right over their heads.

"Blast the Ancients," muttered Foss, just above.

"They cannay see us," said Eliza. "Keep quiet."

"You cannot fool a dragon with a spell of invisibility," said Foss. "We are done for, Eliza Tok. They will do away with me quickly but there is still a chance for you. They will not want you dead, not at any cost! You must not give in to them, Eliza!"

Eliza ignored him, taking his foot by the ankle and moving it from her dagger to a rocky protrusion. Then she pulled her dagger from the rock and held it out out as the dragon opened its mouth in a scream, circling round to face them. The dagger, forged from a dragon claw, enabled her to command dragons, but she could not speak out. She would have to try to enter its mind and there was no time to do so cautiously. Eliza shut her eyes and rushed straight into a clanging, flaming mind, an intelligence and ferocity that flayed her very will. *Don't give us up.* It was a plea rather than a command. She felt her bones would melt. Her thoughts scattered and sizzled. But the dragon veered off and she exhaled. When she opened her eyes she realized with a jolt of horror that she had let go of the cliff face. And yet she was hanging in the air. It took her a moment to realize that Foss was holding her by the arm.

"By the Ancients, Eliza Tok! I felt you let go…what are you doing?"

Shaking away the sparks and pain in her mind she drove her dagger back into the cliff and let herself hang from it for a moment. Her arms ached. She couldn't catch her breath to answer him.

"How curious!" he said as the dragon flew away with Trahaearn on its back. "Did you do something?"

"Yes," she croaked.

The other dragons came soaring out of the Citadel but they followed Trahaearn's dragon and did not give away the two invisible fugitives clinging to the cliff. Foss edged down and stepped on Eliza's hand.

"Ouch!" she shouted.

"Oh, I am sorry! It's difficult, when I cannot *see* you, to avoid *stepping* on you."

An hour later they reached the bottom of the canyon and stood on solid ground with shaking legs, laughing with relief. Eliza was drenched with sweat and trembling all over from the exertion of the descent. She thought she could see the faint outline of herself becoming visible again.

"Can you see me?" she asked Foss nervously.

"I am beginning to," he panted. "Yes, there you are, somewhat. Quickly, then. We must stay close to the edge of the canyon and get ourselves out of plain view."

"Foss." There was no way to say it but plainly. "Aysu is dead."

"Yes." She could hear the weight of his grief in his voice. "I felt it. They came for me very quickly after her murder."

"I've got the Gehemmis."

"Save your breath, Eliza. We must get out of sight. Onto my back again."

She obeyed, saying, "But even if the dragons dinnay give us

away they'll use the Vindensphere to find us. How can we hide?"

"I smashed the Vindensphere."

"What?"

"It was the only thing I could think of to do. When I felt Aysu's death, I knew they would be coming for both of us. I was on my way to warn you. I stopped in the Treasury and smashed the Vindensphere. I thought it our best chance of escape. But they found me there, before I got to you."

"Oh, Foss!"

"They will repair it but it will take time. Long enough for us to get a good distance, I should think. I can repel seeking spells, and the Mancers are not gifted at them in any case."

Eliza stared over his shoulder along the length of the canyon. The dragons were still circling above, shrieking. The canyon splintered off into narrow fissures that wound between sheer cliffs. It was into one of these that they went. It was barely wide enough for Foss to stretch his arms out. The sky was a thin strip of blue far overhead. The path was barely a path at all and so Foss had to scramble over piles of stone where parts of the cliff had caved in. It made Eliza terribly nervous to see these piles and she kept looking up lest another one should be coming down on their heads.

Within an hour or two of scrambling through a maze of deep ravines, they were both entirely visible again. She could not see the sun but she guessed they were making their way roughly north.

"Where are we going, Foss?"

"We will go to Tian Xia," he said. "We must get you to safety. There is no one who can protect you from the Mancers in Di Shang."

"What about the Thanatosi?"

"Your friend is safer than you right now."

The light faded from the sky. Eventually Eliza could make out a few stars glittering in the dark crack between the cliffs above. She was exhausted and terribly thirsty and they had no water or food. Even hanging on to Foss required more strength than she had left.

"I need to rest," she told Foss.

"Ah! Of course."

He stopped and put her down gently on the stony ground. Eliza took the Gehemmis out of her backpack and passed it to him. It was smooth to touch, not heavy, about the length of her hand but narrower.

"This is it."

He held it in his hands and murmured a few spells over it. It took shape, and they examined it curiously by the light of his eyes. It was a white shard with a few black symbols etched into it.

"Is it stone?" Eliza asked. "It's too light, nay?"

"Bone," said Foss.

"What do the symbols say?"

"I cannot decipher them without the Book of Symbols," said Foss. His voice was hushed with wonder. "But it is very old indeed, Eliza. Far older than anything that I have ever held in my hands. It possesses great power, too. I believe this is indeed the Gehemmis given by the Ancients to the Horogarth at the very Beginning and stolen by Lahja in the Middle Days. I did not believe the story until now, but holding it in my hands I cannot deny what I know to be true. Kyreth will not let go of this lightly."

Eliza leaned against the wall of the cliff. Her mind was brimming with too many fears to think of. The Thanatosi, who could not be called off, were waiting for Charlie to leave the Realm of the Faeries. The Emmisariae were out looking for her and for Foss. She could hear the cries of the dragons not far off. And without food or water or money or any form of transportation they had to somehow cross the Republic, for the only ways into Tian Xia that she knew of, besides the Crossing in the Citadel grounds, were in the east.

"What are we going to do, Foss?"

But she was asleep before he could answer.

FOG

CHAPTER
8

Nell and Charlie waited in a grove of apricot trees. The ripe, golden fruit hung from the branches like jewels. In the distance, a castle perched atop a craggy mountain. It was a smallish castle, as castles go, its roof forming a bright peak and swooping out in either direction like wings, as if the whole thing might, at any moment, take off from the mountaintop. It shone blue-green in the soft light.

"I cannay say it's good to be back here," muttered Charlie, rubbing his neck. He was sore from the long flight on the myrkestra.

"Just be glad he's taking us in at all," said Nell.

"I *am* glad," said Charlie, sounding anything but.

"*Am*gla! *Am*gla!" twittered a songbird from one of the trees, cocking its head and looking curiously at the pair.

"Quiet, you," said Charlie to the bird.

"Kwaityu! Kwaityu!" chirped the bird, hopping closer, most intrigued now.

Nell laughed, then pointed into the trees.

"Look, here's Jalo come back."

"That was quick," said Charlie suspiciously.

Jalo strode purposefully through the grove, his cloak flowing behind him. He was followed closely by two other Faeries.

"All is well!" he called to them. "You will stay here with my friend Emin and his wife Mala."

Nell and Charlie exchanged a brief glance and then Nell said, "Wonderful. Thank you so much, Jalo."

They were not surprised or sorry that he was putting them up with a friend rather than taking them in himself. His mother Tariro was not fond of humans and Nell had been dreading the possibility of encountering her again.

Emin was shorter and stockier than Jalo, but he had that lightness of step combined with an eerie inner stillness that was common to all the Faeries. His hair was a dark curling gold and his eyes sparkled warmly. Mala was dressed much more simply than the other two, in a plain blue robe. Her hair was pulled back from her lovely face and she stared at them frankly, the way one might watch a peculiar bug or some other creature one does not credit with much understanding.

"Did you come all the way from the castle?" asked Nell.

"Well...in a manner of speaking," said Jalo, amused. Looking past him, Nell realized that the castle was not far on a mountaintop at all. Gentle hills, not mountains, surrounded the valley, the great cliffs they had seen no more than boulders. What had seemed a castle was more a house with a dramatic roof, right before them among the apricot trees.

"Oh!" exclaimed Nell. She had forgotten how disorienting the perceptual shifts in this realm of Illusion could be.

Emin had obviously been told that handshakes were a common human greeting but had not had much opportunity to practice. He grasped their outstretched hands in a crushing grip and thrust them up and down energetically for a much longer period than felt natural. Nell had to yank her hand out of his to get it back. She rubbed it discreetly with her other hand, hoping it wasn't bruised.

"Thank you so much for having us," she said politely.

"Yes. Thank you," echoed Charlie.

"It is my *absolute pleasure!* Any friend of Jalo's is always welcome in my home."

"We were together at the Academy of Song," said Jalo. "Emin is one of the finest poets in the realm."

Emin waved his hand dismissively and led them into the house. It was the strangest house Nell had ever seen – as if it hadn't quite decided what kind of house to be. The rooms sat at awkward angles in relation to one another. There were an inordinate number of doors and staircases zigging and zagging off in all directions. Each room was over full; paintings crowded together on the walls, great urns and sculptures were propped precariously on glossy tables and chests, tapestries hung wherever space could be made for them, and an odd assortment of furniture filled all the remaining space, so that simply crossing the room required some concentration. Overhead, multiple chandeliers dripped with immense diamonds. The overall effect was dizzying. The power of Illusion, Nell realized, did not necessarily come with a gift for design, or even good taste.

"Lah, how...beautiful," she said, and gave Charlie a nudge.

"Yes," he said, barely suppressing a snort.

Mala reappeared now with a bowl of apricots, which she placed on a piano stool near a velvet chaise longue.

"Please! Enjoy!" cried Emin, rubbing his hands together.

Mala proferred a jug of apricot wine, pulling it out of nowhere like a street magician.

Charlie and Nell sat themselves down on the chaise longue, so startled to find crystal glasses in their hands that they almost dropped them. Mala poured them some wine and the three Faeries stood watching them with interest while they sipped it and ate a few apricots. The wine was light and sweet and the apricots perfectly ripe.

"Delicious," said Nell, wishing the Faeries would sit down and stop staring. It was like being in a zoo.

"I adore apricots," said Emin. "It is the only thing I can bear to eat. And until my poetry is accepted at court, apricots are how I make my living. They are real, you know. Can you tell? Well, you are Di Shang worlders, you probably can't tell."

Jalo looked uncomfortable and Emin laughed.

"My poor Jalo! It is not really respectable, you see, for a member of the nobility to practice a trade."

"Your friends would think it a kindness to be allowed to help you," Jalo protested.

"Lah, there's nothing shameful in having a job," said Nell,

taking another bite of an apricot.

Emin beamed at her. "Quite so! It is my own feeling exactly."

"We'd love to hear some of your poetry," she added. "Jalo recited some Faery poetry to us once. It was beautiful, aye, and so different from our own."

"Why, Jalo! You told me this human was charming and beautiful but I did not believe you. I must apologize, for she is indeed a truly delightful young lady!"

Nell laughed affectedly. Charlie knocked back his glass of apricot wine. He sensed that the visit was going to drag.

They sat in the over-full room chatting as the light faded from outside. Emin suggested having supper on the veranda. Although they had not climbed any stairs, the front door now opened onto a third-story veranda overlooking the fields of apricot trees. The sky was a velvety black, the trees lit with bright lanterns so the orchard swam with light. Supper turned out to be more apricots, lightly stewed this time.

"Do you have family, Emin?" asked Nell.

"I do," he replied. "But I am a stranger to them. Mala was a servant in our home, you see. When I married her, I forfeited my rightful place in Faery society. My family cut me off, and my friends too – all but Jalo. But it does not matter to me. Mala is all my happiness."

Mala was leaning over the railing and looking dreamily at the lights. She turned her head only slightly when he spoke, gave a slow smile, and said nothing.

"I'd think wealth and position and all that would be kind of irrelevant when you can make Illusions," said Nell. "Why do Faeries care about things like that?"

"Oh, it matters a great deal," said Emin with a deep chuckle. "Not all the realm is Illusion, you know! And besides, our laws are very stringent in terms of what one can do with Illusion. One's freedom depends greatly on the wealth and standing of one's family."

Jalo rose and stretched gracefully. "I must go. My mother will be wondering where I am. Nell, may I speak with you?"

Jalo and Emin said their goodbyes and Nell followed Jalo

among the lamplit trees. His myrkestra was waiting at the end of the orchard, where the trees grew tall and thick and dark.

"Emin is trustworthy and will treat you kindly," Jalo said. "He is cut off from the nobility and thus unlikely to attract interest or spark gossip. As I'm sure you can imagine, humans and other outsiders have become increasingly unpopular here since Malferio was deposed. This is the safest place for you."

"This is a lovely place, Jalo. We'll be entirely comfortable."

"You are kind to say so."

He bent closer to her, his beautiful face shining in the lantern light. "I am glad you thought to ask me for help," he said in a low voice. "Since I saw you last I have thought of you often and hoped beyond hope that I would have an opportunity to look on your face again."

He ran a hand lightly over her hair. Nell waited, a little breathless.

"It is remarkable," he said, studying her. "You have changed, I can see. That is the way with humans. I think you are even more beautiful than the last time I saw you."

She smiled, not sure what to say. He bent towards her to kiss her and, much to her own surprise and his, she stepped back, out of his reach.

"I am sorry," he said, confused.

"No, it's all right," she said hastily, annoyed with herself.

He lifted her hand to his lips and kissed that instead.

"I will come back as soon as I possibly can," he said. "It would take a great deal, in fact, to keep me away for long."

"Lah…we look forward to seeing you again!" said Nell. It seemed an oddly formal thing to say. "Thank you again, Jalo. You're literally saving Charlie's life. And mine, aye."

He gave her a look then, as if he knew she was lying. "I am doing it for you, not for him."

"I know."

He mounted his myrkestra and they disappeared in the black sky. Nell turned back and saw Charlie watching from the veranda. She walked slowly back among the lantern-lit trees.

Emin seemed quite content to stay up talking all night. There was no mention of any place for them to sleep and eventually both Nell and Charlie, exhausted from their journey, dozed off right there on the veranda, curled in their chairs. Charlie was only half-sleeping, bothered by the idea of getting up again to find a bed. He roused himself to say, "Praps we should go to bed," and found himself in total darkness. He sat up, alarmed. After a moment his eyes adjusted to the dark and he saw that he was in a large four-poster bed full of rumpled sheets and blankets and pillows, with heavy curtains drawn around it. He heard Nell's voice murmur somewhere outside the curtains: "What did you say?"

He pulled back the curtain of his bed. They were still on the veranda, overlooking the orchard and the dark wooded hills, but their chairs had become beds. Nell was hidden within another four-poster, the curtains embroidered with battling dragons.

"Sorry," he said to Nell. "I woke you up."

"What?" her voice was slurred with sleepiness.

"Nothing."

An exasperated sigh came from her bed. She pulled back the curtain and looked out at him. *"What?"*

"Nothing. I woke up…confused, lah. That's all." He was startled and then saddened by the pale anger in her face. "I'm sorry. I didnay mean to wake you."

She rubbed a hand over her face. "It's fine," she mumbled. "Are you all right?"

"I am, aye. Go back to sleep."

When she didn't move, just sat staring at nothing, he added: "Thanks for doing this, Nell. You're right that Jalo wouldnay have taken me in alone."

"I know. You're welcome."

"You do a fair bit of saving my skin," he added ruefully.

"Oh, I thought praps you'd forgotten that," she said coldly and drew the curtain again.

Startled and beginning to be angry, he asked, "What do you mean?"

"Never mind."

He jumped off his own bed, stomped over to hers, and pulled the curtain back. "That's rude!" she screamed at him, pulling it shut again.

"Nell, let's have it out. What's going on?"

"Nothing's going *on*. What are you talking about?"

"I mean since when do you hardly speak to me?"

She pulled back the curtain again. Her face was white with anger and her lips were tight but he thought he saw tears glistening in the corners of her violet eyes.

"*Me* hardly speak to *you?* Charlie, how many times did you just *drop Eliza off* at my school last spring, or in Holburg over the summer, without even bothering to say hello to me?"

Charlie felt as if she'd slapped him. He fumbled for his answer. "Lah, it seemed like...we got back from Tian Xia last time and you were...you didnay seem to want to be around me. I just thought I should stay out of your way, aye, let you and Eliza be."

"I was *upset*, Charlie! About Ander! That's what this is really about, nay?"

"What do you mean?"

Now tears were spilling out of her eyes and streaming down her cheeks and he felt terrible. She yanked the curtain shut. He didn't have the heart to pull it open again.

"We were supposed to be *friends*," her voice came from behind the curtain, a bit muffled.

"I know," he said. He felt depressed and exhausted. The conversation had gotten out of control and he couldn't remember which direction he'd been trying to steer it in. He hadn't wanted to make her cry. "I'm sorry, Nell," he said.

"I'm going to sleep now."

"All right."

Sadly he went back to his own bed and lay down.

They woke in their chairs with the warmth of the sky on their faces. The Faery realm was sunless, the sky producing a general diffuse light and warmth. A large bowl of apricots was the only thing on the low table between them.

"I hear humans eat every day." Mala was standing in a lopsided doorway that led to several sets of stairs winding up and down.

"Usually three or four times a day," said Charlie hastily. "Or five. Even six, aye. We die, otherwise." He looked at the bowl. "More apricots?"

"Yes," she said, wide-eyed, and fled back downstairs.

Nell did not meet Charlie's eyes as she sat up and began to eat the apricots.

"I hope they have other kinds of food here," he said.

She nodded but said nothing.

"Lah, Jalo seemed very happy to see you," he went on, trying to pretend nothing had happened the night before. "What's it like being romanced by a Faery? You're not still with that boy at your school...what was his name? Julian?"

"That's been over for ages," said Nell shortly. "My boyfriend is Oscar van Holt. He's *frighteningly* clever."

"Really?" Charlie said. *"Frighteningly?"*

"It's nay serious. Sort of on and off, aye. So if Jalo..." she trailed off. "It's nay really any of your business," she finished.

"I spose not," said Charlie glumly. They ate as many apricots as they could in silence.

Emin came up soon after and invited them out to pick apricots with him. Charlie assented immediately, relieved to have something to do. Nell stayed on the veranda with her folder, glad of some peace and quiet to catch up on her studies. She felt rather smug, thinking of Oscar and all the others studying at school or at home, while she, Nell, was in the Realm of the Faeries. She watched Charlie disappear with Emin and Mala into the shining orchard and then opened her folder and got to work.

∞

Jalo's mother Tariro stood in a circle of high stones on a blasted heath, looking into a clear pool of water. There were two figures behind her. One, a Faery dressed in black, her dark gold hair tied back. The other was covered entirely in a brown cloak, only a glimmer of eyes visible within the large hood. In the pool, Tariro watched her younger son Jalo walking with his brother Cadeyrn along a dazzling white bridge that passed over several roaring waterfalls. Cadeyrn was on leave from the Faery Guard and he and his wife were visiting with Tariro. They were very excited because in two more years they would be granted a permit to have a child.

"My Lady."

Tariro did not turn around. It was the other Faery who had spoken, her faithful spy, Miyam.

"Tell me," said Tariro.

"He left the Realm of the Faeries and flew to the lake of the Crossing. There he met a Mancer and three young humans. Two of the humans he brought back here. The other human and the Mancer immediately returned to Di Shang."

"The two humans he brought back. Can you describe them?"

"Male and female. Young. Perhaps in the teen years. The boy is dark-haired, the girl has lighter hair. They are of a complexion neither light nor dark, but somewhere in between."

Tariro made a little gesture of impatience. "The girl. Light brown hair, violet eyes and very beautiful?"

"Yes," said Miyam.

Tariro simmered with rage. Cadeyrn was malleable; he had followed her advice and made a good match with Alvar's daughter. As a result, he had been promoted. But Jalo, her brilliant Jalo, was still carrying a torch for the human girl! He would sabotage any chance of a fine career in the Faery Guard or a beneficial marriage if she allowed the affair to persist.

"Where are they staying?" she asked.

"With his friend Emin."

"Emin!" scoffed Tariro. "The one with the apricots, who married a servant girl?"

"The very one."

She seethed. Why he should have such useless friends and pine for a human girl she could not understand. And he was deceitful, above all else, seeking to hide it from her. But he did not know his mother well enough.

"I want the girl dead. The boy too, why not?"

"By what means?"

Tariro was so irritated that she very nearly turned around. But she did not want to take her eyes away from the pool of water. She was granted only one look at a time and she meant it to last. As soon as she turned around the pool would be empty.

"Any means!" she snapped. "All you have to do is run a human through with a sword or drop them from a great height to kill them. It won't take much. But do it soon."

"It is done."

Miyam bowed but Tariro wasn't looking. She watched her sons carefully in the pool. I am saving you, Jalo, she thought. I am saving you from your own folly. May you one day be grateful to me for it.

CHAPTER

9

"Argh! Can't you hurry up?" Malferio wailed, thrashing on the divan. "It hurts!"

Kyreth sat on a rough bench before a stone desk that emerged from the wall.

"I imagine it does," he replied.

Malferio leaped off the divan and crashed to the floor. "Argh! She Cursed you too; why is my Curse so much worse?"

Kyreth was shaving a twisted root into powder over a flame and did not look up. He said, "Perhaps I simply bear it better. And I have friends. There is that. You, on the other hand, are quite friendless."

"Blast you!" sobbed Malferio. "Blast you and Blast the Ancients too. Why are you going so slowly? You just enjoy watching me suffer, don't you?"

"There are few things more tedious than watching you suffer, Malferio," said Kyreth dryly. He spoke a few words in the Language of First Days, then took a dropper from the desk before him and added three drops of clear liquid to the powdered root. The powder smoked and hissed and absorbed the liquid. Kyreth deposited the mixture into a long pipe, and this he passed to Malferio.

"Flame!" rasped Malferio, grasping the pipe in shaking hands. Kyreth struck a match and held it over the pipe. Malferio put it to his lips, sucking eagerly.

He breathed out a plume of bluish smoke and relaxed.

"Powerful stuff," he murmured. "Ah. The room goes dark.

You look like a goblin, you know, with this spell. All is shadow, and you are a great shadowy goblin with eyes of fire." He giggled and sucked on the pipe again.

Kyreth watched him with vague distaste. Malferio saw the expression and giggled again. "Horrible fire-eyed goblin. You're going to miss me, you know. I'm not friendless at all. You're my friend."

"I am not your friend," Kyreth said. "Nor will I miss you in the slightest. You depress me."

Malferio waggled the pipe at him playfully. "Nonsense! Well, and how is the Magic?"

"Ready," said Kyreth.

"Ready?" Malferio's eyes widened. "It is a potent mix you make me, I must say. No fear of death. But look, you promised me that I could see her…that she would know. There's no fun in dying without getting to see the look on her face, knowing *she's* done for too."

"We shall see how it plays out," said Kyreth.

The embers were dying from the pipe. Malferio sucked up the last puffs of smoke desperately, then crawled back to the divan and lay down, shooting Kyreth a lopsided grin.

"The difficulty is that I cannot kill you," Kyreth went on. "Not I, nor any other Mancer, according to the Oath of the Ancients struck with Nia."

"Well, it shouldn't be hard to find someone who'll do it," said Malferio carelessly. "Say, have you found your little Sorceress yet?"

"Not yet," said Kyreth. "The Mancers are working to repair the Vindensphere. The Emmisariae will go out again with first light."

"You don't sleep, do you? I'd always heard Mancers were such big sleepers," said Malferio, his eyes half-closing.

"No, I do not sleep," said Kyreth in a low voice. He looked thoughtful. "Foss will be weakening," he added to himself. "He has been stripped of his Emmisarius status and he is outside the Citadel walls. He will not last long."

"Ridiculous system," scoffed Malferio.

Kyreth looked up. "The sun is rising. I will see to my wife."

Malferio gave him a greedy look. "Oh yes. You're going to kill her, then? Doing away with your own wife, by the Ancients! I suppose we've a lot in common. Poor taste in women, for starters."

Kyreth gave him a look of disgust. The stones in the floor made way, opening into the spiraling staircase of the tower.

"You're coming back soon, aren't you?" asked Malferio, sitting up, his eyes wide and panicky. "This stuff doesn't last so awfully long, you know!"

"I will be rather busy today," said Kyreth, sweeping down the stairs.

"You've got to come back soon!" Malferio screamed after him as the stones closed and sealed him alone in the room.

Kyreth made his way with swift strides to the south wing, to Eliza's room, as the sun inched up above the horizon and the Mancers began to wake and enter their trances.

"I apologize to have kept you waiting," he said to Selva, drawing a long knife out of his robe. "There was much to do."

"Oh Kyreth," she said, releasing her breath in a long, unhappy sigh. She stood still within the shining barrier, apparently unweary though she had been standing there a day and a night. "I pity you. Truly I do." She cocked her head on one side. "But you will not kill me."

"I do not wish to," he said. "But you have shown yourself too dangerous, my dear. What can I do?"

"No matter, love. Little choice is left to you. They have come for me and you will have to let me go."

He frowned. "What do you mean?"

"They have *come for me*," she repeated. "How strange that it should happen this way. Such a mixed life I have had. And now this next chapter. But what else am I to do, with this Curse, with this Gift?"

Kyreth looked at the knife in his hand, hesitating.

"Your Eminence."

He turned slowly. There was a Mancer in the doorway, a manipulator of water.

"There is…" the Mancer began. Her eyes took in the knife in

Kyreth's hand and she faltered, then started again: "The Faithful are here, your Eminence. A delegation. They are at the shore of the Crossing and they demand that you hand over to them the new Oracle of the Ancients."

Kyreth looked back at Selva. She smiled at him and shrugged slightly. "Strange indeed," he conceded. The barrier around Selva disappeared at a flick of his finger. If the Ancients had claimed her, there was nothing to be done. She stepped close to him, brushing against the blade he still held in his hand.

"Those who know you least fear you least," she whispered in his ear. "It is them you have to fear."

Eliza woke to a terrible thirst, her head pounding and her tongue dry as paper. The sliver of sky showing between the edges of the cliffs on either side of them was a pale blue.

"I need water," she told Foss, her voice a croak.

He was sitting on the stony ground with the Gehemmis in his hands, examining it curiously, but he looked up when she spoke. She thought his eyes seemed dimmer than usual, his face a little drawn.

"Of course," he said. "Another day walking north should bring us to the Noxoni."

The Noxoni was the river that marked the southern edge of the Interior Provinces, joined in recent years by a huge canal to the Arnox, the northern trade route on whose banks Kalla had been built.

"I cannay go another day without water," said Eliza. It was shady and cool in the deep canyon and a part of her wanted to just lie still, let her weariness have its way for once. "There must be streams nearby, or a spring, lah."

"Divining," said Foss. "I have never learned it. We need some wood, I believe."

"You're a manipulator of water. Cannay you…make some? Or find it?"

"I do not manipulate *actual water* so much as the natural powers inherent in water, which I am able to transform into Magic," explained Foss drearily. Eliza stopped listening halfway through the sentence. She closed her eyes and black ravens bloomed behind her eyelids. She saw the terrain from above, this barren rocky land at the edge of the desert. Somewhere a trickling sound, like music.

"How is your foot today?" Foss's concerned voice interrupted her view. She hushed him with a flap of the hand, squeezed her eyes shut again, swooped over the bare hills riddled with gorges. No sign of Mancers, though no doubt they would be sent out again soon. There, that sound again, water running over stone. She swooped downwards and circled until she found it, a spring in the rock, a pool that turned into a damp trickle running down a hill stubbled with short green shrubs, hardy little plants to survive out here.

She opened her eyes.

"I know where to go." She got to her feet and winced. Her ankle was still very sore.

"Let me see it," said Foss. She sat down again and he held her foot in his large gold hands, twisting it gently this way and that.

"Ouch," she muttered.

"A sprain," he said. "You should not walk on it, Eliza. Come, I will carry you."

A raven was perched a little way down the path watching them. As soon as Eliza climbed onto Foss's back it flew ahead a bit further, then stopped in the path to wait again.

"Your Guide will guide us!" said Foss cheerfully. "How convenient."

"I cannay begin to tell you," Eliza heartily agreed.

It was a long hour to the little pool. Once there she climbed off Foss's back and fell on her knees to drink her fill. Nothing had ever tasted as good as this fresh, cold water. She felt instantly revived. Foss stood over her, looking up at the sky.

"The Mancers know about Mt. Harata and some other crossings, but not your volcano," said Foss. "We will go there and seek the assistance of your friends in Tian Xia. I assume we can find a train or a boat going east once we reach the interior provinces."

"I wish I had made more of the potion," said Eliza. "I feel very exposed, aye. It willnay be hard for the Mancers to find us out here."

"Keep your ravens in the sky," said Foss. "The Emmisariae on golden dragons in the sky will be easier to spot than us down below. As long as the dragons do not give us away, we can take cover before the Mancers are able to see us."

Weak with hunger, Eliza half-dreamed as Foss carried her through the heat of the day. Once, she thought she saw Nia out of the corner of her eye, hair piled on her head in an elaborate upsweep, holding the bone Gehemmis and looking triumphant. She startled and woke. There was nothing, nobody.

The low hills were mostly bare but for clumps of determined grass and deep-rooted shrubs. They kept going north until they found themselves, as the sun went down, facing the floodplains of the Noxoni. The hills dropped off dramatically into the broad, flat, fertile plains, a strip of trees running between the hills and the fields. The river was a brown snaking mass with rich green farmland on either side of it. Dilapidated farmhouses dotted the plains, a few muddy roads meandering between them.

"Thank the Ancients," breathed Foss. "We can find food for you here."

"I'll go alone," said Eliza. "You'll be too shocking, aye. People are going to be frightened of you. Wait down below, among the trees. I'll find someone who'll feed me and give me shelter for the night, lah, and see if I can arrange transportation east for tomorrow."

"Can you walk?"

"I'll manage."

They descended the hill and Foss tried to make himself comfortable on the marshy ground among the cypress and tupelo trees. Eliza left the backpack and the Gehemmis with him and limped along the grassy ridges marking out the rice fields, where long, bright green stalks stood tall in the water, their tips waving and rippling in the breeze. She knocked on the door of the nearest farmhouse, an unpainted wood structure with broken steps and a corrugated tin roof. The hungry-looking dog chained up outside started to bark when she approached but soon calmed down and came to lick her hand. She tried to shoo it away; its unnatural friendliness was a dead giveaway that she was Sorma, and people around here were distrustful of the Sorma's mysterious ways. Eliza had been to this region before, when she and her father fled the bandit raids in Quan years ago, and they had not received a particularly warm welcome. But Rom Tok was a grown man and obviously Sorma, whereas Eliza's mixed heritage was more difficult to place and she was still not much more than a child. She hoped she would receive a friendlier reception this time.

A red-faced woman in a stained apron opened the door. Her mouth was a pursed little trap, lines shooting out from it angrily.

"What?" she asked in a bark.

"Pardon me," said Eliza, putting her hands together in a gesture of supplication. "I'm dead tired and I haven't had a bite to eat for two days. I've heard of the generosity of the folks living along the Noxoni and hoped you could spare me a bite to eat and a roof for the night."

"You heard wrong if you think we're generous with what we don't got," snapped the woman. "You're not from around here, so where are you from?"

"Huir-Kosta, originally," improvised Eliza. "I've been living in Quan with my parents, but the town got raided and I had to run."

"Hadn't heard of any raids in Quan lately."

"It just happened."

"Those border towns are dangerous places. Don't know why anybody lives out there. No way to make a living."

Now that she was so close to a place to rest and eat, Eliza's stomach was cramping with hunger and her knees were ready to give way beneath her. She leaned against the doorway, not needing to feign her weakness.

"Please," she said. "Whatever you can spare."

The woman frowned at her.

"Where your folks?"

"We got separated," said Eliza. Tears rose easily to her eyes. She had never lied so effectively in her life. Desperation was a powerful motivator.

"You walked from Quan? Impossible."

"I had a car. I drove partway but it broke down in the hills. I've been walking for two days."

The woman appeared ready to relent.

"Well, I suppose we might be able to do something for you." She looked Eliza over and then her eyes froze around thigh height. Eliza felt a cold despair close around her. She let her eyes fall shut a moment.

"What's that?" The woman's voice had gone hard as flint. Eliza didn't have to look at her to know she had seen the end of the scabbard beneath her jacket.

"Nothing," she breathed.

"Looks like some kinda weapon." There was fear in the woman's voice now. "Thorton!" she bleated.

It was no good. They weren't going to take her in having seen the dagger. Eliza turned miserably and staggered away into the dusk. The immediate neighbors would be no good either, since no doubt the woman would call them and say what she had seen. Eliza walked towards the river, the woman a silhouette behind her in the bright doorway, watching her go. Perhaps she could get somebody to take her across and she could try one of the houses on the opposite side.

It was dark by the time she reached the only light by the river she could see. It was a little boathouse with a bar attached. Two grizzled fishermen were seated at the bar, chatting with the bar-keep. In this part of the world, Eliza knew, the men fished and the women farmed, and still there was barely enough for a family to get by on. She was an odd sight here: a dark-skinned young woman on her own. Nobody came here who didn't live here, because what was there to come for? But fishermen with a few drinks in them might be more hospitable than the woman pro-tecting her home. She tightened the scabbard's shoulder strap and pulled her jacket tight around her. The bar was small and shabby but the glow of light outside made it seem a friendly place.

"What's this?" the barkeep called out when she entered. He peered at her over the counter.

"If you have anything you could feed me," she said, cursing the sob that quavered at the back of her voice, "anything at all, I'd be grateful."

"Got money?" he asked.

"Nothing," said Eliza.

"We don't feed 'em for free, you know," said the barkeep. "This isn't a poorhouse. It's a pub."

"Give the girl a break. Can't you see she's about to pass out?" one of the men scolded him. He fished a crumpled bill out of his pocket and pushed it across the counter at the barkeep. "Here. Give her something to eat."

Eliza nearly wept with gratitude.

"Thank you," she said to the man, her eyes flooding with tears.

"Hey now, no crying," he said. He was in his sixties, or so he looked, with thinning hair and a face like an old potato. His mouth was only half full of teeth, but his eyes were kind beneath straggly brows. "I hope someone'll buy me a meal, I ever get as hungry as you look."

"So where you from?" asked the other man, a yellow-haired fellow with a nose that looked as if it had been broken several times, peering around his friend to get a good look at her. The barkeep had snatched the bill off the counter and disappeared into the back of the shack.

"Huir-Kosta," she replied wearily. She fed them the same story of bandits and her long walk. They gaped at her and took long gulps of their drinks. A few minutes later the barkeep came out with a plate of bony fish, a big spoonful of cold rice, and a couple of tired-looking carrots. Eliza left only the bones of the fish on the plate, sucked dry. The men laughed, watching her eat, and even the barkeep warmed up to her and gave her a glass of cider. It warmed her belly and she began to feel sleepy. As she lifted the near-empty glass to her lips, the man who had paid for her meal said, "Hey, whassat?" He was pointing at her hand.

She put down the glass and put her hand flat on the counter, staring at it stupidly.

She couldn't think of anything to say.

"She got something on her hand," the man told the barkeep, who had come over to see what they were talking about. "Show us your hand!"

"No." She pressed it to the table.

The potato-faced man's eyes turned into slits and his mouth turned down in an ugly scowl. "I buy you a nice dinner and you won't show me your hand!" he snarled.

"Show him your hand," chimed in the barkeep menacingly.

Eliza got up off the stool and held her hand up. They all stared at the tattoo of the black bird.

"Whassat?" he asked, bewildered.

"Something we do in Huir-Kosta," she said. "Thank you for dinner."

"Weird girl," said the potato-face, shaking his head and returning to his drink.

"Hang on there," the yellow-haired one said, sliding off his stool and barring her way as she went for the door. "Hold up a moment. Stranger from out of town, how about you stay and drink with us a while?" He leered unpleasantly.

Eliza met his eyes. They were cold and watery.

"I've got to go," she said clearly. She wasn't afraid of the poor drunk, but if he tried anything she was reluctant to use Magic. If she worked a spell here, everybody all along the Noxoni would hear of her in no time. Something in her voice or her gaze warned him off, anyway. He shrugged and slouched back to his stool, muttering, "Suit yerself."

The night was cold. She had nowhere to sleep and contemplated going back towards the hills to find Foss, but she was too tired to make the walk and her ankle was throbbing. She wandered down among the boats tied up to the wharf and climbed into one. A black cat shot out of a corner of the boat, hissing at her. Eliza stumbled backwards, startled. The cat arched its long back, tail lashing, and opened its mouth in a yowl. Its tongue was red as flame. For a moment, it did not look like a cat at all. An awful voice echoed in her bones: *I am waiting for you, little one. You will bring me your beloved.*

The cat was gone, but the black water lapping against the side of the boat reminded her of the river of death hurtling between the paws of the great panther. Eliza huddled in a corner of the boat, her heart still racing. She pulled a tangle of fishing net around her as if it were a blanket and tried to sleep.

She was woken before dawn by a sharp nudge in her side. A hairy face was scowling down at her.

"Outta my boat!"

She scrambled to her feet and got out, feeling how stiff and cold she was as she did so. She put a bit of weight gingerly on her hurt ankle. It was better than yesterday, at least.

"Any chance you can take a couple of passengers east?" she asked hopefully.

"I can take passengers anywhere they like if they can pay," the hairy fellow shot back. Black teeth and pale eyes showed in his shaggy mane of a face. "Can you pay?"

"Yes," she replied automatically, trying to think how.

"Let's see the money. I want thirty lyrs a day if I'm taking two."

"I cannay pay with money," said Eliza. "But I can pay with fish."

He scoffed. "How's that?"

Her confidence grew. She had eaten and slept. This would work.

"Take me out and I'll show you."

He was just curious enough that he consented. She could see hundreds of little boats pushing out onto the dark water already, to begin their long day competing for whatever meager fish the river had to offer, which was fewer every year.

"I'm Eliza," she told the man.

"Brouton," he replied gruffly. She sat at the bow of the boat and concentrated on what was below. She murmured under her breath, drawing the fish she could feel down there into his net. The will of a fish was a slippery but feeble thing and it was easy to assert her own over it. Within minutes, his net was full. He stared at her with slow-dawning astonishment.

"You're a witch," he said fearfully, making no move to drawn his net in.

"If you want to call it that," said Eliza. This was risky but she didn't know what else to do. "I dinnay mean you harm, but I *will* Curse you if you speak a word of this. I want you to wait for me at the wharf until I come back with my friend. Then I want you to take us as far as you can east. I can promise you netfuls like that all along the way. You can stop to sell where you like."

Brouton nodded, his eyes afraid and his mouth hanging open. He took her back to the wharf and she got out. "Nary a word to anyone," she reminded him sternly. The last thing they needed was a witch-hunt drawing attention to their whereabouts. She walked back to the edge of the floodplains and found Foss where she had left him, in among the trees.

"You look well," he said. "You have eaten. Good. Your foot?"

"Not too bad," she said, thinking that he did not look quite so well. "I found a fellow who'll take us by boat."

"Won't the train be faster?"

"Yes, but we've no money and everybody will be able to see you on the train. You cannay just walk around Di Shang. People willnay know what you are, they'll be terrified, and word will get back to the Mancers right away. This way is easier. You can keep low in the boat, aye, and he'll accept payment in fish. I just have to enchant them into his net."

"Very clever." Foss rose and they crossed the rice fields together. Eliza felt horribly self-conscious; even from a distance Foss was glowing and huge. Surely anyone out and about would spot him from a long way off and know he was not human. The woman from the farmhouse from the previous night was feeding chickens in her yard and saw them pass. She stood staring for a minute and then ran back indoors.

"Quick," said Eliza. The wharf was deserted, all the fishermen already out on the water, except for Brouton, who was waiting in his boat with his big hands dangling between his knees. When he saw Foss his eyes widened. He opened his mouth but nothing came out. Eliza and Foss climbed into the boat. She threw one of the nets around Foss's shoulders, to take the glare out of his robe, and he folded his big body down into the bottom of the boat, where he would be less visible.

"Not taking that!" Brouton whispered.

"Yes, you are," said Eliza firmly. She briefly considered telling him that Foss was a Mancer, but that would require too much explanation and he probably wouldn't believe her. "I promise you it will be worth it. Come on. East."

Brouton obeyed fearfully, starting up the engine. They chugged along the broad muddy river. Foss peered out over the gunwales, curious to see the world. Farms and dirty fishing villages were scattered along the riverbank. Small children ran up and down with barking dogs. Eliza thought back on her own girlhood, so solitary before Holburg, never included in these gangs. If she had felt like an outsider then, she could never have imagined she would come to seem so strange to the world outside, with her dagger and her tattooed palms.

"Their lives seem very hard," Foss commented.

"Not like the north," sneered Brouton, then seemed to remember who he was talking to and shut his mouth. That was all he said all day. Whenever they passed a village with a market he began to shoot Eliza sidelong glances. She filled his nets with fish and he stopped to sell them to a fishmonger. Each time he returned with a tortured grin on his face, pockets jangling with coins.

The river wended its way southeast and then northeast, growing deeper and narrower as they went. The fields on either side became richer and greener, with forest stretching off in the north and low mountains thick with cedars to the south. It was an overcast day, with low rumblings of thunder, but thankfully it did not rain. They slept in the boat and the next morning Eliza made her way into the town to buy bread for breakfast while Foss stayed hidden in the boat.

As she walked through the town the villagers stopped in their tracks and stared at her. That was nothing unusual in itself but she noticed ravens hopping along the tin rooftops and began to get the uneasy sense that something was wrong.

In the bakery, she saw a newspaper lying open on the greasy counter and her heart nearly stopped. There was a very accurate sketch of her and of Foss. She snatched up the paper and read the caption: *If you see these two dangerous Tian Xia worlders, report immediately. Do not approach them. Substantial reward is offered.*

She looked around her in horror. The baker was squinting at her nervously. The few patrons who had been in the bakery were edging out the door. Of course they had already been reported.

"Bread," she said. The baker handed her a loaf. She didn't pay and he didn't ask her to. She took the newspaper as well and hurried back to the docks, still going easy on her ankle. Foss was lying in the bottom of the boat but Brouton was gone.

"The Mancers know where we are," said Eliza. "Or they will soon, aye. We're in the paper, like criminals."

"We are criminals, Eliza," said Foss wearily, looking up. "We've stolen a great treasure from the Mancer Citadel."

His face looked faded, his skin fragile and crumpled like an autumn leaf.

"Are you all right?" She asked, taken aback by his appearance.

"I am fine, Eliza."

"Come on. We've got to get out of here."

She jumped in the boat and started the engine.

"Now we're stealing a boat," said Foss sadly.

"I know, aye, I feel badly too," said Eliza, steering it out into the river and revving the engine to full throttle. "It's a horrible thing to do when he's gotten us this far but I have a feeling he's nay helping us anymore and we just *cannay* get caught."

"We will not be safe for long on the river."

"I know. Keep down."

Eliza maneuvered them out into the thick of the fishing

boats, hoping that nobody was looking at her too closely. She made her way slowly to the other side of the river. A man was getting out of a truck, putting his keys in his pocket and heading into a tobacconist's shop set on the little wharf. She docked the boat awkwardly while a raven dove down and plucked the man's keys from his pocket.

"Eliza Tok!" gasped Foss, shocked.

"The truck," she said in a low voice, scrambling out of the boat. "Before anyone sees you."

Foss hunched low and scuttled after her towards the truck. They scrambled inside and the raven dropped the keys in Eliza's lap. She started it up and drove off before the poor man had come back with his cigarettes.

"Terrible! Terrible! We are boat thieves and car thieves on top of everything else! You've seen how poor the people here are. What will the man do without his truck? Or good Brouton without his boat?"

"We're running for our lives, Foss. I can't think of a nice way of doing this," said Eliza. She followed the narrow gravel road out to a paved road that ran in a straight line with forest on either side. She gunned the engine and they roared eastward.

"I hope the gas lasts," she muttered through clenched teeth. "Why dinnay we have any money? It's been so long since I needed money."

Foss was much too big for the truck. He had to bend over, his long arms folded on the dashboard and his head hunched low. "I didn't know you could drive," he said.

"My da used to let me, sometimes, when I was a kid. We travelled a lot, aye. Lots of wide empty roads like this one."

Indeed, the whole day felt like a flashback to her early life. Run-down towns and people who were just scraping by. The underbelly of the glorious Republic. She'd been on the run from the Mancers then, too, though she hadn't known it at the time.

A dark cloud was following them from the west, making the day seem later than it was. They passed only a few other cars on the drive to Elmount and ate the bread as they drove, but Eliza was soon hungry again.

"Can you make Illusion money?" she asked Foss.

"It would fall apart as soon as somebody touched it," he replied, his head bowed nearly to his knees, which were pressed up uncomfortably against the dash.

"Back to begging," she muttered.

She left Foss and the truck in the woods and walked into Elmount, which was marked out by the huge lighthouse on the bluff, fallen into disrepair along with the rest of the city. People sat at the little cafes along the waterfront eating sandwiches. Eliza was able to scavenge leftovers until she was more or less satisfied. A wind had set up and the grey sea was peaked with whitecaps. The few people left in the streets were holding their hats on and hurrying home. Shops began to close up early. There must be a storm warning out, she thought, and saw that indeed the tidal wave gates were being drawn across the harbor.

She went into a shop and borrowed a pen from the shopkeeper. He didn't seem to recognize her, so she assumed he hadn't looked at the newspaper. She was not so strange in Elmount; all kinds of people passed through this town. She turned over the newspaper clipping she had stolen and scrawled over the pictures of her and Foss: *Call off the Thanatosi and I will return the Gehemmis.* She gave the pen back to the shopkeeper, thanked him, and went outside. A raven was waiting for her, perched on a trash can.

"Take it to Kyreth," she said, rolling up the newspaper clipping. The raven took it with one agile claw and took off into the darkening, stormy sky. If Foss was right and the Thanatosi could not be called off then it was pointless, but worth a try even so. Kyreth was powerful, resourceful, and might find a way Foss had not seen. At least she had something to bargain with now. But it was only a useful bargaining tool if she could be sure she was out of their reach, and that meant getting to Tian Xia and getting help.

She went back for Foss when it grew dark. With no money, and Foss's strange appearance as well, there was no way to get tickets for one of the boats out to the archipelago. It was a matter of stealing or hiring another private boat when the storm sub-sided. The fishermen here were more prosperous, for Ebele's Ocean was still full of fish; they might be harder to buy off with what meager enchantments she could offer.

Foss was glad to see the last of the truck. They made their way up the bluff to the abandoned lighthouse. The air smelled of the coming rain and it seemed as good a place as any to spend the night. The rusted door was open and they climbed up the steps to the top of the lighthouse. It was entirely black but for the dim glow of Foss's eyes. They lay themselves down on the floor and Eliza wrapped her coat around herself for warmth. The rain came then, a great thundering rush of it.

"Just in time," Eliza said, laughing with relief.

A flash of lightning illuminated the room and they saw that they were not alone.

CHAPTER
10

"We've got to say something," said Nell. "Honestly! I cannay eat another apricot."

"I know. And it's horrible being trapped in this body," Charlie grumbled. "I think being human for so long is starting to make me sick, aye."

"It's nay being human, Charlie! It's eating nothing but apricots for days!"

"I dinnay want to be rude."

"I know, lah, but we could be here for…I dinnay know, weeks, I spose. Eliza will come for us once she's sorted everything out and we'll be orange in the face. We'll have turned into mushy little apricots ourselves!"

"Really?" Charlie looked alarmed.

"No, but we're going to get seriously ill if we dinnay eat something else, lah."

"I'll bring it up when we go out today."

"Good. Thanks, Charlie."

They were being terribly polite to each other and had not spoken again of the argument they'd had the first night or the strangeness between them that had lasted over a year. Every day Charlie went out into the apricot orchards to pick the golden fruit with Emin and Mala. The apricots were then sent off by morappus to the Faery City. Nell stayed behind poring over her cream-coloured folder, memorizing formulas and equations and arcane terminology.

A bit light-headed, her stomach grumbling, Nell climbed a spiraling staircase up to Emin's "library." He had told her proudly that he had books on every topic imaginable and she had almost hoped that she would find something useful for her studies. The room itself was usually large and circular, with bookshelves lining the walls and tall windows between them. However, it was clearly a recent and unfinished Illusion. Nothing in it seemed to keep its shape for long. Whenever she took one of the books from the bookshelves and opened it, it turned immediately into something else. She found herself alternately holding a large, hissing raccoon, a diamond-studded tennis racquet, and a big brass kettle before she gave up on the books altogether. The whole tower began to tilt dramatically as the day wore on, the desk where she sat changing size and shape, and sometimes the ceiling began to sag or the walls bulged in a way that Nell found most alarming.

Nell's goal for the past year had been to study cetology, marine mammal science, with the famous cetologist Graeme Biggis. All her life Nell had longed to leave Holburg, to see the larger world, but once she left she came to appreciate the natural splendour she had grown up with. As children, she and Eliza had spent hours sitting on the cliffs in winter watching for whales, cheering whenever they saw a spout or a great dark back surging out of the waves. In the summer they swam with schools of curious dolphins, recognizing individuals year after year by size and scars. They found mushrooms that glowed in the dark and observed the nesting habits of the hundreds of species of birds that populated the island. Biology classes at Ariston Hebe had given her a context for the wonders of her childhood. Cetology in particular – exploring the mystery of those huge underwater mammals, so intelligent, so beautiful – had captivated her completely.

While many students chose to do another two years of secondary school before transferring to a university, the best students usually went on to university after their third year. As a top third-year student at Ariston Hebe she would no doubt win scholarships to any number of reputable universities, but Nell didn't care about that. As far as she was concerned, there was no Plan B. She would go to Austermon and study with Graeme Biggis. He taught select courses at Austermon and chose his top students to be assistants on his marine expeditions. She intended to be one of them, and go deep beneath the sea to witness the lives of the marvelous creatures there. Nothing less would do.

Since she was seeking to enter the Department of Natural Science, the entrance exam would be weighted heavily towards the sciences and mathematics. There would be shorter sections on history and literature but Nell was confident of her ability when it came to the humanities. What she needed to cram were the more complicated branches of physics and mathematics. She wouldn't be given a full scholarship unless she demonstrated excellence in all areas, and the fees were so outlandish that it was simply impossible for her to go without a scholarship.

She spent the morning deep in her notes. At odd moments her mind would wander to Jalo, the way he had bent towards her on the path and how she had stepped away like a fool. When she'd told Charlie her relationship with Oscar Van Holt was "on and off" she had made it sound rather more "on" than it was. In fact, neither of them was capable of a relationship around exam time, and while she was deeply impressed by his intellect, the more she got to know him the less impressed she was by the rest of him. Oscar Van Holt was all brain, without much charm or humour to balance him out. Jalo, on the other hand, well, Jalo was a Faery, unspeakably beautiful, powerful, mysterious. Why hadn't she let him kiss her? What would it be *like* to kiss a Faery?

Angry with herself for wasting precious minutes with such thoughts, she went back to her notes. Kissing Jalo was far from the point. She had to ace the Austermon exam. That was all that mattered for the next three weeks.

Behind her, someone entered the room on silent feet and watched her carefully through brilliant, changing eyes before soundlessly drawing a dagger.

Charlie thought he saw something out of the corner of his eye, a shadow flitting between two trees, but when he looked again there was nothing. He made another attempt to raise the apricot issue with Emin as they walked among the bright little trees, their baskets already overflowing with fruit.

"These apricots are delicious," he began feebly.

"Aprico! Ardelishuss!" a bird peeped cheerfully overhead.

"Yes," said Emin. "Nothing compares to the real thing! Not that you'd know the difference, I suppose."

"Uh huh. Yes. We're enjoying them."

"I am so glad!"

"Ardelishuss! Aprico Ardelishuss!" the bird carried on. Charlie glared at it.

"The thing is, lah, humans need to eat all kinds of things."

"Oh yes!" said Emin vaguely, missing the point yet again. "I can imagine!"

"I'm nay sure you can," said Charlie. "It can be...problematic, aye, to eat the same thing every day."

"Naturally!" said Emin. He had no idea what the human was on about. He picked a gleaming apricot from a low-hanging branch. "This one looks good. Why don't you have it? Since you need to eat so much?" He offered it to Charlie, who shook his head a little, feeling ill.

Mala looked over at Charlie and said in her lazy voice, "Perhaps you would like to eat something different?"

Charlie could have hugged her. He was about to reply when another bird soaring above them sang out, *"Warizagural?"*

He froze.

"What did that bird just say?" he asked.

"What bird?" Emin bit into the ripe, golden apricot. Mala whistled and the bird swooped back.

"Chektacassla. Kwait, kwait."

They all stood still for a moment, perplexed. Then Charlie dropped his basket and began to run back in the direction of the house, which had inconveniently become a castle again, perched on a looming cliff high above. Emin and Mala exchanged a horrified look and everything changed.

Nell heard Charlie shouting and looked up from her notes. She was high above the orchard and she could see him running like mad through the trees, calling her name. She had never heard that note of panic in his voice. She stood up, spilling her notes across the floor. Suddenly the view outside the windows shifted and the house was right in the middle of the orchard. A book-turned-raccoon made an angry chattering noise behind her and Nell span around. A Faery was almost upon her, dagger in hand. Nell threw her bowl of apricots in the Faery's face and tried to run past but the Faery caught her by the arm, dagger hand flying towards her. Before she could move to defend herself, a golden net ensnared the Faery.

"There will be more," said Emin. He and Mala were both in the room. The bookshelves were crumbling to shadow and dust, the walls drawing close around them.

"If they work Illusion? Or Curse us?" Mala's eyes were frightened but Emin shook his head firmly.

"They have no license to work Illusion on my property. I think whoever is behind this would not be quite so bold. I may not be rich but I am still technically a member of the nobility. They are here for the humans, am I right?" He pulled the ensnared Faery roughly from his net. Her bright hair was in a tight knot behind her head and she wore simple silk trousers and a tunic.

"Who are you?" asked Emin, giving her a shake.

The Faery said nothing, staring back at him defiantly. Charlie was at one of the windows, banging.

"There's no door!" he shouted. "Let me in."

The window swung open and he clambered into the room, which immediately began to rise as if the tower were growing. The windows disappeared.

"Are you all right?" he asked Nell breathlessly.

"Emin arrived just in time," she said, looking away. She didn't want him to see that she was trembling. She gathered her fallen notes back into the folder and hugged it to her, gripping the edges to keep her hands from shaking. "What's going on?"

"Assassins," said Emin. "But where are the others?"

There was a whistling sound and Mala spun herself in front of Nell, taking an arrow to the chest. There was a fourth Faery in the room for only an instant. Then both the intruders were gone, straight through the wall.

"Blast the Ancients!" cursed Emin. They went rocketing upwards and the walls fell away. Nell stumbled, dizzy, and found herself clinging to Charlie's arm. They were on top of a stone tower that loomed high over the apricot fields and the hills and the forest. Far below they could see a few figures moving swiftly through the orchard.

"It's nay the Thanatosi," said Charlie. "Though they're about as fast."

"They're Faeries, aye," said Nell faintly. "Why are Faeries trying to kill us?"

Mala pulled the arrow out of her chest with a disgusted look. Thick gold blood trickled down the front of her gown.

"Are you going to be all right?" asked Nell, alarmed.

"It will heal," muttered Mala. She touched her fingers to the blood. "It hurts," she added, as though surprised.

Charlie nodded sympathetically. "I hate being shot with arrows," he said.

Half a dozen morrapi, silken spheres pulled by myrkestras, were soaring over the apricot fields towards the tower. Nell and Charlie stiffened but Emin said, "These are mine. You cannot stay here. I will send word to Jalo. Mala, my love, you will take them?"

Mala nodded, expressionless.

"Take us *where?*" cried Nell. She had her trembling under control now but everything was happening so quickly and the sight of assassins flitting through the orchard made her queasy with fear.

"Jalo arranged a back-up plan in case you were discovered," said Emin. "Our paths part here. Good luck to you both."

The morrapi landed on the tower all around them.

"Come," said Mala. She pulled back the silk door of the nearest one and climbed into the gold-mesh sphere.

"Thank you for everything, Emin!" said Nell shakily, letting him clasp her hand before she joined Mala in the morrapus. Charlie shook his hand as well and they took to the sky, bobbing and floating.

None of them spoke for several minutes. Nell pulled the silk door back just a crack to peer through it. Mala reached over her shoulder and twitched it closed again.

"Don't," she said firmly. "There are several morrapi going in different directions. They mustn't know which one we're in."

"Where are we going?" Charlie asked.

"The Faery City," said Mala. She smiled slightly. "I grew up there. The nobility own land and live in Castellas, but the rest of us live in the City."

"Just one city?" asked Nell.

"It is a very large city," said Mala. She looked down at the bright bloodstain on the front of her robe and passed her hand over it. The mark disappeared. The wound seemed to have closed already.

"I have never been hurt before," she said, looking up at them with her brilliant eyes. "I don't like it."

"I've nary been keen on it myself," Charlie agreed. The way he said it made Nell want to throw her arms around him suddenly. It was such a *Charlie* sort of comment to make at a time like this and she found it deeply comforting.

"Thank you for warning me," she said to him, her voice full of her sudden burst of affection.

Charlie shook his head and his brow furrowed. "I've nary had to run like that. It was horrible, aye. I couldnay turn into anything faster, I couldnay do anything to help you. If Emin hadnay been there…I'm useless, Nell!"

He looked at her, his brown eyes sorrowful and bewildered. There was something so pleading in his expression. Nell didn't know what to say to him. She looked down at her folder. Her knuckles were white from holding it so tightly. She made herself relax her grip.

"Would you like some food?" Mala asked them. "Something other than apricots?"

"Yes!" they both cried.

"What do you like to eat?" she asked.

"Pickled snake," said Charlie immediately. "Black bean cheese! Crab spawn cakes!"

Nell gave him a horrified look and chimed in: "Pancakes, spicy shrimp, cheese WITHOUT the black bean, oh the Ancients, *ice cream!*"

Her mouth was watering.

"I don't know what those things are," said Mala, frowning, but the bottom of the Morrapus filled with trays loaded with food. The Morrapus dipped slightly with the added weight.

"Is it real?" Charlie picked up a spiced chicken leg and bit into it. A look of pure bliss crossed his face. Nell immediately began shoveling delicate canapés into her mouth.

"Illusion food," said Mala, watching them curiously.

"I cannay believe it would have been that easy all along!" groaned Nell. "A whole week of apricots!"

"It will stave off your hunger and keep you alive for a time but you will need real food before long," said Mala.

It tasted real enough. They ate until they couldn't eat anymore. The leftovers simply disappeared.

"What are we going to do in the city?" Nell asked Mala. "Hide?"

Mala shook her head. "Do you know who is trying to kill you?" she asked.

"Nearly everybody, apparently," said Charlie.

"We've no idea," said Nell.

"I do not *know*, either," said Mala. "And perhaps I should not tell you what I *think*, but it seems only fair, given where we're going. I suspect Jalo's mother, Tariro, is behind this. She doesn't want her son's reputation sullied by unsavory friends."

"She nearly killed me last time we were here," said Nell. She could still vividly recall the hate on Tariro's face, her iron grip.

"But how did she know where we were?"

"She tends to know things," said Mala cryptically. "Jalo is at his mother's house now. When Emin's message reaches him, he will leave the house in a hurry, as if going to rendezvous with you. Between them, he and Emin have put together an elaborate ruse to throw any assassins and spies off the scent. Tariro has spies all over the Realm, I expect, but we will be hiding in the last place she would think to look."

"Where is that?" Nell asked.

"In her own Castella."

There was a long pause. Then Charlie said, "That doesnay sound like a very good plan to me."

"What if she *sees* us?" added Nell.

"She will not recognize you," said Mala. She produced a twinkling little vial from a pocket in her dress. "This is a glamour, prepared by a witch that Jalo knows."

"Heilwig, I bet," said Nell to Charlie. He nodded.

"With the help of this glamour, I can work an Illusion on you that not even a Faery can see through unless they look very closely."

Another pause.

"Unless they look closely?" Charlie repeated. "That sounds like a fairly major flaw in the plan, lah. What if somebody does look closely?"

"Nobody will look at you closely," said Mala. "You will be servants like me. Believe me, the nobility barely see their servants as it is. They will notice nothing."

"It sounds dangerous, aye," said Charlie.

"It is," said Mala. She uncorked the vial and tossed the shimmering liquid in their faces.

The journey by morrapus was a long one, made to feel all the longer since Mala would not let them look outside. Nell tried to study but it was impossible to focus. She could feel the changes being wrought by Mala's glamour. Her skin felt different; it tingled and stretched. She kept wanting to rub her face like a sleepy kitten but every time she went to touch her face or run her hands through her hair Mala stopped her and said enigmatically, "Let the glamour do its work."

"It's nice to change bodies a bit," said Charlie cheerfully. "I've been stuck in the same one for so long, I think this'll be refreshing."

Every time Nell looked at him she began to giggle in spite of her fear and anxiety. He was halfway between being Charlie and being something else. The colour of his eyes kept growing lighter and then darker again, and the shape of them wavered. The tips of his eyebrows that turned up at the ends were curving down, she was sorry to see. His features were shifting and his skin brightening. It was most peculiar.

"You look prize strange yourself," he told her as she tried to stifle her laughter. "I'm nay sure how I feel about *you* changing. Especially watching it happen. I'm so used to you looking like... lah, *you*."

At last the morrapus began to descend.

"You can look out now," said Mala to Nell, like an indulgent parent rewarding an obedient child. Nell pulled back the silk and looked out.

The sky was full of morrapi, bobbing and billowing behind grey-white myrkestras. Below them, the gleaming Faery City stretched from horizon to horizon. At first, Nell couldn't believe her eyes. It was as if the City was *rippling*, but as they drew closer she realized that it was changing constantly. Broad promenades and stairs and spangled bridges snaked first this way, then that, winding through the city while towers and spires sprang up around them or faded out of sight. Vast cathedral-like buildings that would have been considered great architechtural wonders in any Di Shang city appeared and grew evermore elaborate before becoming something else. The vast city was in constant motion, but in contrast to the uncertain jumble of Emin's home it somehow maintained a constant balance and harmony through every imaginable configuration. Great Kalla seemed very small and still and dreary in comparison.

"Charlie, look!" Nell grabbed him by the hand before realizing what she was doing. It was an entirely un-Charlie-like hand. She withdrew her hand quickly, glancing at him. He was not Charlie at all anymore and she could tell by the way he looked back at her that she must be similarly changed. His lively face had been deadened to a perfect symmetry, and an expression of haughty nobility had replaced his usual mischievous twinkle. Gold curls framed his face.

"Look at *you!*" she giggled.

"It doesnay feel like *really* changing," he commented. "I feel all wrong, like I could just peel this new face off."

"Don't do that!" said Mala, alarmed. "Remember to try and *move* like a Faery, as much as possible. And you can't bring that." She jerked her chin at Nell's folder. Nell clutched it to her, appalled.

"I cannay leave it behind!" she insisted. "This is the most important thing in the worlds to me!"

Mala frowned, then shrugged. "Keep it hidden," she said. "It will be easier if it's smaller."

The folder was sitting in the palm of her hand, no bigger than a folded handkerchief. Nell gasped and opened it. Her notes were intact, but so tiny as to be barely legible.

"You'll make it big again afterwards, nay?" she said urgently. "I'll go blind trying to read this."

Mala raised her eyebrows. "We're nearly there. Put it away."

Nell slipped the folder reluctantly into a pocket. The morrapus dropped down into a courtyard whose outlying pillars were garlanded in flowers. Charlie and Nell slipped out of the morrapus after Mala, suddenly terribly conscious of how solid, awkward and un-Faery-like their every movement was.

The streets and buildings gleamed, opalescent, like the insides of seashells. Faeries massed about in bright, simple robes. The street moved with them, elaborately carved doorways and shining alleys multiplying all around them.

"Does it nay get confusing?" asked Nell, trying to keep her voice to a whisper and hurrying after Mala. "I mean, if the city is Illusion and it keeps changing, what happens if two Faeries try to make an Illusion in the same place or something? What if you're on a street that disappears? And how do you know where anything *is?*"

"The Architects create the City. There are regulations, a system," said Mala. "Don't talk anymore."

They came to a river as clear as glass. Mala handed a rose-coloured gem to a Faery with long flowing hair and the three of them boarded one of the narrow boats that plied the river. The long-haired Faery stood at the prow and used a pole to punt them along. In spite of the traffic, they moved very swiftly through the water. Charlie and Nell looked around them in undisguised amazement, taking in the fabulous sights and smells and sounds of the city. After an hour they disembarked and Mala led them up a winding staircase lined on both sides with stalls of fruit, silk and jewels. Faeries browsed and bartered noisily.

"This is the Marketplace Liathin," said Mala softly. "Do not speak. Do not look anyone in the eye. Do not draw attention to yourselves."

The staircase wound up and up over the city, the market bustling alongside. It came abruptly to an end facing a pale green marble door. The door was not attached to a building of any kind. It stood alone, framed by the bright sky over the city, which twisted and changed far below. Mala swung the door open. Although there was nothing but sky around the door frame, through it they saw a field of blossoming cherry trees surrounding a shining lake. Blossoms tumbled through the air like snowflakes and banners hung from the trees, each one depicting a different bird. A few blossoms blew out through the door and vanished.

They stepped through the doorway and Mala closed it behind them. At once the city was gone. The doorway stood alone in the middle of the field. Well-dressed Faeries lounged in little groups around the banners, talking and laughing. Mala looked around quickly and then led Nell and Charlie straight to a banner displaying a stylized rendition of a hawk. Three Faeries were chatting and sipping from little jeweled cups. One of them had a gold band around his arm and it was this Faery that Mala addressed in the language of the Faeries, holding out a clear, slender crystal the size of a finger.

The Faery replied in a lazy voice, glancing over the three of them briefly before taking the crystal and examining it. He handed it back to Mala and gave what seemed to be a command. Mala nodded and put her hands behind her back. She shot Nell and Charlie a look out of the corner of her eye. They were standing behind her, arms dangling, mouths slightly open, utterly confused. Her look was enough. They shut their mouths and put their hands behind their backs. Nell felt a mounting hilarity pressing against her chest. She didn't dare look at Charlie or she was sure she would burst out laughing. They stood absolutely still and silent for the best part of an hour while the Faery with the armband sipped at his drink and stared at everything and everyone but them. Then all at once he tossed his cup aside (it disappeared before hitting the ground) and stood up. He gave Mala a curt nod and the three of them followed him to the lake. The shore was lined with waiting morrapi. Two Faeries were struggling to put a large, familiar looking basket into the nearest one. Nell smelled the apricots as she approached but she didn't dare ask Mala about it. Unfortunately, the Faery with the armband got into the morrapus with them, so they couldn't talk at all. Nell glanced at Charlie and looked away again quickly with a flutter of trepidation. The myrkestra pulled the morappus into the air.

CHAPTER

11

Rain pounded against the windows and the flash of lightning illuminated the little room at the top of the lighthouse. In that second of bright whiteness, Eliza and Foss saw a most extraordinary-looking man. He sat leaning against one wall with his legs splayed. His arms and legs were very long and his clothes looked as if they had not been washed in weeks. He had a shock of dirty yellow-white hair springing out around a deeply lined, sunburned face. Several days worth of white stubble covered the lower half of his face and his mouth hung open in an almost comical grimace, revealing a few long yellow teeth. A gleam from somewhere deep among the pouchy wrinkles around his eyes told Eliza that he was awake and had seen them too. A rat ran across the room between them and all was black again. Thunder crashed overhead as if the sky was splitting open. Eliza cringed. Perhaps it was unwise to be in a lighthouse in a lightning storm.

Nobody spoke. The rain roared down. Another flash, and the figure was no longer against the wall. Eliza's heart began to race. She muttered a spell and a ball like a bright lightbulb lit the room. The huge gangling figure was creeping towards the orange glow of Foss's eyes with a brick in his hand.

"Stop!" she cried.

He froze. Foss looked up at the man with a faint chuckle but did not get up.

"Who are you?" Eliza demanded. Her ball of light swooped right in front of the man's face, blinding him. He squinted and turned his face away. The hand holding the brick was enormous and bristled with white hair.

"Ferghal!" he said, in a voice rich and coarse with decades of whisky. "My name is Ferghal Murtagh! What in the name of the Ancients are you?"

His accent was unfamiliar. He used the rough dialect of the eastern coast but there was a lilting cadence to the way he spoke that she had never heard before.

"Drop that brick," said Eliza.

Ferghal laughed a throaty laugh and squinted at her through the light. "Make me!" he said.

"Oh dear," sighed Foss.

Eliza fixed her will on the brick and it flew from his hand across the room, smashing into the wall. Ferghal stared at it and then at her. He broke into another gravelly laugh.

"As the Ancients would have it, am I to be murdered by a young mite of a witch and her wizardish companion?" asked Ferghal. "If it is to be so, well then by all that's mighty, I should like to have a cigarette first."

"Nobody is going to murder anybody," said Eliza, annoyed but beginning to relax. He was no threat to them. "We just need shelter for the night."

"Ah! Then we've a thing or two in common. A need of shelter and no murderous intentions."

This was a bit rich, Eliza thought, given that he'd been creeping up on Foss with a brick in his hand, but she could see how, from his perspective, they might seem rather frightening.

Ferghal reached into his pocket and drew out a pack of cigarettes. "I will celebrate with a cigarette after all."

Eliza settled down on the floor next to Foss. Ferghal hunted in his pockets and then swore.

"No matches." He looked over at them hopefully. "I don't suppose…?"

"We don't have any matches," said Eliza. Of course she could light his cigarette for him, and knew he suspected as much, but she didn't really want to sleep in a room stinking of cigarette smoke if she didn't have to. Every now and then another flash of lightning lit the room and a great clap of thunder made them all jump. She let her light go out and imagined the huge waves pounding against the flood-gates across the harbour.

"And what brings such beings as you to humble Elmount?" Ferghal's voice rumbled in the dark.

"We need a boat," Foss replied.

"Now suppose I knew where you could get a boat," said Ferghal in a sort of drawl. "Suppose I did! What would two such as *you* do for one such as *me* if I were to find you a boat? Perhaps even take you where you're going?"

"Naturally we would find some way to repay you for your help," said Foss. "Is this mere speculation, Mister Ferghal, or do you in fact have a boat?"

"Just Ferghal," he said. "Never met a mister I could stomach and I've no desire to pose as one myself! And *have* is a tricky word, a slippery sort of a word, don't you find? I couldn't rightly say that I *have* a boat, I don't think I could say that, no. But that's not to say I won't have one tomorrow, is it? Indeed, I think it quite likely I might have a boat tomorrow."

"Oh, I see." Foss sounded sad. "Do you mean you will steal a boat? Eliza, I do not like the direction we are going in. There must be another way."

"We dinnay have any money," said Eliza wearily. "And the volcano is way out at sea. What other way is there?"

"Eliza! A fine name!" Ferghal exclaimed. "I had an aunt named Eliza, you know. A hideous spinster and a poisonous cook with a temper like nothing you could imagine. Oh, what a terrible woman she was! Oh, how glad we all were when she gave up her last gasp and ceased to plague the world with her existence. Still, a fine name, a fine name." He crossed the room and sat himself down near Foss. "A volcano is where you're headed then? Not the archipelago?"

Eliza thought longingly of Holburg. "There's a volcanic chain south of the archipelago," she said. "That's where we're going."

"Yes, yes, yes indeed, and why shouldn't you? Peculiar, no doubt, but then it would be even more peculiar if you were doing something ordinary, since as far as I can tell you are both of a peculiar nature. Is that not right? I knew a man once who realized at the age of thirty-five that he couldn't be burned. Have you heard of such a thing? Couldn't be burned! Joined the circus and lit himself on fire for a living after that and drank himself to death with his earnings in under five years. Peculiar, isn't that right? Must have had a bit of mixed blood and never knew it. So long as you mean me no harm then I'm comfortable as can be with your kind, pleased in fact to make your acquaintance. So many folks one encounters these days are the same as the folks one has encountered in days gone by and it all begins to feel a bit repetitive, if you know what I mean. Sleeping in a lighthouse in a storm, I can't help feeling that something just like this has happened before and my life isn't taking me anywhere new, or I'm not taking it anywhere new, but in any case I see the two of you and my first thought is, by the Ancients I am going to be murdered by demons! And then we get to talking and instead I feel that here is something that has never happened to me before. And that's a rare treat, at my age, a rare treat, for I sometimes fear that everything has already happened to me that possibly could and it's going to be repeats 'til the day I die, getting less amusing every time."

Eliza heard a strange low sound and then realized that Foss was chuckling.

"Are you a literate man?" Foss asked Ferghal.

"A what kind of man?" Ferghal sounded wary.

"Can you read?"

"Oh, I can read a bit, yes. I can read the labels on bottles!" he cackled wildly at this joke and in a flash of lightning Eliza caught a gleam of wet tooth in his gaping mouth.

"It seems to me impossible to ever grow bored or to feel that life has run out of surprises if one is literate," explained Foss. "A being of learning, even an Immortal one, could never grow weary of the wealth of wonder, mystery and beauty offered by books." His eyes grew a little brighter, so that Eliza could make out the outline of his face and Ferghal leaning in close. He looked set to continue but for perhaps the first time had encountered someone more talkative than himself.

"Books, you are talking about books!" cried Ferghal. "But I

have no fondness for books! When I was just a child my father used the only book in our home to beat me with, and in my nightmares still a big book chases me around an empty house with the intention of doing me harm! No, spare me your books, my good fellow, I will have none of them! All full of wriggly little words that will tie your tongue and brain in knots trying to work them out, and terrible for the eyesight, they can make you blind in under a week, books can!"

"That is preposterous! Nothing could be more edifying than a book! A life without books is simply unimaginable. My poor man, you have much deprived yourself out of ignorance as to the true and wonderful nature of books!" Foss was most impassioned.

"I say life experienced first-hand is a far superior thing to any kind of story or lie cooked up in a book to fuddle a man and tell him what to do. Why read when one can live? A waste of precious seconds, your books."

"But you are contradicting yourself. Just moments ago…"

"A man's right, self-contradictoriness! Why must I agree with myself all the time? Where is the harm in holding two opposing opinions at the same time? It shows my breadth of mind."

"It shows nothing of the kind. It shows you to be a confused fellow whose intellect has suffered from a lack of books."

"Books! Spare me your books! My father used to beat me with the only book in our house…"

"Yes, you've said that already."

"A man's right, self-repetitiveness! Why must I say something new every time? Where is the harm in repeating the same story twice?"

As the two of them went back and forth like this and the storm raged outside, Eliza drifted off to sleep.

The sun rose over the Citadel and the bare room at the top of the lighthouse in Elmount grew bright. Still Eliza slept. She felt herself on weary wings descending towards the familiar grounds.

The powerful barriers around the Citadel were a mere whisper rustling through her feathers. She flew straight into the south wing, soared over two startled Mancers and through the wall into Kyreth's study. She dropped the little roll of paper on the Supreme Mancer's desk; it landed just inches from his large gold hand. If he was surprised at a raven flying into his study, he did not show it. He unrolled the page of newspaper and read what Eliza had scrawled on the back.

"Have you and Foss neglected your research?" He looked straight into the raven's little black eyes. Eliza felt herself boiling with flame, tossing and turning in the lighthouse. "The Thanatosi, once called, will never rest until their task is completed. They cannot be called off. There are a great many stories of beings calling upon them in a fit of passion and then seeking desperately to call them off, only to fail, every time. Surely you read these tales in the History. There is nothing I nor anyone else can do for your friend, Eliza." He looked calmly at the raven for a few moments. "I will not ask you to come back. The Emmisariae will bring you back and we will speak further then. Do not seek me out in this form again."

Some force blasted against the raven. It opened its beak in a shriek of pain and flew pell-mell straight up through the ceiling, through floor after floor, out the top of the Citadel and into the dawn sky. Eliza sat upright in the lighthouse, her bones aching with the blow. She spat out a singed black feather. She was alone.

She leaped to her feet and ran to the windows. Her ankle was feeling much sturdier today. Foss was down on the bluff with Ferghal. A light rain was still falling but the storm had subsided. Ferghal was a giant of a man, only a few inches shorter than Foss himself. He was pointing down towards the harbour with one of his long arms. Eliza snatched up her backpack and hurried down the stairs and outside to see what they were talking about. By the time she reached Foss, Ferghal was already loping off in the direction of the town.

"He assures me he will not steal a boat," said Foss, smiling down at Eliza. "He will merely borrow one from a friend and return it after our journey. He is a fine sort of man, in spite of his inexplicable abhorrence of books, from which I simply could not sway him. We shall have to think of some form of payment. He seems happy to accept a spell, but of what kind? Whatever it is, you will have to work it, Eliza. I am feeling rather weak."

She looked at him with concern. He was looking grayer and frailer every day.

"Are you going to be all right?" she asked. "Is this…lah, is it because of being separated from the Mancers?"

"A brief separation is harmless for an Emmisarius," said Foss with a sigh. "But I am no longer an Emmisarius. I am like a leaf, Eliza, that has been cut from the plant. I can no longer feed the plant with the natural powers I possess, but the plant will survive for it has many leaves. However, without a connection to the life-giving roots of the plant, I will wither rather quickly, I'm afraid."

Eliza felt her heart plummeting as he spoke. "There must be some kind of cure, something we can do," she said, struggling to keep her voice calm.

"While Kyreth is in power, I will not be welcomed back," said Foss. "There is no cure but that. But do not worry so, Eliza. I have power in me still, and enough to sustain me for a time. I should like to conserve it, however, so if you would be so kind, I will leave the working of Magic to you except in an emergency."

"Of course," she said, trying not to cry. She squeezed his big hand. It was cold.

The rain stopped and they sat on the bluff looking out over the harbour and the sea, grey under the overcast sky. A few hours later, Ferghal returned, looking immensely pleased with himself. He was carrying a canvas bag.

"Friends!" he beamed, waving at them with a big, hairy hand. "I have secured us a vessel and victuals too! Do you eat the same food as we mortal humans do?"

"I do," said Eliza eagerly. Foss declined with a graceful nod.

"I should have guessed, for you look almost human, though not quite, obviously, to a trained eye," said Ferghal cheerfully. He sat down on the grass with them and emptied out the bag of odds and ends he had clearly swiped from grocery stalls: honey rolls, pears, a bunch of carrots, a bag of salted nuts.

"*Almost* human?" said Eliza indignantly. Foss chuckled.

"Well, except for the nose and the eyes," Ferghal said. "In point of fact, you look like one of those warrior women from Boqua, you know, the ones who walk on hot coals all day long to get used to pain. I had a girlfriend like that once, she couldn't bear to wear shoes or walk on the pavement, she had to sprinkle coals ahead of her just so she could walk on the ground. Life was terribly hard for her up north. But my, what a cook! Phenomenal meals she used to prepare! We'd eat a whole pig, buttered and roasted, between the two of us! Daily! Ah, those were the days. But alas, poor thing, she drowned trying to harpoon a giant porpoise. The beast pulled her beneath the waves and I never saw her again, nor tasted one bite of that porpoise. Well, such is life, by all that's mighty! The Ancients have their game with us and then we disappear, is that not so?"

"Well, that is a matter of some debate," said Foss, suddenly animated. "Eliza has some rather odd theories about the Ancients that might interest you. I am of a more conventional mindset myself."

"I should love to hear your theories, witchlet!" cried Ferghal. "I had an Aunt Eliza, you know."

"Yes, you told us," said Eliza quickly. She didn't much want to discuss the Ancients with Ferghal, but he and Foss were already off again, with Foss expounding upon free will and the disappearance of the Ancients and Ferghal quite convinced that the Ancients were peering down upon humankind from behind the clouds, vastly entertained by what they saw.

Once they had eaten the food and drunk the flat beer Ferghal had brought, they walked down the bluff to a cove where he had stashed a small fishing vessel. It looked badly in need of repair.

"Is it really seaworthy?" Eliza asked doubtfully.

"I thought it might not matter much, the two of you being what you are," Ferghal said, leaping in, his white eyebrows waggling at her meaningfully. "You can plug the holes with Magic and command the sea to be calm should it get unruly and we shall be on our merry way. A bit of sunshine might be nice, if you could manage it."

"I cannay do that sort of thing!" said Eliza.

"You can, I'll bet," said Ferghal to Foss. "Eyes like that and a wizardish look about you."

"He cannay do anything right now. He's sick," said Eliza. "We're going to drown in this thing, aye."

"Nonsense," said Ferghal. "She's a fine boat and will bear up well with a little help from her Magical passengers. Come now." He pushed the boat out into the water and held out a big hairy hand to Eliza. She forewent the hand and climbed into the boat. Foss tried to step in but his balance failed him and he swayed dangerously. Eliza leaped to her feet, but before she could do anything Ferghal had steadied him with an arm. He was strong and helped Foss into the boat with all the tenderness of a son helping his aged mother. Eliza began to warm to him.

As luck would have it, the sky cleared and the sea calmed as they headed out of the harbour. The sun was warm on their faces. "Ah, well done, well done!" cried Ferghal, assuming Foss and Eliza were responsible for this change in the weather. Throughout the journey, Eliza bailed frantically with a little rusted bucket to keep the water from reaching above their ankles. Amazingly, the little boat's engine held out.

The sea remained calm throughout the day and the following night. By morning they could see the volcanic islands through which they would reach Tian Xia, small shadows on the horizon. Eliza was beginning to feel confident of their success when a raven on the prow of the boat cawed once, suddenly. She looked up. In the northern sky she saw five glimmering specks and her heart sank.

"Foss," she said softly, and touched his arm. Foss saw immediately what she was looking at.

"They must have fixed the Vindensphere," she said.

"They haven't seen us yet," he said.

"But they know where we are. We cannay hide out here at sea."

"Somebody looking for you?" asked Ferghal, shading his eyes. Eliza pointed. "They'll spot us soon, aye."

"By the Ancients, this is so strange that I half wonder if I'm dreaming! What am I seeing?"

"Mancers," said Eliza unhappily. At this, Ferghal's face split into a gaping open-mouthed cackle, his few teeth unnaturally long in his scarred gums.

"The guardians of Di Shang!" he cackled. "Cofounders of the Republic! They aren't as popular in Scarpatha, don't you know."

All at once Eliza understood his accent and his odd way of talking.

"Are you Scarpathian?" she asked, keeping an anxious eye on the horizon.

"Dangerous to say so hereabouts, isn't it!" he exclaimed. "Oh no, mustn't admit to anything so nefarious as being from that cursed place. Crossed the ocean in a vessel not as seaworthy as this, little witchlet, with twenty others. Three of us left by the time we reached the shores of the Republic, land of plenty. Plenty of what, I wonder? What did I expect? Oh, but I was young and foolish then and such dreams I had. A funny thing, it is, this being human in the worlds. A great joke the mighty powers are having at our expense, it seems to me. Well, I like a good joke as well as any and so I play my part."

The glimmering specks were drawing closer. She could see their wings.

"What are we going to do?" she cried.

"You must hide under the boat," said Ferghal.

Foss and Eliza stared at him.

"How will we breathe?" asked Eliza.

"Magic!" suggested Ferghal, as if she was mad.

"Praps," she said doubtfully. Perhaps she could separate the oxygen from the water for both of them, but it seemed a very tricky sort of spell to work and she doubted she could maintain it for long.

"Well, Magic or snorkels. Take your pick, witchlet." Ferghal pulled open the rusty locker that ran the length of the boat.

Inside was a harpoon that had not been used for a long time, a great tangle of wire and netting, two long battered oars, half a chewed flipper that looked as though a shark had gotten hold of it, and a single snorkel and mask.

"We'll have to share," said Eliza. "Ferghal, turn the boat around. They're going to speak to you, aye, and we're putting our lives in your hands. Do you understand?"

"Am I to speak with Mancers? I never imagined such a thing. Perhaps I will tell them what we think of them in fair Scarpatha."

"You'll tell them no such thing. You will seem dull-witted and speak little. You will say that a being like them and a girl forced you to take them to a volcano and you left them there. All right?"

"Ah! Clever, very clever. They will rush ahead in their pursuit, overtaking you. I see your plan. A being like them, you say...do you mean to say that our friend here is of that despotic tribe?"

"I am a Mancer," said Foss heavily. "Or I was. I do not know for certain what I am now, cut adrift."

"Foss, please. We have to get in the water. Will you be all right?"

Foss smiled at her lovingly. "Poor Eliza," he said. "You are too young to have cares such as these."

"I couldnay agree more," she said, and fit the mask over her head. She put on her backpack with the Gehemmis inside. "We'll take turns with the snorkel. Three breaths each and then pass. We'll need to hold tight to each other and keep it out of view, aye, under the prow." She gave Ferghal a desperate, pleading look. "You willnay give us up?"

"On my life, dear witchlet! I will lie through my four teeth to the Mancers." He was already turning the boat around, so that they were heading back in the direction they had been coming from. Eliza climbed over the bow and slipped into the water. It was very cold. "Come on, Foss!"

Ferghal helped him to his feet and pushed him overboard with a great splash, holding fast to one of his arms.

"I have never been in the sea!" said Foss, with a gasping sort of laugh. Eliza took his hand and fixed it around the painter that dangled in the water, linking her arm through his and getting a firm grip on the painter herself.

"We need to be under the boat so we're nay visible," she said. "Are you ready?"

Foss nodded. He looked grey-faced but strangely serene. Eliza counted: "One, two, three."

They both submerged themselves and slid under the boat. At first the snorkel filled with water, but Eliza managed to position herself so that the tip of it poked out of the water just beneath the prow, where it would not be easily visible. The boat was not going fast but nonetheless the water pulled against them, threatening to drag them right along the bottom of the boat into the engine. They clung to the painter and Eliza wished she had checked it more thoroughly for rot. She blew the water out of the snorkel and took in a breath. The bottom of the boat bumped against her stomach and legs, the water pouring through her clothes, and she saw nothing but a rushing greyness. She took in three deep breaths and then awkwardly took the snorkel out of her mouth and fumbled to find Foss's mouth. His lips closed around it and she held her breath, waiting. She clung to the painter, her arm still locked through his, their bodies jostling together in the water. She wanted to tell Ferghal to slow the boat down, but then perhaps that would look suspicious. It seemed an age of struggling to stay in position, clinging to the painter and each other, breathing in turn, before the bright surface of the water suddenly darkened with the shadows of great dragon wings.

Ferghal Murtagh had seen a great many things in his sixty-seven years of life. He had seen poverty, though he hadn't known at the time that that was what he was seeing, because he had never known anything else. He had seen his little sister die in her bed of a brain fever. He had seen his father, a member of an illegal dissident organization, dragged out of the house, forced to his knees, and shot in the back of the head. He had seen his mother lying at a strange angle on the floor after drinking a bottle of rat poison.

He had seen the inside of Scarpathian work camps, the terrible depths of the coal mines. He had seen the ruined, bombed-out cities attesting to the former glory of the country. And he had seen the sea, for days, on every side. He had seen clean and beautiful Kalla, and he had seen the wretched towns along the border, plagued by bandits. He had seen a man set himself on fire for a living and a woman who ate her own fingers she was so crazy. He'd watched the sun come up and set the snowy peaks of the Karbek mountains alight and he'd seen the most beautiful girl in the world laughing in the grass, her bare feet tangled with his, her long, dark hair hanging in her face. He'd seen beauty and horror and he thought he'd seen it all. But he'd never seen anything like the five green-gold dragons that descended now around his boat. They were much bigger than the boat, with terrible eyes and tongues like fire. The beings riding the dragons were indeed like the wizardish fellow he'd found in the lighthouse. But where that one was dull-coloured, with a muddy robe and burning orange eyes, these ones were so brilliant he could hardly look at them. Looking into their eyes was like trying to stare into the sun. Their skin shone gold and their robes and hair were white.

The dragons landed screaming in the water, pulling their wings back and coasting the waves like colossal, unearthly swans. One of the Mancers leaped with tremendous agility from the back of the dragon and into the boat. Ferghal looked up in amazement at the being. Her voice was the sweetest voice he'd ever heard, high and fine, like a violin singing.

"Excuse us for appearing like this, Ferghal Murtagh," she said. "I am Anargul, manipulator of wood. Here with me is Ka, manipulator of fire, Trahaearn, manipulator of metal, Obrad, manipulator of earth, and Finnis, manipulator of water. Do you know why we are here?"

Ferghal didn't know much about Magic but he knew all about power and authority, and he had known how to lie with every fiber of his being ever since he was a very small boy. He knew how to lie so that while he was lying he believed every word. In another sort of life, he might have been a world-class actor. He trembled now from head to toe and his mouth gaped open in slow-witted amazement.

"Oh the Ancients save me," he babbled.

Anargul looked around the boat and opened the locker.

"They are gone," she said to the others.

"Gone where?" demanded Obrad. "How could they be gone? The Vindensphere showed them to us not seven hours ago, at sea!"

"Do you know whom we are speaking of?" Anargul turned her terrible gaze onto Ferghal and he shielded his eyes with his hands, blinded.

"Ancients save me!" he wept.

"Hush," Anargul bent down and laid a hand on his shoulder. My, but there was something uncanny about that touch, he thought. He peered at her bright face through his fingers. "You had passengers, Ferghal Murtagh. Where have they gone?"

"Oh yes! Oh yes!" he cried. His chin was slick with tears and his hands shook. "A dark little witch and a bright one like you, they made me do it, they made me! Ah, Demons and Giants, I shall be killed, I shall never see my dear wife again!"

"You will see your wife, Ferghal, and there will be no killing," Anargul assured him. "But you must tell us where your passengers have gone."

He pointed, waving his finger in the direction of the volcanic islands, growing ever more visible by the early morning light. "Took them there!" he sobbed. "A volcano! They wanted to go to a volcano! Oh madness! Left them there, by the Ancients, oh I swear by all that's mighty I meant no harm, I meant no harm!"

Anargul stood in the rocking boat. The other Mancers sat straight on the backs of their coasting dragons and looked to the volcanoes.

"There must be a way to the Crossing," said Obrad.

"Then we must hurry," said Anargul. "Eliza has powerful friends there."

She leaped back to her dragon. Ka was watching Ferghal, still peering through his fingers, and he detected in the fellow's teary eyes an intelligent, mischievous gleam. He knew, all at once, without searching the man's mind, that he was lying. He looked at the empty boat, and then noticed that the painter at the bow was taut. A steady stream of bubbles was coming up from the side.

"Come, Emmisariae!" said Anargul. Ka hesitated only a moment. An image of Aysu's body on the Library floor flashed through his mind and he said nothing. The Mancers took to the air, leaving the little boat behind them.

"She is resourceful, I will say that for her," said Kyreth, watching the scene in the Vindensphere. "She has powerful friends, too. They will help her if she reaches Tian Xia, as it seems she will."

"Are you making more of that splendid concoction?" Malferio shifted uncomfortably on the divan. "I think it's wearing off. I've got that pins and needles feeling and something smells rotten."

Kyreth seemed not to hear. Malferio groped at the ground around the divan and muttered, "Where's my pipe. Dropped it." He looked up at Kyreth again with a leer. "If they haven't been able to catch her in Di Shang, they won't fare any better in Tian Xia. She's slipped through your fingers, it would appear. Blastedly clever, isn't she?"

Kyreth gave a thin smile. "I can only hope so," he said.

"Now you are making no sense," said Malferio. "Here is the pipe. Completely empty! Are you making me some more?"

"If the Emmisariae can bring her back then we will have an heir from her. If they cannot, if she eludes them, then perhaps she is capable of giving us even more than that." He strode across the room and snatched the pipe out of Malferio's hands, who wailed in protest. "The Faeries guard one of the Gehemmis. Where?"

"The Gehemmis?" Malferio gaped. "You aren't still hung up about those?"

"I have more of this for you if you tell me," said Kyreth, waving the pipe at him.

"The Master of the Vaults keeps it hidden," said Malferio. "Look, I don't care, I have no reason to lie to you, but I never bothered myself about the Gehemmis. Will you give me more now?"

"Guarded by what? Illusion?"

Malferio grinned. "Enchantments too. Very deep. Your wife didn't get far at all before the Master of the Vaults found her and Cursed her and sent her back to you, a gibbering lunatic."

Kyreth struck Malferio across the face. The Faery sprawled from the divan to the floor with a howl. Kyreth dropped the pipe so it clattered to the stone floor. With the Vindensphere in his hands he swept from the tower, the stones opening and closing for him.

Malferio's screams echoed in the lonely room, diving back down to attack him while the stones loomed and menaced.

When the Emmisariae were nearly out of sight, mere glittering specks over the distant chain of volcanoes, Ferghal leaned over the prow of the boat and tugged on the painter. Eliza's head and then Foss's broke the surface of the water, each of them gasping in a grateful breath of air.

"They're gone?" Eliza managed.

Ferghal thought Eliza and the sick Mancer looked very funny with their hair slicked around their dripping faces. He guffawed, and then said, "Yes, yes! Didn't suspect a thing, not for a moment. They are rushing off to those volcanoes. Come now."

He took Eliza's arm and hauled her on board with ease. "Aren't you a little thing, though!" he said. "You weigh nothing at all. Could carry you round in my pocket." He reached over with both arms, bracing himself with his legs, and hauled Foss into the boat with a grunt. "Him, now, there's another story! Like he's got bricks instead of guts inside."

Foss lay sprawled in an ungainly fashion in the bottom of the boat, drenched, his fair hair clinging to his scalp and face. Eliza felt a stabbing pain in her heart to see him so helpless and weak.

"Thank you, Ferghal," she said, not looking at Foss in case he felt ashamed. She wanted him to be able to preserve his dignity as much as possible. "I promise, we'll think of something we can do for you to make this worthwhile."

"You need not think at all," said Ferghal triumphantly. "For I have already thought of it! The Mancers seeking you seem to believe you are looking for a way to Tian Xia, the world of Magic and mystery, and indeed anyone asking passage to a chain of deserted volcanoes is up to something mighty strange, so I think they must be right. I have decided you will take me with you!"

Wet, cold and exhausted though she was, Eliza managed a weak laugh at this notion. "No," she said.

"Yes, yes!" said Ferghal. "Else I'll smash the engine into bits right now. I've seen enough of this world for one lifetime and I fancy seeing another."

"It's dangerous," said Eliza. She hadn't really the strength to argue. She opened her backpack and checked to make sure the Gehemmis was undamaged. The shard of bone was wet but otherwise unhurt.

"Never mind danger. I have faced Mancers in my day, I might boast! I wish to see Tian Xia. And think, witchlet, a pair of strong arms might serve you well. This Mancer is unwell. I can see it all the better having just come face to face with the healthier variety. Do you think you are strong enough to carry him if he needs it?"

Foss looked back and forth between them, ashen-faced, without comment.

"I'm stronger than I look," said Eliza dryly, but in fact she was wondering if it might not be a bad idea. Ferghal had helped them elude the Mancers and might prove helpful again. One thing was certain, the Faeries would not let Foss enter their Realm, and so she would not be able to stay with him the whole time they were in Tian Xia. Ferghal watched her face closely and saw that it was decided. He clapped her on the shoulder rather too forcefully. She coughed up some seawater.

"Then let us go where your predatory Mancers have erroneously pursued you already! Into the volcano, and another world!"

Ferghal raised his arms in a great cheer, and then the engine died.

CHAPTER

12

Tariro stood on the battlements and watched the morrapus making its journey across the chasm. The outlying battlements of her Castella perched on the edge of a bottomless cliff. The white rock veered down sharply. Clouds whirled in the chasm and great black birds wheeled and screamed far below.

"You sent five Faeries. How could they fail?" Her voice was crisp and cool as usual. One would have to know her very well to hear the rage tightening her vowels. Miyam knew Tariro all too well.

"There was some warning," said Miyam. "They were prepared for my assassins, who dared not use Illusion on a noble Faery's property."

"He is barely noble," spat Tariro. "Born to it, perhaps, but he has nothing to show for it."

Miyam said nothing. The morrapus bobbed closer. They could see the bright eyes of the myrkestra now.

"I want you to finish this yourself."

"I will. Jalo has gone to the City. He will lead us to them."

The myrkestra flew along her high walls and Tariro gave a curt nod to the Guards in the courtyard below. A part of the wall swung open, allowing the morrapus to enter the courtyard. Four Faeries dressed in simple servant garb emerged, staring up at the towering battlements and at the archers looking down from them, arrows tipped with enchanted poisons. A guard with several silver-hounds loping after him went to meet them.

"I wanted it to be quick," said Tariro to Miyam. "It is not good for my son to have it drawn out this way. Now go and see who is arriving."

Miyam ran down the battlements to the little courtyard. Tariro watched the way her bare feet barely touched the ground. Tariro could not have asked for a more dependable servant but in fact she found Miyam disconcerting, with her cold, spinning eyes that sometimes fell terrifyingly still. Tariro often faced away when speaking to her so she wouldn't have to look into those strange eyes, that dead face. Miyam formed the habit of standing behind Tariro to receive instructions while Tariro looked elsewhere. She had saved Miyam long ago from certain imprisonment and Miyam was grateful and loyal. Tariro knew she could trust her; in fact, she trusted no one else. But she could not bring herself to like her.

Miyam exchanged a few words with the passengers. The guard took a covered basket from the morrapus, which he gave to Miyam with some documents. Everybody deferred to Miyam. In authority here, she was second only to Tariro herself. Nobody pretended that Nikias, Tariro's husband, wielded any real power.

Miyam came flying back up the battlements to report.

"Jalo has sent servants for Cadeyrn and his wife. An apology for his sudden departure. They come from the servant house of Illyron." She held out the finger-length crystal as evidence. Tariro examined it.

"And the basket?"

"Apricots, my Lady." Miyam opened the lid a crack to show her. Tariro glanced at it and then looked away again.

"Apricots?"

"There is a letter. For Second Advisor Nikias and Lady Tariro, with warmest regards and much appreciation, your loyal friend Emin," Miyam read. "He has enclosed a poem."

"What is he playing at?" demanded Tariro, bristling. "Are you sure they are just apricots?"

"I will have each one investigated carefully, and the basket too."

"I want a witch to look at them. Search for spells."

"It is done, my Lady."

"Emin will pay for this insolence."

"He is Jalo's dear friend, my Lady."

Tariro spun around to face Miyam. "Are you telling me my business?"

"No, my Lady."

Miyam did not flinch the way most would when facing Tariro's wrath. This was annoying. Even more annoying, Miyam was right. Emin was Jalo's friend. Killing the girl would hurt Jalo. His friend should be left alone, however much Tariro wished to punish him.

"We are done here," said Tariro. "I hope to hear from you soon that the girl is dead."

"So you shall, my Lady." Miyam bowed down on one knee, head bent, then rose in a single fluid motion and disappeared through a well-hidden trapdoor that led inside the walls. The stone walls around the courtyard were real, not Illusion. Now the great door swung open again, this time leading onto a bridge that crossed the chasm, its other end lost in a deep mist. Tariro watched the little group for a moment as they walked along the bridge in a row, then turned and descended the battlements.

Mala presented Nell and Charlie as members of a new group of Illusion-makers who took vows of silence as a means of conserving the powers of the imagination, which sounded completely batty to Nell. They noticed the archers, and the Faery glaring down from the battlements. Nell had had nightmares about Tariro since their last meeting and was less than thrilled to be seeing her again, even from a distance.

They crossed the bridge, into the mist. On the other side, a polished opal floor, smooth and clear and bright as water, stretched as far as the eye could see. Here and there stood isolated archways, and through each, a different scene presented itself. They looked through the archways at opulent banquet halls, gardens and forests and lakes, ballrooms and stormy seas, myrkestra races and extravagant musical performances. But these tantalizing other worlds were not for them. Mala took them through an archway and into a broad corridor hung with clothes. Faeries examined the elegant dresses and murmured gloomily to one another.

"Lady Demetria likes to have her gowns redone every day," explained Mala in a low voice. "She does not like to face the same choices day after day and so her entire wardrobe must be reinvented. This rather taxes the imaginations of her servants and we are to assist."

It was not long before Nell was more afraid of dying of boredom than by Tariro's hand. Mala worked Illusion on their behalf, loading the gaudy costumes with still more gold thread and bright ribbons. By night, they slept in the servant quarters, in a long row of beds. Mala brought them food when she could, some of it real and some Illusion. Throughout the day, they tried to be inconspicuous. All that was required of them was to ponder Lady Demetria's dresses with expressions of great seriousness, follow her about in a big mass when she wished it, and stand by watching while the Faeries feasted and danced in the evenings. Nell thought unhappily of the miniaturized folder tucked in her pocket. She fingered it and ran through formulae in her head.

On the third evening, Nell and Charlie stood side by side watching a Faery ball. Orbs of light circled high in the black sky overhead while unearthly music soared and sang in all directions. The Faeries danced as if they were weightless. And yet Nell couldn't help feeling there was something rather joyless about it all. School dances at Ariston Hebe, the gym decorated with streamers, a mediocre band and over-sweet punch, had more of a buzz of excitement about them than this strange, beautiful, perfunctory performance. She was trying to keep from swaying to the music when a Faery approached her and said softly, "I need you to come with me."

Fear coursed through her like a wave of heat. She had understood him, which meant that the Faery had spoken with intent. He knew what or who she was. She searched his face but it was blank.

"Quickly, please," he said. She glanced at Mala, who gave a little jerk of the chin. She followed the Faery out the archway, leaving the ball behind them. He led her at a brisk pace through the forest of arches, not speaking, and then abruptly through one of them. They emerged into a pleasant glade that reminded Nell of her first visit to the Realm of the Faeries. Jalo was waiting for her there, dazzling in his feathered cloak. She gave a cry of delight. The other Faery stepped back outside the archway.

"I apologize," said Jalo, smiling down at her warmly. "This is risky but I had to see you. We have thrown them temporarily off the scent, I believe."

"Dinnay you think this is a crazy idea?" Nell asked. "Do I look like a Faery to you?"

"The glamour is very good. I can find you through it, but not easily." He touched her cheek with his fingers and she felt herself flush. "There. There you are."

"How long are we going to stay here, Jalo?"

"Your friend, the Shang Sorceress, is in Tian Xia with the Faithful," he said. "She has called for me with your ring and I will leave at once."

"Thank the Ancients!" cried Nell. "Has she gotten rid of the Thanatosi?"

"That I do not know," said Jalo. "But it is too dangerous for you to stay here much longer. You will eventually be found by those that seek your life."

He looked stricken. Nell felt very sorry for him.

"Thank you for everything you've done," she said. "Mala is an absolute gem."

"There is another way for you to be safe," Jalo said earnestly, and then sighed. "I wish I could lift the glamour. I want you to look properly like yourself when I say this. But never mind." He took her hands in his and she felt a distant pounding in her ears. He was going to try to kiss her again and this time she would let him.

"If we were married, you would be safe forever. None could harm you," said Jalo. "I know it is sudden and the circumstances of my proposal less than ideal, but I would make you happy and you would have everything you ever wanted. Will you be my wife?"

This was so unexpected that her first impulse was to laugh. She mastered herself quickly and fumbled for a response that matched the seriousness of his expression. "Jalo...I dinnay know what to say. I'm too young to be thinking about marriage. And... and I'm fond of you but we dinnay really know each other all that well yet, do we? It doesnay seem like a good idea to marry somebody for protection."

"For love, not protection," he insisted. "The immediate danger is what drives me to make this proposal so suddenly, but you and I would be happy."

He bent his lovely face towards her. Before his lips touched hers she found herself inexplicably stepping back again. It was as if she had no control over her own movements. She pulled her hands from his and said in confusion, "Sorry."

Jalo looked sad. "No, I am sorry. I should not be so brash. It is just that time is short and I fear I may not see you again if you leave."

"We'll see each other," said Nell, not because she really believed it but because she didn't know what else to say. It was odd to realize that she didn't want to kiss Jalo, but she didn't. What she wanted, suddenly, desperately, was to be outside, *really* outside, walking or running in the fresh air. She missed the real world. She was sick to death of the sunless sky and the bewildering Illusions here, their unreal beauty masking something ominous.

"Be my wife," he said again.

She shook her head. "I cannay marry you, Jalo. You've been a wonderful friend, but there it is."

He looked confused. "It is a human custom, I think, to put off a suitor or refuse at first. But we do not have time, Nell."

"No, lah, this is nay a custom. I cannay marry you. I willnay change my mind." It came out rather blunter than she meant it to sound but she felt surer by the moment that he would not understand her unless she was very, very clear.

His expression hardened. "It is the other one, isn't it? Your friend the Shade? Though he is nothing but a powerless boy now."

"Charlie?" exclaimed Nell. She did not at all like the icy contempt with which he said *powerless boy*. "This has nothing to do with Charlie."

"Be careful, Nell. I must go meet with your friend the Sorceress." He turned away and she caught him by the arm.

"Jalo! Dinnay be angry. I'm just trying to be honest with you, lah."

He faced her again, his marble-smooth face very bright. He looked a great deal like his mother at that moment, she thought.

"Do you have any idea what you've just refused? It is...I cannot think of a word. You, a human girl, turning down the proposal of a Faery? And not only a Faery, but a Faery from one of the most powerful families in the realm! What do you imagine your life as a human will be? I will tell you, in one word: brief. I could give you Immortality and then everything you could dream of to enjoy for eternity. I think you don't really understand. How could you choose a short and meaningless life in Di Shang, empty and colourless? You will grow old and die so quickly, and that only if you are lucky! You must be mad."

Nell's temper flared. "Why would I want to live forever just so I could be bored out of my mind, away from everyone I love?" she snapped. "I hate this place! It might be very pretty but it gives me the creeps, aye, and I have a lot of plans for my life by the way. I'm going to be a cetologist and go on marine expeditions with Graeme Biggis!"

Jalo stared at her as if she had lost her mind. "I will meet with your friend the Sorceress," he said again in a tight voice. "I will return as soon as I can."

He swept away through the archway and Nell was left feeling sorry and miserable and a little afraid. After all, Jalo was all that stood between them and Tariro; it probably wasn't a good idea to make him angry. She stepped out of the archway but he was already gone. The waiting servant led her back to the ballroom and she slipped into her place next to Charlie.

"Jalo's going to meet Eliza," she murmured to him.

"Thank the Ancients," he said.

"He proposed marriage," said Nell. It sounded so silly she half wanted to laugh again, though in fact she was feeling rather shaky still.

Charlie glanced at her from the corners of his eyes, his expression unchanging. "And?"

"Lah, obviously I said no. We hardly know each other and I dinnay like it here a bit. I've got this exam to take and everything. But he lost his temper, aye. It was a whole other side to Jalo. He couldnay believe I'd turned him down."

"Do you think we can still count on him?"

"I think so. He wouldnay betray us, let us be killed, would he? Just because of hurt pride?"

"I dinnay know. Faeries are notorious for not particularly valuing the lives of non-Faeries."

"We're really nay safe here, are we? But if he's meeting with Eliza, praps it will be all right."

"Praps she's gotten rid of the Thanatosi and we'll be able to go home."

"I hope so. I cannay wait to get out of here!"

His smile, though not his usual smile, was a hint of the real Charlie under the Faery mask. "Still, I'm a little surprised you turned down immortality."

Nell pondered this. The very idea of immortality was so abstract and unimaginable, as was death. She had spoken honestly, for she didn't want to marry Jalo or live in this place. The grander implications of mortality versus immortality had been simply impossible for her to seriously contemplate in such a brief moment.

"I would have had to leave behind my family and my friends and all my plans. I wouldnay be able to go to Austermon. I couldnay give everything up, just like that."

"Not even for a dashing Faery and eternal life?"

"He *is* handsome, aye. I must be crazy. He said as much, actually."

"Arrogant," said Charlie with pleasure. "Although, I spose I'm a little more to your taste like this, nay?"

She gave him a sidelong glance. "It's too strange to see you as a Faery. What about me? Which version do you prefer?"

"The Nell version. No contest."

Nell felt a warm glow when he said this.

"Me too," she said immediately. "I mean, lah, I prefer the Charlie version."

Mala's head swiveled round and she shot them an icy glare. They stopped talking, both of them trying to hide their smiles.

"She was speaking to Jalo?"

Tariro stood in the shadows, the circling orbs overhead never casting their light on her. She was looking at the two servants whispering together.

"Yes," said Miyam. "He has gone now."

"What did they speak of?" Tariro demanded.

"I do not know what passed between them. But look at her and the one she is with. It is a glamour. They are not Faeries."

"Of course." Tariro laughed. "Well, they have made it easy for us. The apricots were a diversion — we wasted our time trying to find spells in them and failed to see the humans in my own Castella!"

"Shall I kill them now, my Lady?"

"No," said Tariro. "If we murder them here...we are well within our rights, but Jalo would be furious. No, arrest them and have them deported to the Faery City for judgment and execution."

"Judgment and execution?" asked Miyam. "Like a witch?"

"They have made illegal use of a glamour," said Tariro. "Jalo need never know that we knew their identities. He will have nothing to hold against me. It is perfect, like a gift."

"As you wish, my Lady." Miyam's face was a blank, her eyes like stones.

CHAPTER

13

The Crossing was hard on Ferghal. At first he slept, for it had been a long day of rowing after dismantling the engine and failing to put it back together again. But when the mist cleared and the cliffs of Tian Xia appeared in the distance, he sat bolt upright, bellowing. He screamed and flailed and begged the Ancients for mercy, then cursed their names in language more colourful than Eliza had ever heard, and finally collapsed unconscious. After bearing the insensible Scarpathian to the healing Cave that had saved both Nell's life and Charlie's in the past, Eliza and Foss went to the temples of the Faithful, and from there Eliza summoned Jalo with the ring.

She was at Foss's bedside now, in one of the smaller temples. Foss's face was dull, his eyes dim, and there was a disconcerting rattling sound deep in his chest when he breathed. Every time she looked at him, Eliza felt her heart twist into a knot of terror.

"We shouldnay have done that spell," she said. "You're too weak."

Foss gave a rasping little chuckle. "So you would venture into the Realm of the Faeries without any kind of protection?" he asked.

Eliza felt the spell humming just beneath her skin. Her blood jumped with it. It was a powerful barrier designed to repel a Faery Curse, and it had taken more strength than Foss had to spare right now.

"It would have been a risk," she admitted. "But it's risky anyway."

"Do not fear for me. This is a good place for me to rest."

"Not for long. Rhianu told me the Mancers looked here

147

before we arrived, but I spec they'll be back. I just hope Jalo gets here before they do."

The priestess Rhianu, Eliza's particular friend among the Faithful, appeared in the doorway.

"Sorceress," she said. "There is someone who wishes to see you."

"Jalo," said Eliza, rising.

Rhianu shook her head. "Come."

Eliza followed her out of the small temple. The Faithful were busy in the fields, cultivating crops and hanging out rows of laundered black robes to dry. Rhianu led her beneath the central Temple of the Nameless Birth and along the narrow flagstone corridor that led to the Chamber of the Oracle. Eliza's heart began to beat faster. Nia had killed the last Oracle. She had never thought to ask if there was another.

Rhianu knelt, whispering, until one flagstone fell away. Eliza climbed down the ladder into the dark room. The flagstone sealed her in and then the room blazed with light.

"And now, here we are!" said Selva. She still wore her black robes, but her fair skin and her white hair glowed with an unearthly light.

"You're safe!" cried Eliza. "How did you get out of the Citadel?"

"The Mancers would not offend the Ancients at a time like this," smiled Selva. "I am tired, my dear, I need rest, so we will speak briefly. You are going to the Realm of the Faeries soon."

"Yes," said Eliza. "The Mancers cannay follow me there. I'm hoping I can persuade Nell's friend Jalo to hide the Gehemmis for me, though I dinnay spec it would be safe to tell him what it is. When it's stowed away I can bargain with Kyreth. Can he call off the Thanatosi if he chooses to?"

"No," said Selva. "That is impossible. The Thanatosi will not rest until their prey is vanquished. There is no way to call them off."

Her half-formed plans and desperate hopes collapsing, Eliza pressed her knuckles against her forehead and took a deep breath, trying not to panic.

"The last Oracle told me that victory would only come at a cost for me," she said. "That I would cut out my own heart.

That mine is the Lonely Road. What does it mean? What do I have to do?"

Her grandmother's hand cupped her cheek. It was a cool, calming touch.

"There is loss and gain with every act," said Selva. "Each moment, you will choose what you feel you must do, and every choice will cost you, and every choice will take you further down the road that is yours. Your heart," she touched her fingers gently to Eliza's chest. "Your heart was made for this task."

Eliza choked on a laugh. Selva was not so different from the last Oracle, in that when it came to the really important stuff she was utterly obscure.

"Maybe Kyreth could do something to protect Charlie in exchange for the Gehemmis?" she said, then shook her head. "No good. I cannay count on him for that. But he might take Foss back if I return it. Praps that's all it's good for. And Charlie will have to stay with the Faeries unless I can find some way to defeat the Thanatosi." Her heart felt like a wave washing against a relentless cliff. What good was any of it? What could she do for those she loved so dearly?

"You must not return the Gehemmis to the Mancers," said Selva severely. "Go to the Realm of the Faeries. Go to the Dragon Isles in the Far Sea. Go to the Hanging Gardens of the Sparkling Deluder. Assemble the four Gehemmis. They have more power than you can imagine, my dear."

"The power to stop the Thanatosi?" asked Eliza.

"Oh, far more than that," said Selva with a smile.

"What kind of power?"

"You must learn how to use them," said Selva. "It is a great and noble quest for you to undertake, as befits a Sorceress!"

Eliza sighed, but hope glimmered again among the looming shadows within her. "Stealing from the Immortal Powers sounds more like an impossible quest, aye, nothing great and noble about it," she said. "But all right. How am I going to get the Gehemmis from…lah, from the Faeries, for starters?"

Selva smiled again, as if fond memories were returning to her.

"You must be wicked," she said.

"As far as instructions go, that's nay very specific," said Eliza dryly.

"Then let me tell you," said Selva, "the secrets of the Faery Vault."

Jalo arrived at night. Eliza was dozing in a chair by Foss's bed. One of the Faithful brought the Faery to their room.

"Thank you for coming," she said, barely awake, stumbling to her feet.

"Never mind that," he replied crisply. "Your friends are in danger. I've hidden them for now but you're going to have to get them out."

"What do you mean?"

"Assassins. Humans are not terribly popular in the Realm of the Faeries these days."

This was a setback Eliza had not imagined. Something about the way Jalo said it told her she was not hearing the whole story. But it didn't matter – she would lie to him too, in a moment. She stood up straighter. She knew how she looked: dirty and tired and terribly young. But she was the Shang Sorceress and Jalo needed to remember that.

"I'll take them with me when I go," she said. "But I have another request. I need to speak with your King."

Jalo looked like he could barely refrain from rolling his eyes.

"That will not be possible," he said.

"Your King will be glad to see what I have to show him," she said. "Have you heard of the Gehemmis?"

Jalo shrugged. "A legend of some kind," he said. "Gifts of the Ancients."

"No legend," said Eliza. She hesitated and then took the strip of bone out of her backpack to show him. She could sense Foss tensing on the bed, no longer asleep.

Jalo took it in his hands and looked over it wonderingly. But when Eliza held her hand out he gave it back to her.

"I can request an audience," he said grudgingly. "I cannot promise it will be granted."

"Good enough," agreed Eliza. "But I cannay go into the Realm of the Faeries without some kind of protection or they will simply take the Gehemmis from me."

Jalo sighed. "What, then?"

"I need to make a brief stop," said Eliza.

Jalo nodded, then jerked his chin at Foss on the bed. "He may not come."

"Give me a moment to say goodbye."

When Jalo had left, she sat on the edge of Foss's bed and took his large golden hand in her small brown ones.

"The Faithful are watching the Cave, aye," she told him. "When Ferghal is better, where will you go?"

"South," said Foss.

"Are you sure the Cave willnay help *you*? It might be worth a try."

"The Cave cannot return me to the Mancer fold," Foss said serenely.

Eliza swallowed her tears and nodded.

"We will go to the Isle of the Blind Enchanter in the inland sea," said Foss.

"I've read about him," said Eliza. "The inland sea is where the Mancer dragons come from."

Foss nodded. "The Blind Enchanter has long held cordial relations with the Mancers, but he is known to welcome all travellers. He may be able to help me keep up my strength for a time. I hope he will be able to help you, too, for he is the only living being to have met the Sparkling Deluder."

Eliza nodded, barely taking this in. She couldn't think of the whole impossible task ahead of her. One thing at a time: the Realm of the Faeries.

"He was known long ago by other names, such as the Wandering Enchanter, the Great Bard, and the Wayfaring Rhapsodist," said Foss, getting the look he often got when embarking on a long tale. "He travelled both worlds, it was said, and made songs of all the things he saw. Before Nia emptied the books, the Mancer Library held all the known transcriptions of his songs. Indeed, much of our collected knowledge of the worlds has been gleaned from them, for he sang about topography, the creatures he encountered, the shape of flowers and their properties, relating not only great tales of adventure but also the tiniest details of life in the worlds."

"I've heard of the Wayfaring Rhapsodist," said Eliza. "I didnay realize it was the same person. He must be very old. Is he immortal?"

Foss frowned. "Of course not. The only true Immortals are the Four Great Powers. But some others, like your friend Charlie before this latest accident, are gifted with great longevity. In his six hundredth year, the Wayfaring Rhapsodist went south and crossed the Dreaming Wasteland to see the Hanging Gardens of the Sparkling Deluder. Many have made the journey and only a few have returned. All but the Blind Enchanter came back raving mad, bearing little semblance to their former selves, sometimes having aged far more years than they were gone, others having been gone a century without aging a day. He was not mad but he was changed. He had walked the world making songs of all he saw, but when he returned from that place, he could no longer sing or see. He was blind, his voice blighted, his wanderlust gone. Now he goes nowhere, sees nothing, and though he welcomes travellers and their tales, he does not tell his own. What happened to him is a great mystery. It will not be easy to get him to tell you anything about the Sparkling Deluder."

"But you'll be safe there?" asked Eliza.

Foss smiled. "The Mancers will be pursuing you, not me," he said. "And south is the safest direction from here. We will go through the yellow mountains."

"The Cra live in the yellow mountains."

"We are both far too old to be palatable to the Cra. They will leave us alone."

Eliza felt a wave of sorrow. She wondered if she would ever

see him again. As soon as she had thought it, she buried the thought. It was too awful to contemplate.

"I have to go," she said. "Be safe, Foss."

He held her hand tightly and smiled up at her. "May the Ancients guide your steps," he said.

She nodded and left him there.

Charlie and Nell were silent for a time, watching the ball, until Charlie could not hold his tongue any longer. Very quietly, he whispered: "I'm sorry, Nell."

She had begun to sway to the music and caught herself when he spoke.

"What for?" she asked.

"Getting you into this. If it were nay for me, you'd be safely studying for your test in Di Shang."

"Lah, that's what friends are for," she said, putting her hand in her pocket to stroke her tiny folder. "And we're still friends, nay?"

"Of course we are. I wish things hadnay been so strange between us this year. I didnay want that. I just felt…"

"Let's not talk about it," she said swiftly.

Charlie gave her an unhappy look.

"Look," she hissed, a little impatient, "I know *why* you were avoiding me."

"You do?"

"Of course. It was so obvious."

"Lah, that's why…I mean, I thought that if you wanted to see me, you'd let me know. I sort of thought it was up to you, aye. I didnay want to *force* myself on you."

"That's ridiculous. But you were angry, I spec. And rightly so."

"I wasnay *angry*. Why would I be angry?"

Nell looked down, could not make herself meet his non-Charlie eyes. "You blamed me. I blame myself, too."

"For what?" Charlie was utterly confused now.

"Ander's death, of course!" she burst out, her eyes filling up with tears. The tears washed away the changing Faery colours and revealed her violet irises. Charlie was confused by her words and the sudden appearance of her own eyes at the same time.

"That's nay..." he began, but Mala had turned to glare at them again. Then her eyes flitted to something behind them and widened in horror. Reflexively, Charlie and Nell followed her gaze.

It happened in the blink of an eye. Five black-clothed members of the Faery Guard swept down upon them, chaining their wrists in silver. Mala was pulled roughly from the group and chained as well. The music rose and the Faeries at the ball kept spinning by the scene, oblivious. They were bundled out the archway and through another, all three of them chained together within a morrapus before the reality had really sunk in. When it did, Nell began to shake uncontrollably.

CHAPTER

14

$\mathcal{J}$alo stayed on the mountainside, preferring not to enter the tower, and Eliza could hardly blame him. The Hall of the Ancients was a ruin, the statues torn from their grottoes and broken across the floor, stones crumbling from the walls. The place reverberated with horror. And there, broken spear in one hand as if poised to throw it, stood Nia, the Xia Sorceress. The Urkleis jerked in Eliza's chest as if it might break loose. At that moment, she almost wished it would. To be free of it.

Nia was unchanged. Her lovely face was white and tense, her red-gold hair coming loose about her shoulders. Her eyes seemed to look right into Eliza's, and the young Sorceress felt, *knew*, that Nia could see her. Frozen within the loop of her own Magic she could neither move nor speak. But she could see, she could think, she could feel. The white tiger, emaciated, slunk from behind his mistress and surveyed Eliza with coal-black eyes. His red tongue hung from his mouth. He looked as if he would like to pounce on her and eat her but did not have the strength. The ravens swirled and screamed. Eliza felt her heart would break with pity, or perhaps that was only the pull of the Urkleis.

"I need something," she said, her voice shaking badly. She had to be quick or the awful rage and longing filling the hall would undo her, split her open and draw the Urkleis from her. She ran to Nia and reached for the vial of brilliant liquid hanging from her neck by a slender chain: Malferio's blood. This had rendered Nia immune to Illusion and would do the same, Eliza hoped, for her.

"I'm sorry," she whispered, unclasping it. She did not want to touch Nia but she could not help it. Her hands brushed the Sorceress's hair, the cold skin of her neck. The moment Eliza touched her, the Urkleis leaped in her chest and Nia's free hand swung down and closed around her wrist. Involuntarily, Eliza looked up into the eyes of the Sorceress.

They were bright green-gold and they bored into Eliza. Her grip tightened. They stood still like this for a moment, the Urkleis tearing against the flesh that held it. The tiger roared and roared, the world was full of its roaring. Eliza's chest burned, her fear crescendoed, and she felt something within her breaking thread by thread. She was lost in Nia's devouring eyes. Her ravens multiplied above, shrieking, *now now now*. She burst free, something snapping. It felt like her body exploding. It felt like threads of fire running through her. She burst away from Nia, clutching the vial of Faery blood in her beak. She shot out of the half-destroyed tower and down the mountain on black wings. She might have continued flying forever, for she had no sense of direction or purpose, only a mad beating desire to escape, but a net of light fell over her and pulled her out of the air. On hands and knees in the snow, she was Eliza again. She turned on her assailant, dagger flashing, cutting free of the net. Ravens poured out of the sky. She forced her enemy back into the snow, driving her dagger into him, again and again. She was hurled off, landed in a snowdrift screaming, the sky swarming with inky ravens. Jalo stood over her, sword drawn. Blood like liquid light trickled from the wounds in his chest, stomach, and shoulder. His face was white with rage.

"How dare you!" he roared. Eliza was sobbing; she could not stop. There was something in her mouth. She spat it out into her palm: the necklace, the vial of blood. The tiger's roar from the Hall of the Ancients carried down the mountainside, echoing. Jalo looked up at the tower and then back at Eliza. She was covered in snow, weeping and shaking.

"What happened?" he asked her, calmer, but she could not speak, even to apologize. She shook her head, fastening the vial around her neck with trembling fingers. She did not look up at the tower on the peak, where Nia was still desperately trying to pull Eliza back to her. She staggered towards the waiting myrkestra and Jalo helped her onto its back, wincing with his wounds. The only cure for this was distance. She had what she had come for.

They paused to rest by a river the following day. Eliza sat at the bank murmuring until a Tian Xia invisible eel leaped into her hands. She had everything else she needed in a little gourd the Faithful had given her. She cut the eel open with her dagger and let its blood drain into the gourd.

"You will be searched before you are allowed to see the King," said Jalo from behind her. He had been a little less cool since they had left the Hall of the Ancients, though his wounds still pained him. Perhaps he had been reminded that in the past she had saved him, too, from Nia. "They will not allow you to carry a potion."

"I willnay carry it," said Eliza. Later, when Jalo was not watching her, a raven appeared at her side. She fed it as much of the potion as it could drink. It faded from sight but she felt it on her shoulder, sharp talons digging into her coat as the myrkestra flew over the witches' forest and the Sea of Tian Xia.

After the long journey over the Sea and the fiery volcanic land on the other side of it, Jalo's lovely, mournful song brought them into the Realm of the Faeries. In spite of the vial she wore, Eliza found herself unable to say quite how it happened – only that the fire and black stone became a general, diffuse darkness and warmth, and when she found herself no longer on the myrkestra but standing in a grove of trees from whose branches white flames danced and flared in place of leaves, it seemed that she had been standing there for some time. The path under her feet glittered with diamonds and at the end of it stood a golden gate. Beyond the gate lay a brightness that made her eyes water.

When she had used Faery Blood to escape Nia's prison in the Arctic years ago, she had seen the Illusion like a semi-transparent veil over the real world of ice and snow. But the Realm of the Faeries was a land of Illusion. With the enchanted vial of Malferio's blood around her neck, hidden beneath her clothes, she *felt* rather than saw how ephemeral the world was, how insubstantial, always shifting slightly beneath her feet. It made her feel a bit seasick and she longed for the stillness and solidity of the world she knew. Shadows flickered here and there, on the path ahead and among the trees. She fixed her eyes on a large shadow just to her left. It became two gorgeously attired Faeries, looking at her in some surprise between the trees, the faint outline of an elegant room around them. She blinked and they were gone. When she looked up, birds span overhead and then vanished. It was dizzying, this sense of a hundred scenes laid over each other, each one haunting the background of every other fleeting reality.

A troupe of the Faery Guard came to greet them. They came and went many times, as Eliza negotiated her visit. The King wanted to see the Gehemmis before he would grant Eliza an audience. Eliza refused. She would show it to him herself, she said. They were unsettled to find that she wore Nia's vial and demanded she give it to them. She would not and they did not try to take it by force. They wanted her to remove the dragon claw dagger before entering the King's presence. Again she refused and the Faery Guard eyed Jalo, who was obviously injured. She began to despair of being allowed to see the King, and yet she was not willing to be unarmed and unprotected in this place.

"He has agreed," said Jalo wearily, at last.

"Good." She let out a puff of breath.

"I will see to the other matter," he continued, and she nodded. They had agreed on a meeting place on the western shore, and he was to take Nell and Charlie there.

He left her there, walking away between two trees and becoming shadow. She followed the Faery Guard towards the gate and the bright light beyond it, feeling very much alone among beings who did not value her life in the least. The invisible raven on her shoulder shifted slightly from one foot to the other.

The Faery Guard led her into and through the light. She felt a shimmer of pain as she stepped through but shook it off. Jewel-encrusted archways stood in rows on a vast stretch of marble, and within each archway was a light as brilliant as the one they had just stepped through. When she looked harder, though, looked at the faint, flickering shadows, she saw the archways were half ruined, ivy twined about them, young saplings bursting up through the rutted, broken stone floor. The Faeries led her quickly through one of the archways, and now she found herself at the bottom of a stairway soaring up into the sky.

"This is the Thousand Steps," one of the Faeries told her. "If you wish to see the King, you must show your desire by climbing them."

So she climbed. For a while she counted, curious to know if there were really a thousand steps, but she gave up after three hundred with the top no closer to being in sight. She focused on her breath, cycling it in and out of her lungs, keeping her eyes fixed only on the steps ahead, clearing her mind so that all her energy might be used for this climb. When at last she came to the top, she looked around in wonder. She was on a broad, open-air platform. White pillars twisted up and then out, forming an intricate lattice across the sky. Rows of black-garbed Faeries stood in formation around the throne at the centre of the space. The throne was carved obsidian, inlaid with gems, and Eliza saw for the first time why Faeries prized their jewels so. They shone with a luster that made their Illusory surroundings seem thin and frail in comparison. The King himself wore a cloak of real feathers and a band of gold around his head. He had a long, haughty face and white-gold hair that fell to his shoulders. The Faery to his right had a sharp, intelligent gaze that he fixed on Eliza. The one on his left wore an expression altogether too cheerful for his august surroundings. Between the pillars she could see the Realm of the Faeries: brilliant rivers weaving between the mountains and sparkling bridges slung between the Castellas perched on every mountaintop. All of it so fragile that Eliza felt she would only have to blow hard to topple the mountains. She stood before the King, at the centre of a phalanx of over-anxious guards.

"The Shang Sorceress," said King Emyr, looking her over in mild surprise. "I had expected someone more...well...that is to say, you are very young."

Eliza would have liked to appear wearing something other than her travel-worn Sorma garb, but she squared her shoulders and gave a brief bow.

"I'm here to ask for your help," she said. "You know that I severed my ties with the Mancers some time ago."

The King nodded. "We know. But you returned to them recently. Why did you go back? And why did you leave again?"

"The Mancers have threatened someone I love," she said, her voice shaking slightly. "I have stolen their most valuable treasure and I intend to keep it from them. There is nowhere safer from them than here."

The King gave her a sly look. "Let's see it, then," he said.

Eliza removed the Gehemmis from her backpack and stepped forward. Here was the moment, her terrible gamble. Selva had been clear that the Gehemmis were worthless alone; only together did they have power. If she could not get the second Gehemmis from the Faeries, this one was no use to her. One of the Faery Guards took it from her and bore it to the King. He looked at it carefully.

"What is this inscription?" he asked. "They look like runes... or something Mancerish."

"The symbols predate Mancer writing," said Eliza. "I dinnay know what it says or even what its use is. Only that it is one of the Four Gifts of the Ancients and that a Sorceress stole it from the Horogarth long ago."

"I never believed that story," scoffed the King. "How could a Sorceress take something from the Horogarth?"

"I dinnay know," said Eliza.

The King looked at her carefully. "And what is it you want exactly? You want us to *keep* it for you? Does that mean you want it back?"

"I'm nay stupid," said Eliza. "If you believe me that this is the Gehemmis, I know I willnay get it back. It's an offering, aye. I want help."

"Help of what kind?"

"My friends are being pursued by the Thanatosi. I'd like to borrow a couple of Faeries...for a short time...to guard them until I can eliminate the threat."

"And your friends are where?"

"With the Faithful."

The King seemed predictably uninterested in this portion of the conversation.

"Well, we will see if this funny trinket is what you say it is. Call the Master of the Vaults!" He clapped his hands.

While they waited, a troupe of very beautiful, brightly dressed Faeries passed through the guards in formation. Five of them stood in a row and began to sing, while the others performed a dance. The King and the Faery on his left watched contentedly, while the Faery to the right, the one with the piercing gaze, kept watching Eliza.

At last the Master of the Vaults arrived and the performers disappeared. He was smallish for a Faery, with very white skin and wheeling, deep blue eyes. He was dressed in a dark red robe, his fingers heavy with glittering rings.

"What do you make of this?" the King handed him the Gehemmis very casually. "She claims to have stolen it from the Mancers."

Eliza knew, from the way that he took the Gehemmis in his hands, that the Master of the Vaults, at least, recognized its value.

"Indeed." The Master of the Vaults looked up at his King. "I should like to examine it. Verify its authenticity."

"Of course. In the meantime, we will make our guest comfortable. Perhaps we can make our arrangements tomorrow?"

"That's fine," said Eliza, her heart sinking slightly. She didn't know how long the spell of invisibility would last on her raven, but surely not much longer.

"Then I take my leave," said the Master of the Vaults, bowing. As he returned to his waiting morrapus, the raven took off from Eliza's shoulder and followed him on silent wings.

Eliza was taken by morrapus to a shady pavilion on an island not twenty feet around. Whichever way she looked, she met an endless stretch of silver water. This seemed a bit silly to her, since they knew she was wearing Nia's vial and could walk across the water if she wanted to. The air and the water flickered with shadows; guards no doubt, but she didn't bother to try to make them out clearly.

There was a long divan in the pavilion. She lay herself down there, closed her eyes, steadied her breathing. She concentrated on her raven.

The Master of the Vaults was walking through deep underground passageways. A large gemstone at his chest lit the way. At various points along the tubular corridors that branched first this way, then that, the Master of the Vaults would pause and turn a ring on his finger a number of times before continuing. The raven followed closely. At first Eliza tried to keep track of the twists and turns of the passageway and the turning of the rings, but eventually she had to give up. This was too elaborate a route to find her way through alone. Eliza could feel the forces that gave way with each twist of the ring and then closed up behind him again. These were not barriers but something else, some Magic she did not know. Selva had been right that the Master of the Vaults himself was the only way in or out. Eliza's grandmother had not made it far into the Treasure Vaults, but she knew there was some great enchantment, something beyond the Magic of Faeries, deep inside.

Eliza's raven was entirely lost in the maze when at last they reached the end of it. The corridor opened up into a spherical room. A long, slender box of Faery Gold, inlaid with diamonds, hung in the air at the center of the room. A woman huddled on the floor, clutching her ragged knees to her chest. She rocked back and forth, muttering. Flaxen hair hung limp around a pale, drawn moon face. Eliza had never been particularly good at sensing power, either in objects or in other beings, but she could feel enough to know this being was a witch.

The witch looked up slowly, first at the Master of the Vaults and then at the raven. Eliza's heart gave a sickening jolt. But no, the raven was still invisible. Yet the witch looked right at it. The corner of her mouth gave a single twitch but her dead eyes gave away nothing. She turned her gaze back to the Master of the Vaults. He was twisting rings furiously now, barely looking at the witch. Then he sighed, as if he were quite worn out, and took the Gehemmis from his crimson robes. The witch locked her eyes on it, still expressionless. The Master of the Vaults spoke a brusque command. She flinched as if in pain. She raised her chin and began a lengthy incantation in a high, quavering wail. Sweat poured from her brow and her claw-like fingers trembled. The golden box descended and opened. The Master of the Vaults placed the Gehemmis in the box. He waited as the witch continued to wail and keen and the box returned to its mid-air position, firmly closed. He gave the witch a curt nod and she fell silent, looking at him with bleak hatred. Then he turned away, plunging them in darkness, the gem at his chest lighting the corridor back. He twisted his rings as he went, disappearing around the first turn.

Eliza breathed deeply and then entered the witch's mind. It was not only easy – it was nearly impossible not to. The witch drew her in with a terrifying, sucking hunger. Her mind was a cavern of flickering flame, strange fanged creatures, a clamour of angry voices. Lights flashed and heavy wings pounded the airless space, every thought steeped in poison.

How often does he come? Eliza asked the witch.

How do I know? What does time mean? He comes often, often, often, perhaps every day, perhaps more than once a day.

Do you know how to work the rings?

A great shrieking and sobbing rose up in the cavern of the witch's mind. It was such a terrible sound that instinctively Eliza tried to pull herself out and found the witch was holding her fast inside. Her heart clenched with fear.

No no no, you won't go running off now, pretty, no no no.

I can't help you unless you let me go.

Eliza felt herself spat out suddenly and opened her eyes. The shadowy forms around the pavilion were flickering nearer. Had she cried out and drawn attention to herself? She rolled over on her side, her heart hammering in her chest. If they suspected her of working Magic, everything would become a great deal more difficult. She shut her eyes again, seeing through the raven in the vaults. She did not want to enter the witch's mind again. She tried to speak through the raven and found to her relief that her own voice emerged from the invisible bird.

"Who are you?" she asked.

The witch made a raw, choking sound that might have been a laugh and said, "Ho! A voice now! The ghost-bird speaks like a girl! You come here and yet you do not know me? Who are *you*, I might ask?"

"My name is Eliza," she said. It might not be wise to tell the truth, but she decided to chance it in the hopes of earning the witch's trust. "I'm the Shang Sorceress."

"Oh yes," said the witch. "There is a Sorceress in Di Shang. I remember."

"How did you come to be here?" asked Eliza.

The witch writhed, tangling her sharp fingers in her hair. "He binds me fast, he does. How I would blast him, wither him, if I could! But I can only obey. Eternity is brutal, Sorceress-bird. I think that you are young, but I will tell you, forever is too long to suffer."

"You're under a Curse," said Eliza, understanding now. "They use your Magic to keep the Gehemmis safe."

"Ho!" cried the witch again. "A clever Sorceress-bird, you are, to find your way here and to know so much! And yet you do not know who I *am*."

"Who are you?"

The witch fairly cackled, and then began to cough. When she could speak again, her voice was a painful rasp. "My name was Amarantha, once. Help me, Sorceress-bird, and I will forever be indebted to you. Help me to be Amarantha again! Then I will blast and wither him, then I will teach *him* what forever means." Her voice rose to a scream at the end.

"Shh," hissed Eliza. The name Amarantha was familiar, but she could not remember where she had heard it before.

"Nobody can hear me," said the witch, and laughter looped from her, mad and high-pitched. "Sometimes I scream for hours and nobody hears, nobody hears, and it echoes through the vaults, and I talk and nobody hears, nobody hears."

"Lah, fine, but be quiet now. I need quiet. Can you work any Magic to help me?"

"None, none! Would I be here if I could work any Magic but that which I am commanded to work? Obedience is my Curse. Forever forever forever!"

"All right. Just…stay still and stay quiet. I'll do my best."

Eliza wished that Foss were here to help her. Amarantha had worked the enchantment keeping the Gehemmis here and so the Curse on Amarantha had to be broken. She didn't know if she was strong enough to work this kind of Magic alone.

The raven stepped onto the witch's shoulder and Eliza began a spell of Deep Seeing. She felt herself poured like a liquid into the body of the witch. Then it was a matter of choosing the right time. How many years back? She tried to hold the years steady as she flashed back through the centuries in the vault. She realized slowly as century after century flew by her that this witch must be Immortal, for no witch could live this long. The Faeries had Cursed her to serve them and then given her Immortality, to keep her here always. Eliza's hold on the spell grew weaker as the years slid by and she began to be afraid she would get lost in the witch's past, never find her way back out. She leaped through time, clinging to the spell, which seemed eager to shake her off. Then she came to the moment she was seeking, and she forced the wheeling Magic to a halt.

The young witch was in an Illusory wood. She wore hide trousers and jacket, but her feet were bare. Flaxen braids hung down her back. Her breath came swift and frightened, her fingers twitched as she whispered spells to protect herself.

The Master of the Vaults appeared suddenly, as if out of nowhere, and uttered a single phrase.

The Curse fell on her like a stone. The forest disappeared. Eliza was impressed by the power and simplicity of the Curse. It was a deep Curse, but it was old too, and the witch had been straining against it a long time.

She tumbled out of the spell, a little sick with the effort of it. When she could speak again, the raven said: "It willnay be easy but I might be able to break it. We need to be ready for him when he comes back."

Amarantha let out a long slow hiss of breath.

"Relax now, and try not to fight me," said the raven. "This may hurt."

Amarantha laughed. "Pain doesn't frighten me."

"Good."

The room filled with ravens.

CHAPTER

15

"Jalo! Thank the Ancients you've returned!" Tariro ran to greet her younger son in the garden. "Have you heard? They found spies in the Castella!"

She tried to embrace him, but before her lips touched his cheek he pulled away from her. The garden shivered and grew cold, a chill wind rushing through it.

"Mother, let us not play games with one another any longer," he said.

"Games?" Her voice was too shrill. She lowered it. By the Ancients, what a look he was giving her! "What do you mean?"

Jalo's lips tightened and his nostrils flared. She could see he knew everything. She dropped the act, for she hated wasted effort. It alarmed her to find that there were some in her own Castella who were loyal to her son. She had always thought him clever, cleverer by far than Cadeyrn, but she had never imagined he might have thought to curry favour or make allies for himself among the servants. Could he have spies in her own house?

"You are more like me than I like," she said with a brittle laugh. "Who told you?"

He took her by the arm and pulled her through the garden to the archway, which stood all twined with roses. Before she could speak to protest he dragged her through it, out into the opaline mass of archways.

"You will put this right." His voice shook.

"No more games, you say," she answered him, shaking free of his grip and stepping back to face him. "Very well. You placed spies in my home. They have been executed."

"They were not spies," he said. "And they are not dead. Do not mistake me for a fool, mother. It is not yet illegal to bring a visitor from the outside world into our Realm."

"It is illegal to do so in secrecy, to disguise them as Faeries, to make use of a witch."

"Nobody consorts with witches more than you do."

"None could prove it even if they wished to. But you have been too rash and careless. You would end in the Faery Dungeons if I were to reveal all you have done these last few days."

"Do you think you can frighten me?" Jalo laughed, an angry, hurt bark. "You care far more than I do what becomes of me, mother. And that is why you will agree to free the humans and Emin's wife."

"I no longer have the power to do so, even if I wished it!" cried Tariro. "It is out of my hands! They are prisoners of the Realm, sentenced to death. I *cannot* stop it, Jalo."

Jalo grabbed her hard by the shoulders. "Show me your secret place," he whispered.

"Jalo!" she tried to throw him off and found to her horror that she could not. He was stronger than her and he was hurting her. He dragged her from one archway to another, each time giving her a violent shake. She gasped, and in a shadowy corner a crumbling stone archway emerged. Through it, only darkness, but he saw her face and pulled her through.

"There's nothing here," she whispered.

Slippery rock under their feet. Blasted trees gaping. He shook her, he squeezed her shoulders so she cried out, and then they were on the windswept heath, among the tall stones. The pool was clear as glass, reflecting the emptiness of the sky. The cloaked figure waiting there bowed in greeting.

Jalo let go of her and stepped away, breathing hard. "You can do whatever you *want* to do, mother. That has always been so. You will make it happen, for me. Release them."

"Do not think that because you are my son I will not make you my enemy if you push me too far," she said through clenched teeth. "And you know, Jalo, you *know* what becomes of *my* enemies."

"Yes, I know." His eyes were pure fire. "This is our agreement, mother. Emin's wife will be sent back to him, all charges against her dropped. You will turn the humans over to me. *I* will take them out of this Realm, with a spy of your choice to ensure that I do so. You will never see them again, and neither will I. If you do this for me then I will join the Elite Faery Guard, I will strive for promotion, and I will woo Emyr's daughter as you wish me to. I will present her with gifts and poetry, I will charm her and I will marry her. I will be ambitious. I will bring you glory and honour. My career, my marriage, all these will be in your hands, and I will swear it by the Oath of the Ancients if necessary. But if the girl dies, then by the Ancients, mother, I will bring such disgrace on this family as you cannot even contemplate. I love her beyond desire for myself. Though I doubt you can imagine such a love, believe that it is real. I feel it. It consumes me. And so in exchange for her life, my life is yours. Now tell me yea or nay, and do not let me hear one word from you but one of those."

Tariro looked into her son's flaming eyes in amazement.

"Jalo," she began, but he roared: "Yea or nay!"

"I will have them freed," whispered Tariro. "But you must take the humans away *immediately* Jalo, and my servant Miyam will not leave you alone for a moment. There will be no sudden, secret marriage."

Jalo laughed shortly. He thought of Emyr's daughter, her chilly eyes and piles of shining hair, her tiny fragile hands that seemed to feel nothing. He thought of Nell's violet eyes, her lovely face that showed everything she felt as she felt it, her bright burst of laughter that so startled him every time. And she would let herself age and wither in a few short years. He could choke on his grief and disappointment. She would die, and he would remain here, forever.

"We are agreed then," he said to his mother. She nodded.

"We are agreed. But I will have to work fast." She sighed. "You have made things very difficult, Jalo."

"Once the girl is safe, I will make things ever easier," he promised.

She embraced him, and this time he accepted it, stony-hearted.

Early the following morning, the King of the Faeries met with his first Advisor, Alvar, and the Master of the Vaults. Nikias was there too, but everybody knew that Nikias had gained the position of second Advisor solely through the maneuverings of his wife, Tariro. They sat around a table on a veranda, looking down on the island where the Shang Sorceress remained.

"They say she has been breathing strangely all night, and cried out once or twice," said Alvar.

"Perhaps that is how people sleep," said Emyr. "She has not been making symbols or speaking. And besides, I am told that the power of the Sorceress lies in some mystical staff. She has that dagger, but she brought no staff with her."

"I suspect she is perfectly capable of working Magic without a staff," said the Master of the Vaults. "We should not underestimate her. She looks young, but she defeated the Xia Sorceress, remember."

"Yes," said Emyr, rubbing his chin. "Do we know how?"

"My son Jalo described the spell to me once," said Nikias eagerly. "Something about turning the Sorceress's magic in on itself. She made use of a creature the Xia Sorceress had Made."

"Clever," said Alvar. "I do not like a clever Sorceress. I think we should not have let her in. She is up to something. Why would she bring us the Gehemmis?"

"No, look, you are worrying too much, Alvar," said Emyr soothingly. "There is no question that her alliance with the Mancers is severed. They are searching all of Tian Xia for her. This thing with the Gehemmis is about vengeance."

"And she wants our help. She says."

"Yes, well, that…perhaps. What shall we do? Is there any danger in sending her back to Tian Xia with a Faery escort, as she asks?"

Alvar shook his head. "When a Sorceress comes to the Realm, it is safe to assume there is more to it than the reason she states. Why would she turn to the Faeries for help?"

"She has come where the Mancers cannot follow her," said Emyr, feeling a little defensive of his decision to put her up for the night. "Still, I do not like that Jalo brought her. That was reckless. He should choose his friends more carefully." The King directed this reproof at Nikias, who hung his head.

"Suppose she is still in league with the Mancers?" demanded Alvar. "Their falling out could be an act."

"The Mancers would not risk the Gehemmis," said the Master of the Vaults with certainty. "Your Majesty, may I suggest, the safest course of action no doubt is to kill her. She has no allies that can retaliate. The real question is what to do about the Gehemmis."

"What to do about it?" asked Emyr, confused.

"Let us come to that later," broke in Alvar. "We must reach a decision about the Sorceress first. I agree with the Master of the Vaults. She is young, but somehow she defeated the Xia Sorceress and stole the Gehemmis from the Mancers. She is more powerful than she looks and she is dangerous. She has come here armed against Illusion and quite possibly against Curses, but she is still human and dies as a human does. We should execute her immediately. Do we have your consent, your Majesty?"

"Oh my!" said Nikias, his only contribution to the discussion.

"Of course," agreed Emyr. "You're quite right. It's the only sensible thing to do."

"Good. Then, the Gehemmis," said the Master of the Vaults.

"I suppose the question is, do we return it to the Horogarth, or keep it?" asked Emyr.

"Your Majesty, may I make a suggestion?" The Master of the Vaults leaned forwards. "If there was a way we could obtain the others, it would be worth any risk. Their power depends on them being together, but there is no doubt that *together* the Gehemmis can generate a Magic greater than the worlds have seen since the Early Days. Enough to return the Faeries to their former dominion of Tian Xia."

Emyr's eyes widened, and he let out a long breath.

"Nonsense," said Alvar sharply. "How would we obtain the others? Go to war with the Immortal Dragons? And what of the Sparkling Deluder?"

"Your Majesty," said the Master of the Vaults, directing his words only to Emyr. "Surely a stealth troop of Faeries could steal an object from the Immortal Dragons. Their power has been waning for millennia. It is said they can no longer cross the Far Sea and I believe it must be true, for they are never seen in Tian Xia. If the Gehemmis was stolen, they could make no pursuit. And as for the Sparkling Deluder of the South...perhaps the Deluder might be offered some exchange?"

"Would the Faeries who went to the Hanging Gardens return?" asked Alvar dryly.

"It is a risk worth taking. These are the very gifts of the Ancients. That the Mancers sought to steal them from the Immortals suggests that they know how to put them to use. We might force them to share this knowledge with us, if we obtained all four."

"Do the Mancers know something we do not?" cried Emyr, indignant.

"With respect," said the Master of the Vaults, "the Mancers know a great many things we do not. The Faeries relied on them too heavily as scribes. When they broke rank and fled our Realm in the Early Days, we did not adequately fill the role they left." The others were looking at him with thinly disguised outrage now, but the Master of the Vaults was undeterred. "It is heresy to say so, perhaps. I believe the Faeries to be the superiors of the Mancers in almost every way but I must concede that in learning, in *knowledge*, they have surpassed us. The Gehemmis would change everything and we are halfway there already."

"It cannot hurt to try," said Emyr.

"Your Majesty," protested Alvar, "We may find ourselves doing battle with the Dragons for eternity, and what peace would Tian Xia have with the Immortals of the East and West fighting one another? And as for the Sparkling Deluder of the South, we would be fools to go into that land seeking anything at all."

"If a mere Sorceress could alone obtain the Gehemmis of the Horogarth," murmured the Master of the Vaults, "why cannot the Faeries obtain all four and secure their dominion?"

Emyr was decided.

"Choose two full Divisions of the Faery Guard," he said to Alvar. "Come to me with a strategy by the end of the week."

Alvar rose and bowed stiffly.

"And give the command for the execution of the Sorceress," added the King.

Nell sat with her back fitted against the curve of the wall. The cell she was in was so small that she could not stretch out her arms or legs completely without bumping up against the other side of it. She called it a cell to herself, but it was unlike any cell she might have imagined. It was perfectly spherical and smooth and dark. No matter how she moved, the entire wall of the sphere had equal gravity. There was no up or down except in relation to where she was, but she could not pull herself away from the wall and so she had to slide along it. This was strange enough to keep her occupied for the first hour or so, but now she was trying to reason out how long she had been here. She did not remember getting out of the morrapus. That part was a blur. She had not woken up, exactly, but rather come to the awareness that she was enclosed and did not know what had happened. Nobody had brought her any food or water. She was terribly thirsty, her mouth dry and sticky and her head pounding, but she was not hallucinating or mad or dead so it could only have been a day or so at the most since she had been left here. In that case, if she was counting correctly, her exam at Austermon was in two weeks. For the hundredth time she touched the tiny folder in her pocket.

She would not have her chance at Austermon. She would not meet Graeme Biggis, she would not become a cetologist, she would not see the underwater world of the whales. Her parents and brothers would never know what had happened to her. Nobody would know that she had died in a little black hole in the Realm of the Faeries, and for what reason? Some mad, jealous mother. She wasn't sure if this was the execution, being left to die of thirst in a hole, or if she was just waiting for some other form of execution. When she thought of dying, of never seeing her family again, or Eliza, or Charlie, of never seeing *anything* again or taking a breath of air in the real world or eating or laughing or stretching her legs or having another thought or feeling, her heart seemed to unspool inside her and she wept, no matter how she tried to pull herself together. With death looming so close, she thought what a fool she had been to turn down Jalo's offer. She didn't love him, didn't want to live in the Realm of the Faeries, but he was right: a human life was too short, so short as to be insignificant, and being a cetologist seemed remote and bizarre from where she was now. What kind of madness would drive her to refuse the chance to live forever, to break the bounds of human mortality and experience the worlds for the rest of time? She wondered if Jalo had had something to do with their imprisonment, and in case he could hear her she screamed once: "I changed my mind, Jalo! I'll do whatever you want!" She was instantly humiliated by her own fearful capitulation. She rolled herself into a ball and sobbed and sobbed, though it hurt to cry when she was so hungry and so thirsty and so afraid.

When she had no more strength to cry or even to really be afraid, when she felt like a dry, thoughtless husk fastened to the darkness of the wall, the sphere split open and light poured in, making her eyes water. Somebody luminous was leaning over her, pulling her out. Her heart began to jackrabbit and she made a feeble attempt at struggling.

"Stop it," said Jalo's voice. "I'm getting you out of here."

She tried to look into his bright face but her eyes were still dazzled after so much time in the dark and she could not read his expression, could not tell if it was the truth. She was being led into a morrapus.

"Nell?" It was Charlie's voice, hoarse but recognizable. She felt his hands on her face and she began to cry again, well beyond the point when she thought she could cry at all. She reached for him, fell into his embrace and held him tight as the morrapus took to the air.

The Master of the Vaults was later than usual due to the morning meeting. He hurried down into the vaults, eager to hold the Gehemmis in his hands again. Daily he made this check, to be sure that every treasure was safe and in its place. He twisted his rings as he went.

Eliza sat up, panting for breath. Every bone in her body ached with fatigue, but she had done it. She had drawn the Curse from Amarantha and she held it now in her own power. The pavilion was transparent. The water and the island roiled with shadows. She knew her time as a guest was almost up. Well, she would see if the barrier against Curses Foss had made was all she hoped. Ravens burst out of the pavilion in a great black cloud and in the same instant the pavilion went up in flames.

The Master of the Vaults reached the vault at the end, twisting his rings. He looked up and froze. Amarantha the witch was hunched in her usual postion, but the box was not in the air. For a moment, the shock of it froze him. He looked down at her. It was in her hands, and a large black raven was perched on her shoulder. She smiled.

The world went up in flames but the fire was shadow, air, nothing. She took a deep breath and called upon the barrier. She felt it burst from her veins and spill around her as the Curses rained down, Curses of transformation, confusion, enslavement and death. Her barrier buckled against the onslaught and she felt the Urkleis hammering against her ribcage like a second heart. Nia's voice in her ear: *Watch your back, Smidgen.* She spun around, dagger in hand, to ward off the blow of a sword. The Faery was far quicker than she. It would be deadly to try and engage. And so she ran, through shadows that barely took shape. The air filled with arrows. With the feeling of tearing limb from limb, of breaking apart, she burst into ravens.

I imagine you'll get used to it, came Nia's voice.

Several of the ravens fell with the arrows of the faeries, and Eliza flew among them, one black bird in a frenzied mass.

You see — it's always good for you when I try to kill you. Motivating. And yet you never say thank you.

Faery nets pulled ravens out of the air and the ravens vanished. Eliza rode the air higher, the pain and panic subsiding, exhilaration filling her. *Thank you,* she thought, laughing inside. She soared.

In the Old Language of the Faeries, the raven spoke the same words she had found through the spell of Deep Seeing: "I bind your will, from now and forever." The Curse that had bound Amarantha, heavy and dark and alive, slipped from her with these words, and took the Master of the Vaults. His eyes widened and he fell to his knees. Amarantha rose over him, her eyes full of murder.

"Wait, we need him!" cried the raven. To the Master of the Vaults, she said: "Get us out of here."

His face contorted with fury. He turned and led Amarantha and the raven through the maze of corridors, twisting his rings.

Eliza, in raven form, searched the roiling shadows, focusing first on this one, then on another. Gardens and salons, servants chattering listlessly, the Faery Guard running through the air, and there, there: a morrapus with another part of her inside. She flew straight for the myrkestra pulling it, landing on its back, and became once more Eliza. The raven with Amarantha disappeared. Eliza let out a breath. The relief of being whole again, herself again, undivided, was tremendous. She began to believe that this would work, that she would pull it off. She squeezed her eyes shut, heart thundering so fast in her chest that it hurt, while the Master of the Vaults took them out of the Realm of the Faeries and into the volcanic land bordering the Sea of Tian Xia.

ASH

CHAPTER

16

Nell and Charlie sat at the treeline, overlooking the choppy grey sea of Tian Xia. Having had some food and water, they were much restored. Both of them were full of things to say but they were made too nervous to talk by Miyam, who stood nearby, her spinning eyes never leaving them. Jalo paced along the shore, watching the horizon.

Nell was still getting used to the idea that she was not about to be killed, though Miyam's presence thwarted her optimism somewhat. The glamour was fading, too. Every time she looked at Charlie he looked more like himself. She had spoken to Jalo only twice, to ask what had become of Mala, and to ask him to return her folder to its usual size. Reassured that Mala was on her way home to Emin, she clung to the folder, felt her heart beating against it. She couldn't bring herself to open it yet. The test was in two weeks and she might take it after all. Her life had been handed back to her, but still it seemed too incredible to be true.

A bright blob on the horizon, moving quickly, became a morrapus. By the time it reached the shore, the sky was full of swift white-gray shapes in pursuit. Charlie and Nell scrambled to their feet. The myrkestra landed not far from where they stood and Eliza leaped from its back. From the morrapus staggered a Faery in crimson robes and a tall, fair-haired woman in rags. Not one of them looked happy.

"Eliza!" Nell ran to embrace her friend. "What happened? You look...you look..." she stepped back, unsure what to say. Eliza looked ill. She was grey-faced and there were deep hollows under her eyes.

"Rough night," said Eliza. She hugged Charlie too, and as she did so she found herself remembering the black panther's open jaws, its bottomless eyes. She drew back quickly.

"The Thanatosi?" asked Charlie hopefully.

Eliza shook her head.

Jalo and Miyam had closed ranks. Amarantha hung onto the Master of the Vaults' shoulder with a bony hand.

"Sorceress," said Jalo, his voice deadly calm. "Explain the situation."

"She was a prisoner," said Eliza, looking anxiously at Amarantha. "You can have the Master of the Vaults back..."

"No," hissed Amarantha. Her eyes grew large and black.

"Do you know who that is?" Miyam asked.

"Her name..." began Eliza. What had she read of Amarantha?

"Centuries before Nia was born, it was Amarantha who wreaked havoc wherever she went and was feared by all of Tian Xia," said Miyam. The witch smiled. "The Oracle of that time called upon the Faeries to stop her. It is written that she was killed. This was clearly not so, but you have freed her from a richly-deserved bondage."

"I had no choice," said Eliza, her heart pounding in her ears like an echo of the sea.

"For a thousand years and more he has ruled me," said Amarantha. "Now he will know for another thousand years what it is to be a slave."

The myrkestras were crossing the sea at great speed.

"We have to go," said Eliza. "There's no time. The Faeries are coming."

"Why are they pursuing you?" demanded Miyam. She looked at Jalo. "What has she done?"

"No time," said Eliza again. She looked around desperately at all of them. "The Faeries should stay here. The rest of us need to go. Now."

"Not without him," said Amarantha hungrily. The Master of the Vaults trembled.

Miyam and Jalo took a pace forward.

"Can you face two Faeries now, in a weakened state?" asked Jalo.

"I am not weak," snarled Amarantha. Eliza felt the shadows of illusion beginning to flicker around them.

"No!" she cried. She caught Amarantha by the arm and then recoiled. The touch burned. "Leave him to them. I'm going to transfer possession of the Curse to Jalo."

"To me," said Miyam coolly, the shadows dissipating.

Eliza looked at Jalo. He said nothing.

"Fine," said Eliza, glancing again at the horde of myrkestras coming ever closer. She reached over and took Miyam by the hand. Her hand was cold. Eliza let the weight of the Curse pass from her to the Faery.

Amarantha emitted a low growl. "I will find you, Master of the Vaults," she said, but the Master of the Vaults did not reply.

Miyam looked at Nell. "Should any of you set foot in the Realm of the Faeries again, I will kill you myself, and quickly. Remember me."

"Fondest memories," muttered Charlie.

"Fine," said Eliza. "We need the morrapus."

"Keep it," said Jalo, not looking at any of them. Not looking at Nell. "You'd better go. Quickly."

"Jalo," said Nell, but he was walking away, towards his own morrapus. Miyam stood facing them all still, the Master of the Vaults expressionless at her side.

"Come on," said Eliza. She looked at Amarantha. "You could help us…"

"I have matters of my own to attend to, things long undone," said Amarantha, a horrible, trembling joy in her voice. "But I will give you a gift."

She took Eliza's hand in hers. It burned like fire. Eliza gasped and tried to withdraw it but Amarantha held her hand hard until the burning had subsided. Her hand looked the same, but she felt the heat beneath her palm.

"A fire spell," said Amarantha. "I was known for burning, once, and will be again." She grinned unpleasantly. "Farewell, and good luck to you, Sorceress-bird."

She raised her arms up in the air with a scream. A thick branch tore off a nearby tree and fell to her, hovering before her. She swung herself astride it, bent to whisper to it. The branch took to the air. The witch disappeared above the trees, her fair hair streaming behind her.

Eliza, Nell and Charlie bundled into the morrapus. Eliza called out to the myrkestra in the Language of First Days. It took off over the witches' forest.

"If we can lose the Faeries, we'll go north of the mountains," Eliza said in a rush. "And then to Lil, aye. The Mancers will be watching Swarn, but they dinnay know about Uri. Praps he can help us."

"The Mancers?" said Nell.

"I take it things have nay been going well," said Charlie.

"Nay well at all," conceded Eliza. "But we have these."

From her backpack, she drew out the diamond-encrusted box and opened it. Inside lay the strip of bone with its rough inscriptions, and a glass sphere. She took out the sphere and held it in her hand. A white fog swirled at its center, forming one symbol after another.

"Hurrah for us," said Charlie. "What are they?"

"The Gehemmis. I'm going to get the other two from the Immortal Dragons and the Sparkling Deluder." She giggled, slightly hysterical. The other two looked confused. "Sorry. It just sounds insane. It prolly is, aye. But we need to get you two to safety first."

"And safety is Lil?" asked Nell.

Eliza began to giggle again. "I doubt it," she said. "Sorry. I'm really, really tired. And the Faeries are coming after us, and the Emmisariae, and…"

An arrow tore through the silken morrapus, skimming between them and tearing out the other side. The morrapus gave a great lurch and began plunging downwards, fast.

"Hang on to me!" cried Charlie, and then it struck him yet again: he couldn't change. He looked to Eliza with fast-dawning horror.

Eliza drew back the silken door. The black trees of the witches' forest were hurtling towards them like iron spikes and among the trees white shapes were moving quickly. The Thanatosi had found them. They had not been flying high enough and the myrkestra had been shot. Hanging onto the delicate gold frame of the morrapus she pulled herself out of the billowing dome and climbed on top of it. They were falling fast for the trees, the weight of the dead myrkestra pulling them down. She drew her dagger and cut the transparent threads that bound the morrapus to the myrkestra. At the same moment a swarm of ravens took up the dangling threads, pulling them back towards the sky. Arrows hissed upwards and Eliza huddled against the top of the morrapus. She could tell already that she did not have the strength to maintain this many ravens for long enough to fly them across Tian Xia, or even across the Witches' Forest. It was exhausting just pulling the morrapus out of range of the Thanatosi's arrows. She would have to come up with something else.

One raven broke off from the others, flying straight for the Irahok mountains. Eliza let the other ravens lower the morrapus, surrounding it as best they could, though many of them fell to the arrows. Eliza clambered back into the morrapus. Charlie and Nell were crouched together, Nell clinging to her folder, their faces white with terror.

"It's the Thanatosi," said Eliza. "I'll hold them off, aye. You need to make a run for it. Get to the Far Sea if you can. I've sent Swarn a message, told her to look for you."

There was no time to talk any more. Nell was screaming questions and Charlie's face told Eliza clearly that a journey all the way to the Far Sea, two humans on their own, was sheer folly. But they had no choice. Eliza built a barrier spell faster than she had ever done before and hurled it over the massing Thanatosi below. It trapped most of them, only seven of them escaping it. The morrapus touched the ground.

"Run," cried Eliza.

Charlie grabbed Nell by the hand and they ran.

Eliza crawled out of the morrapus to fend off the Thanatosi

that had not been caught in her barrier. Those within it were straining against its walls and she could feel that the barrier would not hold for long. The first of the Thanatosi to reach her she felled quickly, driving her dagger into its heart, pulling out her blade and striking off its head with one swift blow. She leaped back into a defensive posture, ready for the next six, which were coming at her as a group. But they paused around their fallen comrade. Their blank faces began to move and darken. Black, misshapen mouths formed slowly. Their fingers grew long and dark. They fell on the dead Thanatosi, plunging their fingers into him, bending their mouths to him. Within seconds there was nothing left of him but his white garments and his weapons. The Thanatosi that had eaten were strangely still now, their mouths disappearing. The rest of the horde was still pressing against the barrier. Eliza needed to buy time for Charlie and Nell, and so she did not attack them but poured all her strength into holding the barrier firm.

"*Help* me, please!" she entreated the trees. The forest was an army of witches under a Faery Curse since the Early Days and it had some powers of its own. But the trees were still and indifferent. The Sorceress and the Thanatosi were nothing to them. The six that had eaten began to convulse horribly. They fell to the ground, twisting this way and that, as if straining against their own skins. And then Eliza witnessed something she had not read about in any of the books, something that had been only vaguely alluded to with the lines: *Death has no meaning for them, though they are mortal in a technical sense, for a single Thanatosi can be killed. However, the power of one belongs to all, and they draw on this and multiply by it.* The skin of the six Thanatosi was stretching, as if something inside was pushing its way out. New arms clawed their way out from the shoulders, new legs from the thighs, another head bulging through the skin of the single head and at last separating. The new body clambered and flailed and pulled itself free, and Eliza found that now instead of six Thanatosi outside the barrier she was faced with twelve. Her horror at the scene shook her grip over her barrier spell. The remaining army of

Thanatosi burst through it.

There was no time to think. She would tell herself this later: that it happened too quickly, that there was nothing else she could have done. But she would wonder, of course she would wonder if she might have done something different, something less destructive. The Thanatosi were rolling towards her like a great white wave spiked with glittering weapons. She opened her palm and spoke to Amarantha's fire spell. A ball of fire burst from her hand, breaking against the mass of Thanatosi and leaping up into a great ring of flame twenty feet high, pouring black smoke, enclosing those who had not been burned. The heat scorched Eliza's skin, made her eyes water. Inhuman screams rose up. At first she thought this was the Thanatosi, but then she realized it was the burning witch-trees. As she dashed back among the trees, away from the blast of the heat, black branches and roots and leaves all poured their wrath towards her. They stole her air and pressed and pulled at her so that she could hardly move or breathe.

"Stop it," she gasped. One of the witch-trees was drawing her towards it. She felt the bark rough against her face, the tug inside her bones, like her skeleton was about to be pulled loose from her body. Ravens swarmed above but could not descend among the trees. She pressed her palm to the tree and fire burst through it. The tree howled, recoiled, and Eliza pulled free. She spun around, pointing her palm at the trees.

"Give me air," she rasped, "or you'll burn." They hissed fearfully, and she found herself able to take a breath. She climbed one of the hateful trees. It tried to shake her off but she held on tight and moved swiftly. From the top of the tree she saw that the Thanatosi were coming through the wall of fire in groups. Roughly ten of them would form a sphere of bodies over three or four and they would roll through in a great flaming ball. Those on the outside would burn, and those on the inside would feed on them afterwards, then split into two, then feed and divide again, as yet more of the balls of bodies rolled through. Eliza watched in horror as the army increased. The tree was shaking violently. She leaped from it to the ground. Nell and Charlie could not have gotten far yet.

The only thing, *the only thing* was to keep the Thanatosi from pursuing them. The terrible screams of the forest filled her ears and she did not notice that she was sobbing. As the first wave of the ever-growing army of Thanatosi began to pour through the trees again, she let another wall of fire burst from her palm.

Charlie and Nell ran until they could hardly breathe and their legs would no longer move. They tumbled to the ground in a tangle, gasping. The trees were thinning here. Behind them they could see the flames and the billowing smoke, and Eliza's ravens swarming over it all.

"Is she going to be all right?" asked Nell tearfully.

"Eliza can handle herself," panted Charlie. "Besides, they're nay really interested in her. They just want to get *past* her."

"We have to keep moving."

"I dinnay know if I can. Ancients blast this feeble human body!"

"You can. Come on, Charlie." Nell got to her feet shakily and helped him up too. They managed a shuffling sort of jog out of the trees. The outline of the Irahok mountains filled the sky. They were facing rolling, bleached foothills. Frost crunched beneath their feet. The air was terribly cold.

"Where are we?" wailed Nell.

"The Northern foothills," said Charlie. "We'll keep north of the mountains, like Eliza said. We cannay cross the mountains on foot, and we cannay go through the land of the Giants without becoming a snack or an ornament."

"We've nay got anything to eat."

"Let's just keep moving."

They followed a frozen creek into the hills. Every few seconds one of them looked back fearfully but they saw only the witches' forest in flames, the sky full of smoke. No sign of the Thanatosi.

"I hope Eliza's all right," wept Nell, crying freely as she stumbled along. She knew she ought to be grateful just to be alive but right now she was only cold and terrified.

Charlie kept walking grimly.

"Do you think it's safe to stop for the night?" asked Nell some time later, noticing that the sun was getting low in the sky. "Oh Charlie! Even if the Thanatosi dinnay find us, how are we going to keep from freezing or starving? There's nothing to eat, nothing to make a fire with out here."

"We'll just have to keep walking, aye," said Charlie, looking around. It was true. There was not even any bracken, just low icy hills that flattened out into the Great Ice Plains of the Horogarth in the north and veered up into the forbidding Irahok mountains to the south. The flaming witches' forest was a full day behind them, the Far Sea still many days on foot ahead of them. After what they had escaped, it seemed almost absurd that they should freeze or starve in the foothills, but he could not think his way around it.

"Yes. Keep walking," Nell echoed. The cold was in her bones now. "What's that light, Charlie?"

A thin blue wave was undulating all along the northern horizon, sending sharp, glittering rays upwards. When she looked at it she got a strange drifting sensation, like her life was wafting up out of her, leaving her body behind. She stumbled. The whole northern sky was made of shimmering blue waves now.

"Dinnay look," said Charlie, grabbing her arm and yanking her to his other side. "It draws you to it. That's the Horogarth."

"Is it?" she said faintly. "It's lovely."

"Dinnay look," Charlie repeated, and she obeyed, watching her feet shuffle through the snow. She couldn't feel her toes.

The sun set and the hard freeze of the night drove into them. They stumbled through the dark, their arms wrapped around each other to share what little warmth they had. When Charlie fell to his knees and then plunged face-first into the snow, Nell shook him and pummeled him and coaxed him to his feet again. When she collapsed sideways, he did the same. Too hungry to be aware of it, too cold to think, they urged each other through the night, and when the sun rose again they were grateful for the little light and little warmth that it afforded.

"What are we going to eat?" asked Nell. The words were thick and strange in her mouth.

"There's nothing to eat. Keep walking."

Soon they were so thirsty they ate fistfuls of snow until their throats ached with the cold. They were not walking anymore so much as shuffling forwards slowly and trying not to fall over.

It was late on this second day that Nell began to hallucinate. She was sure that she saw her house in Holburg perched at an odd angle on the next hill. Her words were too garbled for Charlie to understand but she tried to pull him towards it, while he dragged her back on course, sticking close to the edge of the mountains. Her ears roared with strange sounds that seemed to have no source and she saw her house on every hill now. The sky was crisp and bright with blue light. She knew it could not be real and she cried bitterly. Her tears froze on her face. Her face was made of ice. She felt herself made of ice, moving slowly towards her house where her family would be waiting. Her father would be on the sofa, watching TV. Her brothers would be sprawled around the house being noisy and irritating. There would be food, and Holburg just outside, the warm sea. She would thaw in the sea.

When a snowstorm came blasting from the north, swallowing them in a swirling whiteness, she could not hold herself upright against the wind and the cold any longer. She fell down and this time Charlie did not pick her up. He let himself fall next to her and watched the storm through frozen eyelashes. It was not fair, he thought dully. It was not fair that Nell should die so young because of him. The thought appalled him so deeply that he sat up, shook her shoulder. She murmured but did not stir. Her normally honey-coloured skin had turned white as the snow.

"Please, Nell," he mumbled, then heard crunching snow through the gale, and looked up. He squinted at a blurry, dark shape making towards them through the driving snow. It was several dark shapes in fact, slowly coming clearer through the haze of sleet: hounds as big as horses, with shaggy grey coats. They were harnessed to something huge, baying as they came towards the two fallen humans.

Something leaped from the structure behind the hounds. Something on powerful legs, something clothed in dank furs, something bearded and fiery-eyed with a long sword in its hand. The being came striding towards them on heavy boots, stood over them. The huge iron sword swung up. Charlie watched all this happening as if it were not happening to him, as if he were witnessing a story he had heard long ago. Something came back to him, another language from another life.

"Greetings to the Verr Mon Noorden," he called out in that old language, as the huge sword fell towards them. "I am Bryn-Arr."

The sword halted mid-swing.

CHAPTER

17

When Nell became aware of her surroundings again, she thought at first that she had fallen asleep in the *Confortare* train's dining car. But the movement was all wrong and the powerful smell filling her nostrils was not food. Also, she could not move. This frightened her and she opened her eyes. What she saw first was just a dark mass shifting right overhead. She managed with great difficulty to sit up. She was half-buried under several layers of heavy animal hides, and this was the smell that had infiltrated her feverish dreams. Her face, hands and feet were wrapped in bandages. She lifted her mummified hands to her face, finding gaps only for her eyes, mouth and nostrils.

"Charlie?" she said thickly. There was no answer. She had been wrapped up, piled into some kind of vehicle with a great many furs and, she saw now, some boxes, and she was being transported *somewhere* very quickly. The last thing she remembered was walking through the snow with Charlie. No, that was not right. She searched her memory, using her teeth to pull at the bandages on her hands. She remembered being lifted, a great many gruff voices, fire, and something else…drinking something thick and warm. That was all. Once her hands were free, she pulled the bandages from her face and feet as well. The inside of the bandages was damp and sticky, her face and her hands slick with the same smelly substance. She crawled on top of the furs and felt her way along the edge of the large shifting crate. The domed covering was made of animal hide too. She pushed against the walls gingerly, but she was afraid to push too hard lest she fall out. She began to feel the cold again, so she crawled back under the furs to wait. They had not been captured by Faeries, anyway, and this seemed an unlikely modus operandi for the Thanatosi. Alarming though it was to find oneself bandaged and trapped, there was no doubt that the situation had improved. She had not frozen to death, after all. With this reassuring thought, she fell asleep again.

She woke to a sudden light and a blast of cold air. The hide wall had been pulled aside and a face was staring in at her. It was a huge face, scarred and hairy, with black, cat-like slits for pupils in its large yellow eyes. It opened its jaw to reveal long, wolfish teeth, and made some gruff sounds that must have been speaking. Then it reached under the furs and hauled her out by the arm. Its hairy hand had metallic claws instead of fingernails, and a ferocious grip. The thing strode through the snow, dragging her behind as she scrambled to find her footing. She saw that there were twenty or more covered sleds harnessed to huge, shaggy hounds. The mountains hung almost directly overhead, vicious and white.

Animal hide had been laid in a broad circle around a bonfire. Some of the creatures sat cross-legged on the hide, some sat in wicker chairs covered in furs. Those in the chairs bore more weapons than the others and wore necklaces of bone and teeth. When Nell saw Charlie wrapped in furs and sitting in one of the wicker chairs, her heart contracted with relief. He looked very small among these beasts. The one dragging her let go of her arm suddenly and wandered off.

"You've got stuff all over your face," said Charlie.

She wiped at her face and saw that her hands were covered in something dark and slimy. She wiped her hands on her Faery dress; they left big black marks.

"Yuck," she said.

"Cures frostbite," he said. "Good stuff, aye."

Nell could only think about the cold. She sat next to Charlie's chair and pulled one of the smelly furs around her. The shaggy fellows around the fire grinned at her with their ferocious teeth.

"These are the Verr mon Noorden," Charlie explained.

"Warriors of the Northern Foothills, aye. I had to persuade them not to skin you and eat you, lah, so I said you were my favourite wife. And I said you were a witch who'd been robbed of her powers. I thought it would be easier than explaining…you know, the truth."

"Your *favourite* wife?" Nell said disdainfully. A clay bowl full of stew was placed roughly before her. There were no utensils to eat with.

"Can I use my hands?" she asked, trying to wipe them clean again on her dress.

"That's how it's done, aye," said Charlie. She tucked in, devouring every scrap in the bowl in under a minute. While she ate, she heard and thought nothing, but when she was done she realized that Charlie was talking to one of the Verr Mon Noorden in their own strange, guttural language. His conversation partner wore a necklace of fangs and his clothes were adorned with bone carvings. He laughed and clapped Charlie on the shoulder, nearly knocking him off his chair.

"So, lah, you know them?" asked Nell.

"There's this legendary figure among the Verr mon Noorden," said Charlie. "A warrior named Bryn-Arr. He's appeared throughout the tribe's history and helped them to win battles and hunt the Yrgtha, monsters you find in the foothills and the mountains, aye. One was spotted this morning, actually, so a hunting party has gone after it while we wait here. The Verr mon Noorden fought the Giants in the Middle Days and won with Bryn-Arr's help, even though the Giants outsized and outnumbered them. They're really amazing warriors."

"What does this have to do with us, Charlie?" Nell asked impatiently.

"Lah, I'm Bryn-Arr. Whenever I'd had enough of the worlds or felt like I needed to get away from everything, I'd become this massive warrior hero, aye, and I'd come and spend some time with them. Every Chief knows a few secrets to help him identify Bryn-Arr. Of course, I dinnay look like him anymore, but I know the secret words and I could tell them all the stories of my feats and things I've done. Luckily, they believe me. I can still remember their language, lah, but with a human throat and voice-box I cannay make all the sounds correctly. They understand me, though."

"But how did you explain the way you look?"

"The truth, aye. More or less. I said that I was once able to take many shapes, and Bryn-Arr was one of them. They dinnay know about Shades or anything like that. But I said I'd been cursed and the only shape left to me was this weak one. I explained that the Thanatosi are after me and that we need to get to Lil. They're going to take us across the mountains. We'll have to go the rest of the way ourselves. They willnay leave the north."

"Lah, even though you cannay change, your Shade-self is still very useful, Charlie," said Nell. "I didnay think we were going to make it to Lil." Then something struck her like a thunderbolt. She scrabbled in her empty pockets. "Charlie! Where's my folder?"

He looked puzzled. "What folder?"

"With my notes! The test is in less than two weeks!"

"I dinnay know. We must have dropped it."

"Oh no! No no no! I've got to go back for it!" Nell leaped to her feet. Charlie half-rose, grabbing her by the arm and pulling her back down, which wasn't difficult in her weakened state.

"Nell, we've already been travelling with them more than a day. I cannay ask them to turn around to look for your notes."

"We *have* to! Charlie! Everything I need for the test is in that folder! I have to get it back!"

"You cannay be serious," said Charlie. "The Thanatosi are after me, we're in the middle of the icy northern regions of Tian Xia, and you want to turn around and go look for some notes that you dropped *somewhere* in the last several hundred miles. We'd never find them, lah."

He was right, of course. She thought she must have dropped them when their morrapus started to go down, and they could not go back to the witches' forest. The Verr mon Noorden around the fire rose up shouting. A group was staggering towards them, hounds pulling a carcass as big as a house. It was a shaggy white beast, like a bear but much larger.

"Praps I can still ace the test without my notes," said Nell, her heart sinking. "I mean, either I know the stuff or I dinnay by now, lah."

Charlie nodded absently. The Verr mon Noorden drew fierce-looking knives and set about skinning the monster and cutting the meat into great strips. It was very efficient work, finished in less than an hour. Both the hide and the meat were tied over the tops of the larger sleds to dry out and freeze. The bones were cleaned and put in one of the covered sleds, the organs stashed in barrels. One of the Verr mon Noorden pulled out the monster's teeth with a large metal contraption clearly designed for that purpose. Soon, those working on the poor slaughtered beast were covered in its thick black blood, as was the snow all around it. One of them came towards Nell and Charlie, proffering two bowls. Nell took the bowl and then almost dropped it. Inside it, staring up at her, was a giant bloody eyeball the size of her own head.

"It's a delicacy," Charlie said anxiously. "You'd better eat it, aye."

"You've *got* to be kidding me," she said, turning her head aside. The stench of it nearly overwhelmed her.

"Seriously. Nell, they'll be prize upset if you refuse."

Already a number of the Verr mon Noorden were eyeing her suspiciously and had begun to mutter.

"The whole thing?" she murmured.

"As much as you can."

Charlie dug his fingers into the eyeball in his own bowl, pulling out a handful of eye-jelly and popping it in his mouth. He nearly gagged.

"It tastes quite good when you're one of them," he managed to say. "By the Ancients, this is nay going to be easy."

Nell took a deep breath. She had a strong stomach and she considered herself a pretty good actress. Here was the ultimate test of both. She dove her hand into the eye and felt it squish and roll beneath her fingers. She pulled her fingers out, dripping, and sucked the goo off them, swallowing rapidly and trying not to taste it.

"Speed is key," she told Charlie.

The two of them gobbled down the eyeballs as fast as they could. About halfway through Nell thought she might faint. Her stomach roiled rebelliously but she shut her mind and continued as quickly as she could. The Verr mon Noorden seemed satisfied when she handed back the more or less empty bowl and croaked her thanks. Charlie was green in the face and gave her a miserable look. He was not yet done.

"You're almost there," she encouraged him, and crept behind one of the sleds to throw up. She hastily covered the mess up with snow.

Soon they were off again, racing through the mountains. The hounds tirelessly pulled the sleds along routes known only to them and these strange, large warriors. The snowy peaks were lost in cloud overhead and all around them was white. They sped down and laboured up long snowy slopes, pausing to build fires and eat. At night they slept in the covered sleds with heat-giving lamps burning Yrgtha fat, warm under the heavy furs. On the second day, Nell woke early, helped prepare some stew, and then joined Charlie at the front of a half-covered sled. She was wearing a clumsily stitched hat of Yrgtha fur and was wrapped in a cloak that trailed in the snow. Charlie laughed when he saw her.

"You fit right in, lah," he said. "I think you might have a bit of the Shade temperament yourself."

The hounds needed no direction. They knew the terrain well. The air stung Nell's face as the hounds began to run and the sled skimmed along the ground between the fearsome icy peaks.

"I was part of the anti-fur club at school," Nell said to Charlie. "I wrote all these letters to newspapers about how wearing fur should be illegal. I've been thinking about becoming a vegetarian. And now look at me, eating eyeballs and dressed in Yrgtha skin!"

"Context is everything," said Charlie. "You cannay make

choices like that out here, unless you want to freeze or starve."

"Neither, thanks. Lah, but I'm nay sure I wouldnay end up choosing starvation over a diet of eyeballs. That was horrific."

"I dinnay even want to think about it," said Charlie feelingly.

Nell laughed, and without really thinking she slipped her arm through his and leaned against him. She saw his surprised expression from the corner of her eye and felt suddenly embarrassed, but decided not to move. It was more comfortable and stable than trying to hold herself upright on the fast-moving sled.

So they sat leaning into each other cozily, Yrgtha fur pulled up over their hands, chatting occasionally and watching the mountains wheel by for close to an hour. Charlie glanced at Nell a few times as if he wanted to say something but stopped himself. Her nose and cheeks were bright pink from the cold and her eyes shone. The wind whipped her hair around her face. Charlie reached over and brushed a tangle out of her eyes. She blinked at him. He didn't know what to say then, so he said what was on his mind: "What you said when we were in the Realm of the Faeries..." he began. "Just before we were caught, you said...do you remember what you said?"

He could see that she did. Her cheeks paled a little and she looked down at her hands. "Let's nay talk about it," she said. "It's all in the past, lah."

"I think we *should* talk about it," said Charlie.

She shook her head, hiding her face from him with her hair. "I know what you're going to say, Charlie. It doesnay matter. You dinnay need to say it."

"Of course I do." He put one arm firmly around her shoulders and with his other hand he pushed the hair out of her face and tilted her head up towards him so that she was looking right in his eyes. He held her chin gently between his fingers and thumb so she could not turn her face away again. "You brought Ander to Tian Xia to save my life, Nell. I havenay forgotten that. It's a funny feeling, to owe somebody your life. It's hard to know what to say to a person. And you risked your life for me again, aye, going to the Realm of the Faeries. It almost ended in both of us being killed. I'm grateful for all of it, lah. More than I could possibly say."

"You'd have done the same, aye," said Nell. It was a bit dizzying looking into his face, just inches from hers, while the snowy mountains whizzed past them and the wind howled around them.

"I would," he said. "No question. I would. But Ander dying was nay your fault. Nary a bit. There was nothing you could have done."

Her eyes filled up with tears that fell and quickly froze on her cheeks.

"He was there because of *me*," she said, so quietly he could barely hear her over the wind. "He wanted to leave as soon as you got out of the Cave, aye, but I insisted on this big adventure. I thought we could help somehow, but we didnay do a bit of good. Eliza took care of everything and all I did was get Ander killed."

"He was a grown man, Nell," said Charlie. "You may think you have some kind of power over people, but he didnay have to agree to anything you said, or take on Nia that way. Life is a precarious thing for a human. People die all the time. It's sad and it's terrible but that's the way of things. He was a brave man, he made his own choices, and he got killed in a dangerous situation. Nay your fault."

"His mother moved in with my parents," Nell said, and then she couldn't speak anymore. Tears kept pouring down her face. Charlie tried to wipe them away.

"Do you want to know why I didnay come see you when we got back to Di Shang?" he said.

"No." It came out a little sob.

"Because I showed you my true form, that first time we were in the Realm of the Faeries. I showed you, and I...I thought I made it prize obvious how I felt about you. Do you know what I mean?"

Everything became suddenly very still for Nell. Her sobs died within her. The wind and the mountains and the panting of the hounds were blanketed by a deep hush, a deep quiet in her mind. She didn't feel like she was going to fall off anymore. She stuck her tongue out and licked the icy tears off her upper lip.

"Tell me," she said. Thank goodness he was back to looking like himself, she thought. Thank goodness that false, bright Faery face was gone, and his dark eyes and his funny eyebrows and his about-to-turn-into-laughter-smile were all back. She thought about her notes scattered somewhere in the snow in the foothills or maybe in the witches' forest, and faraway Austermon, and Eliza battling the Thanatosi, shy little Eliza who had come to Holburg years ago and who was so different now and yet so much the same. All these thoughts seemed to exist at once in her mind, hanging still, present and waiting, and she outside them.

"I've been in love with you since the first time we met, aye," he said.

She gave a hiccupping little laugh. "We were *twelve*," she said, but she was barely listening to her own voice. What they said now didn't really matter. She was waiting for something else, a particular moment.

"I wasnay so young," he said. "But I mean it. I didnay recognize it, nay really, until later, but still. I think everybody who meets you prolly feels the same way. Like life is simply less colourful without you. I thought you knew…but then after I showed you my true form you were a bit strange, like you wished I hadnay done it. You were wearing the ring Jalo gave you, and then there was that boy Julian. I thought if you wanted to see me you would say so. But you never did. Eliza never said that you asked about me or you wanted to see me or anything. The way she talked, it sounded like you never mentioned me. She thought it was strange too, I could tell."

"That's why you never visited?" She felt a great weight lift, and began laughing. "Charlie! You're far too subtle for a girl like me! You should have *told* me how you felt."

"Lah, I've told you now," he said, laughing too. "But it's hard making a declaration of love to one of your best friends. I didnay know if you felt the same way. I still dinnay know, come to think of it."

"Dinnay be an idiot," she said. "Of course you know." This was the moment she had been waiting for. She leaned towards him, but he looked up so suddenly that she ended up kissing him clumsily on the chin. A vast shadow passed over them. The Verr mon Noorden were leaping from the sleds, hurling spears up at the sky. Nell looked up too and saw a giant winged creature glittering in the sunlight. A blade of green fire burst from it, sending the warriors leaping out of range. It was a dragon, massive and rust-red.

The covering was pulled off a sled near the back to reveal a huge catapult armed with spiked iron balls. One of these was flung upwards with deadly aim. The dragon dodged narrowly, responding with another burst of fire that set the catapult in flames.

"Charlie, that dragon!" said Nell. "Is it nay…?"

"One of Swarn's!" Charlie finished, scrambling off the sled. Nell leaped after him, waving her arms joyfully.

"We're here! We're here! Tell them to stop, Charlie!"

Charlie shouted out in their language and the Verr mon Noorden paused. The dragon descended, landing right in front of Nell on the snowy mountainside and fixing her in its huge golden gaze.

"It's you!" she exclaimed, running forward to put her hands on its face. She recognized the dragon that she had saved from the dead marsh a year and a half ago, nearly full-grown now. The Verr mon Noorden looked on in amazement.

"Our journey is finished," Charlie told them. "Bryn-Arr is grateful."

"We await the return of the warrior," said the Chief.

"He will not return," said Charlie. "His day is done."

"The stories will be told forever," the Chief promised. Charlie clasped his hand. Then he and Nell climbed onto the dragon's back. It leaped into the air and bore them on powerful wings over the mountains to the cliffs of Batt.

"Is she *still* holding them off?" whined Malferio, peering over Kyreth's shoulder into the Vindensphere.

"You did not know she was so powerful," said Kyreth smugly. "She's not especially *powerful*," said Malferio. "She's just lucky. They would have torn her to pieces if that witch hadn't given her the fire spell, and all she's really doing is doubling their numbers every hour or so. Her barriers are getting worse and worse. And *by the way*, I can't *believe* she's unleashed Amarantha on the worlds! You must be so proud. She locks Nia up in the Hall of the Ancients and then sets free the next worst thing. She's very inconsistent."

"I have read of Amarantha," said Kyreth, smiling. "But Eliza would have found another way if she had not had the fire spell. What is luck but the forces of the worlds aligning with your purposes? Is that not a kind of power too? Why should she be luckier than you?"

"I don't believe in that stuff," muttered Malferio, slinking back to his divan and curling up. He'd had enough of watching the battle. He picked up his empty pipe and looked hopefully at Kyreth.

"She is making use of her ravens," noted Kyreth. "They lift the fallen Thanatosi and take them out of reach of their fellows so they cannot multiply as quickly. Still, she is relying heavily on the walls of fire and their numbers are increasing. They are pushing her back, if slowly. It has been a full day and a night now and she has kept them from pursuing her friends. Of course, her friends will have frozen to death or been eaten by an Yrgtha or slaughtered by the Verr mon Noorden by now in any case."

"Yes, let's have a look at them, that sounds fun," said Malferio, brightening somewhat.

"But no...they must still be alive. If the Shade were dead, the Thanatosi would turn back. How can they have survived? He cannot change."

"Still alive? That's boring."

"Watch – she is very good with the dagger. Now she is disarming them but not killing them. The Warrior Witch has taught her well. Ah! She has something else, another weapon, do you see? She used it yesterday, though sparingly."

"I can't see from over here."

"I recognize it. She used it on the Mancers, too. The Warrior Witch uses such a tool to paralyze her enemies. Ah, that is clever, very clever, but she does not have enough poisoned darts to paralyze very many of them, I think."

"Amarantha free!" muttered Malferio to himself. "Well, there is something for Emyr to worry about. Yes, he'll soon find that being King isn't all fun and games. The Master of the Vaults is a very powerful and clever Faery, you know. I can't think how your little Sorceress got past him. Those vaults are enchanted by...well, I don't know by what exactly but something very powerful indeed."

"By Amarantha's Magic," said Kyreth softly. "Yes, she has done what Selva failed to do. She may yet succeed in her quest. But she is so like Nia, in the end. Her mother was willful, but Rea understood right and wrong. Rea understood duty. Oh, she could be unreasonable and her marriage was folly, but she took her duty seriously, the good of the worlds. This one...she cares only for a few and will let the rest rot. She will unleash a dangerous witch and burn the witch-trees by the hundreds if it serves her purpose. She will die for those she loves, which is noble, but she will lie and steal and kill for them too."

"And you were so keen on an heir. She sounds like she'd be a lovely mother."

"She will produce an heir at the end of this," said Kyreth darkly. "But after that..."

"Oh, I see. What a ruthless son-of-a-troll you are! I understand why the Mancers have thrived."

"She is so weary. She has not slept. And yet she is as quick as they who need no sleep. Oh, but she will tire and fall before they do. She cannot hold them off much longer."

"What about the Faeries? Are they still surrounding the forest?"

Kyreth cupped his hands around the Vindensphere and the scene within pulled away, as if they were seeing it through the eyes of a hawk circling high overhead.

"See for yourself," said Kyreth, but Malferio did not stir.

Faeries with glinting swords stood in formation all around the forest, waiting. They could not enter the witches' forest or work their Magic there.

"I do not know how she will get past the Faeries," murmured Kyreth. "She may need my help. She is being pushed further and further back, towards the edges of the forest."

"How can you help her?" scoffed Malferio.

"I think I shall not need to. The Emmisariae will arrive soon," said Kyreth. "They will not let her die."

"They are no match for Faeries!" cried Malferio.

"You think because you are Immortal you are more powerful than the mortal beings," said Kyreth. "But it is not so. Why did you need Amarantha, then?"

"Look, they can fend off Curses with those barriers, but what can they do against Illusion?" scoffed Malferio.

"How will the Faeries get near enough to them to work Illusion?" Kyreth countered. "A myrkestra cannot approach a dragon."

"Ah!" cried Malferio, growing excited and getting up. "Let me see this part!"

The two of them watched in the Vindensphere as the Emmisariae on their golden dragons soared over the waiting Faery troops and circled the battle between Eliza and the Thanatosi. They saw Eliza look up, the stunned panic on her weary face. She pointed her palm out and a ball of fire shot from it towards the Mancers. Immediately the ball of flame was caught in a barrier, which closed around it, extinguishing it. She held her dagger up and shouted a command at the dragons in the Language of First Days:

"Stay back! Stay back!"

The dragons pulled up, unsure. The Emmisariae commanded them more firmly to go down. The dragons seemed briefly uncertain, circling, and then made another attempt at descent. Eliza ran into the thick of the trees, the Thanatosi behind her. She shot out another firewall to stop them and kept running. The trees snatched at her, recoiling before her hand and her dagger every time.

"She will run straight into the Faeries!" cried Malferio excitedly. "She is done for!"

Kyreth stood up. Indeed, the forest was spreading out, she was nearing the Faery troops, when the Mancer dragons recoiled before a blade of green fire. A dragon far bigger than they, dark red with nearly black wings, came screaming from the clouds and plunged straight for Eliza. It caught her in its talons and shot back up into the sky before anyone had time to react. The Faery myrkestras rose into the air but could not rise fast enough or high enough. The Mancer dragons pursued but they were soon left behind. The great beast took the Sorceress high into the clouds over the foothills and they were gone, leaving behind them the howling witches' forest in flames and the Thanatosi pouring out of the forest after their prey. The Mancers and the Faeries ignored each other, making for the mountains, seeking a sign of the vanished Sorceress.

Kyreth laughed. "There," he said.

"You see!" grumbled Malferio. *"Lucky."*

CHAPTER
18

The cliffs of Batt loomed over the Dead Marsh. Since the destruction of her home and her dragons, Swarn had built a new house high on the cliffs, overlooking the slaughter ground where she had buried the dragons. She was waiting outside her house, a modest dwelling made of clay and bone, when the dragon bearing Charlie and Nell arrived. She stood erect as always, her white hair loose around her shoulders, spear in hand, but Nell thought she seemed much older than the last time they had seen her. It was not that her face was more lined, or that she appeared any less powerful and agile. Rather, it was as if something steely at her center had begun to collapse. Some of the fire was gone from her eyes.

The dragon landed before the witch with a wild scream.

"You got Eliza's message? Her raven, I mean?" asked Nell, scrambling off the dragon's back and slipping to the ground. From the cliffs, they could see over the Dead Marsh all the way to the Ravening Forest beyond. On the eastern horizon the silver-green of the Far Sea shimmered like a strip of watered silk.

"Yes," said Swarn. "I sent the other dragon to assist her."

"Then she's all right," said Nell hopefully.

"I do not know," said Swarn. "She has burned the witches' forest. So many souls! And every being whispers now that the Shang Sorceress went to the Realm of the Faeries to free Amarantha. What is she doing?"

"I spose she's trying to save my life," said Charlie unhappily. "It's gotten very complicated, aye. She thinks if she gets all the Gehemmis she'll be able to do something, stop Kyreth."

"Yes, she has asked for my help in her quest. But why burn the forest? The witches imprisoned in those trees are not her enemies."

"The Thanatosi were right there. I dinnay know what happened. We just ran," said Charlie. He repeated this, as if he couldn't quite believe it: "We didnay stay to help her. We just ran."

"Eliza can take care of herself," said Swarn tersely. "What I do not understand is how the two of you are constantly tangled up in her affairs."

"It's nay on purpose," said Nell. "The Thanatosi are after Charlie."

"I am unsurprised," said Swarn. "We will eat and then I will take you to Lil. It is no more than a day's journey."

Gautelen mon Lil mon Shol was eighteen years old. She spent almost all her time in her father's library. It was a fine library, one of the finest in the worlds, though Uri mon Lil liked to tell of how he had seen the Mancer Library, albeit decimated by the Sorceress Nia, and since then could only see his own library as a few rooms full of second-rate books.

"There is nothing wrong with a young witch spending her time among books," he said to his wife. "She is studious, that is all!"

"She is changed," said his wife, the Storm-Seamstress Ely-Hathana mon Shol, her long amber eyes serious. And Uri knew that Ely-Hathana was right. At sixteen, Gautelen had been full of life and mischief. She had been gifted at music and magic and poetry, quick to laugh, kind to all. Then she spent a year in the Realm of the Faeries as their unwilling Queen. Since her return from that place she was a different girl: quiet, brooding. There was a slow-burning fire in her, and she was tending it.

She returned to them joyfully at first. There was a great party at the house in Lil to welcome her. At the dinner table that night, Gautelen heard for the first time her father tell of his own adventures: how, burdened by a terrible Faery Curse, he had travelled to Di Shang and the famed Library of the Mancers to seek some way to free her from her bondage. She was rapt, reaching to take his

hand, tears starting in her eyes. Then he told how he had helped
the Shang Sorceress to trap Nia with her own Magic and as he
spoke Gautelen's face changed. She withdrew her hand slowly.
Confusion and grief battled across her face. A wind began to howl
outside. She rose to her feet and the dining hall fell silent. Rain
battered the windows – heavy drops the size of a water-ape's head.

"Nia delivered me from the Faeries," she said in a low voice.
"She deposed and punished that...*King.*" She flinched and would
not speak his name.

"But my dear!" said Uri mon Lil, surprised. "The Sorceress
Nia is *evil*. Her revenge on Malferio does not make her less so."

"She freed *me*," cried Gautelen, amber tears rolling down her
smooth dark cheeks. "She did not have to but she did!"

"You were useful to her," said Ely-Hathana briskly. "Do not
be foolish, daughter."

"You don't know her. You didn't meet her. She came to me
and...I know her heart, father! She is not an evil Sorceress! She
is...I cannot describe her, but she is wonderful and she is good
and we must free her at once!"

"That would be folly!" protested Uri mon Lil. "And impossible besides. Only the Shang Sorceress can free her. She has
the...well, she is the only one who can do it."

Gautelen's face hardened. "She has the what? What does
she have?"

Uri mon Lil hesitated. "The power," he said in a small voice.
"My dear...I understand you have been through a terrible ordeal
but you must choose your friends carefully."

Gautelen would hear none of it. She brooded for weeks.
Nothing her mother or father said to her could lift her mood.
Some time later, when Eliza sent word that she was coming to Lil
to return Uri's staff, he arranged for Gautelen to go to the isles of
Shol and visit relatives. She heard about the Shang Sorceress's
visit later, from a wordful water ape, while she was out rowing. A
week of terrible storms followed. The womi of Lil begged Ely-
Hathana to stop the storms, but she thought it best to let her
daughter vent her rage. Then one day Gautelen disappeared in

one of Uri mon Lil's enchanted boats. Uri was frantic. The womi and the wordful water apes of Lil went in search of her. Relatives in Shol were alerted to the young Storm Seamstress's disappearance. Finally, a centaur spotted her in the Irahok mountains and word spread. When it reached Uri, he knew where she was going.

He found her in the ruined Hall of the Ancients, weeping at Nia's feet, half-starved and frozen, having employed every spell she knew. She cursed the name of the Shang Sorceress even as Uri brought her home to Lil. In Gautelen's mind, Eliza was wicked and powerful and ruthless, and Uri thought wryly that the image Gautelen had of her did not at all match the good-hearted, awkward young girl he knew, who did not look as if she could enchant a river rat.

Since then, Gautelen kept to herself, studying in the library. In the Hall of the Ancients she had entered Nia's mind and learned the secret of the spell that bound her: the Urkleis that was lodged in the Shang Sorceress's chest. She poured all her efforts now into preparing to face the Shang Sorceress and obtain the Urkleis from her.

Gautelen ate her supper alone in the library as usual and then walked down to a sandy cove hidden by low-hanging trees on the northeastern tip of the island. She could see the dark heads of the wordful water apes sometimes breaking the surface of the water and she could hear their deep voices murmuring beneath the waves. She sat in the sand with her legs out straight and let the foaming waves wash over her ankles. The tide was coming in. Powers of the Deep controlled the tides, and these powers remained a great mystery. When she was a little girl her father had told her that under the sea there was a world as complex as the one at the surface, as full of different beings, some good and some evil, some powerful and some less so, and as ignorant of the world above as the overland beings were of them. She lay back in the sand and the water washed up her legs. Maybe she would lie here and let the sea take her. The tide would come up over her and pull her down to those mysterious depths she had been so curious about as a little girl. The great beings of that secret realm would help her, give her

Magic; she would return to the world, smite down the Shang Sorceress, bring the Urkleis triumphant to Nia. She would build Nia a castle on one of the lovely uninhabited isles of Shol and defend her against all those who meant her ill. Lost in this fantasy, Gautelen let the waves creep up to her waist, soaking the bottom half of her dress. The dream was shattered when a thousand black-headed water apes surged up and began to bellow all at once around the island, making the sea churn. Gautelen sat up. A massive shape came rocketing through the evening sky towards the island. It was a dragon – far larger than the green-gold dragons of the inland sea or even the long black dragons of the Dreaming Wasteland, illustrations of which she had found in her father's library. It soared over her head, up towards her father's house on the hill. She leaped to her feet and ran back through the jungle, where night birds chattered and huge snakes unwound their bodies and began to look for food. She passed a few of the peaked houses of their womi neighbours as she climbed the hill and saw their faces peering out anxiously. They too had heard the ruckus of the water apes and seen the dragon. Now they watched as the wizard of Lil's strange daughter ran home, half-soaked.

The dragon was sprawled across the front lawn, crushing the rows of flowering bushes her father had planted last spring. It turned its flaming eyes on her and for a moment Gautelen could not move. She had never seen any creature as large or as terrible as this one. But the house was not burning; there were no screams from within. It watched her, but made no move to gobble her up. At last she crept past it, breaking into a run halfway, bursting into the house and slamming the door shut behind her. Her knees folded and she leaned against the door, her heart racing. It was the first time she had ever seen a dragon and she thought she could go a good long while without seeing another one.

There were voices upstairs in the visitors' parlour. She climbed the stairs quietly and knelt at the closed door to peer through the keyhole. She saw a tall white-haired being talking to her father. There were two others with her, slightly smaller, dressed head to toe in heavy furs. They could only be witches of some kind. She had heard of the Warrior Witch Swarn, who rode a dragon. Another enemy of Nia and friend to the Shang Sorceress. One of the smaller beings turned her head, looking around the room curiously. Gautelen could not see very well through the keyhole, but she made out chestnut hair and a youthful face. Her father had described the Shang Sorceress as a human girl a couple of years younger than Gautelen. Gautelen's heart began to pound again as she looked through the keyhole at the pretty girl dressed in furs.

She crept away to the library to think.

They were tired when they arrived that evening, but Nell thought Uri mon Lil's house the pleasantest place they had ever stayed in Tian Xia. Built with black bamboo, it had a great many peaked roofs spiked with chimneys. Inside, it was warm and comfortable, with fires lit in every room and lamps lighting the halls and stair-ways. Uri mon Lil, with his shock of white hair and his shriveled face beaming around bright blue eyes, was a tiny figure next to his towering wife. She had long amber eyes, and her wild hair burst out around a face that might have been sculpted from ebony, so perfect and smooth and black it was. The couple greeted the vis-itors and welcomed them in the parlour with warm food and drinks. Uri and Swarn agreed to immediately work on putting a barrier around the house and trying to hide Charlie's presence with Magic. Charlie and Nell sat by the fire growing increasingly drowsy, fingers interlocked. Every now and then they looked at each other and broke into silly smiles. Sleepy though she was, when their eyes met Nell had to hold back the laughter that bur-bled in her chest. There was nothing funny in particular, and cer-tainly their plight was hardly cause for humour, but she felt so ridiculously happy that laughter seemed the only outlet for it.

"I will show the children to their rooms and then I will assist you," said Ely-Hathana to Swarn. "Come, human children."

"We're not *children*," protested Nell, heaving herself out of the comfortable chair. "I'm sixteen! And Charlie's *ancient.*"

They followed Ely-Hathana down the hall to the guest rooms, still holding hands. She liked the feel of Charlie's cool, rough hand in hers. They walked close to one another, bumping shoulders comfortably.

"You may sleep here," said the Storm Seamstress to Nell, opening the door with a key from a large ring of keys she carried at her waist. The room was small and simple, furnished with a little bed, a fireplace, a bookshelf with an eclectic assortment of things to read, and a porcelain washstand. Fresh clothes were folded on the bed, Nell noticed gratefully.

"It is not much," said Ely-Hathana. "But I hope you will be comfortable."

"I'm sure we will be," said Nell. "Thank you."

"Your room is down the hall," said Ely-Hathana to Charlie. "Sleep well," she said to Nell.

Parting was painful. In spite of all the long looks, hand-holding, and silly grinning, they hadn't had a moment alone since Swarn's dragon had swooped out of the sky and frightened the Verr mon Noorden. Nell let go of Charlie's hand reluctantly. He gave a helpless shrug.

"I will lock the door behind you," said Ely-Hathana. "You will be quite safe here."

Nell stood alone in the center of the room while the key turned in the lock. She heard Ely-Hathana's sweet, low voice murmuring spells outside the door, and then her footsteps and Charlie's disappearing down the hall. She washed herself off at the washstand and left her furs heaped on the floor. She decided to sleep in the clean dress they had put on the bed, since there was nothing else to wear. It was a simple, cotton sheath, and fit her well enough, though made for someone taller. She lay down and stretched out luxuriously. How good it felt to lie in a bed, to be safe and clean and fed.

She expected to fall asleep quickly, but her mind was too busy and would not let her rest. She was worried about Eliza, but hopeful that Swarn's dragon had arrived in time to help her. She wondered about the dark-headed creatures she had spotted in the water as they flew over the Far Sea to Lil and the deep bellowing noise they made. This was some kind of sea mammal entirely unknown in Di Shang. She was relieved to be with Swarn, who was surely powerful enough to protect Charlie from the Thanatosi. And above all, she was preoccupied with kissing.

Nell had been kissed before. It had been pleasant, if faintly absurd, with Julian, and then rather too sloppy and wet with Oscar, whose breath was further not reliably fresh. For some reason she had feared Jalo's kiss even while she'd been curious about it. But in each case she had been passive, accepting or refusing the kiss of another. She had never understood what it was to *want* to kiss somebody until now, and the thought of it had been present every moment since Charlie had brushed her hair out of her eyes as they raced through the Irahok mountains. She laughed thinking of the clumsy kiss she'd planted on his chin while he looked up, and she felt she would not be able to wait until tomorrow to have a moment alone with him and kiss him properly. She knew it would be something entirely different from what she had experienced before, and to lie here all night, *not* kissing him, seemed simply unbearable. She got up at one point and tried the door, thinking to go down the hall and see if he too was still awake, but the doorknob was enchanted and she could not turn it. It was all very well to be protected from intruders; she was less pleased at being trapped.

She went back to bed, but sleep came slowly. She was finally beginning to relax, her mind emptying and her body growing heavy, when she became aware of a soft muttering outside her door. She rolled onto her side and said, "Charlie?"

There was the sound of the lock clicking aside and the door opened. A shadow crossed the room, swift as a bat. Before Nell could move she felt a strong hand around her throat, pinning her to the bed. A blade glinted in the moonlight that came in through the window.

"Now, Sorceress, I will cut the Urkleis from your very chest," hissed Gautelen.

CHAPTER
19

$\mathcal{E}$liza felt a breeze on her face, heard the swish of the waves washing against the shore. For one blissful moment, she imagined she had dozed off on the beach at Holburg. But the air was acrid here and the very ground hummed with Magic. This was not Holburg. She opened her eyes.

Beneath a fringe of overhanging leaves, she saw the pebbly shore sloping down to the sea. The water was a dark, metallic grey, ridged with pointed waves. A huge dragon, rust red, skimmed over its surface, turning and swooping. Eliza crawled out from under the bush and found the white bones of last night's supper, a fish she had enchanted out of the water. Every part of her hurt, but she felt refreshed in her mind, and hungry again.

She remembered, now, how they had come here. Like an arrow shot from a giant bow, the dragon had borne her into the mountains, leaving the Mancers and the Faeries flapping uselessly behind on their smaller dragons and myrkestras. They had flown over the foothills and the land of the Giants, where battles raged and great fortresses smoldered. She had clung to the black spike on the dragon's neck with what little strength she had left, her only thought being that if this dragon had found her, then the other dragon would surely have found Charlie and Nell, and they would be safe, for now, from the Thanatosi.

She took the Faery box out of her backpack and opened it to make sure she still had the two Gehemmis. There they were: the flat sliver of bone and the glass orb full of fog. The fog formed symbols, and symbols were scratched on the surface of the bone, but they were not the same symbols and she did not recognize any of them.

The dragon coasted over the water on its huge wings and landed near her on the shore, lowering its head so that she could climb onto its neck. It swiveled its head round to look at her and she pointed the direction with her dagger.

The Isle of the Blind Enchanter was a sickle-shaped island at the southern end of the inland sea, its white cliffs jutting high up out of the water. Covered in wildflowers and birds, it was largely uninhabited but for the dragons that nested there and the Blind Enchanter himself.

As they neared the island, Eliza saw that the pebbled coves and ravines were crowded with small gold-green dragons. They lifted their heads and screamed as the rust-red dragon of the Cliffs of Batt soared over their island. The Yellow Mountains on the southern shore of the inland sea, so-called for the golden flowers blanketing their slopes, created a dramatic backdrop. A stone cabin stood at the highest point on the island. Swarn's dragon landed there, swiveling its head around defensively. As Eliza leaped to the ground, the door of the cabin opened and the Blind Enchanter strode out to meet her.

He was not what Eliza had expected. He looked like a body-builder, tall as a Mancer and twice as broad, his head a clean-shaven dome. He had a great square face with a powerful jaw, and beneath beetling black eyebrows, his eyes were white and sight-less. He wore a sleeveless leather vest that was giving out at the seams and a pair of threadbare trousers. He approached her with enormous hands stretched out in welcome and sniffed the air once or twice with a long, agile nose to determine her direction.

"We have been...expecting you...Sorceress," he said. His voice cracked and wheezed, and it seemed to cost him a great effort to get the words out. "Welcome."

"Then Foss is here?" she asked, relieved. "He's well?"

"He is as well as a...Mancer can be...in exile," said the Blind Enchanter. "Which is to say...he is...still alive."

He placed his hand over Eliza's face, his big fingers feeling her features. His palm smelled of some kind of oil or sap.

"You are...young," he said, his voice giving out on the final word and collapsing into a whisper that made it sound rather sinister. He turned abruptly and led her indoors.

The cabin was as simple on the inside as it was on the outside. There was a large hearth with some rough-hewn chairs around it at one end, and a bed at the other end. A long wood table took centre space, and there sat Ferghal, pulling the hard shells off a heap of nuts and popping them into his mouth by the handful.

"Witchlet!" he cried, rising and spilling shells everywhere. "Though I have been told numerous times by our good host that you are *more than that*, he says it so, *more than that*, and tells me you are a Sorceress. Well, and I say, my people of Scarpatha have never been averse to a Sorceress! So if you be a pint-sized Sorceress with powers more formidable than I have seen then I congratulate you, for it is good in such worlds as these to have some power to set one apart and defend oneself against disaster. I have never been able to defend myself against disaster and yet I have a capacity for carrying on in spite of disaster that I think is likely rare…ah, but you are looking past me, you are worried about the sickly Mancer. Well, see for yourself, he is not well at all. It grieves me, for I have become quite attached to him. The blind chap is not much help, though it is generous of him to put us up and put up with us. Do you know, there are dragons all over the beaches so you must be careful. I dare not venture far from the house, for they are very fierce-looking indeed…"

Eliza had already crossed the room to the bed. Foss lay very still, breathing shallowly. His skin was ash-grey, stretched thin over the bones of his face, his hair limp and lusterless. When she touched him he opened his eyes. Dim light glimmered out as if from a great distance, a fading red, like the last glow of an ember before it goes out. Eliza put her backpack down next to the bed.

"I have the Gehemmis from the Realm of the Faeries," she told him.

Foss wetted his lips and struggled to speak.

"It's all right," she said. "Just rest, lah."

But as she drew away his hand came out from under the

covers, reaching for her. She leaned down and he whispered in her ear, a faint rattle: "Good girl."

Her eyes were warm with tears. She squeezed his hand. "You need your rest."

Foss wetted his lips again and whispered something she could barely make out, but she thought he said *Get the others*.

She couldn't bear to see him this way. She patted his shoulder and turned away from him. The Blind Enchanter and Ferghal were eating nuts at the table. She sat down next to the Blind Enchanter and said in a low voice: "He's much worse. Isn't there anything you can do for him?"

"No," said the enchanter bluntly. "Such is the...nature...of the Mancer. He will...not live much...longer."

"You must not let him die, little witchlet," said Ferghal urgently, leaning across the table towards her and throwing nuts into his mouth at great speed, as if he could save Foss by eating. "I sometimes fancy I can see the soul of a being, it is a sort of gift that I possess. He is a noble one and he must live. You must work some clever Magic and save him. This blind chap, he can hardly speak a word, he cannot see, what can he do? *You* must save him, witchlet."

Eliza took some nuts. Her mouth was dry and her appetite gone, but she needed to keep her strength up. She wished the Blind Enchanter would offer her a hot meal.

"I'm going to go South," she said to the enchanter. "I need your help, if you'll give it. I need you to tell me how I can reach the Hanging Gardens. And...what is the Sparkling Deluder?"

The Blind Enchanter shook his head a few times, opening and closing his mouth. His white eyes rolled about in his head. It was tremendously difficult for him to make the small speech. Sometimes his voice broke on a word like a wave against a rock, scattering. Sometimes it cracked and soared unexpectedly, and sometimes he lost all breath so that no sound came out at all, but Eliza managed to get the general gist of it.

"There is no...song. There are no...words. What more...can I see...after what I saw...there? What can I...say...of that which is...beyond language? But I will...tell you...what I can. There are four…lakes…Sorceress…and you must…go…to each of them. The first is…the Lake of Sweet…Lies. The second…is the Lake…of Hope. The third is…the Lake…of Awful…Truths… and last of…all is the…Lake of the…Deep…Forgotten. If you go to each…lake and…learn what it…has…to show you… without…surrendering to…delusion or…despair…then you will be…taken to the…cave of the…Beginnings. There…you will know…what you are. If you are…worthy the…Vermilion Bird… will take you across…the Dreaming Wasteland. You…cannot cross it…alone. Those that returned…mad…never saw the… Hanging Gardens…but lost themselves…in the Dreaming Wasteland. Only…the Vermilion Bird…can take you to…the Hanging Gardens."

"And then?"

"Then you…give yourself up. What else can you…do? If you go…you go with faith…and you surrender yourself…to what will be. Your will is…nothing."

"But you *saw* the Sparkling Deluder? What kind of being is he…or she?"

"All song and…sight I…left there," said the Enchanter. "There is no…more for me to…see…or sing. You are…young. You should not…go."

"I have to," said Eliza.

"She has to!" echoed Ferghal. "To help the poor dying Mancer!"

"Wait," said the Enchanter. He got up and left, striding out into the bright afternoon. His physical vigor seemed such a surprise, compared to his weak and failing voice.

Eliza looked at Ferghal, who was still shoveling nuts into his mouth. She took a few more.

"Thank you for bringing Foss here," she said.

"'Twas a great adventure!" Ferghal enthused. "We were given donkeys by those peculiar people in black. They have no eyelids, had you noticed? Most unsettling, when you can see nothing but the eyes, and the eyes have no lids. Your Mancer was weak, but we went on donkeys all along the great black cliffs, ah, for days!

Through the mountains we travelled, hunting and foraging for our food. We came to the sea and I built a raft with my own hands! Thought I had seen all there was to see of the world, and now here is another world. Terrible creatures live in the mountains, nasty things with black wings, but they seemed afeared of the Mancer and left us be. I fear for him, little witchlet, for he gets weaker by the day. We have not had a conversation of any kind since we reached the sea, and while this blind chap is a decent sort, it grates the ear to hear him talk."

Ferghal continued to relate the adventures they'd had on their journey for some time, until the Blind Enchanter returned with four stones in his large palm.

"This is the…most I can do…for you," he rasped. "I have… enchanted…the stones. Throw one…in each lake…to clear the… image and…pass on. It will…speed your journey."

"Thank you," said Eliza. She took the stones and put them in her pockets. "I'd hoped I could rest here tonight, but I dinnay think there's time. I should go right away, lah."

"Yes indeed, witchlet. Go and find a cure for our friend here," Ferghal urged her.

Eliza longed to stay the night but she was terrified that if she did, Foss would be dead when she woke up. And so she said goodbye, returning to Foss's bedside to kiss his cold cheek. This time he did not open his eyes, but he found her hand with his and clasped it with a weak pressure.

She left her camel hair backpack containing the two Gehemmis in the care of Ferghal and the Blind Enchanter and told them to hide it, reckoning it was as safe with them as with her, if not safer. Swarn's dragon carried her over the strip of grey sea between the island and the shore, and as dusk fell it flew into the Yellow Mountains, following a stream of ravens that cried out in the dark. The Hanging Gardens of the Sparkling Deluder twinkled on the southern horizon. They seemed just as far as they had always seemed, the glimmer of an unreachable world. Eliza's heart thudded in her chest as she imagined herself returning changed, unable to speak or see, perhaps, or unrecognizable as her former self. But there could be no turning back now. What kind of life would be left to her if she lost both Foss and Charlie? What would be the point, then, of remaining Eliza? They spent the night in the mountains and carried on before first light.

The ravens landed at last on the shore of the first lake, and the dragon a little further back. Eliza had seen these lakes on rough maps of Tian Xia, though they were named only in the Songs of the Wayfaring Rhapsodist. This first lake, the Lake of Sweet Lies as he called it, was the largest, almost like a small sea. The Yellow Mountains surrounded it, soaring high and gold into the brightening sky, the first light of dawn glimmering to the east. Birds sang and bees buzzed and dipped among yellow, white, and purple wildflowers. A gentle breeze was blowing. The ground was wet with dew that soaked Eliza's shoes. A myriad of small creeks ran down from the mountaintops and fed into the lake, and Eliza had to leap over a number of these to get close to the water. The dragon knew better than to get too close. It had landed a fair distance from the lake, and the next time Eliza looked over her shoulder she saw it had taken to the sky again, a dark shadow against the mountains. Her heart sank. It was leaving her here.

A short distance down the shore she saw two figures walking hand in hand. Their heads were close together and they were talking softly. There was something familiar about them. She reached into her pocket and took one of the Blind Enchanter's stones in her hand. The pair did not seem dangerous, however, and she was loath to disturb them, for they seemed so intimate. So she stayed still as they drew closer, and gradually she could make out their faces. Her heart began to beat a little faster.

There was herself, smiling and soft-faced, walking hand in hand with Charlie. She knew without asking that the danger was gone, that he knew everything and felt as she did. The Eliza holding hands with Charlie looked up at the Eliza surrounded by ravens and laughed kindly. "You didnay need to be so afraid," the other Eliza said. "All you had to do was tell him, aye."

Charlie looked up at her too, tearing his eyes away from the other Eliza.

"It's funny to think that all that time we were thinking the same thing, lah, but too afraid to say so," he said. The Eliza holding his hand laid her head on his shoulder.

"You could stay with us if you wanted to," said Charlie. "We owe her that, nay?" he said to the other Eliza, who murmured something into his neck.

Eliza felt her heart harden as she watched them. "But you are sweet lies," she said in a clipped little voice. She tightened her fist around the stone in her hand.

"What would you prefer?" asked the other Eliza. "Bitter truth? Life is too short."

"Reality is all in our perception of it, aye," said Charlie. "Who are you to say what is real and what isnay? How can you judge? Look."

He leaned to kiss the other Eliza, who tilted her head up to meet his lips, her mouth soft, her body bending into his. Eliza could not watch. She turned away from this happier self and hurled the stone the Blind Enchanter had given her, into the clear water of the lake. Where it splashed, a slender boat emerged.

"Are you leaving?" she heard Charlie's voice behind her. She felt his hand in hers. "If you go," he said, "I'll never see you again."

She could not see through her tears. She splashed through the water to the boat and climbed in. The boat carried her across the lake as the sun rose high into the sky, leaving her beloved Charlie and that other, happy Eliza hand in hand on the shore.

The lake narrowed, and the leafy trees on either side of it bent over the water, creating a sort of tunnel. Then the passageway widened out again into another lake. The water here was clear and still, reflecting the Yellow Mountains and the verdant shore, shimmering in the sudden summer heat. A breeze disturbed the surface of the water, breaking the mountains into streams of gold light, and when the lake stilled again Eliza saw something altogether different reflected there. Now she saw her mother walking freely along the path that led from their old house to Holburg town. She could see her father's garden flourishing, and the little house that had been home once. She could almost hear the buzz of the bees. She leaned over the edge of the boat and another breeze smoothed the image away. She saw Charlie and Nell skipping rocks and she heard their laughter echoing over the water. Nell's voice said clearly: "I passed the test, aye, so I'll be starting at Austermon in the fall. You two will have to visit." She leaned further, then caught herself and sat up suddenly. Foss was in the boat with her, his back straight, his eyes white fire.

"You're nay real," she said, her voice catching.

"A strange notion," he smiled, kindly. "Of course, I am dying on the Isle of the Blind Enchanter, but it doesn't necessarily follow that here I am not *real*."

The lake widened into a blue sea, and the sky overhead was blue as well. She looked up at it gratefully. How she missed the Di Shang sky when she was away from it! The boat bobbed on the waves, and Holburg lay green and beckoning on the water. Her heart leapt.

"If it's real in some way, can we go to Holburg?" she asked, plying the oars.

Foss glanced over his shoulder at the island. "I don't think you can go there," he said. "This is hope, not the fulfillment of hope."

"I dinnay see the point of this," she said wearily, letting go of the oars. "I want my friends to be safe and happy, aye. I want my mother to be well, aye. I want you to be well, aye. I wish I could go back to Holburg, aye. I know all that. Why do I have to row along a lake and see visions of it?"

Foss looked at the island again. "Why only *wish* you could go back? Surely you can go back whenever you like."

"But not to live. Lah, I spose I could live there, but it's different now. My father isnay there. Nell isnay there."

"So the people, not the place, are most important to you. And you have them in your life even without the island."

Eliza laughed. "You must be real after all," she said. "That's some very Foss-like logic. Lah, all right then, I wish for that time in my life when the people I loved were together in the place I loved."

"Before you knew you were a Sorceress," said Foss.

"Yes."

"And back then, what did you hope for?"

"I dinnay know. I was twelve. I wanted to stay in Holburg forever. Nell was the one plotting all the things we'd do when we grew up, aye, all the places we'd go. I didnay want anything to change."

"But this is not the lake of nostalgia, or the lake of longing, or even the lake of wishes. This is the lake of hope. How can you hope for that life? You are not a child anymore."

She clenched her fist around a second stone. "I didnay pick the vision," she said.

"But it is your task to understand it, is it not?" said Foss.

"Or I could just use this." She took the stone from her pocket.

"Certainly," he agreed mildly. "But would you be worthy, then, of the journey to follow?"

She gazed at the island across the water, the lookout tree clearly visible on the southern cliffs.

"Holburg is stillness," she said at last. "And safety. All my life I'd travelled with no purpose. We were fleeing and hiding, but I never knew why. And then we were home, and we were safe. At least, that's how it felt, aye." She looked straight into his brilliant eyes. "Until the Mancers came."

"That is what you hope for? To feel safe again?"

"For my world to have limits again. To be finished with all this. I hope for an end point, a destination, a place to belong. To feel like I've arrived and I can stay."

"The life of a Sorceress is perpetual struggle," said Foss. "With forces both external and internal."

"I know," she said. When she looked at the water it raced with images of those she loved. She stood up in the boat and took one last look at Foss, strong and powerful, as she might never see him again. Then she hurled the stone at the island. It broke apart and she was alone in the boat, which carried her swiftly across the length of the lake and down another narrow corridor of water.

This next lake was the smallest yet. Brilliant leaves fell from the trees along the shore and swirled in the chilly wind. She did not look at the water. She held the third stone firmly in her hand and stared straight up.

The sky over her was a glass dome. Through it she saw Kyreth, like a giant looking down on her, his eyes great pools of white fire. Malferio's pale face sneered behind him. They were looking at her, she understood instantly, through the Vindensphere.

"I wondered if we would meet here." Kyreth's voice resonated through the trees and the shore and made ripples on the lake. "It appears that I am to be the teller of truths you would rather not hear. Fitting."

"Who are you talking to?" Malferio looked confused.

"Does he know what you're planning to do?" Eliza demanded, and Malferio looked down at her, shocked.

"Can she hear us?"

"He knows," said Kyreth. "I could not do it without his consent. Immortality is not easily stolen."

"We're getting rid of Sorceresses," said Malferio. "It's our campaign. A noble cause to die for."

Eliza noticed how glassy his eyes were, his cheeks slack. She felt sick.

"Tell me the awful truth, then," she said. "I want to get out of here."

"To begin with," said Kyreth, "you are doing very well. You have two of the Gehemmis already. This third will be the most difficult, I think."

"What do the Gehemmis do?"

Kyreth smiled again. "I am not an Oracle. I am not here for you to ask questions of. I am here to tell you the truth, not necessarily what you want to hear, but what you need to know."

"Right," she said flatly. Malferio had retreated, bored. "The awful truth."

"Let us begin with the Book of Barriers," said Kyreth. "You

took it to Nia in exchange for your father's life. It didn't work out the way you had expected, in the end, but you knew that the Book of Barriers might enable her to free herself, and that, free, she would be a force of massive destruction. Did you ever wonder if what you did was right? If your father's life was worth many lives?"

"Oh," said Eliza. "We're going to go over my mistakes? That's nay so bad. No, I didnay give it much thought. I couldnay know what would happen if Nia had the book, I just knew I would do anything to help my da. But obviously, it was stupid of me."

"Stupidity is far from the point," said Kyreth. "Your father's life was all that mattered to you. The consequences, the price that *others* might have to pay as a result of your actions, you did not deem worthy of consideration."

"I thought he was going to die," said Eliza. "I'm nay making excuses…I didnay know what else to do."

"Indeed," said Kyreth. "What of the Cra?"

"The Cra?"

"They have a name for you, you know. *An-murth*. It means blade of death."

Eliza said nothing.

"Abimbola Broom. You considered the merciful option, I am sure. Handing him over to the Sorma. But instead you punished him, and his family with him."

Eliza clenched her jaw. "Dinnay ask me to feel sorry for him."

"I am not asking you to. Merely pointing out that you don't. Do you think Jalo will go unpunished for your theft of the Gehemmis? He helped you."

"If I'm in an impossible situation, that's your fault," she replied.

"Amarantha is back in the worlds. Witches will have a name for you too, when word spreads about the forest. Will you stop at nothing?"

She lifted her chin. "Nothing," she said.

"You would kill me without hesitation if it would save your friend, I don't doubt."

"It wouldnay take that much."

"Ah! There is my girl. Do you think you can claim to be *good*, Eliza?"

"I try to be," she said. "Which is more than can be said for some."

"No points for effort!" came Malferio's voice. "How much longer is this going to take?"

"What is most important to you?" asked Kyreth. "To know love, to be good, or to *do* good?"

"To know love," she answered immediately. "But that's not to say I dinnay care about being a good person. I try, lah. I do. You should come down here and see what the lake tells *you*. I spec you'd be surprised. Or praps you wouldnay be."

"Rea would have said that pure intent is the most important thing," said Kyreth. "To *be* good. She and I differed there. I took the longer view. Our actions are all that touch the world, all that will be remembered when we are gone. To *do* good has been my aim, and whatever I had to *be*, myself, to achieve those aims, I accepted. But when history judges your actions, Eliza, when your story is written into the Chronicles of the Sorceress, what will it say? There will be a list of careless, selfish acts. You will go down in history as a lying, murdering thief who cared only for her friends and family and did nothing for the worlds."

"Praps," said Eliza. She shook with the echoes of the screaming trees, the bones of the Cra breaking, their black blood, the Kwellrahg stumbling in the sand, Abimbola Broom on his knees before her. Nia saying *Eliza, don't do this to me.* "Praps."

"But perhaps all of that will be overshadowed, forgotten," said Kyreth. "When you bring me the Gehemmis."

She hurled the stone at the sky, shattering it. The world rained down in pointed shards and the current carried her fast to the next lake, which was half-frozen. The sky was hidden by a dark reddish cloud covering. The boat moved for a while among shifting plates of ice and eventually got stuck. There was somebody waiting among the evergreens on the snowy shore. Eliza got out of the boat and made her way carefully over the ice, across the lake. She knew who was waiting long before she was close enough to really see her. She knew because the Urkleis in her chest had begun to throb.

"Hello, Smidgen," said Nia when she reached the shore. "The Lake of the Deep Forgotten! Fancy seeing you here."

CHAPTER

20

Kyreth rose, the Vindensphere in pieces at his feet.

"That was strange," said Malferio, who had scuttled back towards the wall when it shattered. "How did she do that?"

"It is almost finished," said Kyreth. His hands were trembling and the brilliance of his eyes turned the room almost white. "I must go."

"Go?" shrieked Malferio. He snatched up the empty pipe and waved it at Kyreth. "Go where? You can't leave me! I need my dose. I can feel this scratching behind my eyes and the shadows are turning nasty again."

Kyreth looked at Malferio almost as if he was looking through him.

"You will be taken care of, too, Malferio. That is one of my errands. I have chosen a suitable killer for you."

"Don't talk about it!" Malferio screamed, panicking. "Give me my dose!"

"Soon we will have the four Gehemmis and the Shang Sorceress here in the Citadel," said Kyreth. "If she succeeds…she *must* succeed."

"You're not listening to me!" Malferio hurled the pipe at Kyreth. Kyreth knocked it aside with a casual wave of the hand.

"It is a pity about the Vindensphere," he murmured. "I had hoped to take it with me. Never mind."

"Take it where?" Malferio had curled up on the bed and was looking at Kyreth like a miserable dog.

"To Tian Xia," said Kyreth.

The floor opened up into stairs and Kyreth swept down them.

"Don't leave me without my dose!" wept Malferio as the floor closed up again.

Swarn, Uri, and Ely-Hathana stood on the hill looking down on the dark island.

"The Thanatosi may not be susceptible to Magic affecting the senses," said Swarn. She was not satisfied with the spell they had worked, which was supposed to refract the essence of a being so that seeking spells and enchanted objects such as the Vindensphere could not locate them. "Nobody knows how they find their prey. It may not be the essence at all that draws them, but some other kind of knowing."

"Well, if it doesn't work, there are the barriers we raised around the house," said Uri cheerfully.

"I do not have great faith in our barriers," Swarn answered. "We would need a Mancer to keep them up for long."

"They won't manage a sneak attack with the barriers up," said Uri. "And remember, we have two Storm Seamstresses here! They can bring a typhoon down on the Thanatosi, a gale that will sweep them away. No doubt you have a few tricks up your sleeve as well." He eyed her shrewdly.

"You should rest," said Ely-Hathana, laying a hand on Swarn's arm. Swarn wanted to shake off the friendly touch, but resisted the urge. There was no point offending her hosts. They meant well.

"I will keep watch," said Swarn.

The wizard and the Storm Seamstress returned to the house, arm in arm, and Swarn remained on the hill. It was a beautiful island, but she was uncomfortable with beauty. She missed the barren marsh.

The marsh was a mass grave now, her dragons buried in the swampy ground. After the battle with Nia that had nearly killed her, she had rebuilt her house high on the cliffs, the Irahok mountains hanging over her threateningly, and she relearned what it was to be lonely. She felt she had come to the natural end of a confused and arid life. But she did not die. She lived, wounded, weaker, with only two dragons remaining. The emptiness ahead yawned open every morning when she woke from her dreamless sleep.

Swarn was born with the fight in her. As a young witch, she found relief only in battle. She could not bear to be still. She could not bear company. Her power was a tumult in her veins, a storm that had to be released, one way or another. When facing a dangerous opponent, the restlessness and rage that chafed her unforgivingly in her ordinary life fell away. It all narrowed down to the fight, only the fight. She did not fear death. She did not fear anything. That steely stillness at her core was the closest she came to knowing peace, and victory, every time victory, the closest she came to joy.

The dragons of the cliffs of Batt were the most beautiful creatures she had ever encountered, and the most deadly. In her first battle with a dragon, she brushed up against death and discovered her will to live. She wanted to live! It seemed a revelation. The dragon was wild and vicious and full of magic – like her. She stretched her power to its very limits to defeat the dragon, and for the first time she felt real kinship with another creature.

Swarn did not give the notorious Sorceress Nia much thought until Nia murdered Swarn's sister, Audra. Swarn and Audra had never been close, but they understood each other, and there was something in that. She wanted to go and fight Nia – a great battle such as those she had known in the past. But together Malferio and the Oracle persuaded her that this was useless. Nia was Immortal and possessed the power of Illusion. She was far more powerful than Swarn and would surely defeat her. They could not kill her, but together they could banish her.

Taken aback by her own grief and rage, Swarn accepted the proposal. She took her sister's place in the Triumvira, and so Nia was banished. Swarn returned to the marsh with a sense of failure and a deep loneliness weighing on her heart. Who was she, if not a warrior? Who knew her, now Audra was gone?

One day there was a terrible battle on the cliffs. A witch and a dragon, she heard. When she arrived, the dragon was already bowed in submission. A young woman of no more than fifteen or sixteen years old stood before the creature, her pale face flushed with triumph. She wore a black tunic and her long red hair hung in a thick plait down her back. She bore no weapon but a white staff.

"I've heard of you," said the girl, speaking the Language of First Days. "My name is Rea. I want you to teach me."

Swarn refused, but Rea was not to be put off. She claimed to be the Shang Sorceress, ward of the Mancers. She had sought Swarn out in secret to learn the secrets of combat and potions. Intrigued, flattered, disarmed, at last Swarn agreed to take her on as a pupil. It was immediately apparent that the girl was brilliant, far more powerful and intelligent than anyone Swarn had ever encountered. She lacked only experience.

They talked more than Swarn had ever talked, but it was not idle conversation. Every word had weight, *meant* something, and Rea knew how to be silent too. It was companionship of a kind Swarn had never known. She liked to cook with Rea and hear her tell of Di Shang. They learned each other's languages. Swarn felt her world expand with an entire new vocabulary. Soon she found herself missing Rea when she was gone, looking forward to her return.

Yes, it was fair to say that she had loved Rea. Perhaps she had never loved anyone else but Rea, in her long life. Eliza had invited her to come to Di Shang and visit her mother but Swarn did not, could not. Perhaps Rom was content with what little remained of his wife, perhaps the mere reminder of the woman she had been was enough for him, but not for Swarn. The Rea she loved had been crushed, and that was the end of it. She developed a fondness for her daughter, a sense of responsibility, but Eliza was not nearly so gifted, nor so pure in heart and thought and deed. She was a confused, emotional child, overburdened with her power, out of place in the worlds. Swarn felt a kind of warmth and a kind of pity for her, but her tired old heart could not bear to love again.

The loss of Rea left her bitter, brittle; Nia's slaughter of the dragons broke something in her. Their beauty had been what bound her to the world; now they were gone. She went to face Nia to die and Eliza saved her, saved her life. Swarn returned to the marsh with the last of the cliff dragons, but she was changed. She had become old. Swarn thought she was waiting to die, but now, in Lil, she realized it was not death she was waiting for. It was something else whose time had come around.

She had survived all these years in order to perform a greater task. Not to die in a vengeful battle. If there was such a thing as destiny, her destiny was beckoning. She felt it. And if nothing was preordained, then her own free will tugged her in one clear and obvious direction. She had waited too long, stayed too still. Now it was time to act.

Her train of thought was shattered by a high scream coming from the house. She drew her knife from her belt and placed it between her teeth as she ran across the lawn, climbed swiftly up the outside wall, and hurled herself through the window, rolling across the floor and back to her feet in a shower of glass, the knife in her hand now.

Gautelen screamed a Curse at Swarn, but it was clumsy and half-formed, easily brushed aside. She was on top of Eliza's friend, a blade in her hand. Nell was holding her wrists, struggling and screaming.

Charlie burst through the door and Gautelen swung Nell in front of her, holding the blade to her throat now and facing the other two.

"No Magic!" she cried. "If I hear a spell I will cut her throat before you finish!"

"Wait," Swarn commanded her. "Do not be foolish. I will show you something to change your mind."

"Don't!" cried Gautelen. Her eyes were panicked and the hand that held the knife was trembling. Nell was staring straight at Charlie, who looked from her to Swarn with a desperate, pleading expression.

"Do you see this?" Swarn pulled something white and oblong,

like a small flute, from her belt and showed it to Gautelen.

"Stop it!" cried Gautelen, pressing the knife to Nell's throat. "Put it away!"

Nell and Charlie recognized the object, for Swarn had given Eliza one just like it. The poor girl, thought Swarn – she was so young, she had never hurt anybody before – she hardly knew how. Before any of them could move or speak, Swarn had the object at her lips and blew softly. A dart struck Gautelen in the neck and she fell to the ground, paralyzed.

Nell ran straight into Charlie's arms and he held her tight. They were both shaking. Uri mon Lil appeared at the door moments later.

"What has happened?" he cried, running to Gautelen.

"I can only assume she took Nell for the Shang Sorceress," said Swarn. "She is paralyzed. It will wear off in a few hours."

Ely-Hathana followed in an elaborate white nightdress and looked murder at Swarn. Uri mon Lil stood hastily between them.

"We will get Gautelen to her room," he said.

They spent the rest of the night in the visitor's parlour, sipping hot tea made from wildflowers native to Lil. Nell was not inclined to feel particularly charitable towards the young woman who had held a knife to her throat, hoping to murder Eliza. She wanted to ask what in the worlds was the matter with Gautelen but she held her tongue, looking from Uri mon Lil pacing back and forth with his crinkled brow to Ely-Hathana hanging onto the arms of her chair as if she thought she might fall out of it. Swarn stood straight-backed and expressionless by the door. Charlie nodded off on the sofa, the teacup tipping out of his hands. Nell gasped, but before the cup spilled it righted itself and flew across the room to the table. She supposed there was not much danger of spills or accidents in such company.

"What?" Charlie mumbled, waking up at her gasp.

"Nothing." Nell smiled at him in spite of herself.

He looked at Uri and Ely-Hathana, rubbed a hand across his face, and said: "I spec it must be hard for you to understand why she's acting this way."

Ely-Hathana gave him a poisonous look and said nothing.

"What do you mean?" asked Uri mon Lil.

"I mean, lah, I dinnay think either of you have ever met Nia, have you?" said Charlie.

"I *saw* her, in her final battle with the Shang Sorceress," said Uri. "But we were not, ah, formally introduced, so I suppose I cannot say I have *met* her."

"I have not met her," said Ely-Hathana. "But she has enchanted my child somehow."

"Nay enchanted, exactly," said Charlie. "A long time ago Nia freed me, too, from a different kind of bondage. I thought I was going to be trapped for all eternity with no free will..." He glanced uneasily at Swarn, who showed no sign that she was listening. She knew his history with her sister Audra, and with Nia. "And then Nia gave my freedom back to me. When she's on your side, she's really prize charming. I served her for a long time, willingly, because she was the face of my salvation. I did some terrible things on her behalf, aye, the worst of them being that I almost got Eliza killed. So I can understand a little what your daughter is going through."

Nell could not keep quiet any longer. "I'm so glad you're able to sympathize with someone who had a knife to my throat an hour ago," she snapped.

"She didnay know who you were," said Charlie. "She doesnay even really know who Eliza is. She thought you were some kind of all-powerful Sorceress and that she was doing something really dangerous and brave to help Nia. Before I met you, when it was Nia against the Triumvira and Nia against the Mancers, it was easy to see her as a victim, lah, up against impossible odds. It was easy to take her side. It wasnay until she was gunning for Eliza that I started to see things differently."

"So you think there is hope for her? That she will come to see the truth of the matter?" said Uri eagerly.

Charlie shrugged uncomfortably. "Prolly. Eventually. Of course, I served Nia for about sixty years before changing sides, so it could take a while."

Uri's face fell. At the same moment, the water-apes set up a baleful howl around the island. Ely-Hathana rose and pulled aside the curtain, looking out.

"I cannot see," she said. "The night is too misty."

"Oh no!" Nell leaped to her feet and ran to the window. The mist was creeping up the hill.

"The barriers," said Uri, confused. "They have fallen."

"The Thanatosi could not have done it so quickly," said Swarn, feeling it too. "There is another power on this island. A great master of the art of barriers, I'll wager." She said this between gritted teeth.

"Away from the windows," said Ely-Hathana as the mist surrounded the house. "There is a secret passage in the basement, it travels under the island..." but she did not finish her sentence. The large windows shattered. White shapes with flying limbs and swinging blades came through them in a rain of arrows. Nell pushed Charlie down behind the broad cushioned settee, throwing herself over him to protect him. One of the Thanatosi, hair flying, leaped onto the back of the settee and swung his great shining sword down towards them. Then something came between them and the sword, deflecting the blow. Swarn swung and thrust a double-headed spear, placing herself before the settee and fighting off all comers.

"Get up!" she cried to Charlie and Nell. "We must go!"

They scrambled to their feet. Swarn tossed a handful of powder into the air. Everything went suddenly very black and still. Nell and Charlie each felt a hand close over their wrists, felt themselves pulled through the thick, heavy darkness, their thoughts swimming slowly: *Something is happening, but I dinnay know what. I dinnay remember.* By the time the potion wore off they were on the hillside, the Thanatosi coming after them, struggling out of the potion's hold. Swarn threw her head back and screamed, a raw and terrible sound. Out of the jungle surged the dragon. It breathed green fire into the mob of Thanatosi. Swarn, Charlie and Nell leaped onto the dragon's scaled back and it took off into the air. They left Lil behind them as the Thanatosi streamed down the hill towards the water.

For a time, Gautelen's mind was frozen. When it began to thaw and stir, she was in her own bedroom, on the bed, the door and window enchanted shut. She wiggled her fingers slowly. They hurt. Everything hurt as it came back to life, the poison within her dissipating. She sat up, nearly weeping with the agony of it. A grinding anger was working deep within her too. Her parents had betrayed her. They were playing host to Nia's enemies and had allowed a witch to harm her. She crawled from the bed to the floor to the door, and laid her hands flat against it. Strong enchantments. She knelt there and whispered spells to break the lock, but she was too weak still and collapsed, trembling, on the floor. Through a haze of tears, she saw a door appear in the wall where there had been no door before. The door opened and a shining being stepped through, all white and gold. She sat up again, pulling herself back against the wall.

"I know what you are," she said helplessly, her voice thick and slow in her mouth. "I have read about you. You are a Mancer."

"I am," agreed Kyreth. He went to the window and looked out at the night. "The Thanatosi are coming," he murmured, and glanced at Gautelen over his shoulder with a faint smile. "They have a task I would like to see finished."

Gautelen trembled. He had eyes like twin suns and a voice like a tolling bell. She did not know what he was talking about, but she knew Mancers were the Sorceress Nia's great enemies. The water-apes began to howl.

"Oh, you are wrong there," said Kyreth. He showed no sign of hearing the water-apes. "It is true that we were long at war with Nia, but some of us had reason to oppose the war. You see, I am her father."

"I don't believe you," whispered Gautelen. "Did my parents send for you? The Mancers are the guardians of the Shang Sorceress."

"Again, you are misinformed. Surely you have heard that the Shang Sorceress broke all ties with us? But that is not important. Your parents have no idea that I am here. I would not be welcome in the least. I am not here to discuss Sorceresses, Gautelen. They do not concern me now. I am concerned, rather, with a task that Nia left unfinished. I cannot finish it myself and so I need your help."

"What task?"

"Ending the life of Malferio, former King of the Faeries."

She drew in a sharp breath and tried to get to her feet. Her knees gave out beneath her and she sprawled at Kyreth's feet. He knelt swiftly.

"The Warrior Witch has served you a dose of her poison," he said. "We will see to that. Let me help you."

She felt his strong arms lift her up.

"I need you to be willing, Gautelen," he said. "Will you come to Di Shang with me? The Magic to end Malferio's life is prepared but I cannot administer the killing blow. Will you do it?"

"Gladly," she replied.

"Good. Look," he carried her to the window. She saw a mist swarming up the hill and around the house. There were white figures in the mist, leaping and spinning.

"What is it?" she asked.

"They will not harm your parents," he replied. The windows downstairs shattered. "Now we must go."

He took her out through the new door. Doors appeared wherever he seemed to wish them. In no time he was striding through the jungle, alive with night sounds, carrying her like a child down to a sheltered cove where a dragon waited.

Nell clung to Charlie, seated behind him on the dragon's back. She imagined falling and falling through the early morning sky to the sea below. She had read somewhere that when falling from a great height the shock kills you before the impact, and wondered if it was true.

"Where are we going?" Charlie shouted, for they had left all of Tian Xia behind them and the sea stretched to the horizon in every direction, a disc of green as far as the eye could see, ringed around with the fiery sky.

Swarn looked over her shoulder at him and said: "Where none will follow us."

They flew throughout the day, high over the sea, descending occasionally for Swarn to spear fish, which the dragon roasted for them with a single breath. As the sun began to sink towards the horizon, the green sea was flecked with crimson and gold. The dragon began to descend.

"Look!" Nell shouted, pointing.

Charlie had seen the same thing. "Islands!" he cried.

These must be the mythical dragon isles, thought Nell excitedly, although she saw no dragons. The islands were bright gold and the setting sun gave them a fiery tinge. They bore no sign of vegetation but soared up out of the water, barren and gleaming with jagged rocks. Swarn's dragon descended further, letting out a wrenching cry as it circled over the nearest island.

The island beneath them stirred. The tip of the island lengthened, more and more of it appearing, lifting up out of the water. Nell saw eyes as green as the sea, a terrible head at the end of a seemingly endless neck, which lifted higher and higher, water streaming off it. The head opened into a mouth, a mouth large enough to swallow them all, including the dragon they rode upon. Swarn's dragon was like an insect to this colossal creature. It let out a sound that rent the air, a sound that made Nell's heart stutter and her mind go black. And then all the islands lifted their heads, all of them dragons as big as cities. Vast wings opened up over the green sea and the air was full of unearthly cries.

CHAPTER

21

The white tiger snarled, baring red gums and tongue, slinking along the shore. Nia was wearing a fox-fur coat like when Eliza had found her in the Mancer Library. Her face was very white and she was shivering a little from the cold.

"Are you all right?" Eliza asked.

Nia raised her eyebrows. "A funny question, coming from you," she remarked. "I must say, it seems a cruel sort of irony that it should be winter here, as if I hadn't had enough of snow. And it appears that one can't work Illusion at the four lakes, so we'll just have to bear the cold."

"I'm sorry." Eliza wasn't sure what she was apologizing for. It came out before she thought about it.

A fallen tree lay along the shore, its upper branches disappearing into the ice of the lake. Nia brushed a patch of snow off the trunk and sat down. Eliza sat next to her.

"You've had a rough time, I suppose, with the last three lakes," said Nia. "And not enough sleep these past couple of weeks. Poor Smidgen. It's all over your face. You never were any good at covering up your feelings. So tell me: What did you see?"

Eliza hugged herself against the cold and fumbled for words that did not come at first. She felt strangely that in all the worlds, Nia was the only one to whom she could tell her secrets.

"The lake of sweet lies…" Nia prompted her.

"He doesnay love me," said Eliza. "Nay…like that."

"No, of course not. Oh Smidgen, how blind are you? It's touching but a bit pathetic. You'd better just get over him."

"How?"

Her tears turned cold on her cheeks. The white tiger paced up and down in front of them, growling.

"It seems impossible at first," said Nia. "You think that this one person's love is all you want, all you need to be whole. You think that without it you'll hunger your whole life. But here is the truth, Smidgen: you'll hunger your whole life anyway, no matter what. Someday it will be somebody else, but you'll find that the heart breaks a little easier every time, and heals a little faster each time too. I remember how it is the first time. For better or for worse, you'll never feel it again in quite the same way."

Eliza wept until she felt entirely empty, lighter than air. She slept a while, leaning against Nia. When she woke, she was lying on the ground wrapped in Nia's fox fur coat. The tiger was sniffing at the frozen lake and Nia was still sitting thoughtfully on the fallen tree trunk.

"What about the next lake?" Nia asked, almost as soon as Eliza's eyes had opened. "The lake of hope?"

"Everybody was safe and all right," said Eliza sleepily. "I saw Holburg, aye." She reached into her pocket for the final stone. Nia's hand was on her wrist, quick as a snake.

"Give it to me," she murmured. Eliza handed it over without thinking.

"Good girl. I must say, your hopes are modest. This is fascinating to me, you see. I've always longed to see the Hanging Gardens and the Sparkling Deluder. I went to visit the Blind Enchanter once, to see if he could help me, but he wouldn't speak at all. I thought about Cursing him horribly as punishment but it seemed sort of overkill, considering he's blind and can't sing a note anymore. I could have given him stabbing gut pains for the rest of his life but in the end I just left him be, thinking I'd try again another time. I don't see when I'll have a chance now, thanks to you."

"I'm sorry."

"Stop apologizing, it doesn't help a bit. Well, go on. What about the lake of awful truths?"

"Kyreth told me I'm a bad person," she said dully, sitting up and pulling Nia's coat tighter around her.

"Kyreth told you?" said Nia, her eyes flashing. "He should not be able to tell anybody anything. He should be living in the grip of a mindless, implacable terror."

"We got him out of that place," said Eliza, not looking at Nia. "After…afterwards. We took him back to the Citadel to free the Mancers from your Curse, and then…they've been helping him, aye. He's still Cursed, but nay like you meant him to be, I spose."

Nia's nostrils flared but she controlled her voice. "You know what he did. To me and to my mother."

"Yes," said Eliza.

"And now he is the bearer of an unwelcome message. Your idea of evil, come to tell you that you are not so perfect yourself."

"I nary thought I was," said Eliza. "At least I try to do the right thing. You nary tried."

"Perhaps that just makes me more self-aware, not more wicked," said Nia. "But you're welcome to think of yourself as the good Sorceress and me as the bad Sorceress, if you find that kind of thing comforting. So Kyreth was the messenger of Awful Truths. The Shade you're so fond of told you the Sweet Lies, I assume? Oh Smidgen, *do* control yourself. There is nothing less appealing than a powerful Sorceress with a trembling lower lip. Who brought you the message of hope?"

"Foss," Eliza managed.

"Poor thing, you're really on the edge, aren't you? I'm not even going to ask about it. But in any case, it makes sense, doesn't it? He was your teacher and, unlike the other Mancers, he always accepted you for yourself. What he wanted most was your happiness, I imagine, and so of course he should bring hope. Now we are at the lake of the Deep Forgotten. So why are you seeing me?"

"I dinnay know. Are you really here?"

"As much as I can be anywhere," said Nia with a shrug. "Come on, Smidgen, don't be obtuse. Why would *I* be *here?*"

The snowy trees were full of ravens looking down at them.

"What have you forgotten, Smidgen?"

"My ma," said Eliza. "I dinnay remember my ma from when

I was a baby. And what she was then…is mostly inside you, now."

"Clever girl."

It was not Nia's voice. Eliza looked at her in astonishment. Nia was gone. A red fox sat alertly where the tiger had been and Rea stood in the snow, looking down at Eliza. Not Rea as she was now – this Rea looked more like the portrait of her in the Mancer Citadel. Her face was younger, pale and serious, but mostly it was the way she carried herself that was unfamiliar. Eliza was struck by the resolute way she put her shoulders back, her feet planted on the ground with a kind of righteous certainty, her hazel eyes intense and penetrating, like she was not merely looking *at* Eliza or the lake or the trees, but looking *into* them.

Rea knelt swiftly and cupped a hand around Eliza's face. Her hand was very cold and her breath puffed out in plumes of white mist.

"So like your father," she said. "And I don't just mean the way you look. I mean the way you love. If it weren't for the power, I'd hardly believe you were mine."

Eliza could not move. This was her mother before she was beaten and broken and unmade, but even seeing her here could not bring back the memories that were buried too far in the past to retrieve, hidden behind everything that had happened since.

"You were so young, just a baby," said Rea. "I was your world and you were mine. That's how it is between a mother and child at that time. But I knew about the rest of the world, too. I couldn't stop living in it even if I wanted to. I didn't have the right. It was my duty, my calling, to protect the world before even my own daughter."

"I know that," whispered Eliza. "I'm nay angry."

She knew as she said it that it was a lie. Rea smiled wryly at her. She did not look as if she smiled much. She stood up and squinted out over the lake. Eliza staggered to her feet as well.

"I was your world, and I left you and never returned. That was what you grew up with: that lack, that loss. You don't remember the loss, not exactly, but you cling to those you love with such ferocity, you would die for them, because the memory of that first loss is buried within you, and it defines you."

It felt like cracking up the center. It felt like death. Some memory stirred, somewhere deep.

"It's nay really you," said Eliza desperately.

"Of course not," said Rea. "I'm gone forever."

A wave of fury washed over Eliza, washed away everything else. Her voice burst out of her like a wild thing from a cage: "How could you leave me? Why did you go?"

"I believed I would come back," said Rea. "I believed I would win. I'd never had cause to doubt my strength. But even if I'd known what would happen, I would have gone. What choice did I have? I could not turn my back on my task."

"You left me! You just left me behind!"

It came back like a great wind, like a tempest that tears up the earth and leaves behind a ruin: the memory of her mother, the memory of her mother's disappearance, the bottomless terror and grief and confusion of it. Tears blinded Eliza, blurring the image of Rea watching her with pity but also an unmoving calm, an unshakeable certainty in herself. She howled like a baby. Her heart smashed against her ribs, again and again. She returned to herself cradled in Nia's arms. Nia was rocking her back and forth gently, whispering, "sh, sh, sh."

Eliza pulled free of Nia's embrace, wiped the tears from her face. "Where is she?"

"You know where," said Nia. "Parts of her are in me. Parts of her remain in the body left to her. And parts of her are simply gone. She can't be whole again."

"Unless I can find a way to take back what you stole from her," said Eliza.

Nia laughed sympathetically. "One thing at a time, Smidgen." She held out the fourth enchanted stone. "I'm going to tell you a secret: You can survive the loss of all you love, of all you *think* you are, and yet still be Eliza. You knew it when I tried to rob you of yourself. You knew it then, but you have forgotten it again."

"But what would I have to live for?" Her sorrow was too big for her. It filled the ravens in the trees, so all their hearts overflowed with it.

"That is the mystery," said Nia. "That is what you live to find out. If you strip everything away, what is left at the core? What are we? I wish I could go with you, Smidgen, I'm *dying* of curiosity. But if anyone can go to meet the Sparkling Deluder and come back to tell the tale, I'll bet it's you. Here, eat this."

She grabbed Eliza by the back of the neck and shoved the rock into her mouth. Eliza struggled and gagged. Without wanting to, she bit down. A heavy darkness filled her throat. Nia was gone. She saw the shadows of the trees as if she was looking through fogged glass or her own tears. Some shadow whose form she could barely make out moved towards her and touched her, and the touch was ice and fire at once. It turned and moved, changing shape as it did so and yet no shape fixed enough that she could name it, limbs more than she could count and then perhaps none at all, it moved and she followed, and the trees folded and fell and the ground softened and swallowed her.

She was deep in the earth. She felt the beating hearts and the clamour of consciousness all around her. She felt great bodies folding against each other, and she was the sorrow of the Ancients, because they loved life, they loved the world. She slid like a tear from an eye into the earth, and the earth was made of slumbering bodies. She crawled, two hearts beating, four legs and four arms. She pulled herself up out of the earth and as she took in her first gasp of air she tore apart from her other self. She lay gasping in the dark and the cold. The earth stirred once more beneath her, and was still. She was bound in flesh and time and space. Blazing-eyed they came to her, tall and gold and white. They formed a ring around her, begged her to come with them. They gave her shackles and they gave her love, and she took both with a grateful heart, for she was too unmoored, too much alone.

Eliza opened her eyes and saw only darkness. The ground was hard and cool beneath her. She sensed immediately that she was in a cave. It was a very long cave, deep in the earth, and narrow too. She could not stand up, and so she slithered and crawled towards the glimmer of light in the distance. She crawled out of the opening and found herself high in the Yellow Mountains.

Bright flowers blanketed the slopes. Far below she saw the four lakes, one in spring, one in summer, one in fall, one in winter, unchanging. At that moment the world seemed impossibly beautiful and she felt grateful just to be alive and witness to it.

Beyond the lakes lay the Dreaming Wasteland. It was a white moonscape, a barren expanse cut through with rivers that gleamed like quicksilver. Long black dragons with tattered wings swung over the terrain, letting out high, mournful snatches of song. A faint haze, like steam, rose up from the ground, forming swirls of cloud.

A crimson bird as big as a myrkestra swooped out of the sky and landed next to Eliza. It looked at her, expectant. She thought of the great Panther waiting for her to return what she had taken and the terrible prophecies the past Oracle had spoken of her. She thought of all the powerful beings in pursuit of her. She thought of Charlie fleeing the Thanatosi and Foss slowly dying in the Enchanter's cabin. She felt little hope that it might all come out right, but she had set her course and she would follow it through. She climbed on the bird's back and left the beautiful world behind her.

CHAPTER

22

Watching the immense Dragons surge up out of the water, Nell was, for a few moments at least, entirely free of fear, so great was her amazement at their size and beauty. Many of them had been entirely submerged but surfaced now, like islands springing up out of the sea, and the water churned and rocked with the movement of the great beasts. They formed a circle and Swarn's dragon descended and landed at the centre of it, floating on the water quite comfortably, unafraid.

Nell saw that Charlie had his hands over his ears and then realized that she was doing the same thing. The sound of the Dragons was like the sky being torn open. Her head was ringing with it. Swarn, however, was standing up on the head of her dragon. She held her double-sided spear up in the air and was emitting an awful wail of her own. One of the Dragons leaned its head down towards them, casting a huge shadow, and let out a whistling reply that nearly knocked Swarn off the head of her dragon. She seemed to understand whatever the dragon said, for she looked sharply to the west. Charlie and Nell looked also. They saw a whitish line moving just over the darkening horizon.

"What is that?" shouted Nell.

"Ten thousand or more myrkestras," replied Swarn.

"What? How?"

"The Faeries are coming," said Swarn. "The Dragon tells me that there was an attempt at theft just days ago – an attempt that failed. Now the Faeries are out in full force. They are waging war on the Dragons."

"What for?"

Swarn smiled grimly. "The Gehemmis. It seems everybody has decided it would be a good idea to collect all four."

Charlie looked around at the sea full of colossal dragons and laughed a little. "What could the Faeries possibly do against *these?*" he asked.

Swarn's dragon lurched up out of the water and flew over the expanse of foreleg and shoulder of the Dragon that had spoken to them. It settled on the hard, bright scales between the wings.

"Come." Swarn's face was bright with joy. "They will take us to see the Dragon Lord."

"Oh. Do we want to…see the Dragon Lord?" asked Charlie nervously, but Swarn did not reply. With a great roaring of water, the Dragons emerged from the sea like islands being uprooted, and wings many kilometers long beat the air. The Dragon's back was so huge there was little fear of falling as it flew eastward, towards the dimming horizon.

As they flew through the night, many more islands that proved to be Dragons rose into the air to fly with them. They could no longer see the approaching Faeries in the dark.

When dawn came, the sun inching up over the horizon, they saw what appeared to be the end of the world. The sea poured over the edge, and nothing lay beyond it, nothing at all but the sky. The horde of Dragons flew out into the nothingness, shut their wings, and began to drop.

They plunged, dropping with the sea, for miles. There was a faint, echoing roar, perhaps the sea landing somewhere far below, but they could not see. The roar grew louder and the air was hazy with spray. Another world came suddenly into view. The Dragons stretched their wings out again and coasted over bottomless, twisting towers of rock, cliffs and arches, all gleaming like the inside of a seashell, smoothed and shaped by wind and water. Vast caverns hung with glistening moss. Dragons sat poised upon clifftops or curled in canyons and caves. The shining stone was everywhere cracked and riven with black lines. Here and there, empty black calderas smoked. A mist of sea-spray hung over it all.

The Dragon landed high on a cliff and stretched out its foreleg, enabling them to scramble and slide to the ground without injury. Swarn remained standing on the creature's great claw and said to Nell and Charlie:

"Wait for me here. If I do not return, my dragon will know the time for you to go."

Her face was changed. She seemed younger, almost. Not less weathered and lined – but rejuvenated.

"What do you mean, if you dinnay return?" cried Nell. "Swarn –"

But the witch was gone. The Dragon rose above them and they cringed in its shadow. The wings came down and the wind knocked them to the ground. It soared away, lost quickly in the spray, leaving Nell and Charlie to scramble to their feet, push their damp hair out of their faces, and look around at the marvelous world they found themselves in.

"It's incredible," said Charlie.

"Even if I dinnay get back in time for my test," said Nell, "it's worth it, aye, just to see this."

"You'll make it back," said Charlie. "You'll ace that exam and get a huge scholarship to Austermon and become the best cetologist in Di Shang. I cannay imagine anything stopping you, Nell, short of the end of the worlds, and praps not even that."

And there, finally, with the Immortal Dragons filling the sky, atop a shining cliff at the end of the world, she put her arms around his neck, pulled him to her, and kissed him.

The Dragon took Swarn further east, to a plateau ringed by smoldering dark calderas. There sprawled a monster of unspeakable size. Swarn had felt the power of this creature calling to her before they had come across the first of the Dragons in the Far Sea. She thought she had felt it from as far away as Lil – perhaps she had felt it her whole life. This was the Lord Dragon, first among the Immortal Dragons, the Child of the Ancients. It lay across the plateau and did not stir as the Dragon that bore Swarn to it landed a short distance away. Swarn had been riding on its foot, her arm clinging to the ridges of its bony talons. When it set down, she leaped to the ground and strode towards the Lord Dragon, knelt and bowed her head. The Dragon blinked slowly, wrinkled lids closing over eyes like black lakes and then rising again. Swarn had been pleased to find that the strange, archaic language of her cliff dragons was indeed derived from the language of the Immortal Dragons and that she could communicate with them. But with the Lord Dragon, there was no need of language.

Master of the Flame.

This was the Dragon's greeting to her.

Lord Dragon, why do you call me master? I am only your servant, was her reply.

If my servant, then I am Master of the Flame. But our land is without fire. The sea comes and encroaches and our power wanes.

Can you repel the Faeries? Swarn asked the Dragon. *They are coming for the Gehemmis.*

The Lord Dragon showed no sign of perturbation.

Those who come are Faeries only in name. The First among the Faeries, my brothers and sisters, are gone further west than even the Faeries of Tian Di know. They are stronger, greater, purer than the Faeries of this world, who are but shadows of what they will become. Likewise are we but shadows of what we were, since the Mage stole Flame from us. Without Flame, we are too weak even to fly across the Far Sea to Tian Di. Some Dragons go by sea to seek our stolen Flame, but they do not return. I think that on the journey, they become creatures of the Deep and forget their first allegiance. Tian Di was a wasteland that became a world, now two worlds, and our world disappears slowly, swallowed by the sea. But you have come to us, Master of the Flame, and so there is still hope for us.

Yes, hope. Swarn felt it fill her up, like taking a deep breath of air after being long submerged underwater. She thought she was beginning to understand.

So the old stories are true – the Dragon Mage stole the source of your power, the Flame, and used it to Make the mortal dragons.

It is true. Though we are Immortal, a Dragon without Flame is barely worthy to be called Dragon. Our Realm is robbed of Magic and we are weak. How the Mage took our Flame, what Magic he employed, we do not know. How to regain it, also a mystery. But I have felt you coming. I know what you command. What can you offer us, Master of the Flame?

All her life, Swarn thought, her flesh had bound her Magic too tightly. Her power had been struggling from the day of her birth to be free, to exist as a force only, to perform this task. That was the battle within her, the endless struggle against her self, Magic pushing against constricting bone and skin. Stirring within her now was a Magic she had never learned, something that had dwelled within her all this time, waiting for this moment.

I offer myself. To return the Flame will require Great Magic. It will require all my power. All that I am.

The Lord Dragon blinked his black lake eyes at her slowly.

You will become one with the Flame.

She felt something unfamiliar opening up within her: joy.

Yes. But in return, I ask for the Gehemmis.

If you do this, you can never return to what you were.

She found herself holding a folded sack of thinnest dragon scale, small enough to fit in the palm of her hand. (Goodbye, palm of my hand, she thought, and tried to stop herself from whooping with laughter). She opened the sack and looked at the black dust inside.

Ash, said the Lord Dragon. *What was burned in the Making.*

Charlie and Nell passed the earlier part of the day in a state of stunned, joyful wonder on the cliff. As the day waned, however, they grew damp and cold from the spray that filled the air as well as terribly hungry, and Swarn had still not returned. So it was with great relief that they spotted her standing on the head of a Dragon flying towards the cliff, wings spread so far they seemed to have no end. It landed on the cliff and Swarn strode down between the two vast ponds of its eyes, along its long nose, and leaped to the ground as if casually jumping off a roof.

"Thank the Ancients you're back!" Nell began eagerly, rushing forward, and then she stopped, her mouth dropping open.

"What in the worlds…" murmured Charlie, just behind her.

Swarn was changed. Her white hair shone like strands of pure light. Her skin, which had always looked like worn old leather to Nell, was smooth and dark and glowing. Her eyes shone like black jewels and her flesh almost seemed to flow, as if she were not made of bone and muscle anymore but a kind of liquid that held her shape.

When she spoke, her voice resonated, clear as a bell.

"This is the Gehemmis of the Dragons," she said, handing it to Nell. "You must take it to Eliza."

"OK," Nell faltered. She took the folded sack in her hand. "Are you nay coming?"

Swarn smiled — not her usual wolf-like grin, but a real smile.

"Tell Eliza to have patience. She is young and has borne much, but we all become what we must. Wish her farewell from me."

"Farewell? Swarn, what's happening?"

"Balance is being restored," said Swarn. She threw back her head. A terrible screeching sound burst from her throat. Swarn's dragon's head shot up and the creature came to her swiftly, bowing its head towards her. Her high, wild keening continued. The dragon swayed its head almost as if it was dancing to the awful sounds she made. Charlie and Nell backed away, putting their hands over their ears. Then Swarn's dragon emitted a long sigh and green flame poured out of it and onto Swarn.

"No!" shouted Nell, starting to run towards them, but Charlie grabbed her and pulled her back. Swarn did not appear to be burned by the flame. It flowed into her, flickering in her and around her. The dragon was keening now, the two of them swaying and wailing together, until the last of its fire flickered out of its mouth and it dropped its head, exhausted. Swarn screamed a command. The green fire burned in the air all around her, burned on her skin and her hair without consuming her. The dragon turned to Nell and Charlie and bowed its neck.

"Come on," said Charlie. "It's time for us to go."

"But..." Nell gestured helplessly towards Swarn. "What's going on?"

"I dinnay know," said Charlie. "But we've got the Gehemmis. Whatever happens next, I dinnay think we want to be part of it."

Nell scrambled up onto the dragon's neck behind him. The dragon took to the air, flying up through the spray. Nell looked back at Swarn. She was glowing brighter and brighter with green flame, her chanting rising and filling the air. She became a white light at the center of the flame, and then the chanting crescendoed and she burst into fire. The green fire ran along the dark cracks in the rocky cliffs and leaped from the smoking calderas. The land of the Immortal Dragons was suddenly alight, and all the Dragons were roaring together.

"What just happened to her?" cried Nell, but she could not hear her own voice.

Swarn's dragon shot straight up, followed at a distance by the Immortal Dragons. Over the edge of the cliff of falling water, they could see the legion of approaching myrkestras, line after line stretched across the sea. Swarn's dragon continued to rise, straight up into the clear reddish sky, high above the Faery army. Below them, the Immortal Dragons roared, their green flame bursting onto the green sea.

The sea surged up and Swarn's dragon still rocketed skyward, out of reach. The sea turned back in a giant wave that grew rapidly, higher than a mountain, higher than ten mountains, and still Swarn's dragon rose above it. Nell and Charlie clung to the dragon's neck, dizzy and terrified, as the sea chased them ever upwards. The rows of myrkestras began to scatter and rise, but not fast enough. The sea roared towards them, loomed over them, then hurtled down and swallowed them.

The sea roiled and churned, fire and water, and when it settled Charlie and Nell and the cliff dragon were alone in the sky.

STAR

CHAPTER

23

The Vermilion Bird's feathers were softer than anything Eliza had touched before. She longed to caress it, bury her face in its softness, but she did not dare. It was a being of great power after all, and great intelligence too. It might be proud enough to throw her off if she were so presumptuous as to stroke the feathers she held now in a firm grip.

The Yellow Mountains fell away almost immediately. A voice like a soft brush of wing told Eliza, *Don't look.* Steam rose up from the Dreaming Wasteland. The black dragons circled and sang far below them. Eliza closed her eyes. She drew breath into her and pushed it out in a slow, circular rhythm.

"The battle is won or lost in your breath," Swarn had taught her. "If you control your breath, you control yourself, physically and mentally."

The song of the dragons drifted up, beautiful and sorrowful. Eliza felt tears sliding out from under her closed lids. She felt the pull from the Dreaming Wasteland, a tug at the heart. Clinging to the Vermilion Bird, she tried not to think of letting go, for at that moment it was sorely tempting. To slip from the soft back and fall. Finally, to let go and fall. Into that song. Her grip loosened and the voice came again, soft as smoke: *Do not listen.*

She breathed in time with the gliding swing of the soft wings. Her only thought was *Don't fall off.* She forgot her purpose, her destination, everything but *Don't fall off.* As if this was all of life, as if she had never done anything else.

And then she was not on the back of the bird. The sweet, sad song was gone. They were not flying. She breathed. She waited until she was sure. She had not fallen. She had arrived. She opened her eyes and marveled.

She was at the foot of a staircase made of light. Levels upon levels of the Hanging Gardens were suspended in the blackness of space all around her. The light moved, changing shape. Brilliant spires became bright forests, which in turn became a waterfall of light flowing into yet something else. The shining stairs passed up through all these levels, and Eliza climbed them. She did not feel tired here, though the steps seemed to go on and on. Climbing was effortless; she was nearly weightless. The stairway led her into a vaulted cathedral of light. Luminescent pillars soared upwards. The light formed latticework and intricate detail along the pillars and the walls and around the vast ceiling. There was faint music, notes absolutely pure, and she walked among the pillars looking for its source before realizing that this sound came from the light itself.

She heard her name. Coming towards her among the pillars was a being of pure light. The being was as tall as a Giant, but far more shapely and graceful than those brutish creatures. Any features it might have had were obscured by the light that emanated from them. It was as if a star had taken the form of a colossal Faery.

The being called her name again, in a voice that was neither male nor female, neither song nor speech. It was a beautiful voice, gentle, sure, so full of warmth and kindness that Eliza felt immediately safe. She felt welcome.

Eliza, are you lost?

"No," said Eliza. "I came looking for you."

A pealing laugh seemed to come from every direction at once. The Hanging Gardens fell away suddenly. Lights plunged and doused themselves in the inky blackness of space, the pillars around her tumbling to nothing. Everything before her and behind her was collapsing, disappearing. Eliza dropped to her knees. She was perched on the edge of a long strip of light stretched far out over black space, like the edge of a plank stretched out from a pirate's ship. Somewhere in the emptiness out there, an echoing roar – the Panther waiting, poised.

The Sparkling Deluder (for who else could it be?) curled softly in the darkness as if the darkness was a nest. It looked at Eliza, or so it seemed, though Eliza could not find eyes in the flare of brilliance that was its face.

Eliza, do you want to tumble too?

There was menace in the voice now, and amusement. The gentleness with which it had spoken her name had been deceptive. This was a being who meant her harm.

"No," she said, and her voice shook. "I want to be safe."

She was startled by her own pronouncement. It seemed she had never spoken words so true, so completely from her heart. For this was all she wanted, all she wanted in the worlds right now: only to be safe. Not to be perched at the edge of space, not to tumble at the whim of this being.

That's all anybody wants, when they lack it.

The Sparkling Deluder reached towards her with a shining hand. The hand went right through her, into her body. It was the strangest sensation, as if her flesh were not substantial, merely a clamour of atoms being pushed aside. The hand withdrew, a black raven in its palm. The Sparkling Deluder opened its hand wide and the raven took off, disappeared into the black.

I could pull them out of you for the rest of time and there would still be more, I suppose.

"I dinnay know," said Eliza.

You don't know what you are. You see, I was right. Lost, poor thing.

Eliza felt a cold sweat breaking out along her hairline and her upper lip. She couldn't look at the wheeling blackness waiting to swallow her. There was nothing out there, no way back to the worlds she knew.

"Please," she croaked, her voice failing her. "I'm frightened."

The darkness seemed to sway and beckon. The hand swept through the darkness, dusty particles of light tumbling from it and winking out.

The Immortals are stirring. The Faeries of Tian Xia are looking for the Gehemmis. They wander the Dreaming Wasteland and their armies are lost in the underwater realms, disturbing the Deep. The

Dragons are rising in the East and who can say what they will do now their power is restored. Amarantha walks the world again. All this because of a mortal girl on a quest to save the boy she loves. Can you see it?

"I cannay see anything," said Eliza.

The Sparkling Deluder pointed with one bright finger and drew a circle of light in the air. Through the circle, Eliza saw Tian Xia, the lake of the Crossing, the Far Sea to the east. She longed to leap through it, just to be in the worlds again. She could leap, become a raven, be safe. But no, she couldn't leap, she could hardly move, clinging to this strip of light over black space, terrified.

The Warrior Witch has given herself to the Dragons, said the Sparkling Deluder. *Look.*

The view through the circle of light changed. Eliza saw a world of soaring white stone half-obscured by a mist of sea-spray. Dragons of unfathomable size nested there. And she saw Swarn, brilliant with green fire, burst into a shower of light.

Grief, Eliza knew, could come in many ways. It could be a shadow that clung to you, or a fist around the heart. It could come all at once, washing over you like a wave and then disappearing, or it could approach with soft footsteps and linger close and quiet. It could gnaw at you with tiny teeth or crush you like a block of stone. Now it came like a blade, bright and sudden, twisting. She cried out in startled pain, then closed her teeth over it and breathed. Like Swarn had taught her, Swarn whom she would not see again. She breathed slowly, forbidding the sobs that clamoured in her chest, forbidding the tears that rushed to her eyes. Later, later she would weep for Swarn, if there was a later for her. For now she had to keep still, breathe, be ready.

"She was my friend," said Eliza.

Yes, I know. The Sparkling Deluder emitted a high whistling sound, like a sigh. *You don't need to tell me. I've been watching. And you came here, all this way, for the Gehemmis. What good does it do, the struggle and the pain?*

"I dinnay know what you mean," said Eliza.

You see everything up close. You have no perspective. It's not your fault. It's the nature of what you are. But I will show you the larger picture and then we will see if you still care so much about finding the Gehemmis.

The darkness seemed to fold, cave in. The Vermilion Bird shot out over the Yellow Mountains, wings spread wide.

She could see everything at once, or so it felt. It was not like watching, exactly, for there was no passage of time. Simply, she saw everything in fullness and at once, from no particular direction or perspective.

Foss lay like an ashen shadow on the narrow bed where she had left him, the last faint glimmer of his eyes gone out. Ferghal knelt by the bed and wept over him. The Blind Enchanter dug a hole among the flowering bushes outside the house, sweat gleaming on his muscled shoulders. He slung Foss's brittle and deflated body over his shoulder, carried him out and put him in the ground. Ferghal followed him out, still weeping. They covered him with flowers and shoveled the dirt overtop.

"Nay Foss!" Eliza cried out. "Please dinnay take Foss!"

Who has taken him? Who are you calling out to? He has simply ceased to be.

Eliza found herself standing on the strip of light again, suspended over the empty universe. "The river," she croaked. "I'll bring him back."

You caught the boy as he was crossing between life and death and you brought him back to life. This one has already crossed. There is no bringing him back. This is the way of things. Why can't you let go?

"I cannay," she whispered. "Nay Foss."

The Vermilion Bird winged over Di Shang now, and though her eyes were pressed shut Eliza had no choice but to see what it showed her.

The Citadel soared white and proud as ever at the edge of the desert. A beautiful young witch with black skin and amber eyes received a small, jeweled blade from Kyreth. Eliza recognized it. It was Malferio's blade. Malferio knelt before the witch and Kyreth, his expression dazed, stupefied. The young woman grabbed him by the hair and drove the blade into the back of his neck, uttering an incantation as she did so. He gave a few rapid, stunned gasps, looking up at the triumphant girl in miserable disbelief. Kyreth watched, expressionless, as Malferio crumpled to the ground. At the same instant, Eliza saw Nia frozen in the Hall of the Ancients, her eyes widening almost imperceptibly before she fell. Eliza felt the Urkleis in her chest give a desperate throb and then crumble.

Charlie was running through a wood.

"I cannay watch!" screamed Eliza, unable to turn away or shut the vision out. "Dinnay show me!"

An arrow pierced him, and then another. He stumbled and fell and in an instant the Thanatosi were upon him, blades flashing. Nell came staggering through the woods after him, bleeding heavily from a wound in her shoulder. The Thanatosi ignored her, leaping away and vanishing, leaving Charlie on the forest floor. Nell was sobbing. She threw herself over the dead body of her friend. "Eliza!" she cried. "Where are you?"

Eliza could make no reply.

Your worst fears will come to pass. Everything you dread. But he met his end after hundreds of years. Is it so terrible? An end must come for us all, even for we Immortals. We all will pass. The question is only when.

She saw her Grandmother Selva laid out by the Faithful, who sang their mourning songs around her funeral pyre. She saw her parents, old and frail, playing chess together in their tent. She saw the Sorma funerals, her parents buried in the desert, the graves unmarked in the Sorma tradition. The endless sands swept over them, their bones lost forever.

She saw Nell, but so much older that it took a moment to recognize her. There were spidery lines around her violet eyes and her bright chestut hair had faded to grey. She was wearing a lab coat and her hair was pulled back as she examined a series of slides. The room was swaying – she was on a boat of some kind. A bearded man wearing a yellow raincoat entered the room suddenly, saying something with great excitement. Nell looked up from what she was doing and it seemed as if she was looking right into Eliza's eyes.

The world continues without you. The survivors will grieve for you and live on, and then they too will pass and be mourned. What can you do? What is it you fear so? Some few extra years of life for some, if you fail or if you succeed? Does it make any difference? In the end, it is the same for us all.

She saw Nell with grown children laughing around a table, a man whose face she did not recognize. She saw the children, grey-haired and with children and grandchildren of their own, burying their mother. The funeral was in Kalla and there were hundreds of people there. Of course, in a lifetime, so many would come to love Nell.

She saw Kyreth in his passing, and Ka succeeding him as Supreme Mancer – the Citadel unchanged, but without a Sorceress.

You disappeared from the story. It carries on without you.

The Vermilion Bird blinked its black eyes and centuries flew by.

Four hundred years after you left the worlds, what do you see?

The Mancers doing their Magic in the Citadel. The Faeries recovering from their disastrous failure to obtain the Gehemmis. Emyr deposed, Alvar crowned. Another wizard, far less benevolent than Uri, lives in Lil now, and most of the womi have left. A young witch in Tian Xia hears for the first time the story of the last Sorceress. How the Shang Sorceress defeated the Xia Sorceress and then disappeared in the South. Legend has it she became one of the lights in the Sparkling Deluder's Hanging Gardens. That one, you see, that winking light at the top of the spire: we call that one Eliza. Immortal Amarantha still wreaks havoc from her home in the Irahok mountains.

The Vermilion Bird blinks again. Millenia pass. Amarantha offends the Horogarth and he topples the Irahok mountains, trapping her beneath them forever. The visionary King Jalo, son of Nikias, leads the Faeries to the land in the west, all of them together, their Realm of Illusion abandoned. The old stories are forgotten.

Do you still wish to go back to the changed world?

Her heart thrums. She wants to go back. Even now, even thousands of years too late, with no one who will know her or love her, she wants to go back.

"Yes. Send me back."

You can stay here if you wish. My brightest star. Eliza.

"I want to go back."

You want to live.

"Yes."

For a few years.

"However long I can. Yes."

But look. There is more.

The Vermilion Bird blinks. Eliza feels herself wheeling away from the worlds, their past and their future, into vast, empty space. Beyond the sun and the circling planets, and out and out, galaxies spinning, and then nothingness, nothingness, forever nothingness. She can't hold on to this strip of light. She slips away from it. The vastness is unfathomable. Her mind bursts into black winged shapes that flee the awful truth. Life is dwarfed by emptiness, lifelessness; it is a quivering speck in an endless dead sea. She opens her eyes, slow, like a newborn. She is lying in a pool of light. No. She is cupped in the hand of the Sparkling Deluder. The bright face overhead. Still, even now, beauty can fill her up.

"You dinnay know what it's like to love," says Eliza. What a tiny voice. What a fragile little body. She almost wants to laugh at herself for bothering to speak at all. And yet.

Perhaps that is why I brought you here. To teach me about love.

She feels as if she is coming to pieces slowly. She holds out a hand and watches, fascinated: a darkness forms on her skin, swells wetly, like black water dripping out of her. It takes shape and as it drops away from her becomes a raven. It happens again and again, not just in her hand but all over her. She is leaking ravens. They disappear into space. There is nowhere they can fly to. There is nowhere to go.

I know what pity feels like. You feel it now.

For the ravens with nowhere to go. For herself, lost from her own life. For those she loves who will die in fear, clinging to their one brief life. For those she does not love or know, who live and die baffled and hoping, but for what? For life, wonderful and strange, marked with sorrow. Time and Space are unthinkable but they are barren too. Only life is truly beautiful, truly pitiful.

You can step out of the story and it continues without you, and it is not so terrible. Do you remember, even, what you meant to do, or why you came?

Eliza thinks. The ravens slipping out of her, slipping away, make her feel weaker by the moment and it is difficult to think straight. There was a reason, something important. She came for an object, but she can't think why she should need it. She remembers a boy running in a wood. She wanted to help him. That was it. She wanted to save him. She came here to save him. But he is dead now. They are all dead now.

Come.

She is on the solitary strip of light again, standing at the edge of it, looking out over the emptiness of space. The Sparkling Deluder is behind her, beckoning her back towards the Hanging Gardens.

You will be my purest star, Eliza, so full of pity, so full of love. You will shine here forever, until the end of the worlds, when the universe closes up again, folds itself up and disappears.

"I want to go back."

Look at you. You are too old now. You would not live long in any case.

She looks at her hands. They are shriveled and wrinkled, speckled with liver spots. She snatches at her hair, which hangs to her waist, ash-grey. She touches her face, feels the grooves and lines. She has grown old here, an old woman.

"How long have I been here?"

Again, that pealing laugh. The Sparkling Deluder shines brighter and brighter.

Come, Eliza. They are all gone. It is finished. Be my purest star.

"Send me back."

Send you back to die?

"Yes."

I will send you back mad, with a wild stutter and terrible visions. You will stumble to and fro, a crazed old witch, until you drop dead or some other being puts you out of your misery. You will be a warning to all. They will know you came from me and that I am not to be approached lightly. You come and say you are in love, you ask me to give you the gift of my parents, the Ancients, and I show you time and space and still you want to go back, you want to go back. Then go back. Go back toothless and gibbering and remembering nothing. Go back sick and frail and ridiculous. Go back and be mocked and spurned. You may enjoy a sunset or two before you die.

"I havenay asked you for the Gehemmis yet."

I won't send you back. I will put you atop that spire, my purest star, lovely Eliza. The last Sorceress, from the last days of Tian Di. I will go and call the Mancers back and the Crossing will dry up. Di Shang will be alone, as it was meant to be. The end. The end of the story. Eliza. Come.

Her heart ached. Ravens dripped from her skin. What was there to fear, now? This was only what she knew would happen. That it would all end here. But she would not go and be a star. That would be surrender.

"You dinnay know pity," she said. "You are cruel and pitiless. I willnay be your star. You dinnay deserve me."

Justice! A very human notion. Well then, old woman, what will you do?

Eliza jumped.

The Hanging Gardens reeled above and she fell into the blackness, ravens pulling out of her skin, peeling themselves out of her veins, her blood all dark feathers and wing and claw now, her flesh disappearing into a thousand ravens or more, becoming one with the dark.

She fell forever, until the last of her became a bird, became the dark, and nothing, nothing at all.

It's funny that you think you have a choice.

(To be light. Not like the stars of the galaxies, vast orbs of gas and flame, but light itself. A brilliance among brilliance, unfading forever. There is consciousness, too, though of a different kind. The star holds certain things within: the sensation of flight, the smell of the sea, her father's voice. These are the clearest. And then there is the boy running through the wood; that is important. Again and again memories rise up and fade. Certain among them repeat over and over. A beautiful woman in red pajamas eating ice-cream on a divan. She throws aside the ice-cream, leaps to her feet crying out joyfully, *Eliza! I'm so glad you've come!* And she is so glad too that for a moment she is almost Eliza, almost a girl standing there, cold and frightened. But why frightened, when this woman is so warm in her greeting? Why be afraid? She can't remember that. She shines with longing.)

You still want to go back.

(She smells the sea. She tastes honey on her tongue. She hears her father laughing. Sand between her toes and the sizzle of the barbecue.)

The Sparkling Deluder is holding a box. The box is made of darkness and symbols are etched on it with light. Inside the box is the first star.

You imagine you can use the Gehemmis to stop the Thanatosi.

(She sees the boy running through the wood. An arrow cuts right through him and she wants to scream but can't.)

But nothing can stop the Thanatosi. Not the greatest Magic in the world. Pursuit is what they are and to stop them you would have to stop them existing. Some things, once done, cannot be undone.

(Sand between her toes. The running boy. She wants to scream. The taste of honey. Laughter. Send me back.)

Eliza, your love is terrible, beautiful. It is selfish and giving at once. It can survive time and space and all things. Love is what you are. To snuff it out, I would have to stop you existing. Some things, once felt, cannot be unfelt.

(Blue sky, blue sea, two girls on the cliff. A voice, her own? "I seriously doubt that Nat Fillion really jumped off here." The other girl looks at her with violet eyes, adjusts the straps of her swimsuit, and opens her mouth to reply.)

Though it will not be what you hope or expect it to be, I will give you the Gehemmis and send you back to the world, to the very moment you left it. But you must make me two promises.

(The way his eyebrows turn up at the ends. Her father on horseback, grinning down at her. A shining being beams at her, "Do *not* be discouraged!" Anything. I'll do anything.)

You must separate the worlds. Then you may live out your life, be it a few days or a hundred years. When your time comes, I will send the Vermilion Bird to bear you back here. Then you will become my brightest star and remain here always.

(Hope like a salty breeze, something almost forgotten. I promise.)

You will not like what must be done to separate the worlds. But if you break your promise to me, I will pluck you out of the worlds as if you had never existed.

The Sparkling Deluder walked out into the blackness, the star in its palm of webbed light. They left the Hanging Gardens twinkling behind them. With one finger, the Deluder drew a circle in the black and through it they saw the world again. The star became a raven.

I will see you soon, Eliza, my purest star.

The Sparkling Deluder cast the bird out through the eye, and the eye winked shut.

She was not a bird. She was *on* a bird and the world wheeled beneath her. Oh the world! The crimson soft feathers under her cheek, the Yellow Mountains below, bright gold in the sun, the throb of the Urkleis in her chest, the weight of her body and the smell of the air. Beyond the mountains was the inland sea and the sickle island of the Blind Enchanter. It all came rushing back to her, everything she had lost and been given again, love twined close to its shadowy twin, fear, and the painful squeeze of *hope.*

She wept and laughed and wept.

Only when the Vermilion Bird landed outside the stone cabin did she realize that in her hands she held a dark box inscribed with light, the Gehemmis of the Sparkling Deluder.

The door of the cabin opened and Ka stepped out.

CHAPTER

24

Bees buzzed in the flowers around her ankles and the breeze carried the sharp, salty smell of the sea. It felt as if a hundred years had passed since she had been herself in the worlds, and it felt as if no time had passed at all.

"Is Foss alive?" she asked, and her own voice sounded strange to her, like a voice she had not heard in a long time.

"He lives," said Ka. "But he has little time left. A day, perhaps two."

His flaming eyes fell on the box in her hands, darkness inscribed with light.

"The Gehemmis," he said. "Eliza, you are more remarkable than any of us gave you credit for."

She felt strangely calm. What could frighten her now? She had lost the worlds, her loved ones, she had lost everything, and now it was all returned to her. Perhaps only to lose again, but all was not lost yet, it was not too late.

"Kyreth murdered Aysu," said Eliza. "I saw you find her, aye. You know he did it. He would have given me to Obrad against my will. He has stolen books from the Library about Karbek's spell. He has Malferio in a tower. He's insane, and a liar, and dangerous."

Obrad stepped out of the house and joined Ka. Eliza fell silent.

"Our Sorceress has turned up after all," said Obrad, his voice betraying no feeling.

Eliza spoke only to Ka. "Dinnay let Foss die," she begged.

"Eliza, we are Mancers. We cannot be something else," said Ka. "Do you think that Foss's treachery is noble? I know about

Malferio. Kyreth intends to rid the worlds of Nia and we have been lending him our strength that he may complete the Magic necessary to do it. If Foss didn't know, it is because nobody trusted him enough to tell him. He has brought this exile on himself. He is beyond our help."

"Coward," Eliza spat out clearly. Ka's eyes flickered.

Anargul, Trahaearn, and a young Mancer Eliza did not recognize stepped out of the house. Ka and Obrad immediately stepped aside to let Anargul face Eliza. Ka murmured something to her.

"Where are the other Gehemmis?" demanded Anargul.

So they had not found the Gehemmis she had left with the Enchanter, thought Eliza. She gave no answer, closing her mind against the Mancers.

Anargul looked at Eliza closely. "Very well. I will ask you only once to give me the Gehemmis you hold in your hands."

The moment Eliza reached for her dagger, something twisted her arm back sharply. Ravens burst out of the ground like big black flowers, shrieking. But Anargul had the Gehemmis already.

"Now the others," she said grimly.

A lovely, fluting voice overhead called out an unfamiliar word. Eliza looked up. Eight myrkestras were descending on the island. Golden-haired Faeries in flowing, feathered cloaks sat astride them. She looked to the Mancers but they were entirely still, did not even react.

"Faeries!" she shouted. Anargul did not move.

"Cursed them with immobility," said a Faery cheerfully, leaping from the back of his myrkestra and striding over to Eliza. "Works particularly well on Mancers, since they rather tend to stillness anyway. Mind you, it will only last the day. We don't want to do anything more extreme until we know for sure whether they're in league with you, little thief."

He was still smiling, but there was something dangerous in his eyes. The other Faeries joined him, prodding the frozen Mancers gleefully.

"Very exciting to be the first to find you. No doubt there's a fine reward in it for us," the Faery continued jovially. "There will be others coming soon, but things will go better for you if you give us the Gehemmis you stole right away."

"I gave it to the Mancers a few days ago," said Eliza, her mind racing. "A liaison was waiting for me in the Irahok Mountains and he took it back to the Citadel."

"So you are working for them!" the Faery cried. "What treachery! The Faeries will crush them!"

"*Was* working for them," said Eliza. She saw that a couple of the Faeries had noticed the dark box in Anargul's hands and they were murmuring to one another. "But then they sent me south to face the Sparkling Deluder. I couldnay even make it to the Dreaming Wasteland. It was a waste of time. I'm nay that powerful."

"Of course not," said the Faery. "The Mancers have always put far too much stock in their Sorceresses, if you ask me. Well, so they've taken our Gehemmis to the Citadel. How do we know you're telling the truth?"

"You dinnay think the Mancers would let me carry it around for long, do you?" she asked.

"Then what are you doing here? And what's *this*?" he reached towards the box in Anargul's hands.

"I wouldnay touch it if I were you," said Eliza.

The Faery hesitated.

"My punishment," she lied quickly. "The Mancers made it hundreds of years ago. They're the only ones that know how to use it, how to control it."

"What does it do?"

"When it's opened, it draws the Magic out of its target," she said. "If you try to take it from the Mancers, it will open up and take *your* Magic. Mine is already gone. They had just finished using it on me when you arrived. Another blast would probably kill me. They're the only ones that know how to close it."

"Nonsense," said one of the Faeries. "She's just trying to scare us off. It's obviously something important."

Eliza shrugged. "Go on and grab it then," she said. "I spose

I'm to be killed anyway."

"I will!" cried the Faery, pushing forwards.

"Wait, wait!" said the one who had done most of the talking. "No need to be hasty. We just need to send word, have it investigated. It won't be long. Better safe than sorry! You," he pointed to one of the Faeries, who was putting flowers in Trahaearn's hair. "Send word to the General. Tell him we'll stand guard here until our orders come."

The Faery bowed and took off on his myrkestra.

"What about her?" one of the Faeries asked.

"Shut her in the house," suggested the leader.

Eliza hated to leave the Sparkling Deluder's Gehemmis in Anargul's frozen hands, surrounded by Faeries, but she had no choice. She followed the Faery into the house. It looked much more run down than she remembered, as if nobody had lived there for years. Foss lay in the bed, his eyes closed. Ferghal and the Blind Enchanter were nowhere to be seen.

"Is that one dead?" the Faery asked, pointing at Foss in alarm.

Eliza's heart began to beat like a jackhammer in her chest, but she managed to keep her voice steady: "He opposed their using the box on me. So they used it on him too. Twice."

The Faery shuddered and strode back out into the sunshine, shutting the door on her. She ran to Foss's bedside.

He opened his eyes. They were like dark caverns with a faint light glimmering at the back. His skin was loose against the bones of his face. He stirred very slightly when he looked at her.

"Hang on, Foss," she pleaded. "I'll think of something, aye. Where are Ferghal and the Blind Enchanter?"

Foss's lips stretched slightly into what might have been a smile. He lifted a shaking hand and pointed at a tall lamp by the wall. Eliza looked at it, puzzled. It was not a very attractive lamp. It was odd and bulky and…she paused and looked again. It was not a lamp at all, but the Blind Enchanter. He held her backpack in his hands. He winked at her.

Eliza leaped to her feet.

"How did you do that?" she asked, impressed.

"A kind of...Deep Seeing...in reverse," he rasped out. "With a...glamour...effective if no one...looks too hard."

"And you still have the Gehemmis?" she whispered. He handed her the backpack.

"You have seen the...Hanging Gardens," he said. The last two words were voiceless, breath only.

Their eyes met and she nodded. They spoke no more of it. The Blind Enchanter went and lifted his large wooden table aside. Then he stroked the earth floor, murmuring. A trapdoor appeared and opened.

"By the Ancients!" Ferghal boomed, falling silent when Eliza shushed him. He scrambled out, his grizzled face covered with dust. "Cold down there," he whispered. "Good to see you back in one piece, witchlet! Sooner than we'd expected, but not a mite too soon, may I say." He indicated Foss with his head. "Why are we being quiet?"

"Faeries outside," said Eliza.

"And your friends...are coming," said the Enchanter.

Eliza looked at him in surprise. "My friends? How do you know?"

He smiled at her. "I always know...when someone is coming...here."

"How will they get past the Faeries?" she asked, her fear returning.

"Send them a...message," said the Blind Enchanter. "We will create...a small diversion. They must go around...to the west... keeping low and...out of sight. The cliffs...will hide them. There is a...cove there...and...a small cave. The cave leads...to this... passageway." The long speech cost him a great deal. He leaned against the wall, gasping for breath.

Eliza opened the trapdoor and sent a raven down it, bearing the message to Nell and Charlie.

"What kind of diversion?" she asked. The Blind Enchanter grinned and followed the raven down the tunnel.

Eliza heard the Faery approaching from outside. Hurriedly she shoved Ferghal into the tunnel with her backpack and pulled the table back into place just as the Faery opened the door and entered.

"Not up to mischief, are you?" he asked her.

"There's nothing to eat in here," she said. As soon as she said it, she realized how hungry she was.

"They want me to check that this one's really dead," he said, uninterested in her remark about food. Eliza watched apprehensively as he went over to Foss's bed and prodded him. Foss did not stir. The Faery shrugged, leaned down, and pulled a long, shining knife from his boot.

Eliza half-flew across the room, dagger in her hand before she knew she'd reached for it. She clamped one hand over his mouth so he could not cry out and with her other hand she drew her dagger across his throat. Shining blood poured from the wound. She threw him to the ground, voiceless with his throat cut, and drove the dagger deep into his heart, again and again. She knew he was struggling to make a Curse and so she continued to stab him until he gave up. Then she drove her dagger right through him, pinning him to the ground through the chest.

"Blast the Ancients," she muttered. She shoved aside the table again and opened the trapdoor. Ferghal was crouched in the tunnel, wide-eyed. She pulled her dagger out of the wounded Faery and dragged him to the opening.

"Get him out of here," she whispered. "Take him to the Blind Enchanter, fast. See if he can think what to do. If he shows any signs of getting his strength or voice back while you're taking him, then drop him and run, fast."

"Powers that Be!" breathed Ferghal. The Faery looked murder at him. Ferghal hefted the wounded being over his shoulder and hurried away down the passage. Eliza dragged Foss out of the bed, whispering apologies as she pulled him across the floor and lowered him into the passage as well. Then she shut the trapdoor over him and pulled the table back into place.

She waited alone in the house, heart thundering. The thought that came to her again and again was: I am not strong enough. I can't defeat them all. I am not strong enough. Again and again, she pushed the thought away. I've come this far and I can go a little farther yet.

Two Faeries came in this time.

"Where is he?" One of them demanded.

"He took the dead Mancer," said Eliza.

The Faeries gaped at her.

"Took him where?"

"I dinnay know," said Eliza. "He just took him."

"Nobody's come or gone," said one of the Faeries.

"Lah, he left a few minutes ago," said Eliza.

The Faeries looked at her some more and then at each other.

"Were you watching the door?" one of them asked in a low voice.

"No," conceded the other. "But we would have noticed."

"What, do you think I made them both disappear?" asked Eliza sarcastically. "I dinnay even have any powers anymore."

"So you say," said the first Faery, then turned to his partner. "You watch her, don't take an eye off her."

"Why me?"

"Just watch her."

Half an hour passed with different Faeries coming in and questioning Eliza. She stuck to her patently false story: that the Faery had simply taken Foss's body away with him.

"She's not going to tell us anything different," said the one who seemed to be the leader. "But I've heard humans respond to pain very quickly." He gave Eliza a cold look.

"So? What kind of pain?" The other Faery in the room drew a sword.

"Don't kill her," said the leader. "That won't get us anywhere. Try burning her."

Flames licked around Eliza's ankles, but they were illusion flames and she was still wearing Nia's necklace. She hesitated a moment too long, trying to decide whether or not she was good enough an actress to feign being burned.

"We need some real fire," said the leader, scowling. He drew a firestick from his cloak.

At that moment there came a great screeching noise outside and the sound of myrkestras crying out. It took Eliza a minute to recognize the screeching: dragons. The Faery grabbed her by the arm and dragged her outside.

Gold-green dragons were swarming in the air around the eastern end of the island, diving and feinting in the direction of the myrkestras.

"Is this your doing, Sorceress?" demanded the leader.

"I cannay *do* anything!" Eliza insisted. "I've no idea why they're acting up!"

"Look! One of them's got Ildor!"

Indeed, the Faery Eliza had attacked was hanging and flailing from the talons of one of the dragons. Eliza almost laughed with relief.

"Those are Mancer dragons!" she said. "They must have seen him with the dead Mancer and gotten angry."

"We'll have word soon enough. We will wait for our instructions," the Faery leader ground out between his teeth. "Back inside."

Another Faery dragged Eliza back into the cabin. She waited there, every muscle tense, the Faery watching her hatefully. What happened next occurred so quickly that Eliza couldn't quite piece it together in her mind afterwards. The trapdoor was open and the Blind Enchanter hurtling out. The Faery was turning, rising, hand reaching for his sword, as some powder caught him in the eyes. He stood there a moment, frowning, blinking, and then went back to glowering at Eliza as if nothing had happened.

Eliza sat frozen and bewildered on the bed as Ferghal followed the Blind Enchanter out of the trapdoor, lifting Foss. Behind them came Charlie and Nell.

CHAPTER

25

Eliza could not help herself. She leaped up and ran to embrace her friends. For a moment they were all laughing and talking at once. The Faery showed no sign of seeing any of this.

"What did you do to him?" Eliza asked the Enchanter. "And keep your voices down," she murmured to the others.

"Potion," said the Blind Enchanter. "For one hour...he'll see just what he saw...a few moments...before I threw it at...him. You on the bed...the empty...room."

"The dragons'll be settling, I reckon," said Ferghal. "Clever, that, how he set them off! And with the body of that Faery, so he can't squawk!"

"I've been trying to get this one to explain who he is and what he's doing here," said Charlie, raising his eyebrows at Ferghal.

"He helped me and Foss," said Eliza. Her heart ached looking at him. She thought of him running through the wood, the arrows whistling after him, the Thanatosi upon him.

"What is it?" he asked, seeing her eyes well up with tears. "Lah, we're all fine, Eliza. Trapped in a house with Faeries outside, not a fantastic situation, aye, but still."

"We've got to get out of here quick, I reckon," said Ferghal. "We'll run down that passageway and escape on the dragon these two arrived on. I've never ridden a dragon, that'll be something new. Quite a story for the grandkids, not that I've met any of them, but I reckon I've got several and if I track them down it will be quite a tale to tell. Hello, I'll say, I'm your granddaddy, and have I told you about the time I escaped murderous Faeries on the back of a dragon? That shall impress them well enough, I should think."

"But...go...where?" demanded the Blind Enchanter.

"We need a plan," agreed Eliza. "We cannay just take off with Faeries and Mancers out looking for us. We willnay get far."

"Will this help?" asked Nell. With a look half-proud, half-shy, she handed Eliza the dragon-skin pouch. Eliza took it.

"The Gehemmis?" she asked wonderingly.

"We have a lot to tell you," said Nell. Her smile fell away. "Swarn..."

"I know," said Eliza swiftly. She put the Gehemmis in the backpack with the other two. "We need the last one, the one Anargul's holding outside. Then we'll have all four."

"Then what?" asked Charlie. "We become all-powerful masters of the universe?"

"I'm nay sure," said Eliza. She looked at the Blind Enchanter. "Do you know how to use the Gehemmis?"

He shook his head.

Eliza laid the three Gehemmis out on the table and examined the symbols, but she could not read any of them or identify any patterns. The Blind Enchanter lifted the strip of bone and sniffed it with his long, agile nose. Ferghal picked up the sphere full of fog and turned it over in his hands.

"Old," he said, nodding sagely.

Charlie and Nell exchanged a look, a slight roll of the eyes. There was nothing unusual in it, exactly, but the look they gave each other and the way they stood together, shoulders touching, was so intimate and so complicit somehow, so different, that Eliza understood, suddenly, what had passed between them in the last few days. She turned aside quickly and gulped for air.

"Are you all right, Eliza?" asked Nell anxiously.

"Give me a minute," she replied. She walked to the other end of the long cabin and pressed her forehead to the stone wall by the fireplace.

What a joke I am, she thought to herself. What a stupid girl. Not to have guessed. To have ever thought...she clutched her hands together to stop them shaking.

"You're nay all right," said Nell, right behind her. "What's happened? What are you nay telling us?"

"I'm fine, lah," said Eliza. "Just scared."

"There must be somewhere we can go," said Nell. "What about the Faithful...?" but she trailed off.

"We cannay use the Gehemmis. We cannay read the symbols," said Eliza, barely hearing what she was saying. "The Book of Symbols is nay even in the Citadel. Or, it is, but it's empty, Nia drained it." Her face changed. It came to her then, what they had to do.

"You and Charlie," she said flatly.

Nell flushed and she broke into a silly grin.

"I wanted to tell you right away, aye, but with everything so dire and serious..." she whispered in a happy rush.

Eliza felt her face crumple. She couldn't help it. Tears slid out of her eyes. She covered her face with her hands.

Nell stopped, confused, and then turned very white.

"Eliza?" she whispered. She pulled Eliza's hands away from her face. Her eyes were wide with horror. Neither of them said anything for a minute.

"You dinnay...? Oh Eliza!" said Nell, her voice trembling slightly. "You nary told me! If I'd known..."

Eliza drew a sharp breath and pulled herself together quickly. *That's right, Smidgen*, she seemed to hear Nia say.

"Charlie must nary know," she whispered, almost angrily. "You have to promise me, Nell. Swear that you'll nary tell him, no matter what."

"Eliza..."

"Promise me." It was a command from a Sorceress, not a plea from a friend.

"I promise," said Nell, her face creased with misery.

"Good." Eliza strode back to the table, where the others were helplessly examining the Gehemmis for nonexistent clues. "We need to get the fourth Gehemmis from Anargul," she said, directing this at the Blind Enchanter. "Can you use that potion on a group of Faeries at once?"

The Blind Enchanter nodded. "But after…that?"

"Then I'm taking all four Gehemmis to the Hall of the Ancients," she said, "and freeing Nia."

There was a long silence.

Nell was the first to speak, her expression still pained. "That's looped, Eliza," she said.

"Oh dear," sighed Charlie.

"That's what I'm doing," said Eliza.

"You *cannay!*" Nell cried. "Have you forgotten that she killed Ander?"

"And a great many others, aye," said Eliza, not looking at Nell. "That's nay the point. We're outmatched. The Mancers. The Faeries. The Thanatosi. We dinnay even know how to *use* the Gehemmis. She's the only one who can help us."

"She's nay *going* to *help* us!" shouted Nell. "You must be looped to think she would!"

"I know her better than you do, Nell," replied Eliza. "If our interests align, she'll help us. And at the moment, the Mancers are enemies to all of us."

Nell looked at the others, throwing her hands up. "Tell her! Tell her she's looped!"

Charlie gave a weak little shrug.

"I'm with you, witchlet! Bring back the Sorceress!" cried Ferghal.

"Shut up, you're nay part of this," snapped Nell. "I know you're upset, Eliza, but…"

Eliza turned a furious gaze on her and Nell fell silent.

"This is what I'm doing," she said again. "This is my plan. I can create a stir out there with ravens. Once I've distracted them, will you use the potion on the Faeries and get the Gehemmis for me?" she asked the Blind Enchanter.

He nodded.

"What about you?" she asked Charlie, not quite meeting his eyes. "Are you with me?"

"As always, Cap'n," he said bleakly.

"Charlie!" cried Nell. "It's…she's…"

"You dinnay have to be part of this, Nell," said Eliza. "But dinnay think for one second that you can stop me."

Charlie rose and put his arm around Nell, pulling her close. Eliza averted her eyes and Nell immediately looked down at her feet.

"This is Eliza's decision," Charlie said.

The passageway was cold and dark. They hurried along it in single file, Ferghal and Charlie carrying Foss together. It reminded Eliza of scrambling through the caves in Holburg with Nell when they were children. It led them in a straight line down to the cove at the western tip of the island, where Swarn's dragon was waiting. The Blind Enchanter was moments behind them with the dark box in his hands, which he gave to Eliza.

"You'll have…an hour's…start on them…if that," he told them.

The Blind Enchanter bound Foss to the dragon's neck with bands of leather. Nell and Charlie scrambled up onto the dragon's back, and after some hesitation and speechifying, so did Ferghal.

"What about you?" asked Charlie, looking at Eliza.

"I'll keep up," she said.

He raised an eyebrow. "That's new," he said, and then gave a wry smile. "I spose you really dinnay need me at all anymore."

She could not bring herself answer that, and so turned to the Blind Enchanter instead. They shook hands warmly.

"Will you be safe when the potion wears off?"

"They will not…find me," he replied.

"Thank you," she said.

He nodded. Eliza broke into ravens, dark wings scattering across the sky. The dragon followed.

The journey was not as peaceful as they might have hoped. They flew northwest over the inland sea and the mountains. As they neared the lake of the Crossing they spotted myrkestras in the sky but the swift dragon lost them, weaving through canyons and ravines. They camped that night in the Ravening Forest. Smoky wisps began to tumble from the trees, but Eliza gave a fierce command to the trees and the wisps rolled away, murmuring. Ferghal and Eliza took the first watch, Charlie and Nell the second. Eliza had barely fallen asleep when she heard Charlie cry out. Mist was creeping among the trees. The Thanatosi had found them. Eliza deflected a storm of arrows with a barrier while the exhausted group scrambled onto the dragon's back again. They flew low over the forest and then over the Dead Marsh. The other cliff dragon met them there, crying out joyfully to find its partner. They spotted myrkestras in the distance again but the dragons outpaced them easily.

A day or two, Ka had said. Eliza's heart was cold with dread that Foss would die, strapped to the dragon, before they reached the Hall of the Ancients. It was late in the day when they arrived, the sky clanging, the snow and the sky alike bright white. The Hall of the Ancients loomed on the ragged mountain peak.

She did not want to stop being the ravens. She did not want to be Eliza again; Eliza with her broken heart. But the Urkleis was in Eliza's chest and so Eliza she would be.

The dragon landed just outside the Hall.

"Wait here," Eliza told the others. "If something goes wrong, go back to Lil and find Uri. He'll help you."

They nodded silently. They all knew that if something went wrong, they were finished.

Nia was staring at nothing, her eyes dead, her hair lank, her lips cracked. Eliza reached tentatively towards her mind but withdrew before a sucking, swirling darkness. She spoke instead.

"I need your help," she said.

Nothing. Not a flicker.

"I need you to help me to defeat the Mancers. To use the

Gehemmis. I have them. All of them. In here." She held out her camel-hair backpack. "And I have to separate the worlds."

For a moment, there was no response. Then a faint glimmer returned to Nia's eyes. Her cracked and broken lips twitched into the beginnings of a malevolent smile.

It was easier to let the Urkleis go than it had been to take possession of it. She put her hand on Nia's bare arm. Her skin was cold. She felt the Urkleis pounding in her chest. You can go, she thought. Get out. She could feel it pushing, yearning towards Nia, and Nia was drawing it to her. It was quick and painful. Her chest opened and the Urkleis, a burnt black ball, rolled out. Nia's arm swung out and the Urkleis landed in her palm. Eliza fell to her knees with a cry of pain, her flesh and bone closing up over the empty space where the Urkleis had lodged. Nia's fingers closed, the Urkleis melting into blackness and then nothing, as if her skin simply drank it up. She was doubled over and gasping for breath. Eliza looked up at her, almost giddy with the relief of being free of the Urkleis, awash in the old, familiar, irrational love she bore the Sorceress.

"Do you *ever* bathe, Eliza?" Nia gasped out. "I thought we'd spoken about this."

Before Eliza could say anything in response, Nia's hand shot out and she had Eliza by the throat, rushing back, pinning her to the stone wall. The Hall span around her as a thousand icy knife-like little hands dove into her, cold shadows searching, grasping, pulling her apart.

CHAPTER
26

Eliza broke into ravens, all of them flapping up towards the vaulted roof, past the broken carvings on the walls. From above, Nia looked small and pale and very old. She raised her arms with a livid shriek and the mass of ravens were pulled down by a force they could not resist, pulled back together into one struggling shape, back into Eliza.

"That's clever, Smidgen," hissed Nia. "But tricks like that won't help you."

And again the diving, clutching fingers, the snipping and seeking deep inside her, where dark wings beat against dark air. Her Magic was pinned, stifled. She felt the tremendous force of Nia's power pushing against her own, felt how quickly Nia would crush her.

She tried to speak but no words would come and so she fumbled for her dagger. Nia's grip around her throat cut off her breath. The world was closing up into a small, dark, spinning circle. She pulled the dagger from its scabbard and drove it into the Sorceress's belly.

Nia screamed, staggering back a step or two. All the prying little hands inside Eliza vanished. Nia gave her a shocked, white-faced stare, then struck her hard across the face.

"You horrid little…" she put her hand over the bleeding gash. The wound closed up.

"*Please* listen to me!" Eliza spoke as fast as she could. "You can drain me of my power, we both know that, but it will take time too. And…"

Nia struck her again with the hand she'd touched to her

wound. Her flat palm smeared blood across Eliza's face. Eliza fell back against the wall. Nia grabbed her by the wrist with a burning grip. Unwillingly, Eliza felt her fingers loosen and she dropped the dagger. With her other hand Nia grabbed Eliza's face and squeezed.

"Shut up, Smidgen," she snarled. Eliza saw the lines riving Nia's pale face, the torn and peeling skin of her lips, the web of broken blood vessels in her eyes. All this swam before her and again the cold grip within, tearing at her.

"Kyreth has Malferio," she managed to croak.

Nia let go of her and Eliza fell to the ground, gasping for breath.

"No," said Nia.

"There isnay time," said Eliza. "He has Malferio and he's been preparing the Magic to kill him."

"He can't," said Nia. "He swore by the oath of the Ancients. You were there."

"He'll find a way," said Eliza. "Malferio is helping him."

Fear flickered across Nia's face. She opened the locket around her neck and looked into it. Immediately she was restored, her hair shining, her face young and lovely, her eyes bright.

"Important to face the worst with one's best face," she said to Eliza, her tone more cheerful. "All right, Smidgen. You've got yourself a few minutes. Why are you here telling me this?"

"You drained the Book of Symbols," said Eliza. "You have all the knowledge of the Mancer Library and I have the Gehemmis. You can use the Gehemmis to stop Kyreth. And then I have to use them…I need you to show me how to separate the worlds."

"Honestly, Smidgen. You must be joking. You come here and offer me objects of tremendous power and what do you expect? That I'm going to spare you? Let you share the power?"

"I made a promise to the Sparkling Deluder," said Eliza. "I said I would separate the worlds. If I dinnay do it, I'll be taken back to the Hanging Gardens with the Gehemmis. I dinnay think even you can afford to have the Sparkling Deluder as an enemy."

She had no idea if the Sparkling Deluder would take back the Gehemmis as well or hold Nia responsible if Eliza failed in her promise, but lying was coming more and more easily to her the more desperate she became.

Nia smiled. "You never cease to amaze and delight me, Eliza," she said. "But I have conditions too. If I am going to help you, I want to finish what I started when you interrupted me last time. Swarn."

"She's dead," said Eliza stonily.

Nia sighed. "Typical. And Kyreth is free of my Curse?"

"Nay free of it. But nay completely bound by it either. If you want to kill him, I'll help you this time."

Nia burst out laughing. "You *are* full of surprises! Very well, a spot of patricide in the afternoon and then we'll see where we stand. I'm curious, though. This eagerness of yours to separate the worlds seems a little out of character and I don't for a minute believe you're just keeping a promise. Since when do you care so much about separating the worlds?"

"Humans would finally be safe," said Eliza. Nia arched an eyebrow at her. "And my friends would be safe. Right now we've got the Thanatosi after us, and the Faeries, and the Mancers, under Kyreth. If you kill Kyreth and we separate the worlds, we can stay in Di Shang and be safe from all of them."

"And safe from me too? Is that what you think? That I won't demand of you the power that is mine?"

"It's nay yours, it's mine," said Eliza. She took a deep breath. "But if you let me live, I'll give it to you. No fighting. The power only. Nothing more."

Nia gave her an appraising look.

"I have to admit that my experiment with Rea was hardly successful. I don't particularly enjoy having all her memories clamouring about in my head, and the power...well, I've managed to make use of it well enough, even without taking her whole. If you're going to offer me your power without a fight, your life and self seem a fair price. Then, as you say, you and your little friends can stay in Di Shang and lead your little human lives, and I...well, I will have all of Tian Xia, with the power of three Sorceresses and the Gehemmis."

Eliza's heart gave a little lurch. She thought of what Kyreth had said at the Lake of Awful Truths. Here she was, planning to leave Tian Xia at Nia's mercy. Nia and Amarantha, both Immortal and terribly powerful, would make Tian Xia a very dangerous place indeed. But what else could she do?

"I imagine that Kyreth has some idea of what you're up to, however," continued Nia. "I suggest we hurry. Give me the Gehemmis."

There was no turning back now. Eliza took off her backpack. At the same moment, Nell came racing into the Hall.

"The Thanatosi!" she cried. "They've found us!"

Charlie and Ferghal followed, dragging Foss.

"Faeries, too," Charlie panted. "They've just come up through the clouds."

"I must say, it surprises me that Kyreth sent the Thanatosi after you, Smidgen," commented Nia. "That seems rather extreme, even for him. I thought he wanted an heir from you."

Mist poured into the Hall and Eliza fixed her eyes on Charlie, holding her hands out and garbling a barrier spell. Arrows bounced off the barrier and the Thanatosi came spinning and swirling through various entranceways, surrounding Charlie. Eliza quaked with every blow from every sword against her weak barrier.

"They're nay after her," said Charlie from within the mist. "They're after me."

Nia raised her eyebrows meaningfully at Eliza. "Ah. I *see*."

"Help us," begged Eliza, grabbing Nia by the hand. She felt the barrier shudder and give a little. "I'm begging you. Help us, and I'll do whatever you want."

"You'll do whatever I want *any*way," said Nia with an irritated shrug, pulling her hand away. "And don't grovel. It's depressing."

"We were friends once," Charlie called out to Nia. "I was a good friend to you for a long time."

Eliza and Nell exchanged a startled look. It struck Eliza how little she really knew of Charlie's history and the long alliance he'd shared with Nia. She had always assumed he was bound to her by obligation and fear. To hear him describe their relationship as friendship was rather unsettling, and she could see that Nell felt the same way. The Thanatosi were slashing at the barrier ruthlessly now, feeling its weakness. It was buckling, folding.

"Please!" she cried to Nia.

Nia looked at Eliza almost pityingly for a moment and then Eliza felt the weight of the barrier lift. It ballooned out around Charlie, pushing back the Thanatosi. They continued to whirl around it, swords flashing, but it held firm against them.

"Thank you," she gasped.

"We've still got Faeries coming any moment and we won't be able to get much done with these ridiculous things performing acrobatics," said Nia with a gleam in her eye. "The situation calls for something more extreme, I think. Lend me your power, Smidgen."

"What for?" Eliza felt a cold fear creeping under her skin.

Nia gave her a fierce look. "Do you want my help or not?" she demanded. She took Eliza's hand in hers. Eliza felt everything inside her suddenly surging with an intensity beyond anything she had ever felt.

"*You* two?"

The tone was one of utter disbelief. A little boy stood facing them, arms folded. Eliza recognized him. It was the curly-headed little moppet she had spoken to in the desert before defeating the Kwellrahg. The one who had told her to go back. He stuck his finger in his mouth and glowered at them.

"*Together!*" added another voice. A pigtailed girl was perched on the stump of a broken statue in one of the grottoes above them.

"I hate her," said the little boy irritably, pulling his finger out of his mouth and rolling his soft eyes towards Nia. "She's so bossy."

"She can't boss *me* around," the little girl sniffed. "She tries to but she can't." She looked down at Eliza curiously. "Aren't you the Sparkling Deluder's purest star?" she asked.

"I suppose I...was. Or will be," said Eliza cautiously.

"The Sparkling Deluder is my best friend," said the little girl happily, and her two pigtails lengthened into long slender snakes, swinging and hissing. She leaped down into the Hall.

"Oh. That's nice," said Eliza.

"Make it stop," said Nia to the little girl. "Everything but us."

Eliza stared at the Sorceress, baffled. The little girl shook her head firmly, and then she was not a girl at all but a huge black cobra, coiled right around the hall. Her dry scaled flesh heaved and her hooded head waved above them. She looked down on them through flickering eyes. Nia did not seem in the slightest perturbed. She pointed at the little boy cowering now at the far end of the hall and commanded him: "Come here."

"I'm not helping you!" he shouted tearfully. "That's my sister!"

Eliza felt a tearing and wrenching within. Ravens swirled around the head of the cobra.

"Stop it!" shouted Eliza, pulling her hand free of Nia's. The ravens disappeared.

"Don't be a baby," said Nia through clenched teeth, sweat breaking out across her brow. "I need power."

She grabbed Eliza's hand again and once more Eliza felt herself torn open. Her body jerked back rigid, her mouth opened wide, and ravens poured out of her throat. She heard Nell screaming as if from another world and from the corner of her eye she saw Nia's raised arms flickering with black light. The black light spiraled out from her arms and twisted around the cobra, pulling it this way and that. The little boy was at her side, looking miserable. There was no air in the hall, only a soundless flaring struggle, which finished with a popping sound.

The little girl with pigtails lay on the floor, bleeding from her nose, her eyes full of tears. The little boy ran to her side but she pushed him away angrily.

The arrows of the Thanatosi were frozen in mid-air, as were the leaping assassins themselves. They were suspended, swords raised over their heads, their featureless faces all turned towards Charlie, who was looking up at them in alarm. The mist around them was frozen too, like a photograph of a cloud. Nell was stopped in mid-run, feet hardly touching the ground, mouth wide, making towards Eliza. Ferghal was huddled protectively over Foss's prone form.

"Marvelous!" said Nia, her eyes shining. "Let's look outside. Come on, Smidgen!"

Aching inside, as if she had been pulled out of her own skin and then stuffed back in, Eliza stumbled after Nia. Twenty or more myrkestras were but paces from the Hall, stopped in mid-air. There was an eerie stillness all around, no breeze, no whisper of air. Nia turned to Eliza with a look of triumph.

"That girl is the Guardian of Time," she said. "I've never been able to get her to concede to anything before but it would appear that with your power added to my own and your mother's, I've just enough. Which is…a *very* exciting notion. Think what I'll be capable of!"

"What about the boy?" asked Eliza numbly.

"The Guardian of Magic. Supposed to set its limits and so on, but he's a bit of a pushover really. Well, come on. I don't know how long this is going to last. I'll put a barrier around the Hall just in case, much as I dislike them. We don't want to be interrupted."

"Can we move the Thanatosi outside?" asked Eliza. "I dinnay like them…hanging over Charlie like that."

"Poor Smidgen," sighed Nia. "Yes, of course."

The Thanatosi, limbs still unmoving, came drifting out as Nia murmured under her breath. She stood them on their heads, smirking to herself, and then raised a barrier behind them as she and Eliza re-entered the Hall.

Back inside, Nia noticed Ferghal and Foss for the first time. "You always have the oddest hangers-on," she noted. "A Scarpathian indigent? Honestly, Eliza. And what in the worlds is wrong with the Mancer?"

"He rebelled," said Eliza. "He stood up to Kyreth and he's dying now. Cannay you help him?"

"Nobody can help a Mancer but the Mancers," said Nia with a shrug. "I'm sure he knew what it would cost him. Trying to keep a Mancer alive when it's been cut off from the others is like trying to keep a flower alive in the dark. There's not much that can be done. Give me the Gehemmis."

Without waiting for Eliza to hand it to her, Nia snatched the camel-hair backpack from her and took each of the Gehemmis out in turn, looking them over carefully.

"Can you read the symbols?" asked Eliza.

Nia smiled. "Of course. Thanks to the Mancer Library. You know, it's as if this was meant to be, Smidgen. You and I, here. It's perfect. I don't believe in destiny but sometimes random chance offers up something so sublime that you almost want to believe it *had* to be this way."

She held up the Gehemmis of the Horogarth. "Bone," she said in the Language of First Days. "What was broken in the Making."

The fragment of bone flew from her hands to a faint carving on the northern wall, a long undulating line. It fit perfectly into a notch in the stone. Nia picked up the dragon-skin sack.

"Ash," she said. "What was burned in the Making."

The black ashes swirled out of the bag and scattered themselves across the eastern wall, where the broken, carved head of a dragon looked down from the highest grotto.

"Fog," she said, taking up the glass sphere of the Faeries. "What was obscured by the Making."

The glass shattered and the fog inside it streamed up to a grotto on the west wall that had once held the carving of a Faery King. There it took the shape of a crown where the head was no longer.

At last she lifted the dark box from the Sparkling Deluder. Her hands trembled slightly.

"The first star," she said, "that illuminated the Making."

The box opened. Eliza threw herself to the ground, arms over her head, to shield herself from the light that poured out. The Hall shuddered, and for one panicked moment she feared that it would fall on them. When at last the light began to dim, Eliza opened her eyes, still seeing sunspots. She and Nia were alone in the Hall but it was not the Hall as she knew it. The stone was a deep black, unfaded. The symbols, once worn and difficult to make out, were etched clearly into the stone, and the statues and carvings were brightly painted, a riot of colour against the black walls. She and Nia got slowly to their feet. Nia's eyes were bright with wonder and joy.

"Where are we?" asked Eliza.

"I think the question is *when*, not where," said Nia. "And I've no idea."

The Hall shuddered again. Something emerged from the wall. Its large eyes, wet and bright and moving, held both Sorceresses immediately. The rest of it seemed only partly formed – or perhaps that was wrong; perhaps it was just in perpetual flux, changing and moving. Swirls and shadows suggested a body but Eliza could not look away from the eyes to really be sure. Even the face around the eyes seemed little more than a kind of spreading, gleaming darkness. The stones of the Hall spoke to them, in a voice that only stone could ever make:

Have you come to wake the Ancients?

"Wake the Ancients?" murmured Eliza.

"I'm fairly sure that's *not* what we've come for," said Nia.

But that is the power of the Gehemmis.

The Hall vibrated strangely when the stones spoke. Whether it was the vibrations, the stepping outside time and place, or the peculiar eyes she could not look away from, Eliza felt faint and queasy. Nia, however, seemed unaffected.

"I hadn't realized the Ancients were…ah…sleeping," said Nia. "I thought they'd gone off somewhere."

They are here, said the stones. *They are us, and you, and all of this. They sleep in your bones and in your breath and in the oceans and the earth.*

"So if we wake them up…"

They will become what they were, not what they are now.

"Well, let's let them keep napping a bit longer then, shall we? What else can the Gehemmis do?"

That is the power of the Gehemmis.

"That's all?" Nia looked at Eliza a bit petulantly. "How disappointing."

"What about separating the worlds?" said Eliza. "The Sparkling Deluder told me…"

The giant, wet eyes seemed to throb and flash. The stones grated angrily.

It needs no power to separate the worlds. It needs power to keep them together. Power still dwelling in Di Shang, power that Tian Xia cannot pull away from.

"What does that mean? What are you talking about?" Nia sounded angry, impatient, but Eliza thought she understood.

"I should have known," she murmured. "I should have guessed, when Foss told me about the spell slowing down, how there was no record of it."

Magic wanted form, said the stones. *Magic wanted to live in the world, and so it took shape. It wanted love, and so there were more. You call them the Ancients. They lived and loved, and when they grew weary, they did not want to leave the world, and so they became part of it, part of Tian Di. Then Tian Di broke into two. It is the way of worlds, sometimes. They draw apart, they multiply, occupying different planes of existence. It should not take so much time, but the Mancers have been sowing their Magic deep into Di Shang, housing Tian Xia treasures, binding the worlds still. So long as beings and objects of great power remain in Di Shang, it cannot pull apart from Tian Xia.*

Nia reacted first: "I knew it! I just knew the Mancers couldn't have managed such a spell! Those mangy, sneaking liars, pretending *they* separated the worlds."

"So the worlds would separate naturally if the Mancers left Di Shang," said Eliza.

The Mancers. The Citadel. And the Sorceress.

Eliza's heart plummeted. Then she remembered her agreement with Nia. She would give up her power. She felt suddenly dizzy. What would it be like to once again be simply a girl, with no Magic at all? To live in a Di Shang that was no longer connected to this strange and terrible world, a Di Shang with no need of a Sorceress? What would she *do?* She had missed years of school… She reined in her wild imaginings, forced herself back to the present.

"But *why* would the Mancers do this? All this time, they've been keeping the worlds connected on purpose? To what end?"

They are ignorant – most of them. Fooled and manipulated by the Supreme Mancer.

"Kyreth," said Eliza bitterly.

Karbek, said the stones. *When it began, Karbek alone understood what was happening and misled the others. He knew that if Di Shang pulled away from Tian Xia, the power of the Mancers would be much diminished. They draw their power from the natural world, not the magical. He led the Mancers to Di Shang and began the Magic they have worked ever since, to keep the worlds together, while claiming to do the opposite. He still held ambitions of Mancer dominion over both worlds. Some Mancers since have known the truth. Those that pursued the Gehemmis knew it would serve their cause. All the Gehemmis in Di Shang would be powerful enough to draw the worlds back together, remake Tian Di. One world for the Mancers to rule, with humans as their foot soldiers.*

"Humans," snorted Nia.

They were feeble and powerless long ago. Not anymore. They are so numerous, and their modern weaponry far more sophisticated than anything in Tian Xia, where beings rely so entirely on magic.

"So that's Kyreth's plan," said Eliza, shuddering.

But now the Gehemmis are here in the Hall of the Ancients. They are put to use. I ask for the last time: Will you wake the Ancients?

"No," said Nia swiftly. "We don't want to do that."

Then the Gehemmis are returned to their rightful owners until such time as they choose to wake the Ancients.

The moist, moving eyes blinked and were gone. The Hall was a ruin again, Eliza's friends still frozen in time.

"Well!" said Nia. "*That* is a surprise, I must say."

For a moment they said nothing more. Then Eliza felt something give and Nell was running straight for them and yelling. She stumbled and paused, confused.

"What happened to the giant snake?" she asked.

Charlie was looking around in bewilderment. "What happened to the Thanatosi?"

"Giants' Oaths!" cried Ferghal, sputtering. "Ancients' Spit! What in the name of all that's Immortal is going on?"

"We have to get the Mancers out of Di Shang," said Eliza to Nia.

"Priorities, Smidgen," tutted Nia. "Patricide first. Speaking of which − " her head shot up and her eyes flashed. "Somebody is tampering with my barrier."

An entrance groaned open and Kyreth stepped into the Hall. At his side was a slippery grey creature with a giant, bald head and lurid yellow eyes. It looked as if it were half fish, half ogre.

Nia's lip curled. "I should have known a barrier wouldn't keep *you* out," she said. "Did you know Eliza's offered to help me do away with you? Isn't she sweet?"

"Where are the Gehemmis?" His voice was like thunder.

"Gone," said Nia blithely. "They weren't much use, as it turns out. We did discover that you've been telling some rather shocking lies, however! I really shouldn't be so surprised. Take my hand, Smidgen."

Nia reached for Eliza, and Eliza hesitated.

"Even together, are you a match for all the Mancers, powers combined and Magic prepared?" asked Kyreth.

"I don't see *all the Mancers*," retorted Nia. "Eliza! Take my hand!"

"I...."

"She is not a murderer," said Kyreth. "Whatever else she may be, she will not be able to bring herself to kill me."

Nia spoke in the Language of First Days, her voice resonating terribly. "Your bones break, your heart be still, your breath be gone!" The black light was unspooling from her fingers, lacing around Kyreth, but a white light poured out of him and dissipated it almost instantly.

"I am ready for you this time," he said, holding up a hand. "Eliza, you have achieved what no Sorceress before you could achieve, but you are nonetheless terribly predictable. I knew you would seek help from Nia. I knew that I would find you here. I had hoped..." he drew a sharp breath here, "that the Gehemmis would not yet be put into use. Your manipulation of time *was* unexpected, though most impressive. But all is not lost. We are here. Before you arrived, I enchanted the Hall of the Ancients."

"What...?" began Eliza.

"That's the Guardian of Space with him," said Nia grimly.

"Long allied with the Mancers," said Kyreth.

The Guardian opened his awful mouth. No sound came out but the Hall began to spin. It span faster and faster, until it was only a dark blur. Then it fell still suddenly and they all staggered, trying to adjust their eyes to the scene. They were in the grounds of the Citadel, surrounded by Mancers. Malferio knelt on the grass, his eyes dull and hooded, and Gautelen stood behind him, holding his dagger. She and Malferio spoke in unison: *"Life becomes Death."*

Then she drove the dagger into the back of his neck.

CHAPTER

27

Eliza reeled, trying to keep her balance. The world had only just stopped spinning, and she could not quite believe what she saw. As the stroke fell, she heard Nia's voice, a stunned whisper: "No!"

Malferio fell forwards on the grass. He looked up at Nia with shining eyes. "Do you see what you have done to me?" he gasped. "King of the Faeries! To die like a groveling mortal!" A look of amazement crossed his face as the Magic worked through his blood. "There it is. To *die*, to be no more. It isn't fair. I feel it. It isn't fair."

Nia ran to him, kneeling and taking his face in her hands.

"Malferio," she whispered, her eyes full of tears.

"I wish I had never known you, wretched fiend," he murmured. "Ah! It touches the heart."

Nia looked up and her eyes fell on Gautelen. Her tears were gone as quickly as they had appeared. "You blasted little fool," she hissed. "Will you let anyone make use of you?"

Gautelen's look of triumph fell to bewilderment. She dropped the dagger in the grass.

"It is done," said Kyreth.

A barrier sprang up around Eliza, binding her arms fast so she could not reach for her own dagger.

"Yes," said Nia, rising and stepping back. She looked from Malferio gasping in the grass to Kyreth standing over him. "But not quite finished yet."

With a wild, terrified look in her eyes, she plunged her hand through the barrier that held Eliza and pulled her free.

"Do you trust me?" she whispered. The Mancers had all begun chanting at once. Without a thought Eliza gave her power over to Nia. The girl with snake pigtails and the slippery grey ogre stood before them, reaching out. Clinging to each other, Nia and Eliza grasped their hands. The two Guardians gave a sharp yank and the Citadel was gone.

They are in the desert, by the Lookout Tree. The little boy sits high up in the branches, looking down at them silently. Selva is there, holding Rea cradled in her arms. Not Rea as she was at the shore of the Lake of the Deep Forgotten, but Rea as she is now: broken, haunted.

Nia leans against the tree and looks at Eliza with wide, brilliant eyes.

"They've beaten me," she says. "After everything! The blasted Mancers!"

Rea says hollowly, "Now you know how it feels to lose."

"Yes, I left you with that memory, didn't I?" says Nia. "I...I don't think the Guardians will let us stay here long, so I suppose I'll be dead in moments. But Kyreth is mistaken if he thinks he can get away with this. If he thinks he can stamp me out and be safe." The golden fire in her green eyes shines more brightly than ever as she looks at each of them, Selva, Rea, Eliza. She begins to whisper something, curling in on herself. The white tiger comes leaping out of the desert towards them. It paces circles around the Lookout Tree, tail lashing.

When Nia looks up again, she holds two little wrapped bonbons in her hand.

"This one is for you," she says to Eliza, giving her one of them. "Yummy sugar-coated centuries of dark Magic. My power. Ironic, isn't it? Use it to avenge me. Promise me."

"I promise." Eliza replies without thinking.

Nia turns to Rea. "And this is yours. Everything that I took."

Rea reaches for it with a trembling hand.

Eliza looks at the bonbon in her hand. Nia's power. She sees again the Oracle of the Ancients, her clear eyes and her small pointed teeth, and she hears her hissing voice: *You will cut out your own heart.* And finally she understands. That time has come.

"If you take back your power, you'll have to leave Di Shang forever," she tells her mother. "We have to separate the worlds. All the beings of power will go to Tian Xia, and the humans must stay in Di Shang."

"Rom?" asks Rea, staring at the bonbon, brow furrowed.

"He must stay," says Selva quietly. "He belongs to this world."

"You *can't* be thinking of…" Nia begins.

Rea hands the bonbon swiftly to Eliza. "I can't leave him," she says.

Nia rolls her eyes and slumps against the tree.

"You must make your choice quickly, my dear," says Selva to Eliza. "Time will not wait for us much longer."

"You could have it," says Eliza, knowing it's useless.

Selva shakes her head. "Mine is another road. You know yours. You have only to choose it."

Nia has turned very white. "Smidgen, you promised! You'll punish him, you said…"

"Yes," says Eliza. "I will."

"I wish I could see their faces when you turn up! You know, I always thought…well, if anybody was going to do me in, I'd have thought it would be you."

"I couldnay have done it," says Eliza.

"Oh, you might've had to. I was going to wreak the most terrible havoc. But that's all done now." The pendant around her neck is fading, darkening. The white tiger gives a low moan and bows its great head to her. She puts her arms around its neck.

"Oh Smidgen," she says, tears shining in her eyes as she looks up at Eliza. "The fun I've had!"

"Go on," says Selva gently.

Eliza puts the bonbons in her mouth, one after the other, and bites down. Trust Nia, they are delicious, but there is not much time to notice that. She feels the wind and the ocean thundering through her veins. She feels the emptiness of space in the marrow of her bones. She looks up into the branches of the Lookout Tree, where the little boy is staring down at her with wide, frightened eyes. He points, and she follows his finger.

A dark river cuts through the desert. In the shadowy distance the great panther looms, crouching over it. The river rushes between its giant paws. *You will bring me your beloved.*

Eliza finds she is weeping as she lifts Nia into her arms. The sand turns to darkness beneath her feet as she carries the Sorceress to the river. The white tiger pads behind her.

Charlie, Nell and Ferghal huddled together in the grass around Foss, staring at the spot where moments before Eliza and Nia had joined hands and then vanished. Malferio lay dead just paces away. The Mancers were silent and still.

"A seeking spell," Kyreth threw over his shoulder at last. "Find Eliza."

"The Vindensphere…" a Mancer began tentatively.

"In need of repair," said Kyreth with a harsh laugh. "Again."

Gautelen sank to her knees in the grass. She looked at Nell in stunned bewilderment.

"You are not the Shang Sorceress," she said.

"No," said Nell coldly.

"I do not like this place," muttered Ferghal. "Hello! My friend awakes!"

Foss was sitting up slowly, painfully, a faint glimmer returning to his dark eyes.

"Kyreth!" he called out, his voice still weak.

The Emmisariae were standing directly behind Kyreth and started when Foss spoke.

"It is Foss!" Finnis cried out joyfully; then he fell to frightened silence.

"You are leading the Mancers astray, Kyreth," said Foss. He tottered to his feet.

From somewhere in his flowing robes, Kyreth drew a long, gleaming sword.

"See what becomes of a traitor!" he called out to the assembled Mancers.

"Will you stand by and watch murder?" cried Ferghal, outraged, leaping to his feet. "Defend your fellow from this monster!"

The Mancers looked at one another fearfully. Kyreth strode towards Foss, sword aloft. Ferghal snatched up the dagger Gautelen had dropped.

Before they reached each other, the earth moved, as if the Citadel was perched atop the back of a sleeping beast that was now stirring. The great walls and towers trembled. For a moment they all froze, waiting in the strange hush that fell for what would happen next.

Ravens poured out of the sky. Ravens burst from the ground and the white walls. The world was a mass of them, seething. They covered the grass, they covered the walls, they filled the trees. They formed a doorway against one of the walls, and through it stepped Eliza.

Her eyes were black pools, her hair dark cords that snaked around her shoulders. Light trembled from her fingers.

Kyreth span towards her, sword raised, and Ferghal lunged at him, driving Malferio's enchanted dagger into his back.

The Citadel shook again. Kyreth staggered. Ferghal was backing away from him, eyes wide, mouth working soundlessly. The walls groaned. The earth gave a jolt and they all staggered. Great cracks began to run across the walls and the ground.

Kyreth stumbled towards Eliza, the light draining from his eyes, his bright gold skin fading rapidly to white and then to grey. She stood still as he grabbed her by the shoulders, towering over her.

"Eliza," he whispered. "The greatness of the Mancers depends on Di Shang. You must not...you must not..." His voice faded. He fell to his knees.

"There are many kinds of greatness," said Eliza.

He looked up at her, unseeing, his eyes black caverns, and then toppled sideways, dead. The walls and towers tumbled with him. The Inner Sanctum cracked and fell. The Mancers and the humans covered their heads and ducked among the trees for shelter from the falling stone. When the sound had abated and the dust cleared, they began cautiously to emerge. The Citadel lay ruined.

Ferghal helped Foss climb onto the rubble of the Inner Sanctum, where he addressed the Mancers.

"I would like to call an emergency council," he said weakly. "With all Mancers in attendance."

Once Eliza had explained her side of the recent events, she left the Mancers to their council outside the ruined Inner Sanctum. Foss was getting stronger every moment that he stood among his fellows, she was glad to see. They had all been stunned by the revelation that their Magic had for eons connected the worlds rather than pulled them apart, and a great many of the Mancers were still insisting that this was impossible. Most of them, however, saw the truth of it as soon as they heard it. Eliza hoped that they would agree to go to Tian Xia peacefully, but had made it clear that any who refused would have to contend with her. They all looked at her fearfully now; Obrad in particular avoided her gaze. She had other things on her mind for now.

With some trepidation, she joined her friends sitting under the trees. The ravens were mostly gone, just a few of them here and there pecking at the dust. To her relief, they looked at her as if she was unchanged. As if she was still Eliza.

"Nia's really dead?" asked Nell.

Eliza nodded.

"I'm sorry about...before," said Nell. "On the Isle of the Blind Enchanter. It's just, lah, when you said you were going to *her* for help..."

"It's all right," Eliza said quickly. "I understand."

"And look at you now," said Charlie. "The power of three Sorceresses! How does that feel?"

There were no words for it. What could she say? The power she felt trembling within her and around her was terrifying. She was connected to everything, or so it seemed, but not in a nourishing way. She could pull the sky down with her fist, stop time. It felt destructive, too large and too dangerous for this quiet, gentle world. She felt as if she had been swallowed by Magic and was looking out of it from a great distance at everything that had once been familiar. Her friends.

Thankfully, when she didn't answer, Charlie kept on talking. "So, separating the worlds. I used to be opposed to the idea, but being human now, I've had a change of heart, aye. It's awful how vulnerable humans are. It might be the right thing to do after all. I mean, if you think it is, then I'm all for it."

"I dinnay know if it's the right thing to do or nay," said Eliza. "That's too big a question for me. But it's what would have happened naturally if the Mancers hadnay been stopping it. It's also the only way to keep the Thanatosi away from you for good, aye. I'm guessing they're on their way to Di Shang right now."

Charlie grinned, a little nervously. "How many people can say that their best friend sundered two worlds on their behalf?"

"And all that needs to happen is the Mancers need to leave," said Nell. "That means you'll be the only being with any power left in Di Shang!"

There was a short pause. The truth hit Nell and Charlie at the same moment.

"No!" said Nell.

"Eliza!" said Charlie.

She looked down at her hands. Light still flickered around her fingertips. It was unsettling.

"It's the only way, lah," she said. She couldn't look at them.

"But...how will we see each other?" cried Nell.

Eliza stood up. Her own grief felt dangerous to her, tinged as it was with this terrible and unfamiliar power.

"We willnay," she said shortly. "But it's the only way. I'm going to see how Gautelen's doing."

The young Storm Seamstress sat huddled by herself under an

oak tree, her dark face streaked with tears. She looked up when she heard Eliza approaching.

"I don't understand," she said dully. "I thought you were her enemy. Now it seems you were her friend."

"A little of both," said Eliza, crouching down next to her.

"And Malferio...she hated him. I thought she'd be... grateful."

"It's complicated," said Eliza. "It always is."

"Is she dead?"

Eliza nodded and Gautelen buried her face in her hands. Eliza put a hand on her shoulder.

"We'll take you back to Tian Xia," she said. "Your parents will be worried."

She sat with the weeping girl until Nell and Charlie came and joined her. Nell's eyes were red and puffy.

"They've all agreed," said Charlie. "The Mancers, I mean. They're going back to Tian Xia. They need to go through the ruins for books and enchanted objects...that'll take a while I spec. And they've just voted Foss Supreme Mancer."

"What?" Eliza leaped to her feet.

"At first they all assumed it would go to Ka. But then he said he wasnay worthy because he'd known Kyreth was wrong and suspected him of killing Aysu but hadnay done anything. He said the only one who had been willing to do the right thing was Foss and he should be Supreme Mancer. I cannay say everyone looked happy about it, but they agreed."

"There must be some way you can stay here," Nell burst out, almost before Charlie had finished.

"I dinnay think there is," said Eliza. "And I've done a lot of damage in Tian Xia. Amarantha is still on the loose. Now I have all this power, praps it's time to do...something good. Something useful."

"You can be good and useful in Di Shang!" cried Nell.

"And be the last thing linking the two worlds, aye," said Eliza. "If anything crossed over from Tian Xia, it would be my fault. Besides, I spec the Sparkling Deluder would be as good as its word, or as bad as its word, and take me back like it threatened to. I know what I have to do and it's nay easy. Dinnay make it harder."

They were all silent for a while, finding it difficult to look at one another. At last Nell said, "By the way…it's nay the best timing, praps, but do you spose we could borrow a dragon from the Mancers?"

Eliza and Charlie gaped at her.

"What for?" asked Eliza.

Nell shifted uncomfortably. "My test is tomorrow."

The following weeks passed in a blur. Shortly after Nell left for Austermon on Ka's dragon, the Thanatosi appeared. For the first time, Eliza performed the Magic that would have been her duty as the Shang Sorceress, the Magic her ancestors had performed. She banished them, forcing them with Magic to return to the Crossing and to Tian Xia, never to come again to Di Shang. Of course, as Foss had said, there were always more, like the Cra. Until the worlds were severed, they would keep coming.

For several exhausting days in the desert, Eliza returned her mother's memories to her. Nia had been right that the power was deeply entwined with memory and other aspects of self. Returning Rea's memories and thoughts and fears and strengths without returning any power to her required a very strenuous, meticulous kind of Magic. She could not return it all in the precise form it had been when it was taken. Rea's old self was returned to her fragmented and altered, not quite what it had been, but nevertheless the change in her was remarkable. She could walk unaided at last, and some of the pride and certainty Eliza had seen at the Lake of the Deep Forgotten returned to her.

In the ruined Citadel, she returned the knowledge Nia had drained from the Mancer Library. The many treasures of the Mancers as well as the thousands of books were piled around the dark wood that still stood at what had been the northeast corner of the grounds.

They repaired the Vindensphere and searched out the few Tian Xia worlders remaining in Di Shang. This included, among others, a fair number of the Cra, several womi, one very shy wizard who had, for over a hundred years, disguised himself as a snow-covered rock in the Karbek mountains, three witches, one of whom was the president of a major corporation and was not at all pleased at being forced to abandon all her holdings, and a community of trolls living underground in Huir-Kosta. Besides banishing all of these, Eliza had, every few days, to contend with new hordes of the Thanatosi. When Charlie was not with her, he had to remain within a barrier.

And yet in all these endeavours she felt she was using but the surface of a Magic that went deeper than she dared yet to plumb. She was weary, but she knew there lay within her a vast, dark well of power, and when she was quiet and alone, she felt something from its depths stir and whisper unintelligibly.

Ferghal was granted use of a dragon to return to Scarpatha. Without the Mancers propping up the Republic, he said, he was interested to see how the politics of Di Shang would shift, and he wanted to stand with the Scarpathians. Foss wrote him a letter presenting him to the Prime Minister of Scarpatha, currently in prison, and allowed him to take three treasures from the Citadel. He chose a goblet of Faery Gold, for, as he said, he was short on cash and it was no doubt worth a fortune, a crystal ring that turned dark when danger approached, ("There is nothing worse, by all that's mighty, than having danger sneak up on you unawares!") and Foss's portrait, which they managed to retrieve unharmed from the rubble of the Portrait Galleries. He and Foss said long and emotional farewells, but the other Mancers seemed very relieved to have him gone and Eliza heard a number of them commenting on how nice and quiet it had become.

Eliza thought once or twice that she would like to see Holburg again before leaving, but in all the activity there was no time, and the day she had to say her farewells crept up on her faster than she had expected. Perhaps it was better that way, she told herself.

In her tent in the desert, she looked over her few possessions, wondering what to pack. Here was the chess set her father had carved for her, and the little amber dropper Uri mon Lil had sent for her birthday. A good dream. *The Legends of the Ancients* – its author had not been so far from the truth after all, she thought. Foss was now eager to work on a commentary to the text. She unfolded a piece of paper and saw it was Charlie's map of the island he had named Eliza. She would never see that island now. Seventeen waterfalls, he had said.

Her father entered the tent and sat down with her. When she had told him what had to be done, pain had closed his face, but he had not said one word to dissuade her. Unlike her friends, he was used to accepting the decision of a Sorceress. He knew, more than she did even, what it meant, and the sacrifices that were required. Now he said nothing, but waited for her to speak.

"I dinnay feel like myself," she said. "With all this power, am I still even Eliza?"

He took her chin between his thumb and forefinger and turned her face towards his, looking deep into her eyes. She looked back. If I cry now, she thought, I won't stop. And she pushed her sorrow deep down again, where the Magic was waiting.

"You're Eliza," he said firmly, releasing her. He looked around the tent. "What are you taking with you?"

"Nothing," she decided.

He followed her out of the tent. There on the hot sand, she found herself inescapably in the moment she had been dreading above all others.

They stood before her. Her mother, still half a stranger to her. Her beautiful Charlie, her beloved Nell, holding hands. Nell was crying and Charlie had a puzzled look on his face, as if he didn't understand what was happening. And her father. It was impossible.

"I cannay say goodbye," she told them. "I'm sorry, but I just cannay."

Her father's face crumpled and he reached for her. She fell into his embrace, breathing in for a brief moment the familiar smell of him, then pulled away. She couldn't speak and she only hoped that they would understand. *You will cut out your own heart.*

She turned away from them and became a single raven, flying north, straight as an arrow over the desert.

The Mancers were waiting for her.

"Where will you go?" she asked Foss.

"We will build another Citadel in the Yellow Mountains," said Foss. "And we will turn our power to the accumulation of knowledge and the recording of history, our true strengths. But what about you, Eliza Tok?"

"I dinnay know."

"You are welcome with us, of course. Whatever the relationship between the Sorceress and the Mancers is to be in the future, you and I will forge it together. There will be no Shang Sorceress henceforth. You will be the only Xia Sorceress. Nia's heir, ironically, and also the most powerful Sorceress ever to have lived."

"I wish I knew what I should do with all this power."

"I hoped you might help us build the new Citadel. But you have just cause to be wary of the Mancers."

"So do you," said Eliza, smiling. "Helping with the new Citadel will give me something to do to start out, aye. Plus it's a good way of making sure I know what's in all the secret rooms and towers! Then I'll go see my grandmother. Praps she'll be able to help me figure out what to do next."

Foss nodded gravely and turned to the assembled Mancers.

"It is time."

Eliza went first into the dark wood. It made way for her and she came quickly to the silver shore. Hundreds of boats emerged from the mist. The Boatman bowed in wordless greeting to her. The Mancers set about loading the boats with their treasures and books. Eliza, Foss, and the Emmisariae boarded one boat.

Di Shang slipped away.

The Crossing seemed briefer than in the past. Long before Eliza expected it, the mist parted and the countless boats made their way across the green water to the great black cliffs. Steps opened up before them.

"My time is done, Sorceress," said the Boatman, with a respectful bow. When she looked back, she saw that the thick white mist at the centre of the lake was gone. It was only a lake now. There was no way back.

"Come," said Foss.

He held out a big golden hand and Eliza took it. Together they climbed the steps into Tian Xia.

EPILOGUE
Many Years Later

Nell makes her way up the windswept hill, holding her coat tight around her. Seabirds call out to each other from the rocky shore behind, skimming the water and landing on ice floes. She bends down and picks a tiny purple sprig. *Ellis Mosapa*, native to these islands off the northern coast of Scarpatha. While most would consider it a barren place, Nell will miss it. The islands are bleak and icy, but the sea here throngs with life. Now winter is setting in, and they cannot stay. Her assistants all left a few weeks ago, and the few islanders remaining will soon take the boat for the mainland and pass the winter there.

She tucks the sprig into the buttonhole of her coat and shivers as an icy gust sweeps over her again. The research centre stands at the top of the hill, sturdy and squat against the wind. She can see Charlie readying the little plane that is his pride and joy. *The Gryphon* is painted in bold black letters across its side. She smiles and climbs faster.

"Boo!"

She shrieks, nearly jumping out of her skin. The two little girls who had been hiding behind a rock are laughing uproariously now.

"Frightened you!" shouts one, a skinny, swarthy little thing with corkscrew curls, no more than ten years old, and for half a second Nell's heart swells hugely in her chest. She shakes her head and laughs at the girls.

"You'd better get on home," she says to them in fluent Scarpathian. "The wind is rising. I'll see you again in the spring!"

"Where will you go?" asks the little girl who reminded her so of Eliza.

"South," she says, smiling at them. "Where the whales are."

The two girls run off, holding hands and giggling. For a moment, she stands still and looks after them. It happens often, more and more it seems, that she sees shadows of Eliza. As if she is waiting for her, as if at any moment she might come around a corner. What would she look like now? What is she doing?

A shout from up the hill. The plane is ready and Charlie is waving at her to hurry. Smiling and waving back, she climbs towards him up the hill.

ACKNOWLEDGEMENTS

Many thanks to my editor, Laura Peetoom, and to all the kind, talented, witty people at Coteau Books, for turning my stories into beautiful books. Watching Tian Di go from stuff-in-my-head to books-in-the-world has been a great joy. I could not have navigated the new waters of Being An Author without guidance from the inimitable Amber Goldie and my glitch-fixer Kelsey Koshinsky.

Love, gratitude and cake, so much cake, to those who read my terrible drafts and support my peculiar life choices, starting with Egans large and small, presented here in order of height: David, Joshua, Michael, Kieran, Susanna, Jordan, and Janice. More love / thanks / cake to my grandmother Kato Havas, Jonathan Service (also mapmaker extraordinaire), Gillian Bright, and the ridiculously patient Mick Hunter, who keeps this ship afloat and looks good doing it.

And you, whoever you are, for reading this far: here is some cake for you, as well. Thank you.

ABOUT THE AUTHOR

Catherine Egan is the Gold Moonbeam Award-winning author of *The Last Days of Tian Di* trilogy. Her short fiction has been published in Canadian and US journals. Catherine is a world traveller who has lived in Canada, the UK, Japan and China. She currently resides with her family in Connecticut. Follow Catherine on Twitter @ByCatherineEgan and visit her website at www.catherineegan.com

ENVIRONMENTAL BENEFITS STATEMENT

Coteau Books saved the following resources by printing the pages of this book on chlorine free paper made with 100% post-consumer waste.

TREES	WATER	SOLID WASTE	GREENHOUSE GASES
25	**10603**	**1172**	**2310**
FULLY GROWN	GALLONS	POUNDS	POUNDS

 Calculation based on the methodological framework of Paper Calculator 2.0 - EDF